ENCHANTED *in*

Regency *Society*

ANN
LETHBRIDGE

MILLS
BOON
&

Published in Great Britain 2014
by Mills & Boon, an imprint of Harlequin (UK) Limited,
Eton House, 18-24 Paradise Road, Richmond, Surrey, TW9 1SR

ENCHANTED IN REGENCY SOCIETY
© 2014 Harlequin Books S.A.

Wicked Rake, Defiant Mistress © 2009 Michèle Ann Young
The Gamekeeper's Lady © 2010 Michèle Ann Young

ISBN: 978-0-263-25011-4

052-0215

Harlequin (UK) policy is to use papers that are natural, renewable and recyclable products and made from wood grown in sustainable forests. The logging and manufacturing processes conform to the legal environmental regulations of the country of origin.

Printed and bound
by CPI Group (UK) Ltd, Croydon, CR0 4YY

Ann Lethbridge has been reading Regency novels for as long as she can remember. She always imagined herself as Lizzie Bennet, or one of Georgette Heyer's heroines, and would often recreate the stories in her head with different outcomes or scenes. When she sat down to write her own novel, it was no wonder that she returned to her first love: the Regency.

Ann grew up roaming England with her military father. Her family lived in many towns and villages across the country, from the Outer Hebrides to Hampshire. She spent memorable family holidays in the West Country and in Dover, where her father was born. She now lives in Canada, with her husband, two beautiful daughters, and a Maltese terrier named Teaser, who spends his days on a chair beside the computer, making sure she doesn't slack off.

Ann visits Britain every year, to undertake research and also to visit family members, who are very understanding about her need to poke around old buildings and visit every antiquity within a hundred miles. If you would like to know more about Ann and her research, or to contact her, visit her website at www.annlethbridge.com. She loves to hear from readers.

Wicked Rake, Defiant Mistress

ANN LETHBRIDGE

I would like to dedicate this book to my husband, Keith, and my wonderful critique partners, Molly, Maureen, Mary, Sinead, Teresa and Jude. My special thanks go to my editor, Joanne Grant, whose skill and patience is gratefully acknowledged.

Chapter One

Sussex, England   May 1811

The anger burning in the Marquess of Beauworth's throat tasted of bile and bitter regret. While the horses thundered through shadows and moonlit tracts of rolling Sussex landscape, Garrick fought the urge to turn back for London.

He swallowed his ire and the carriage raced on. Home to Beauworth. The place he hated most in the world.

Not even the person closest to him, Duncan Le Clere, understood his hatred of the place. Sometimes he didn't understand it himself, but lack of knowledge didn't lessen the tension in his shoulders or the foreboding.

The pain of bruised tendon and bone reminded him of the reason for his return. One by one, he unclenched his fingers, forcibly relaxing his hands in his lap, breathing deeply and slowly, regaining control. He lounged deeper in the corner, stretching his legs along the gap between the seats, a picture of insouciance.

After all, the Marquess of Beauworth, idle rake, reckless gambler and bored dandy, had a reputation to uphold.

The carriage swayed violently. He grabbed for the strap beside his head. The vehicle slowed, then stopped.

'*Mon Dieu!* What now?' He let down the window and stuck his head out.

The carriage horses tossed their heads uneasily, their shapes indistinct in the shadow of the high hedges lining the road. The sound of their hard breathing and jingling harnesses cut through the warm stillness. Garrick narrowed his eyes, staring ahead into the dark. 'What do you see, Johnson?' Probably a puddle. The poor old fellow should have retired years ago.

Something white gleamed eerily in the shadows ahead. A white horse walking in the centre of the road, moonlight slipping luminescent over a dappled coat. At first he saw only the horse. Then another dark shape, a slight figure clutching the bridle. A woman in a black riding habit. Walking alone? Bloody hell. She must be in trouble.

He wrenched open the carriage door, leapt down and started forwards with an offer of help on his lips. The sight of a pair of long-barrelled pistols in her hands, one aimed at his forehead and the other at his servants, stopped him short.

Cold moonlight revealed a black mask covering all but her mouth, while a point-edge cocked hat adorned a curled and powdered peruke. Black lace frothed at her wrists and throat.

'Good God.' The exclamation exploded from his lips as recognition struck. Lady Moonlight, the daring cavalier's lady from Cromwell's time, forced to take to the High Toby to feed her family. Her exploits were legendary in this part of Sussex as were the sightings of her spirit after she'd hanged.

'Stand and deliver!' Her husky voice, tinged with the accent of the dregs of London, echoed off the over-arching trees. The grey minced sideways and she checked it with a low murmur.

No ghost this. Merely a common criminal.

Garrick glanced up at the box where Johnson and Dan sat wide-eyed and motionless, apparently taken in by the clever ruse.

'Hand over yer valuables or the boy is dead meat,' she called out.

There was a desperate edge to the coarse voice he didn't like, but the pistols remained steady enough and both were cocked and ready. Damnation, but he wasn't in the mood for this tonight. A rush of anger roared through his veins, a red haze blurring his vision, his fingers curling into fists.

He inhaled long and slowly.

Control. Anything else and someone less innocent than he would die. Behind her mask her eyes glittered. Courage or fear? Would she shoot an unarmed man?

Dan, fear bleaching his cheeks, rose in his seat. One pistol tracked his movement.

'Curse it, lad,' the thief said. 'Yer want to die?'

Nom d'un nom. Garrick might be prepared to take a chance with his own life, but he would not risk the boy. He, more than anyone, deserved better. 'Sit down, Dan,' he ordered.

Scared eyes found Garrick's face. He nodded encouragement. The boy subsided on to his seat beside the rigid Johnson. Garrick shook his head. 'Be still, both of you.'

Clearly realising Garrick's dilemma, the little witch

kept one pistol fixed on Dan as she slipped the other
into a saddle-holster beside a cunningly wrought sword
sling. The intricate hilt protruding from the scabbard
fitted her costume well enough. His lip curled. He'd like
to see her try to best him with a sword.

She tossed her hat on the ground near his feet.
'Throw yer trinkets in there.'

A shimmer of light surrounded her face and body as
she moved. A ghostly light. Was he going mad? Then
he saw the sequins. They covered her mask and reflected moonlight from her coat and waistcoat. The
little wretch looked like a reveller at a masquerade, and
for such a deadly purpose.

An elegant twist of wrist and flutter of black lace
drew his attention to the upturned hat. 'I ain't got all
day.'

Garrick bowed with a flourish, acknowledging her
impatience with charm and grace. 'Your wish is my
command, milady.'

As he straightened, her full lips curved in a quick
smile. She bobbed a curtsy. 'Yer too gracious, sir.'

'Ah, a polite Lady Moonlight.' He raised a brow.
'I'm waiting, *chérie.*'

Her smile fled and oddly he found himself regretting
its loss. 'For what?' she asked. 'A bullet in yer brain?'

'For my kiss. Lady Moonlight always kisses the men
she robs if she thinks them handsome.'

'Just put yer valuables in the 'at, milord.' A hint of
laughter coloured her nasal voice.

Aware of the astonished gazes of those on the box,
he spread his arms in a mock gesture of appeal. 'Are
you saying you find me lacking? How cutting. You
break my heart.'

She chuckled, soft and low and very feminine, but

the pistol steadied in the region of his chest. 'Now, milord.'

He put a hand to his pocket as if seeking his watch and cursed silently. He had left his travelling pistol in the coat lying on the carriage seat. Perhaps it was as well. He had no wish to harm the wench. He kept his voice calm and soft. 'This is dangerous work for a woman. If you get caught you'll hang, whereas I could offer you gainful employment.'

'Hah. I know yer sort's idea of work. Enough gabbing or you'll be joining yer ancestors.' Underneath the bravado, her voice shook with the tremor of tightly stretched nerves.

Much as he didn't care if he joined his ancestors, he didn't want her nervous and threatening the servants again. He pulled out his fob and dangled his watch between them. Slowly, he twisted the gold links in his fingers. The diamond-encrusted case winked and glittered like moonbeams on water.

The pistol trembled. She wouldn't use it. He was certain.

She reached for the prize, her head no higher than his shoulder as she snatched at the watch with her leather-gloved hand. Garrick caught her fine-boned wrist in one hand and restrained her pistol arm tight against her side with the other. He crushed her slender body hard against him, encircling her waist.

Her exhale of shock was warm, sweet and moist on his neck. Soft breasts compressed against his ribs. She smelled of vanilla with undertones of leather and horses. An oddly heady combination. He lowered his head and planted his lips firmly against her mouth, pleased when her lips drifted open in surprise.

The air around him warmed and swirled, sending his

blood pounding and his senses alert to her response. Her delicate lithe body, at first inflexible, softened just enough to let him know she was not unwilling. Indeed, her body moulded most deliciously to his. He ran his hand down her slender back and savoured the soft curves of her buttocks.

Somewhere in this exchange, his earlier fury had softened to the heat of desire. Another passion requiring control. And control it he would. He deepened the kiss and inched his fingers towards her hand, feeling for the pistol.

The little hellion broke free and leapt back, breathing hard, her eyes in the slits in the mask sparkling with reflected sequins or some deeper, hotter fire. Chest rising and falling in quick succession, she levelled the barrel at his chest. A point-blank shot. 'Stay back.' Her glance darted to the servants. 'All of ye.'

Laughing, he reached for her. 'Surely we can find a more amenable way for you to earn a living? One we would both enjoy.'

She stilled, those rosy just-kissed lips curving in a saucy grin. She curtsied, full and deep. 'I think not.'

'Look out, my lord,' Johnson called.

Garrick caught a blur of movement at the corner of his eye. With a curse, he whirled around. A large masked man, a pistol clutched in his fist, raised his arm high. Garrick dodged. The blow hammered against the side of his head. A blinding light flashed. He fought descending darkness. The ground hit his knees as he fell into black.

Blood rushed in Lady Eleanor Hadley's ears. Her head swam. Her heart raced. At any moment she would measure her length beside the man at her feet.

She took a deep breath, crouched at her victim's side and found a strong steady pulse in his wrist. She stood upright, glaring at Martin. 'Did you have to hit him so hard?' she muttered.

'What the devil are ye doing, letting him get so near?' Martin's deep, low mutter rang harsh with anger. He levelled his pistol at the men on the box.

Panting, she stared at the inert body on the ground. What had she been thinking? That he was tall and impossibly handsome under the soft light of the moon? That the easy smile on his lean, dark face held no danger? If not for Martin, she might have fallen into his trap like a wasp in a jam pot. He had to be cocksure of his abilities as a lover if he thought to overpower her with a kiss. A laugh bubbled up. Hysterical, born of nerves and the strange sensations he'd sparked in her body. Never had she felt so horridly wonderfully weak, as if her bones were liquid and her mind was mush. Not her normal self at all.

If it wasn't for his grab for the pistol, he might have swept her off her feet.

'Where were you, Martin?' she muttered. 'Weren't you supposed to be covering the driver?'

'I never saw you start forrard. The plan was for me to give the signal.'

Even in the dim light, she saw his skin darken. Poor Martin. The best man to lead a charge, according to her father, but he made a terrible highwayman. She'd tried to send him away after their first foray. He'd refused point blank. Dear loyal Martin.

'Never mind.' She pointed to her victim and raised her voice. 'See wot 'e's got on 'im before 'e wakes.'

As Martin bent to do her bidding, the coachman fumbled under his seat. Oh God, this could get out of hand very quickly. She jerked her pistol in his direction. 'Don't try it.'

He straightened and raised his hands again. The angelic-looking boy beside him sat rigid, his shoulders shaking, his teeth biting down on his bottom lip. No heroics there, thank heavens.

Martin rolled the man on the ground on to his back. He moaned, his head lolling against his shoulder, his brow furrowed as if, even unconscious, he was aware of pain. The strong column of neck disappeared into a crisp, elegantly tied neckcloth and merged with powerful shoulders encased in a snug-fitting dark coat. Dark hair and olive skin gave his strong features a foreign cast.

Her heart pounded a little too hard. He was beautiful. Not an adjective she normally used about a man. They were usually either rough, or gentlemanly, or they were simply men she saw every day and gave no thought to at all. This one was beautiful in the way of a bronze sculpture: a perfectly moulded jaw, smooth plane of cheek, straight dark brows above a noble nose. Her fingers itched to trace his features, to feel the texture of bone and skin, much like one might run a hand over a fine statue. The line of his full bottom lip echoed the feel of his mouth on hers, warm and unbelievably exciting. And his voice, with its faint French accent, had brushed across her nape like the touch of velvet.

Madness.

He moaned again. She jumped back. To her relief, he did not open his eyes. Martin had struck him hard. She swallowed. Hopefully not a fateful blow. She didn't want him badly hurt, for all he'd seemed so careless with his life. Nor did she want to face him again. 'Time to go. Into the coach with him. You,' she said, pointing

at the coachman, 'get down and lend a 'and. And no
tricks.'

The coachman heaved his portly frame over the side.

Martin went to his head. 'Pick up his feet,' he
ordered the coachman, who bent with a grunt and
grasped the man under the knees above black Hessians
polished to an impossibly glossy shine.

'Hold,' she said.

'What now?' Martin said in a growl.

'Take his boots.'

Stiff with anger, he dropped the man to the ground.
He pushed the coachman aside with a grunt of disap-
proval and heaved off the tight-fitting footwear. He
returned to his post at the man's head.

Eleanor opened the door of the carriage and stood
back. The two men hoisted their burden on to the floor
of the coach. Martin slammed the door.

'Be off with you,' she said to the panting coachman.
'As fast as you can before I change me mind.'

The coachman wasted no time in climbing up and a
moment later the carriage sped down the road. Its
swaying lamp disappeared around the corner.

Martin bent and cupped his hands and boosted her
on to Mist, her steady little gelding, who had waited so
patiently all this time.

Eleanor struggled awkwardly with her skirts as she
settled into the saddle. 'Next time I'll wear William's
breeches.'

'There ain't going to be no next time.' Martin stuffed
their booty into his saddlebags and climbed aboard the
chestnut. 'Mark my words, you'll end up like her, my
lady. On Tyburn tree.'

Eleanor's stomach twisted at the worry in his voice.
'Do you have a better idea?' She dug her heel into

Mist's flank and they galloped swiftly into the protection of the woods. Eleanor used to love the freedom of riding at night. Many times, she and William, her twin, had slipped out to roam the countryside around their Hampshire estate after midnight. They'd been best friends in those days. She'd borrowed his clothes. And why not? She'd ridden as well as, if not better than, her brothers, shot as well as they did. And that was her downfall. She thought she knew better than them.

Look at tonight. This victim had been wonderfully rich, but the night had almost ended in disaster. Everything she touched went horribly wrong. William was on his way home, his ship due in Portsmouth any day now, and he'd come home to find himself ruined.

All because she couldn't leave well enough alone. Heat flooded her body. He'd think her such an impetuous fool.

Unless she could put things right before he arrived.

It didn't take long to reach the barn where they hid their horses. Eleanor slid out of the saddle and led Mist inside. She swept off the mask, wig and hat, casting them to the floor, scrubbing at her itchy scalp as her hair cascaded around her shoulders.

'Do you know who he was?' Martin asked, following her in.

'A dandy with gold in his pocket and jewellery to spare.'

'It was Beauworth. I recognised the coach.'

'What?' A cold, hard lump settled in her stomach. Beauworth? The man bent on destroying her family. She'd flirted with him, let him kiss her. Her face warmed at the memory. How demeaning. She yanked the leading rein through the metal ring in the wall. 'You should have told me.'

'Weren't much time for talking,' Martin said, turning

from the task of lighting a lantern hanging from a beam. His voice sounded disapproving. 'He's a gambler and a libertine. Cuts a swathe through the ladies like a scythe through hay, I'm told. The way he took hold of you fair makes my blood boil. We should never have held him up, neither. His uncle is the magistrate. We'll be knee deep in Bow Street Runners in a day or so.'

Eleanor grimaced. 'Without money, we'll starve and what will I tell William? That I carelessly lost his home and fortune?' Her stomach dropped away, her skin turning clammy, the way it did every time she remembered. William had trusted her to look after his interests until he returned. By forging his signature, she'd spent every penny in the bank. And then, out of nowhere Beauworth had demanded repayment of a mortgage she'd known nothing about. Damn him.

When he realised they couldn't pay, he'd sent in the bailiffs, forcing her and Sissy to seek refuge where they could.

If only the ship into which she'd sunk all William's money would return from the Orient, everything would be all right. The stupid thing seemed to have disappeared without a trace. Her heart picked up speed. What if it never returned?

And she needed money so they could eat. Blast it all. She had thought she was so dashed clever. Instead, she'd brought them all to the brink of ruin.

Miserably, she pulled a carrot from the pocket of her coat. Mist's warm breath moistened her palm as he nuzzled it free.

'Perhaps if I went to speak to the Marquess, he would listen to reason,' she said.

'Take pity on a helpless woman, you mean?'

Phrased in such bald terms, it sounded thoroughly

dishonourable. William would never approve. But then he wouldn't approve of her taking to the High Toby, either. A career that she'd discovered all too quickly, lacked the romance and adventure of legends. If they were caught, the authorities would respond without mercy. 'Ask for more time.'

'Jarvis said he needs the money. Got debts of his own.'

They always did, these fashionable men. Michael, her eldest brother, had had huge debts when he died. They were what made her invest in the ship.

There had to be some other way out. 'We need something to trade for the mortgage.'

'Too bad you didn't think of that an hour ago. We could have traded his lordship.'

Jaw slack, her eyes wide, she gazed at Martin's broad back. 'Blast. I walked away from the perfect solution.'

Martin swung around. 'Oh, no. I was jesting, my lady, and badly. I promised your father my loyalty to his children and I've kept my word, but I'll not be party to abduction.'

'You are right. It is far too dangerous.' She tossed an old blanket over Mist's back. Martin did the same for his mount.

'Why didn't you tell me the rest of that stupid legend?' she asked. 'The kissing business?' A kiss as sweet as sugar and as dark as the brandy on his breath. Not to mention strange delicious shivers deep in places she never knew existed. His body, where he pressed her close, had felt satisfyingly hard. She had wanted to touch him. All over. At the thought of her fingertips on his skin, her stomach tumbled in a strangely pleasant dance.

Blankly she stared at the plank wall with limbs the

consistency of honey. She clapped a hand to her mouth. How could she feel this way knowing what this man had done?

Martin scratched his chin. 'My brother never mentioned no kiss, my lady.' Which meant it probably wasn't true. She felt the heat rise in her face as Martin turned to look at her. 'Why did you take his boots?'

Eleanor still didn't understand the sudden teasing urge she'd felt and she certainly wouldn't tell Martin about the way his wicked smile and brush of his lips had turned her insides to porridge. 'They were new and he's a dandy.' She shrugged. 'It will annoy him. You know how ridiculous William is about his boots.' Besides, he'd been too bold, too reckless for his own good. A real criminal might have killed him. A lesson in humility would do him good. 'Throw them in the pond.'

She picked up her hat, tucking the wig and mask inside it. She stripped off the coat and waistcoat and handed them to Martin, who hauled the bundle up to the rafters in a net by way of an old block and tackle they'd found in the hayloft. 'We will have to ride out again.'

'Please, my lady. You are risking your neck for naught but a few baubles and a handful of guincas.'

She winced. As her father's sergeant in the army and later his steward, Martin would have given his life for her father. Now he held doggedly to his promise to serve his children, but she couldn't ask him to take any more risks. Not when everything she touched went wrong. 'It would serve William best if you returned to Castlefield. Keep an eye on the house. Make sure the bailiffs don't steal anything.'

'And let you risk your neck alone?' Martin glowered and shook his shaggy head. 'Your father always said you was a handful.'

A tomboy, he meant. Too competitive for a girl. Too impetuous, Father had said, when Mother defended her. And she'd been so sure she'd show William how well she could handle things in his absence. Pride had definitely ended in a fall. And if she didn't do something soon, she'd drag the rest of the family into the pit.

Garrick groaned and sat up on the floor of the carriage. Cursing, he pulled himself on to the seat and investigated the bump behind his ear with his fingertips. A knot as big as an egg. Blast the woman.

A comely female at that, if he hadn't been mistaken. He recalled the spiralling heat between them and her delicate trembles beneath his touch with a searing jolt of desire. For one heady moment, he'd thought he'd wooed her out of her villainous purpose. He might have, too, if she'd been alone. His luck was definitely out. First he'd taken the bit between his teeth to tell Uncle Duncan the bad news, and then he'd been robbed.

Head aching, he probed the tender spot on his scalp. Brandy might help. He fumbled in his cloak pocket and pulled out his flask. He rubbed some of the alcohol on the lump, hissing at the sting, then took a swig. The servants must have been terrified.

The abominable pounding in his head increased. He closed his eyes and leaned back against the squabs, uttering a sigh when, some twenty minutes later, the carriage crunched on gravel to a gentle stop.

Beauworth Court.

Johnson pulled open the door and let down the steps. 'My lord? Are you all right? I darsen't stop on the road.'

'I'm perfectly all right,' Garrick said, forcing a smile.

He allowed the coachman to help him out of the carriage and glanced at the house. Stone lions guarded

the wide granite steps to the front door. Columns, illuminated by torches, rose up to the first floor with Pal-
ladian grace and the lower windows blazed with light.
Uncle Duncan must be entertaining. Garrick bit back a
groan. *Merde.* He really did not want to be here.

'Dan,' he called out. 'Bring my coat, please.'

Dan jumped down with alacrity and dived into the
coach for the garment. ''Ere, my lord.'

'Good. Stay close to me.'

The gravel stabbed into the soles of his feet as he
hobbled up to the front door. 'Damn, blasted wench.' Why
the hell she had stolen his boots he could not imagine.

On cue, the door opened. The butler, a slick-looking
fellow Garrick didn't recognise, stared down his nose.
Recovering swiftly, he stepped back with a bow.
'Welcome home, my lord.'

Hah. 'Thank you.' He handed over his greatcoat and
headed for the arching sweep of staircase leading to the
first-floor chambers.

A door opened. Light spilled from the dining room.
A heavily built figure, his military bearing obvious,
strode purposefully across the black and white tiled
floor. Duncan Le Clere, his father's cousin, and
Garrick's trustee for twelve more months.

Dan ducked behind Garrick as Le Clere's stern gaze
took in the scene. 'The devil. What is the meaning of
this?'

'Got held up.' His uncle stiffened. 'By highwaymen.' Garrick chuckled at his pathetic humour.

Le Clere quickened his pace. 'Are you injured?' He
must have caught a whiff of the brandy because he
recoiled. 'Or drunk? Is this one of your pranks?'
Nothing slipped past Uncle Duncan with regard to
Beauworth and its heir.

'I might be a trifle foxed, but I am fully in possession of my faculties, I assure you. The damned rogues relieved me of my valuables and my boots.'

Two more men hurried into the vestibule: Matthews, the Beauworth steward, and Nidd, his father's ancient valet who did for Garrick on the rare occasions he came home.

'Johnson told us what happened,' Matthews said. 'These villains need teaching a lesson.'

And the beefy Matthews was ready to mete out the punishment. The thought of the saucy little wench in his hands did not sit well in Garrick's stomach.

'Send for the constable,' Uncle Duncan said, taking in Garrick's stockinged feet with raised brows.

'Not tonight.' Garrick put a hand to his head and winced. 'The morning will be soon enough. Right now, I'm for bed.'

Uncle Duncan's lips flattened. He glanced toward the dining-room door. 'I expected you for dinner. It takes more than a contretemps with the lower orders to keep a man from his duty.'

'Johnson said they struck his lordship on the head,' Matthews said.

The hard expression on Le Clere's face dissolved into concern. 'I'm sending for the doctor.'

The doctor who would poke and prod and wonder. Garrick put up a hand. 'A small lump, nothing more. I'll be well by morning.'

The broad back stiffened. 'A knock on the head, Garrick... I'm only thinking of your welfare.'

'Don't fuss.'

Le Clere recoiled. 'But your head, Garrick...'

A black emptiness rolled out from the centre of Garrick's chest. He knew what Le Clere was thinking, knew from the wary look in his eyes what he feared, and Garrick honestly couldn't bear it.

Garrick rubbed his sore knuckles. Le Clere hadn't yet heard of the latest débâcle. 'I'm sorry, Uncle. I know you mean for the best, but I do not need bleeding or quacking tonight.'

His uncle blew out a breath. 'As you wish. But if there is any sign…' He had no need to finish the sentence; his gentle smile said it all.

Garrick nodded. 'I'll see the doctor.'

'So be it,' Le Clere said. 'I cannot tell you how good it is to see you come home. There is much to be done, much to learn in the next twelve months, my boy.'

Hardly a boy. And the rest of it would wait for the morning. 'Good night, Uncle. Oh, and I brought my tiger.' He gestured to Dan, who moved closer to Garrick.

Uncle Duncan glanced at Dan with pursed lips. 'He belongs in the stables.' He waved off Garrick's response. 'We will talk tomorrow when you feel better. I must attend my guests. Take good care of him, Nidd. Matthews, I'll see you in the library later.' He hurried back to the dining room. The stolid Matthews bowed and wandered off.

Nidd's cadaverous face was anxious. 'He worries about you, my lord. You know how he is.'

Garrick sighed. 'Yes, I know. But I wish to God my father hadn't tied up my affairs so tightly.'

'You were but a babe then, my lord. He never dreamed he and your mother would go so early.'

A regretful silence filled the empty hall. It pressed down on Garrick's shoulders with the weight of a granite mountain. He started up the stairs.

In Garrick's chamber, Nidd eased him out of his

coat and went to work on his waistcoat. Garrick gestured at the boy hovering by the door. 'My wits were begging. I should have sent him to the stables with Johnson.'

'Leave him to me, my lord. I'll see he gets there. Johnson was only saying the other day as how he could use more help.'

That was another thing. Why so few servants in the house? In the old days there had been a footman stationed in every corridor. Was something wrong? Did he care?

Sometimes he did, and then the old anger he worked hard to contain erupted.

He leaned back in the chair and closed his eyes, seeking distance. 'Take him now, Nidd. I can manage the rest.' Since he had no boots to be pulled, undressing presented no difficulty. He opened his eyes as Nidd headed out of the door with his hand on Dan's bony shoulder. 'Tell Johnson to treat him gently. He's had a rough go of things.'

Eyes closed, he unbuttoned his waistcoat. His fingers sought his fob. Gone. He stared down at his right hand in horror. His signet ring, a family heirloom handed to him by his dying father, had also been stolen. Rage surged in his veins like a racing tide. This time he let it flow unchecked.

To lose the family signet ring now, when he'd finally made his decision. Damn the woman to hell. Damn him for falling under the spell of her kiss.

He pulled off his shirt and glared at the tester bed with its carved insignia of the Beauworth arms, the shield and white swan, a motif repeated on the moulded ceilings here and in the dining room. The same as the insignia engraved on his ring. He would have it back if he had to search the length and breadth of England. And when he found the woman, she'd rue the day she'd crossed his path.

Chapter Two

The next morning after an early breakfast, Garrick traversed the second-floor gallery and made his way down the sweeping staircase. Marble pillars rose gracefully to support the high carved ceiling above a chequerboard floor he couldn't look at without cringing. He took a deep breath, determined to keep his composure. He was twenty-four, not a scared child. Nor would he allow his uncle's cautious solicitude to get under his skin.

He knocked on the library door out of courtesy and entered. A polished oak desk dominated one end of the long room. Immersed in the papers before him, Uncle Duncan did not look up.

While Garrick waited, memories curled around him like comforting arms. He could almost hear the sound of his father's voice, the feel of his arm heavy on Garrick's young shoulders as they poured over maps or Father told him stories of military engagements.

On a warm spring day like today, the bank of French windows leading to the balcony would have been thrown open, a breeze heavy with the scent of roses from the garden beyond billowing the heavy blue curtains into the room.

He hated the smell of roses.

Garrick blinked, but the recollections remained imprinted in his mind like a flame watched too long: a young boy wide-eyed with imagination, his father, jabbing at the air with his cigar to emphasise some important point of strategy, until Mother chased them out into the fresh air. How his father's face lit up at the sight of her as she swept in, her powdered black hair piled high, her hands moving as she talked in her mix of French and broken English.

Mother. Like an icy blast from a carelessly opened door in mid-winter, the warmth fled, leaving only a cold, empty space in his chest. Hell. He would have sent Le Clere a note if it had not been cowardly.

It seemed to require every muscle in his body, but somehow Garrick slammed the door on his memories. He locked them away in the same way his father's old maps were locked behind the panelled doors of the library bookcases and focused his attention on Le Clere instead. Uncle Duncan, as Garrick had called him since boyhood, had grown heavier in the past four years. His ruddy jowls merged with his thick neck. His hair was greyer, but still thick on top and he looked older than his fifty years, no doubt dragged down by responsibility. As if sensing Garrick's perusal, he raised his flat black eyes. Garrick resisted a desire to straighten his cravat. Damn that the old man could still have that effect on him.

'Well, Garrick.' The deep voice that had once reached to the far reaches of a parade ground boomed in the normally proportioned library. Garrick winced as the harsh tone reverberated in his still-sensitive skull.

'What can you tell me about these villains that set upon you last night? This is the second time they've robbed a neighbourhood coach.'

Le Clere took his responsibilities as local magistrate seriously, but Garrick was not going to let the morons who stood for local law and order frighten off the cheeky rogues before he recovered his property.

He shrugged. 'They were masked. I barely caught a glimpse of them before I was struck.' He was certainly not going to admit being bested by a woman and he trusted Johnson to say nothing about that kiss. Damnation. Was he smiling at the memory?

A sour expression crossed his uncle's face. 'I had hoped you would be of more help. The last man robbed babbled on about a ghost.' He inhaled deeply. Garrick recognised the sign. Control. Uncle Duncan hated it when things did not go according to plan. Apparently in command of himself once more, Le Clere smiled. 'No matter. I am simply glad you are here, ready to devote yourself to duty at last.'

The old man's hopeful expression twisted the knife of guilt in his gut. He didn't like to tell him that the command to come back to Beauworth and take up his responsibilities had tipped the scales on his decision.

'I've decided to join the army.'

Le Clere sat bolt upright in his chair. 'You can't mean it.'

The anger, always a slow simmer in his blood, rolled swiftly to a boil. He let it show in his face. 'I certainly do.'

Bushy brows snapped together. Red travelled up his uncle's neck and stained his cheeks, the same signs of anger he experienced himself. The old man opened his mouth and Garrick awaited the parade-ground roar that had cowed him as a boy, but now left him cold. Le Clere inhaled a deep breath and when he finally spoke, his voice rasped, but remained at a reasonable pitch. 'What brought about this sudden decision?'

'I found one of Father's campaign diaries in the library in town. I'd forgotten how much he loved serving his country. I want to follow in his footsteps.'

Le Clere slammed a fist on the table. 'I should have burned them. Your father should never have risked his life in that manner, neither should you.'

'Father never got a scratch.' Only to come home and die in a hunting accident. Garrick rose to his feet. 'I have made up my mind. There is nothing you can say to convince me otherwise.'

Le Clere sagged against the chair back. 'All these years I've worked to safeguard your inheritance and you treat it as if it is nothing.' He pressed his fingers against his temple.

More guilt. As if he didn't have enough on his conscience. 'I have to go.'

'Why?'

'You know why.'

'Nothing has occurred since that incident at school. You've been all right. Got it in hand.'

It. The Le Clere curse. Something they'd never spoken of since the day Garrick had learned what it meant.

'No.' He stared at his bruised knuckles. If his cousin Harry hadn't pulled him off the bullying bastard beating Dan with a pitchfork, Garrick might have been facing charges of murder instead of spending every penny of his allowance to pay the man off.

'I see,' Le Clere murmured, his brow furrowing. 'Then you've wasted these past few years. Learned nothing of the estate. The war cannot continue much longer, surely, and when you come home I may not be here. I'm getting old, Garrick.'

Garrick tugged at his collar. 'I'm going.'

'Wait until my trusteeship is over. Twelve months is not such a long time. Learn all you can. Set up your nursery, get an heir, then go with my blessing.'

The older man's anxiety hung in the air like a sour London fog. If it hadn't been impossible, Garrick would have sworn he smelled fear. He could not let his uncle sway his purpose. Staying in England as he was, a short-fused powder keg waiting to go off at a stray spark, was asking for trouble.

'I've made up my mind.'

Le Clere ran a hand through his hair. 'What if you are killed? What will happen to Beauworth?'

'Cousin Harry is the heir.'

His uncle stilled. He seemed to have turned to a block of granite. His face reddened. The veins in his neck stood out above his neckcloth. Dear God, was he going to have an apoplexy? 'Uncle, please. Don't upset yourself.' Garrick strode for the table beside the hearth and poured a glass of brandy from a decanter. He took it back to Le Clere. 'Drink this.'

His uncle accepted the brandy with a shaking hand. It hurt Garrick to see the liquid splash over the side. Le Clere took a long swallow. He stared into the bottom of his glass. 'How long will this visit last?'

He'd planned only to collect his mare and bid his uncle farewell. The loss of the signet ring meant a delay. It must be there for Harry. At least his cousin didn't carry the Le Clere taint in his blood.

'A week.' Plenty of time to run the little vixen to earth.

Uncle Duncan straightened. 'Then we will use what little time we have to good purpose.'

Inwardly Garrick grimaced. If the old man hoped to use the time to change his mind, he was in for more disappointment. More guilt. Ah, well, if he was going to be here anyway... 'All right.'

Le Clere beamed. 'Good. Very good. Let us get started right away. After all, we don't have much time.'

Garrick hid his sigh of impatience. What he really wanted to do was question the local people about the thieves. It would be hours before he could make his escape. 'I'm looking forward to it.'

Eleanor bore most of the weight of the basket swinging between her and her twelve-year-old sister, Sissy, as they trudged through Boxted toward their cottage. After the hour's walk from Standerstead on a fine spring day, a trickle of sweat coursed down between her shoulder blades.

Her stomach tightened. Time was running out and here she was having to spend it buying supplies instead of doing something about her predicament.

As they passed the Wheat Sheaf across from the village green, a tall man with broad shoulders in snug burgundy velvet stepped into their path. The Marquess of Beauworth. No one but the local lord of the manor would cut such an elegant figure in the humble village of Boxted. And he looked lovelier in bright sunshine than he had beneath the moon.

Eleanor's heart skipped and her breath caught in her throat as she fought not to stare at him, tried to pretend he wasn't there. But when he bowed with elegance and a charming smile, she could pretend no longer. She halted.

'Good day, ladies.' His deep voice sounded intimate, seductive.

A disturbing surge of exhilaration heated her cheeks and sent shivers tingling from her chest to her toes. The man was downright dangerous if he could do all that with a smile. And she did not like the puzzlement lurking in his amber-lit brown eyes. Please, don't let it be recognition.

She bobbed a small curtsy. 'Good day, my lord.'

'May I help you with that heavy basket, miss?' he asked.

Before Eleanor could respond that he need not trouble, Sissy piped up with a cheeky grin and a look of relief in her dark brown eyes. 'You can help me.'

Eleanor groaned inwardly. Why couldn't the child hold her tongue for once? 'Sissy, please. You must excuse my sister, my lord, she is too forward.'

'Why, I believe she is just truthful. It would not be at all out of my way, you know.' With a smile warm enough to melt an icicle in mid-winter, he grasped the handle of the basket.

Fate in the shape of a black-haired imp had taken the decision out of Eleanor's hands. 'Thank you, my lord.' She released the handle and he hefted the basket as if it weighed nothing at all.

'It is a remarkably fine day, is it not, Miss…?'

'Brown. Ellie Brown, sir, and this is my sister, Sissy.'

'Miss Brown, Miss Sissy Brown.'

He bowed politely to each of them in turn as if they were gentry and not simple village misses. If it was possible, her heart beat a little faster. For the first time in weeks, she felt valued. Her cheeks flared hotter than before. Lord, what would he think?

'You have just come from the market?' he asked.

'Yes, my lord. For baking supplies.'

'Ellie makes the best biscuits in the whole world.' Sissy added, 'I think she should sell them.'

Eleanor wanted to put a hand over her sister's mouth. She was far too ready to confide anything to anyone. She quelled her irritation as the Marquess smiled winsomely at the vivacious child peeping admiringly up at him. Clearly he applied his charm to any female who crossed his path. She resented the pang of something unpleasant in her chest as he directed his lovely smile at Sissy.

'I hope I might try some one day,' he said.

Outwardly polite and ineffably charming, while inside there lurked the worst sort of rake. A man who had done untold damage to her family. The strangely weak feelings she had around him were inexcusable. She scowled at Sissy behind his back.

Seemingly impervious to Eleanor's stare, Sissy gave a little skip. 'Perhaps you would like to buy some.'

Now the child sounded like a merchant. Access to Beanworth Court might solve their problems, but not at the cost of involving her innocent sister. 'Silly girl. The Marquess will not be in the habit of purchasing food.'

'Very true, Miss Brown, but I will mention your talents to Mrs Briddle, our cook.' His dark gaze searched her face. Against her will, her gaze roved over the elegant lines of his bronzed features. Definitely foreign looking. And that French accent made her toes curl. Mortification dipped her stomach. This must stop.

'Miss Brown, I have the strangest feeling we have met,' he said. 'Before I went away to school, perhaps?'

Surely he would not recognise her as Lady Moonlight. 'It is not possible, my lord.' How breathless she sounded. She inhaled deeply, willing her pulse to stop its gallop. 'We only moved here recently.'

'In London, then?'

'I've never been to London.' Fortunately she hadn't. With the deaths in her family, her come-out had been postponed for three years in a row and if she didn't sort things out soon, would probably never occur. Not that she minded. Primping and simpering had never suited her temperament.

'We lived in Hampshire—' Sissy announced.

Eleanor gave her a little pinch to stop the flow of words.

'Ouch,' Sissy cried. She rubbed her arm and glared balefully at Eleanor.

Eleanor bent over her. 'Oh dear, have you hurt yourself?'

'No. You—'

'Good.' She straightened 'This is our cottage, my lord.' She pointed at the last dwelling in the row of five. Beyond it, fields of hay and ripening corn spread as far as the eye could see. 'Thank you so much for your help.' She took the basket from his grasp. 'Come, Sissy.'

Uncomfortably aware of his gaze on her back, Eleanor kept her shoulders straight and her eyes firmly focused on her front door. She would not look back. Next time they met, she would be ready for him and his winsome smile.

Like a connoisseur of fine wine, Garrick savoured the gentle sway of Miss Brown's hips and her proud carriage as she negotiated the wooden plank across the sluggish stream running alongside the road. As if she'd forgotten him completely, she opened the gate and walked up the short path through the unkempt patch of garden.

With guinea-gold hair pulled back beneath her plain straw bonnet and her serious expression, she presented a delicious picture of demure English womanhood. Somehow she put the sophisticated ladies of London in the shade. Prim and proper as she seemed, the confused blushes on the creamy skin of her face indicated an interest. None of his former loves had ever coloured so divinely. Although her wide-set, dove-grey eyes set in an oval face observed him coolly enough, they warmed to burnished pewter when she smiled with a heart-stopping curve of two eminently kissable lips.

How extraordinary to find such a beauty in sleepy Boxted.

The feeling that he knew her remained. He combed his memory without success. Eventually he would remember. Miss Ellie Brown was not a female a man would easily forget. Not when the mere sight of her had pulled him away from his purpose at the inn. An instant attraction that was not plain old-fashioned lust, so swift to rouse when he'd kissed Lady Moonlight. Rather, the purity shining in her face had evoked a different kind of admiration. Not one he'd had much experience with. And yet the spark of innocent passion he'd sensed running beneath the modest appearance offered an irresistible challenge, even if it could result in no more than harmless dalliance for a day or two.

He returned Miss Sissy's cheery wave as she followed her sister inside.

He frowned. The cottage, like the others in the row, sagged like an ancient crone. Mortar crumbled around the windows and patches of stone showed through the rendering. Nesting birds had pitted the moss-covered thatch, while the stench of stagnant water hung thick in the air. He narrowed his eyes. He hadn't noticed any problems with the estate's finances during his session with his uncle this morning, but in his father's day, these cottages had been well-kept abodes. Perhaps he needed to look a little closer.

He turned his steps for the Wheat Sheaf where he'd abandoned his horse and his tankard of ale for a pretty face and a well-turned ankle. The local men must know something about the highway robbers. A glass of heavy wet should loosen their tongues.

Her heart having settled into its normal rhythm after her encounter with the Marquess, Eleanor set a batch of cakes to cool in the pantry. The sweet smell of baking reminded her of helping her mother in the medieval kitchen at Castlefield. The servants had grown accustomed to the sight of their Countess, the daughter of an impoverished gentleman parson, in a starched white apron over her gown and flour up to her elbows. As soon as Eleanor had been old enough to stand on a stool, she had loved helping Mother, breaking the eggs into a little cream-and-brown china bowl, learning the art of baking the lightest of confections, creating something from nothing. It was the only thing she and William had not done together, though he wolfed down the results of her efforts cheerfully enough.

Sweet memories. Best not to let them intrude. She shivered and rubbed her arms briskly against the chill. The fire, the bane of her existence, had gone out again. It seemed to have a mind of its own. A mean mind. Every time she turned her back, it died. Or it smoked.

She opened the outside door. Cuddling Miss Boots, a tabby cat of questionable heritage, Sissy sat reading in the shade of a straggly rosebush.

'Fetch some wood, please, Sissy,' Eleanor called out.

The child glanced up with a pout. 'Why do I always have to fetch the wood?'

'Please, don't whine. I need your help. It's not too much to ask.'

Sissy grumbled her way to her feet. Eleanor returned to her nemesis. This time she would make it behave.

For once, the paper spills caught with the first spark of the flint and the slivers of kindling flared to light with a puff of eye-stinging smoke. Where was Sissy?

Eleanor ran to the front door. Her jaw dropped. Sissy had her head beneath the bush apparently trying to rescue Miss Boots.

'How could you?' Eleanor cried. 'You know I need firewood.'

Sissy jumped guiltily and dashed for the pathetic pile of logs against the wall. 'Coming.'

'Really, Sissy. I had it lit. Now the spills and the kindling are burned and I have to start over.' Eleanor wanted to cry. She snatched the logs from her sister's hands and hurried back inside while Sissy ran back for more.

Jaw gritted, she laid the fire once more. The tinder-box shook in her hand. She struck and it failed to spark. Calm down. She took a deep breath and struck it again. A tiny glow dropped on to the tight twist of paper.

'Please light,' she begged. The fire flared. 'Hah.' She nodded in triumph and balanced the logs on top. Now for tea. She marched to the pantry. Hearing Sissy's steps behind her, she called out, 'Put the rest of the wood on the hearth and then set the table.' She tucked a loaf of bread under her arm and grabbed a pat of butter and a jar of jam.

Sissy screeched. Eleanor whirled around. A lump of soot lay on the floor, a black monster writhing with red glow-worm sparks. The rug at Sissy's feet smouldered. At any moment it might burst into flame.

'Sissy, move.' Panic sent her voice up an octave.

The child remained glued to the spot, coughing as choking black smoke rose around her.

Heart pounding, Eleanor dropped everything and ran. She caught Sissy by the arm and thrust her out of the front door. She flew back inside.

Rubbing her eyes, Sissy poked her head in. 'The rug is on fire.'

'Stay there.' Flames played among the ragged ends of the rug. Glowing soot took flight in the draught from the door and landed on the tablecloth. It flared up. Oh God, soon the whole place would be alight. She glanced wildly around. Her father's calm voice echoed in her ears. *Smother a fire.*

She ran to the bedroom, pulled a blanket off the bed and ran back to toss it over the flames. Smoke billowed up. Vaguely, she heard Sissy screaming, 'Fire!'

The door burst open. A tall figure loomed through the rolling smoke like a warrior wreathed in mist. He wrenched the blanket from the floor and beat the flames into submission. The burning tablecloth went out of the window. Water from the bucket by the sink sluiced over the rug.

Eleanor peered at her rescuer through streaming eyes.

The Marquess of Beauworth flapped the singed blanket, chasing the last of the smoke out through the open window. 'Good thing I was riding by. It looks like the day King Alfred burned the cakes.'

She stiffened. 'It was the chimney, not my baking.'

He grinned. He was teasing. She tried to smile back, but as her gaze roved around the disaster, her shoulders sagged. The rug was naught but a charred ruin. A few minutes more and the house might well have burned to the ground. Sissy might have been hurt. Her legs turned to water. Heart racing, she dropped down on the sooty sofa. 'Thank you, my lord. I dread to think what might have happened had you not been on hand.'

He shrugged. 'You seemed to have things under control.'

She hadn't, but she was grateful for his kind words. Her heart slowly returned to normal and she looked around at the mess.

Sissy's head appeared around the door. 'Is it out?'

'Yes,' Eleanor said. 'But don't come in. There's soot and water all over the place.'

'Your horse is loose on the other side of the stream,' Sissy said. 'Won't she run away?'

'She won't go anywhere without me,' the Marquess replied with a smile.

Sissy's head disappeared.

Eleanor pulled herself to her feet, her knees shaking and her hands trembling. She began to roll up the remains of the evil-smelling carpet.

'Let me.' The Marquess took the rug from her hands. It followed the tablecloth into the front garden, as did the blanket.

He glanced curiously around the room. How he must scorn their poverty, whitewashed plaster bellying from the damp stone walls, sticks of furniture acquired by Martin from who knew where. Lit by a lattice window, the room looked positively dreary. She hoped the shame did not show on her face.

'I'm sorry I couldn't save the rug.' He sounded sorry. She hadn't expected that and she smiled.

He grinned, his eyes crinkling at the corners, his

teeth flashing white against his soot-grimed face. He looked nothing like the elegant Marquess she'd met earlier. She giggled. 'You look like a sweep.'

He dragged a sleeve across his brow. 'No doubt.'

Taking the bucket to the door, she called out, 'Sissy, fetch water from the well. Bring it back and then come inside.'

She turned back to her rescuer. 'Will you take tea with us?'

He hesitated. What was she thinking, inviting someone like him to take tea? In her present circumstances, she was far beneath his touch. She tried to hide her chagrin with a diffident shrug.

He smiled and her heart did a back flip. 'Yes, thank you.'

She knew she was beaming at him, but she couldn't help it. She dashed for her pitcher of water in the bedroom. She filled a small bowl, setting a cloth, soap and towel alongside it.

'Please,' she said. 'Use this to wash. There is a mirror above the sink.'

The Marquess stared at his blackened hands. 'Good idea.' He took off his jacket, something no gentleman would do in the presence of a lady, but she couldn't hold it against him. Not when he'd saved them. He rolled up his shirtsleeves and she saw that his forearms were strong, corded with sinew that shifted beneath his tanned skin as he scrubbed. A shimmer of heat rose up her neck. A little squeeze in her chest made her gasp.

She shouldn't be looking. She shifted her gaze to his back. It didn't help. The way his broad shoulders moved beneath the fine cambric of his shirt created more little thrills. Her heart gave a jolt at the weird sensation. What on earth was wrong with her? This man was her enemy.

Do something else. Tea. She'd offered him tea. Set the table. That was it. Gaze averted, she hurried for the dresser. Where was Sissy with the water?

'Miss Brown?'

'Yes, my lord?' She turned.

As he wiped his jaw with the damp cloth, his gaze travelled over her face in a long, slow, appraising glance. Heat rushed to her cheeks.

'You look quite smutty yourself,' he said with a smile. He reached out with the cloth and dabbed at her nose. She couldn't breathe. She snatched at the cloth.

Laughing, he caught her hands in his large warm one and wiped them clean. Such strong hands. She seemed bereft of the will to move.

He stepped back, his head cocked to one side. 'You know, you have a streak on your chin. If you will allow me?'

Her heart thundered in her chest. Her body clenched with another delicious thrill as the tips of his fingers, feather light on her jaw, tilted her chin towards the light. She held perfectly still, afraid she might do something rash like place her hands on his shoulders for support. Her pulse raced unmercifully as gently, softly, he dabbed her chin, her cheek, her nose, the water delightfully cold on her heated skin.

Long dark lashes hid his eyes as he lowered his gaze to his task. The scent of sandalwood cologne and smoke filled her nostrils. His expression softened, then his glance flicked up and caught her watching.

Amber glowed like sunbeams in the depths of his warm brown eyes. He bent his head and his parted lips hovered above hers. Heat radiated from his body and her heart skipped and thudded.

She struggled to catch a breath, as if something tight

restricted her ribs, and feared he would hear the soft pants for air she couldn't control.

His cheekbone filled her vision, clearly defined above a lean suntanned cheek. A whisper away from her skin, his dark brown hair curled at his temple. She held her breath, while her heart raced wildly. For the life of her she couldn't move. Didn't want to.

He brushed his lips across her mouth, warm and dry and soft. A mere whisper of the kiss he'd given her in the dark on a moonlit road.

A lightning bolt seemed to shoot through her body, hot yet pleasurable. She stiffened in shock.

'I've been wanting to do that since the moment I saw you,' he said, his voice carrying on a warm puff of breath against her chin.

She shivered, her mind a blank to everything except trembling anticipation.

A smile dawned slowly, lazy and sensuous. She could not tear her gaze from his mouth. He slid one hand behind her neck. 'You are very pretty, Ellie.'

His husky voice seduced her ears. He was the sun and she the moon, pulled inexorably into his orbit. She leaned closer. He dropped the cloth and enfolded her in his arms, his hand spanning the arch of her back, his breath warming her lips.

What was she doing? It felt so right, but was very, very wrong.

The door crashed back on its hinges.

Eleanor jumped back. The Marquess turned away, but not before she saw a glimmer of rueful amusement in those warm brown eyes.

'Here you are,' Sissy announced. Water from the bucket slopped over her shoes. She glanced around. 'Gracious, and after you spent all day yesterday cleaning.'

Eleanor busied herself clearing the table and wiping away the soot, praying that Sissy would not notice her heated face or agitated breathing. 'Put some water in the kettle and the rest in the sink.' Her voice sounded different, throaty, rough.

The Marquess grabbed the bucket. 'Let me. That is far too heavy a load for such a small person.' He poured water in the kettle and hung it over the traitorously merry fire.

Eleanor laid the table and, while the water boiled, she covered the old wooden table with another threadbare cloth, dusted off the bread and pot of jam she'd dropped unceremoniously on the floor and brought cakes from the pantry. The Marquess helped Sissy move the chair and two stools to the table. Somehow he didn't fit with Eleanor's idea of a rake. He seemed no different than her brothers. Well, not quite like a brother, but nice, friendly and fun.

'Goody,' Sissy said, 'cakes. We never have cakes unless Martin comes, and not always then.'

'Martin?' The Marquess looked enquiringly at Eleanor, but it was Sissy who replied.

'Mr Martin Brown, he's—' began Sissy.

'A relative of ours,' Eleanor put in swiftly. Sissy knew the story they'd woven, but sometimes she forgot. 'He works nearby on his cousin's farm.'

'Please sit down, my lord.' Eleanor bobbed a curtsy and gestured to the chair. She and Sissy took the stools. Eleanor poured tea and Sissy passed him the plate of cakes.

'Special cakes,' Sissy said.

He popped one in his mouth. 'They are delicious.' He took another and Eleanor smiled. It was nice to have a compliment from someone like the Marquess.

'How long have you lived here, Miss Brown?' he asked in formal conversational tones.

'Almost one month.'

'I see.' He glowered at the hearth. 'That chimney should be cleaned.' His gaze roamed the room. 'The walls are damp.'

'The roof leaks a little,' Eleanor admitted.

'And the stream outside overflows,' Sissy said, placing her cup in its saucer with a decisive clink. 'We had water running right through the kitchen. And frogs.'

'Please don't think I am complaining,' Eleanor hurried to say. 'We were lucky to find a place we could afford so close to the village.'

He looked at her curiously. 'Miss Brown, you are not from around here. Your accent is not from Sussex. Indeed, you both sound almost...'

What had he been about to say. Educated? Noble? She'd made no attempt to change her or Sissy's speech. Not in this particular role. Once more he'd surprised her, this time with his perception. She tried to keep the guilt from her voice and face while the lies she and Martin had concocted tripped glibly from her tongue. 'We were brought up on a great estate, similar to your own. Our mistress was fond of my mother and allowed Sissy and me to be taught with her children. I plan to become a governess, but have as yet to find a suitable position.'

'I like it here,' Sissy said. 'I found Miss Boots in the garden.'

'Miss Boots?' the Marquess asked with a raised eyebrow.

'My cat,' Sissy said. She ducked under the table and pulled out the kitten. 'See, she has little white boots.' She pointed to the cat's tiny white feet and legs.

'So she does,' he said. He pulled out his watch, a

plain silver thing. Nothing like the glittering piece she'd stolen. 'You will forgive me,' he said. 'I have another engagement this afternoon.'

And here he was listening to a child's artless chatter. Eleanor tried not to let the chagrin show on her face. 'Please, do not let us keep you. Thank you for allowing me to pay my debt in some small measure.'

He shook his head. 'The pleasure is mine, I assure you.'

And she believed him. Despite their apparently different stations, he showed not a smidgen of condescension. Why could she not have met him in her old life?

Oh, Lord, what was she thinking? This man had ruined her life. But somehow she no longer felt any hatred. After all, he'd saved them from a fiery fate. Her change of heart had absolutely nothing to do with all those other hot sensations. Or his kisses.

He shrugged himself into his jacket and picked up the hat and cane he had dropped on his way in. 'I will certainly tell Mrs Briddle that Boxted village boasts one of the finest bakers in all of Sussex. I am sure you will hear from her very soon. Good day, Miss Brown, Miss Sissy.' He bowed and, with a touch of the head of his cane to his forehead, departed.

Eleanor, with Sissy at her side, watched him stroll down the path from the doorway. He paused briefly on the wormy plank across the stream, looking down into the water for a moment, before mounting his horse.

'Eleanor, that's it,' Sissy said. 'You can bake cakes for Beauworth Court and we will be rich again.'

The hope in Sissy's voice brought Eleanor down to earth with a painful jolt. If she didn't find a way out of this morass soon, things were going to get a great deal worse. 'He's a dangerous man.'

'I liked him,' Sissy said. 'He has nice brown eyes.'

'You only like brown eyes because you have them, too.'

Sissy laughed. 'Well, he likes you. He looked like he wanted to eat you instead of the cakes.'

Eleanor put a hand to her lips as she recalled the way she had melted at the brush of his mouth. The man was a practised seducer. How many other young women had he brought to ruin?

Not to mention that if he hadn't called in the mortgage, they would not be in such desperate straits. Perhaps Martin's ransom idea had merit after all.

Chapter Three

Arriving back at the stables, Garrick found Johnson in the barn mending tack. 'Where's Dan? I want him to come with me on a small errand.'

'I sent him to the kitchen for summat to eat. Got hollow legs, that lad 'as. Needs feeding up.'

Garrick nodded. 'Saddle the quietest thing we've got for him, would you? I'll look after Bess.'

They worked in the side-by-side stalls in silence for a few minutes.

'Bright that lad 'e is,' Johnson said to the jingle of a bit.

Garrick knew he meant Dan. He grunted agreement as he lifted his saddle on to the mare.

'Good with the horses,' Johnson continued. 'You don't have to tell him a thing more than once. 'Ad some rough treatment somewhere, I reckon.'

No point in keeping it a secret. 'Apprenticed to a bad master. I convinced him to let him go.'

'With your fists, I hear, my lord. Served the bastard right.'

A sick feeling roiled through Garrick's gut. When

he'd caught the bully laying a stick across the boy's back, he'd seen red. The blood red of terrible rage. If Harry hadn't separated them, the man might have cocked up his toes.

When it was over, he'd paid handsomely, both for Dan and for the damage he'd wrought, yet his gut still churned when he recalled his desire to spill blood. After years without incident, he'd lost control, let the inner beast slip off its chain. He'd been a fool to think he could beat the Le Clere curse. He wasn't fit for civilised society.

If it wasn't for his lost signet ring, he'd have left for Lisbon today.

'Dan should not have said anything,' Garrick muttered.

'I winkled it out of him, my lord. I couldn't understand why he flinched every time I raised me arm. Won't do him any good around your uncle.'

Garrick patted Bess's neck. 'Keep the boy busy and he'll do well enough. I'm surprised you don't have more help.'

Johnson shrugged. 'Mr Le Clere don't like to spend a shilling when a groat will do.'

At that moment, Dan entered the stable whistling. Garrick leaned out of the stall. 'Give Mr Johnson a hand, lad. You are riding out with me.'

Dan's angelic face lit up. 'Yes, my lord.'

From his side of the stable wall, Garrick listened to Johnson giving instructions. He'd been right to bring the lad here to Beauworth. He'd learn a useful trade as well as grow strong away from the foul London air. Today, he'd explain his plan for the boy's future.

He finished saddling Bess and led her out into the sunshine. Dan followed a moment later, the old nag Johnson had found for him chewing on its bit.

'Ready, boy?' he asked.

'Aye, my lord.'

They mounted and rode out of the stable yard towards the place where they'd been held up the previous night. If luck was with him, he'd find some trace of his attacker. Attackers, he amended. Damn it. He should have expected an accomplice. Her husband, perhaps? Or was she his doxy? A repulsive thought. Just thinking about the man with his hands on the saucy wench made him go cold.

What the hell was the matter with him? To be attracted to two women in one week seemed overly debauched even for him. Two very different females, too. One sweet, innocent, barely aware of her feminine appeal. The other, coarse and brash, a lure to the brute every civilised man held at bay.

What a base cur he was, to look forward to meeting the lady highwayman again.

Leaving the lane, they entered the woods. Ancient oaks and elms rose above their heads, the cool air smelling of leaf mould. A breeze stirred the branches and gold-dappled shadows shifted on the track. Here and there the damp soil revealed the passage of two horses travelling fast, one large and one smaller.

When they emerged into open country again, Garrick lost the tracks. Forced to dismount, he cast around.

Dan slid warily from his horse a short distance off. 'There are hoof prints in the dried mud over here, my lord, leading that way.'

Garrick inspected the prints. They were the same as those he'd seen in the woods. 'Well done, Dan. Let's see where they lead.'

Walking their horses, they continued on. In the

distance, hedgerows seemed to stitch the patchwork of green-and-gold fields together, and the dipping sun gilded the tops of emerald trees. Once in a while, a patch of soft earth, or dried mud, revealed evidence of their quarry.

Tucked in a valley near a copse of trees they came across an ancient-looking barn hunkered beside a stream-fed pond. 'This looks promising,' Garrick said.

Dan shifted in his saddle. 'Do you think they are in there?'

'Doubtful. But in case, I want you to remain here out of sight with our horses. Ride back to Beauworth if anything goes wrong.'

Straightening his thin shoulders, Dan dismounted and grabbed the bridles with a determined expression. The lad was tougher than he looked. He had to be, or he wouldn't have survived.

Garrick cautiously crossed the clearing to the sound of twittering birds in the nearby trees. He peered through a crack in a wooden door barred and padlocked from the outside. He made clicking noises with his tongue and listened with satisfaction to the sound of stirring feet and the huffing breath of animals tethered inside. The faint gleam of a white coat in the shadowy interior confirmed what he had hoped. He had found their hiding place. And if they were keeping their horses in the neighbourhood, they no doubt expected to strike again.

He returned to Dan, his mind busy forming a plan. If this worked, he'd be leaving in a day or so. He looked into the face of the anxious boy and remembered why he'd brought him along. 'I have some bad news for you, lad.'

The day after the fire, Martin's bulk overflowed the wooden chair at Eleanor's kitchen table.

'Beauworth has been making enquiries,' he said, glancing out of the window to where Sissy was sitting reading to Miss Boots. He lowered his voice.

'Really,' she said, hoping he wouldn't hear the sudden increase of her heartbeat in her voice.

He nodded. 'According to my cousin, he was worried they might try to steal the gold expected from London tonight.'

Eleanor straightened.

Martin's eyes narrowed. 'It's a trap, my lady. Stands to reason.'

Traps sometimes closed in more than one way. 'I think you are right.' She crossed her fingers in the folds of her skirt. 'And besides, I wouldn't dream of trying a robbery while you are gone.'

A sceptical expression passed across Martin's rugged features, but he said no more. He flung a small leather pouch into her lap. It landed with a soft clink. 'This is all the money I got from the first robbery. Not much, considering the danger.'

She nodded and gestured to the valise on the floor. 'We need to make sure Lady Sissy is safe before we think of doing anything else.'

'Did I hear my name?' Sissy wandered in with Miss Boots draped across her shoulders. She rubbed her cheek against the cat's soft fur.

'Martin is going to take you to Aunt Marjory,' Ellie said.

Tears pooled in Sissy's eyes. She dropped to her knees by Eleanor's feet. 'No. You said I could stay with you.'

With a wince, Eleanor looked at Martin. He shook his head. He didn't like this any more than Sissy did, but Eleanor could not let the little one stay any longer.

She ruffled the dark curls on the bowed head at her knee. 'You like Aunt Marjory. She has cats. Miss Boots will have company.'

Sissy clutched Eleanor's skirts. 'Please don't send me away, Len. Everyone else has gone. I'll fetch the wood every day, I promise.'

Not even the loss of her parents to influenza or Michael's freakish carriage accident had caused Eleanor so much pain in her heart as Sissy's tears did now. Until William returned to take up his title, she and Sissy were all that were left of their once close-knit family. 'This is just a visit, dearest. You always visit Aunt Marjory in the summer.'

A hiccup emerged from the face buried against her lap. 'You won't leave me there forever, will you? Cross your heart and hope to die.'

'I promise.' When Sissy looked up, she made the obligatory sign over her chest.

'All right.'

The tone was grudging, but Eleanor breathed a sigh of relief. She kissed the top of her sister's head, stroked the glossy dark brown curls into some sort of order and blinked back her own tears. 'William will be home soon, don't forget.' Anguished, she looked at Martin. 'Time to go.'

He swung Sissy up into his strong arms. Eleanor handed up Miss Boots and followed them outside to the waiting gig. Martin lifted the child, her kitten and her bag into the carriage and climbed up beside her. He touched his hat. 'I'll return tomorrow.' He set the horse in motion.

'Give my regards to Aunt Marjory.'

Sissy stared at her mournfully. 'I will.' The child looked over her shoulder all the way down the road and

Eleanor waved cheerfully until the gig was out of sight. Eyes burning, she closed her front door. If things went wrong, she might never see her family again. But she had to try to put things right.

Moisture trickled down her cheeks, hot at first, then cold little trails. Crying? She never cried.

She wiped her eyes and lifted her chin. This would be her last chance to make amends. She must not fail.

After pushing the bolt home in the door, she drew the curtains across the windows in the parlour and the bedroom. She pulled the trunk from beneath the bed she shared with Sissy and placed the pouch of money among the articles they'd stolen. Items she'd rejected for sale as too distinctive. One such sparkled in her hand. The Marquess had tried to seduce her in order to keep it. And she was a numbskull to be swayed by the charm of a man who had ruined so many lives.

She sat back on her heels, staring at her ill-gotten gains. She would do well to keep that in mind.

Dinner over, Garrick sauntered out of the house with his father's sword under his arm. After a full morning going over the estate's ledgers in his uncle's absence, he now had an inkling of why Beauworth seemed less than healthy. Over the last decade, rents had declined. Why, he wasn't sure. Le Clere would no doubt have the answer, but would he have a solution?

Modernisation might be the key. He'd heard others talking about new farming methods. He'd mention it to Uncle Duncan when next they met. Right now, he had to deal with the robbers.

In the stables, Johnson had Bess ready to go.

'Some lucky lady you're keeping warm tonight, my lord?' Johnson said with a leer. 'Not that nice Miss

Ellie in the village, I hope. I heard as how you'd been showing an interest in that quarter.'

Garrick frowned. Blasted gossipmongers. In a small place like Boxted, it didn't take much for rumours to fly. 'Quite a different sort of entertainment.' He showed the old man his sword. 'Going to pay a call on Appleby. I've been promising him a return match since the last time I was home.'

Johnson nodded his head. 'No doubt 'e'll regret it.'

Garrick grinned. He had no intention of letting his coachman guess what he was about. He buttoned up his coat and pulled his beaver hat down low. 'You know how Appleby is, so don't worry if I'm gone for a day or two.' It might take some time to track down the ring. If they'd sold it, he might have to follow it as far as London. Heaven forefend that they'd melted it down.

Dan must have heard his voice, for the boy came galloping down the ladder to the loft. 'Can I come with you, my lord?'

'Not this time, Dan.'

The boy's face fell. 'But you'll be gone soon and—'

'Don't argue with his lordship,' Johnson said. The boy flinched.

It only took one sharp word and the old fear resurfaced. Garrick's ire rose, curling his hands into fists. The boy stepped back. Afraid of him, too. And rightly so, yet it cut him to the quick. 'Lead the horse out to the yard, lad,' he said quietly.

Dan hurried to comply. Garrick followed him outside.

With only the lamp above the stable door to light the courtyard, Garrick took the reins from a miserable-looking Dan. The lad was all alone and clearly worried about Garrick's departure. 'Can you keep a secret?'

The boy nodded.

'I've laid a trap for our highwaymen.'

'At the barn?'

He'd decided against laying in wait at their hideout. Things might get ugly if he cornered them both. He wanted to separate them. Catch one of them out in the open. Divide and conquer. Not something he had time to explain to the lad, so he nodded agreement. 'Not a word to anyone, if you please.'

The boy's face brightened. 'And you're takin' yer sword, too. I'd like to see a sword fight.' He lunged, with one arm straight. 'Stick her with it.'

Bloodthirsty little wretch. 'Perhaps,' Garrick said, holding back the urge to laugh. 'Be a good lad and obey Mr Johnson as you would me.'

Dan stepped back and bowed with an innate dignity that seemed at odds with his rough upbringing. He'd miss the lad when he left for the army, he realised. Enough maudlin thoughts. He had work to do.

With a nod he mounted and urged Bess into a canter. Beyond Boxted he found a rise not far from where Lady Moonlight had held him up two nights before. From this vantage, he would see the villains when they set up their ambush for the non-existent Beauworth coach. They were in for a nasty surprise.

Clouds fled from the moon and Mist stood out like a patch of snow on a bare mountain. Eleanor edged deeper into the shadows. As usual, her stomach tightened like a windlass and her mouth dried to dust, but tonight her nervousness was pitched far higher than normal. She missed the stalwart Martin. She tightened her grip on Mist's reins.

The horse pricked his ears, flicking them in the direction of the field on the other side of the hedge. She held her breath, listening. A rustle of leaves, barely noticeable above the sound of the wind in the trees. A crack of a twig. It had to be him.

A rider broke through a gap in the hedge at the same moment the pitiless moon chose to reappear. Bad luck for him. 'Now, Mist. Fly.' She crouched over his neck and they galloped for the woods.

After a few minutes of dodging trees and bushes, she reined in. The pursuit crashed through the undergrowth behind her. She smiled. He'd taken the bait. A heady rush of excitement filled her veins, buzzing in her ears. He'd come alone, too, so she didn't have to worry about leading more than him astray.

She guided the horse off the well-worn path and into the tangled bushes. Low branches kept her ducking, but Mist required only the lightest touch as he followed the path she'd mapped out earlier in the day.

The clearing came up fast. She stopped and glanced back. Nothing. No sound or sight of anyone. Dash it. She'd been too clever and managed to lose him. She started to turn back.

'Hold.' The harsh word came from in front, not behind.

She whipped her head around. There, across the moon-drenched space, pistol drawn, he waited, his horse breathing hard. He'd circled around instead of following. Her heart thundered, her mind scrambled with the alteration to her plan. She gulped a breath. Things would go very ill if she made a mistake.

'You may observe,' the Marquess said coolly, 'that I have my pistol trained on you. So I suggest it is your turn to stand and deliver.'

She walked Mist into the middle of the clearing.

'Throw down your pistols,' he demanded.

No fool, then. She pulled them from their holsters one at a time and tossed them at his horse's front hoofs. The animal rolled its eyes, but remained still. Damn.

'Dismount,' he said, his voice cold, his hand steady.

A chill ran down her spine. He looked dangerously angry. She turned, preparing to dismount with Mist between them.

'Oh, no, you don't. Get off on this side or I'll shoot the horse.'

Blast. He obviously knew that old cavalry trick. She bit her lip. She had no choice but to obey. Cautiously, she slipped out of the saddle, retaining her hold on Mist's bridle.

Still mounted, the Marquess walked his horse to stand directly before her. The big-boned mare towered over her and Mist. Raising her gaze, Eleanor watched his eyes, ready to drop to the ground if he decided to fire. You didn't grow up with older brothers and a soldier father without learning something useful.

Atop his horse, his face stern, he looked like some avenging god of war. Beautiful in the way of a cold marble statue.

'Well, wench, we meet again.' His gazed raked her from her head to her heels. 'An interesting costume. You don't expect me to believe you are a boy, do you?'

She'd opted for the freedom of breeches for the work she had to do tonight. She cast him the saucy half-smile she'd copied from Lizzie, the upstairs maid at Castlefield. A lass with an eye for the lads. 'Well, well, if it ain't the Markiss Boworthy. So we meets agin', milord. Come for another kiss, 'ave yer?'

Casually, he gathered his reins in one hand and prepared to dismount. The nodcock. Underestimating her because she was female. She tensed. As his foot touched the ground, his body turned and his pistol moved off target. She tore her sword from the scabbard on her saddle and clutched the blade in her left hand. As he squared up, she lunged. A swift arc with the hilt knocked his pistol up. It exploded harmlessly into the air. A flick and she tossed the sword into her right hand, ready to run him through.

'Stand back,' she ordered.

Steel hissed as he drew a sword from the scabbard at his side. He was carrying a sword? Only the military carried them these days, or those with nefarious intent. He must have noticed hers on her saddle the other evening. Damn it. Now what?

He must have seen her surprise, because he laughed. 'Nice move, wench, but I am an expert swordsman. You might as well give up now.'

The way he said swordsman, almost like a caress, sent a shiver down her spine. Arrogant man. She would dashed well show him a thing or two before she presented her nice little surprise. 'Damn yer eyes, Markiss.' She slashed at him, testing his skill.

He stumbled back, yet parried the unexpected thrust. He chuckled softly. Was he enjoying this? He had the reach, without question, but he was nothing but an idle rake, whereas she had practised for hours with William every day before he left for his regiment. She hacked at him in a flurry of blows.

At first, Beauworth gave ground to her attack. He fought lazily, his tip dropping time and time again. Always managing to recover before she broke through. He kept glancing around. 'Where's your accomplice?' he asked in insultingly conversational tones as he parried a particularly tricky thrust with seeming ease.

'Takin' care of business in Lunnon.'

'So you thought you'd try thieving on your own?'

'Like taking lollipops from a baby it is.' In spite of her bravado, her heavy breathing meant she found engaging in a conversation difficult. She'd tried every trick she knew. Sweat trickled into her eyes. She dashed it away on her sleeve, circling her opponent and taking advantage of a brief reprieve.

'Had enough, wench?' he jibed.

Enough? She'd almost pinked him twice. She had the upper hand, despite her tiring arm. She gulped air into her desperate lungs. 'Not 'til I have yer 'ead on me spit.'

His husky chuckle drifted maddeningly into the night. Damn him. She was wilting and he seemed not the slightest bit discomposed.

Without warning, he changed his stance, attacked her hard and fast, lunging and stabbing. No more did his sword point waver, it flashed in a quicksilver blur. The grate of steel on steel screeched into the silence. Forced back by his superior strength, she retreated toward the great oak tree, which had stood guard over this clearing for centuries. She bit her lip. Had she been too confident?

His sword tip closed in on her throat. She defended and recovered. Again, he forced her back. She tripped on a root, staggering back, her arms wide.

He flicked his wrist and her coatsleeve was cut from elbow to shoulder. They both knew it could just as easily have been her flesh. She could see it in his eyes and the arrogant tilt of his head.

Air scraped her throat dry. Trembles shook her hand. Her wrist ached. The point of her blade wavered badly. *Tip up. Tip up.* Her father's laughing voice rang in her ears. Her wrist refused to comply. This man was dangerous and she was running out of time. She glanced over her shoulder, lined herself up.

The Marquess's grin exuded arrogance. At any moment, he would have her. He knew it. She knew it. He was far better than he'd let her believe. She should have been more wary right from the beginning, more focused on what she needed to do.

The tree trunk loomed behind her. She thrust at him one last time. He twisted his wrist. Her sword spun free. He caught it neatly and effortlessly in his left hand and crossed both blades at her throat.

Her heart beat wildly. Her stomach pitched. She swallowed dust. This was not supposed to happen.

His teeth flashed white and his eyes gleamed. While her ribs ached with the need for air, his chest barely rose and fell. 'Now, Lady Moonlight, we need to talk. But first, let's see your face.' He tossed her blade aside.

Eleanor's knees shook so hard, she feared she might stumble on to his point, yet somehow she dodged his hand. 'Put up...I concede.'

He gave a little ground, but his sword point did not waver from the base of her neck. 'So, you thought you would have my head on a spit, did you? I wonder how yours will look stretched on the gallows. Give me the mask.'

She lifted her hands away from her sides in an extravagant gesture of defeat, felt the dagger slide into her palm. She flicked it free of her sleeve. The blade flashed wickedly.

His jaw dropped, then he laughed. 'You think to defeat a sword with a hat pin?'

God, she hoped so. She cast it underhand at the branch behind his head. He dodged. The net dropped, tangling his sword in the mesh. He cursed. Sawed at the ropes to no effect. She ran for the coil of rope behind the tree, hauled it through the block and tackle she'd nailed above his head. The mouth of the net tightened, trapping him and his sword inside.

She ran for her pistols and spun around. 'Methinks…yer took o'er long, Markiss,' she gasped. She wrapped the length of rope around his torso, while he glared at her through the mesh. 'You should 'ave finished it when you had the chance.'

A net. The little hellion. Garrick's face heated. She'd caught him like a cod fish. No matter how he twisted, he couldn't break free and could get no leverage with his blade.

'Drop yer sword,' she said, pointing her pistol at his head. With his legs free, he could try a flying leap and no doubt one of them would get shot. Trouble was it was more likely to be he with his arms trapped against his body. He released the hilt of his sword, and she extracted it from the net, kindly not slicing him in the process.

He tried stretching the ropes with his shoulders and elbows.

'Save yer strength,' she advised, tying the free end of the rope to her horse. 'You've a long walk ahead of yer.'

'Like hell.'

'Yer choice. Walk or be dragged.' She mounted the grey and gathered up Bess's reins.

Bloody hell. He was going to see her hang for this.

It was a long walk back to the barn he'd found the day before, but she took it nice and easy, and if he hadn't been bundled like a sack of washing, he might not have minded the exercise.

Inside the barn, she bade him sit.

'What now?' he asked as she tied his ankles and fastened the rope about his waist to a metal ring on the wall.

'I would think a Markiss ought to be worth a guinea or two.'

That he hadn't expected. He forced a laugh. 'So it's a ransom you're seeking, is it?' He tried to ease the pressure of the ropes, but there was no give. 'My uncle won't fall for it. 'Tis well known that once the ransom is paid, abductors kill the victim. He will, however, hunt you down like dogs.'

She kicked at his boot. 'Looks like yer the dead man, then.'

She left him in the dark with his thoughts, his growing anger and the scent of hay and horse manure in his nostrils.

He struggled inside his bindings. Nothing he did made them any looser and he found nothing within reach to serve as a blade.

The more time passed, the more fury filled his heart until his head ached. He imagined his captor swinging from a gibbet, or hanging by her arms in some dark dungeon. But each time he got to the point of murdering her, he found himself kissing her instead. More frustration.

What would Uncle Duncan do when he received their ransom note? He'd be worried mindless. He'd probably pay the damned ransom, too. Something the estate could ill afford, apparently.

She'd have to set him loose at some point and then he'd find a way to break free. In the meantime, it would be better to think of something other than his captor if he wanted to remain sane.

The delightful vision of Ellie Brown floated across his mind's eye. Now there was a maid worth thinking about. She reminded him of untouched spring mornings and pristine golden beaches—all that was good in the world—whereas Lady Moonlight was dark nights and silk sheets and the heat of lust—pure wickedness.

Given the choice, which one did he want? Both. Together in one bed. He groaned as his body expressed approval of the image then let his mind take him where it would. Better to be driven mad by sexual frustration than rage.

Garrick opened his eyes to the sound of raised voices. Two voices, one male, one female, outside the barn. A falling out of thieves? He blinked to clear his vision. He must have slept. His neck and back were sore and his hands and feet were numb. The barn door swung open and sunlight streamed into his prison. He squinted at the large figure outlined in the doorway. Her accomplice had returned. He looked furious.

Pistol in one hand, knife in the other, the masked man slashed through the net and then the ropes. He yanked Garrick to his feet. Blood rushed into his extremities. He bit back a protest. 'Outside,' his captor said.

Struggling to regain his wits, Garrick shuffled out on feet pricked by a thousand pins, and every joint in his body complaining. Outside in the dazzle of a fine morning, the woman, also masked, bent over a pan on the fire. The blankets piled nearby suggested she'd camped there.

As usual, her hair was covered with her peruke. She looked up as Garrick sat down cross-legged against the wall of the barn. 'You walk like an old man.'

He glared at her. 'So would you if you'd been tied like a parcel all night.'

She collected more wood for the fire from a pile at the

side of the barn. On the way back she sniffed as she passed him. 'You stinks. Ben, take 'im to the pond to wash.'

So her partner's name was Ben.

'On your feet, my lord,' the man said.

'Why bother?' he said, glowering at Ben. 'You're just going to murder me.'

Ben picked up his rifle, grabbed Garrick by the upper arm and marched him down to the pond where he untied the ropes at his wrists.

'Strip.'

Garrick glanced at the woman. 'No.'

'Then I'll do it fer ye while she holds the rifle. Leave your damned breeches on if ye must.'

Garrick huffed out a breath. No point in arguing for the sake of it.

He removed his coat and dropped it at his feet. His shirt followed, and he sat to remove his boots and stockings. Retaining his breeches, he stood. With a wary eye on Ben, he backed into the water.

'You'll see my bullet coming,' Ben said.

Garrick didn't trust either of them and let disbelief show in his face. When the water was deep enough, he sluiced the water over his arms and face. The woman strolled to the water's edge and tossed him a bar of soap, then she picked up his shirt and stockings, rinsed them and hung them to dry over the fence.

'I'll have those back, wench,' Garrick called. She ignored him.

Although the mud on the bottom oozed between his toes, the water was cool and reasonably clear. Garrick could not help but enjoy the freshness after his ghastly night. He kept an eye on Ben who, while he held his rifle casually, held it with the assurance of a man prac-

tised in its use. Garrick was sure the man had seen
military service from his disciplined movements and
ramrod carriage. A hard man, who would not make
escape easy.

He soaped his hair and sank beneath the water to
rinse. When he came to the surface he saw Ben alert,
his rifle cocked. He stood up slowly, aware of the wench
watching from the bank, her gaze travelling over his
torso, her lips parting slightly as if she'd never seen a
man without his shirt.

Heat pooled instantly in his loins. Damn her. She'd
done it on purpose. He splashed more water over his
face, forcing his body under control before he could
think of leaving the water. Fortunately, she returned to
her cooking.

So Garrick made his way out of the pond and headed
for his clothes.

'No need to be shy,' the woman said. 'Put them on
when they are dry.'

Ben looked scandalised. He muttered something
under his breath, but gestured for Garrick to go ahead.

The scent of bacon assaulted his nostrils. Whether
because it was being cooked outside, or because he was
ravenously hungry, his mouth watered. He kept his face
impassive and returned to his place against the barn
wall.

'Sit by the fire,' she ordered. 'We don't want yer
catching a chill.'

He curled his lip. 'Not before you get my money, at
least.'

Ben jerked the rifle. 'Sit near the fire.'

Garrick cursed and sat as directed.

The woman slapped the eggs and bacon on to a slab
of bread and handed it to him. She did the same for Ben.

It tasted as good as it smelled. It would do no good to starve himself. He'd need every ounce of strength to escape these two.

She stood up. 'We need fresh water.' She walked away.

Moments later, he heard her gasp behind him.

Ben looked up from his food. 'What is it?'

Garrick knew what had caught her attention. It was the reason he never removed his shirt in public. He glowered, but said nothing as she placed a cup of water beside him, her gaze still fixed on his back.

'Look at this,' she said to Ben.

Unfolding his brawny body with a grunt, Ben stood up and joined her at Garrick's shoulder. He whistled softly through his teeth.

'Who did this?' she asked.

Garrick heard the pity in her voice and cringed. He did not need her sympathy, damn her. 'An accident, years ago.' Uncle Duncan had lost his temper. He'd expressed his regret as Garrick lay on his stomach, bandaged and medicated. Le Clere had never lost control like that again but it always served to remind Garrick what lay beneath the surface.

'An accident?' She stared at Ben, her face full of incredulity. 'Have you ever seen…?'

'In the army, I have. An officer's cane can do that kind of damage.'

She reached out and pressed a finger on his back. Garrick jumped with a curse.

'Sorry,' she said, whipping her hand away.

'Forget it,' he ground out through clenched teeth. 'Just give me my shirt if the sight troubles you.'

But once again she touched him, gently now, tracing the three straight diagonal lines across his back. His skin jumped and flickered, although her touch was as gentle as a butterfly, as light as a whispering breeze, almost a caress. He felt his chest constrict. The women he had known in London were interested in only one thing and it did not involve tenderness. No woman had ever touched him so softly, not since his mother…

Garrick squeezed his eyes tight, forcing down the memories. He pulled away from her questing fingers.

Ben shook his head. 'They're old, but no accident.'

She paced away. 'If he's to spend another night here, you will need to find a better way to make him secure.'

He glared at the woman. How long did they expect to keep him here? 'Le Clere won't pay you. He is not such a fool.' He hoped.

'I'll find something.' Ben's voice sounded kindly, less harsh. 'Up you get, lad. Sit over by the fence.'

Garrick rose to his feet. Silent and grim, Ben tied him to the fence with enough rope to shift his position. Tied up like a wild animal. Like one of his nightmares. He clenched and unclenched his hands, forcing himself to hold back the anger rising in his gullet. He took a deep breath. Then another. Control. Sooner or later they'd make a mistake.

Ben left them on foot, meaning he was headed for somewhere nearby. Were they in league with one of the local farmers? One of his tenants? An interesting and disturbing thought.

Forced into idleness, he watched the wench groom all three horses. The skin-tight breeches hugged the flair of her hips, and her slender thighs above riding boots were the stuff of pleasurable dreams. The full shirt and open waistcoat didn't hide her narrow waist, but gave no impression of the size of her breasts. Those he'd felt, small and firm, when he'd kissed her.

He shifted, furious and uncomfortable at his body's arousal. No doubt she knew how incredibly sensual she looked in her boy's garb. He wouldn't give her the satisfaction of knowing he'd noticed. Instead, he closed his eyes to picture her face behind the mask, light eyes, certainly. But what colour hair lay beneath her ridiculous old-fashioned wig? Her eyebrows were fair. But her hair could be anything from red to gold. The sun warmed his skin. A bee bumbled by in a soft drone on air scented with grass and sweet clover.

Having finished with the horses, Eleanor decided to feed her prisoner before Martin returned and they left for the night. A platter of bread, cheese and pickles seemed a somewhat meagre offering for a man who must be used to the finest dining. On the way, she gathered up his now-dry clothes. The Marquess needed to get dressed. The sight of him sprawled on the grass like some Adonis really was too much, especially since he had fallen asleep, leaving her free to peek all she wanted. The way he had watched her from beneath half-lowered lids, while she groomed the horses, had made her feel hot and awkward. She'd been glad when he'd drifted off to sleep.

He looked so peaceful propped against the fence, his head lolling against a naked broad shoulder. Like an angel. A fallen one, with that sensual cast of his lips and the body of a heathen god. And there was just so much of him. Even stretched out on the grass, his male virility was overpowering.

Her breath became shallow as she stood just looking at the rogue. What would they have thought of each other if they had met under different circumstances? In London, perhaps? Would they have met? A proper young lady wouldn't be introduced to a rake with his reputation.

Whereas a real lady highwayman might well take advantage of a handsome prisoner tied up at her mercy. A little thrill shot through her insides at the image. Dash it. How could she be so wicked? She really wished she'd never started along this path.

She set the plate beside him and the pile of clothes. He must have sensed her presence because he opened one eye, then the other and stretched. 'You'll forgive me for not getting up.'

Polite to a fault, even if there was an edge of sarcasm in his voice. 'I'll forgive ye. Eat. It's all you'll get today.' She flopped down against the fence. 'So you thought to trap us with yer talk of gold at the inn?' she asked as he munched on the bread.

He swallowed and she watched the rise and fall of his Adam's apple in the strong column of his throat with utter fascination. 'I wanted my signet ring back,' he said.

'Not the watch?'

A glimmer of a smile curved his lips. 'A gift from a lady with rather flamboyant tastes. You are welcome to it.' His face sobered. 'The ring was my father's.'

The hollow note in his voice made her cringe—she knew how awful she'd feel if she lost her mother's locket. But he only had himself to blame. If he'd not proved so intractable about the repayment of the mortgage, none of this would have happened.

Something moved at the edge of her vision. By her knee. A spider. Big and black and hairy. Walking up her leg.

She froze. A shudder ran down her spine. Held her rigid.

'Looks like you've made a new friend,' he said, grinning.

'Get it off,' she gasped.

He laughed. 'It's only a spider.'

'Get it off me,' she said through stiff lips, afraid to breath in case it moved. 'Please.' Her voice shrilled.

With a muttered curse, he leaned forward and brushed the horrid thing away with his bound hands. It scuttled into the grass. 'There. It's gone.'

Her skin prickled as if it was crawling all over her. Trembles shook her body. Her teeth chattered. 'I hate them.'

'It's gone.' He tipped her chin with the back of his hand, smiling. 'I promise you.' He lifted his arms, dropped them over her head, around her shoulders and drew her on to his lap. 'You are all right.' He pressed his lips to her jaw below her mask, let her nuzzle into his shoulder where she drew on his calm, comforted by the steady sound of his heartbeat.

Slowly her trembles dissipated. She felt safe, protected, for the first time in many months. And being held in his arms seemed like the most natural thing in the world. The chills of revulsion lessened. Heat rushed to her face. 'I'm such an idiot,' she muttered against silken skin smelling of soap and smoke from the fire, and another scent. Him.

'We all have our fears,' he said gently, as if he really understood. He tipped her chin with the back of his bound hands, the sight of the rope making her cringe. And when she met his gaze, his warm brown eyes showed concern. 'All right now?' he asked, then frowned. 'Tears?' He smoothed her cheek below the mask with his thumb, then bent his head and pressed his lips to the place he had rubbed as if to kiss away her fear. Like an adult with a child. Sweet. Kind.

An ache squeezed her chest. Guilt. And something else she didn't dare name.

She dropped a kiss of gratitude on his cheek, missed and landed on the corner of his mouth. He angled his head and captured her lips full on, licking and tasting, while his forearm supported her nape. Tingles raced across her breasts. Her insides clenched.

Oh, heavens. At any moment, Martin would return. Yet she didn't want to stop. Couldn't stop. Not yet. Soon. She opened her mouth to his questing tongue. And she was lost. Lost in pleasure. Dizzy with the rapid beat of her heart. The lack of air. Sensations rippled though her body, pleasurable little thrills, warmth, and languid melting.

Her hands clung to his sun-warmed shoulders. Satin skin, firm muscles rippled beneath her fingers. Pure strength. Lovely wicked flutters deep between her thighs held her enthralled.

She lay her hand flat against the haze of beard on his jaw. He broke the kiss, turned his head, the roughened skin grazing her palm, and licked the base of her thumb, hot and wet, followed instantly by cool. A shiver of delight danced across her breasts.

She moaned at the sensual onslaught.

This is wrong, a little voice whispered. You will never be the same again. Get up now.

He shifted his weight and eased her on to the ground, cushioning her shoulders with his forearm. She opened her thighs at the nudge of his knee and a sweet burst of pleasure fired in her core.

'Untie me, *chérie. Vite.* Quickly. Free my hands.'

Eleanor stared at him blankly.

'Cut the rope,' he pleaded, his breathing ragged and shallow, his voice hoarse. 'Set me free. I'll do nothing to hurt you.' His soft, accented voice was an urgent enticing whisper in her ear. His thigh ground against her, pushing between her legs, creating hot surges of sweet agony.

'A promise you will keep, my lord.'

Ah, no. Martin. Face scalding, she slipped under the loop of the Marquess's arms and rose to her feet, breathing hard. What had she been thinking?

Martin cocked his rifle with a loud threatening click and the Marquess struggled to a sitting position.

Bewilderingly, her mind seemed to be full of molasses, thick and syrupy and deadly. He'd comforted her and she'd dissolved like butter in hot milk. Mute with embarrassment, she stared at Martin weighed down by a necklace of iron chain and shackles. He levelled his rifle.

The Marquess stiffened, as if bracing for… Oh God. Martin was going to fire. 'Put the gun down,' she yelled. 'He is unarmed and bound. No harm was done.'

Martin held her stare for a long moment, then grimaced. He let the rifle fall to his side, but his body remained stiff, his movements jerky as he set the rifle against the fence. He pulled the Marquess to his feet. 'Back to the barn for yer lordship.'

'Take your hands off me,' the Marquess said, steadying himself on his feet, his face as flushed as hers felt.

Was he ashamed of their kiss? And why did it matter? Once this was over, she'd never see him again. A pain she couldn't fathom filled her heart. Oh, God, what was wrong with her? Kissing him like a wanton, all the while knowing Martin would return at any moment. She had lost her mind.

He'd been so kind about the spider, not laughing the way her brothers always had at her stupid female fear, that she'd forgotten they were enemies. And now Martin looked ready to commit murder. Something she would not allow. She picked up the Marquess's clothes and the rest of the food and followed them into the cool depths of the barn.

Martin fixed the iron chain to the ring in the wall and fastened the shackle to the Marquess's ankle before cutting the ropes free.

'That'll hold you,' Martin said.

The Marquess glanced up from inspecting his chain. 'Your accommodations leave much to be desired.' The lazy drawl seemed at odds with the revulsion she glimpsed in his eyes. 'Why not shoot me and have done? I'll be damned if you'll get any money.'

Bravado, she thought. And yet…

'We'll see,' Martin said, stepping back.

'Leave me alive and I'll hunt you down like dogs,' the Marquess said, in matter-of-fact tones.

He meant it. Was he taunting Martin deliberately so he'd shoot? Did he hate those chains so much? Bile rose in her throat, a sour taste of guilt. Her heart sank. She couldn't see it through. She could not keep him chained here day after day, thinking they were going to kill him and watching his hatred grow.

She gazed down at him. He winked. More bravado.

Martin growled a curse.

In her heart she knew the Marquess would try again to charm her into setting him free. And she wasn't sure how long she could resist, unless she kept away from him completely. It would be best if she left him to Martin. Best for her. Not for him, given Martin's present mood.

Coward.

And what if his uncle wouldn't pay the ransom? What would they do then? Not only would they not have the money they needed, they'd have the Marquess bent on revenge. If only she had something he wanted in exchange for the mortgage.

There was one thing he seemed to want. Her. And that was out of the question. Wasn't it? Was it really too high a price to pay for what she'd done?

She inhaled a deep breath. 'Bring 'is horse inside,' she said to Martin. 'We needs to talk.'

They did very little talking on the way back to her cottage after leaving their horses at Martin's cousin's farm. Anger surrounded Martin like a wall Eleanor could almost touch; while she regretted causing him upset, his grim silence left her free to mull over her options.

The Marquess did like her. He kissed her when she was Ellie. And he kissed her when she was Lady Moonlight. And instead of kissing her, he could easily have overpowered her before Martin came back. He'd been too busy kissing her to save his own neck, the rake, and she'd thanked him by chaining him to a wall. She winced.

But if she took this step, she'd be well and truly ruined. Wasn't she already far beyond the pale of what was acceptable? A thief, and, if this afternoon was anything to go by, a wanton. Her stomach gave a horrid little lurch, the kind that stops your breath at the knowledge of the inevitable. It didn't matter. She was the one who'd created the mess, she should be the one to pay the price. Not the Marquess. Certainly not Sissy and William. And definitely not Martin. It also would not lead to prison.

But she'd have to get Martin out of the way.

Once inside the cottage, Martin put his hands on his hips and glowered. She braced herself for a lecture. She was actually surprised he'd lasted this long before taking her to task.

'What is it you want to say, Martin?'

'I'd like to know what you thought you were doing

with that lordling. Don't you understand? He could…'
He took a breath. 'You don't know what these men of
the world are like.'

A flash of heat scalded her cheeks. Martin thought
of her as an innocent, but what had happened out at the
barn wasn't all one-sided by any means. Where the
Marquess was concerned, it seemed she didn't have an
iota of control.

'It wasn't what you think,' she muttered. 'There
was a spider.' Martin knew how she hated the horrid
crawly things.

'Well, if you hadn't been rolling around the grass
you wouldn't have seen a spider. I know what I saw, and
he had his hands on you.'

And she hadn't resisted. Not for a minute. Shame
flooded through her at the look of disgust in his eyes,
even though she knew he was trying to hide it.

'Give up this nonsense, my lady,' he pleaded.
'Before you end up on the gallows, or worse.'

Unfortunately, worse seemed to be the only alternative. She avoided his gaze, fearing he would sense
something amiss. 'You are right. This is not going to
work.'

Martin let go a long breath. 'Thank God. I'll go and
set him free.'

'No. I'll do that first thing in the morning.' She took
a deep breath. 'I need you to take a message to William.
Right away. Then go to Lady Sissy and wait.'

'You will be there when I get back?'

'No.'

He looked startled, then worried. He opened his
mouth to argue.

She forestalled him. 'It is all in the note to William.
I'm going to Scotland to visit Molly MacDonald—you

know she's been begging to see me for weeks. I can't risk the Marquess discovering my whereabouts.'

The worry on his face didn't ease. 'I suppose you're right.'

'I know I am.'

She pulled out paper and a quill and sat down at the kitchen table while Martin paced back and forth, as if he couldn't quite make up his mind. She ignored him. First she wrote a short note to Mr Jarvis, telling him the money was on the way. Next a note to Molly, asking her to forward her letters on to William when they arrived and promising to explain the whole when she arrived in a few weeks' time. 'I want you to post these for me in the morning.'

Martin halted and nodded.

The next letter was to William. Explaining the mess she'd caused and begging him to wait with Sissy until he heard from her that all was resolved. She sanded and sealed the note. 'You will take this to Portsmouth and leave it with the harbour master. Stress that it must be put into William's hands the moment his ship arrives.'

'Don't worry. I'll make sure he understands. You will take care, my lady? Setting him free and all?'

'Yes, Martin. I know exactly what I have to do. Give me the key.'

She handed him the letters and he gave her the key to the Marquess's shackles.

'I'll wait until you have time to get well on the road,' she said. 'Tell William not to worry when you see him. And, Martin, whatever you do, do not bring him here. The Marquess is not to blame for this.'

He narrowed his eyes. 'Something tells me you are keeping something back. You should go to your brother yourself. Tell him the whole story to his face.'

No fool, Martin Brown. 'Martin, do this and I promise I will never ask you for aught else. Now make haste. You don't want to miss William's arrival.'

He sighed. 'Very well, my lady. But I will keep you to your word.'

Chapter Four

Another night in the pitch black with only his mare's soft breathing for company. Instead of kissing the wench, he should have forced her to untie him. Used her as a hostage. Instead he'd let his lust overcome reason.

That and her tears. He hated to see any woman cry. Something that had cost him dear over the years in farewell trinkets.

Where the hell was Le Clere? Surely a ransom note would have had him scouring the countryside? And Dan knew of this place. He would have told Johnson where to look.

An owl hooted. Had something disturbed it? Garrick listened. Nothing. He returned to his fingertip exploration of every board in the wall behind him, every crevice within reach on the floor. One little nail to poke in the padlock was all he asked.

A splinter drove under his fingernail, sharp and agonising. He cursed.

'Is that you, my lord?' The whisper came from the direction of the door.

Puzzled, Garrick peered into the impenetrable darkness. 'Who is it?'

'It's me. Dan.'

Thank God. 'Have Johnson or someone break open the door, boy.'

'There's only me, my lord. You told me it was a secret.'

Not what he wanted to hear. 'Go for help. Hurry up.'

The sound of splintering wood drowned out his words. Would the lad never listen?

'Where are you, my lord? 'Tis so dark, I see naught.'

'Over here.' Garrick kept talking until Dan stumbled into him. He grasped the boy by the arm. 'Has there been no hue and cry at Beauworth? No one out searching?'

'No, my lord. Everyone thinks you are visiting friends.'

No ransom note? How bloody odd. 'Very well. Take my horse and ride back to the Court. Tell Le Clere he will need a hammer, a chisel, tools.' Garrick rattled his chain.

'Nay, not so much, my lord.' Pride filled the boy's voice. He fumbled with the chain, his breathing a dry rasp in Garrick's ear. 'Gimme a tick,' he muttered. The sound of metal against metal, scratching, a click. The padlock fell with a clunk, followed by a rattle of iron.

'Good God. I had no idea you were so accomplished.'

'No, my lord.'

Garrick got to his feet. 'Come on, show me where you got in.' He followed as Dan felt his way along the walls to the broken plank. By widening it, Garrick was able to crawl out.

'What on earth brought you?' Garrick asked, looking around for signs of his captors. The waning moon lit a silver path across the pond and stars winked a greeting.

The boy shuffled his feet. 'I was afeared you was

goin' to tip the old fellow a double. I thought you'd gone off and left me.' He wiped his nose on his sleeve. 'I weren't goin' to stay there on me own. So I followed. I didn't know where else to start.'

Garrick ruffled his hair. 'Well, I'm bloody glad you did.'

'I brought this.' Metal glinted as Dan handed Garrick a pistol. 'I *borrowed* it from Mr Johnson. If yer joining the army, I wants to go, too.'

The weapon dated from the last century, but looked serviceable and clean. 'Did you ask Mr Johnson?'

He shrugged. 'He would've said no.'

Incorrigible. 'I don't suppose you thought to bring bullets and powder?'

Dan's teeth flashed white. 'That I did.'

'Damn me, boy, you are a marvel.'

'I got a blade, too.' The boy pulled forth a knife. A sliver of steel with a bone handle. A deadly weapon in the right hands, and also useful in opening padlocks.

'Where did that come from?'

'It's mine.' Dan caressed the blade with a fingertip. 'A friend gave it me. I were going to use it on *him* if you 'adn't come along.'

'Then I saved you from hanging. May I borrow it for a while?' The more he thought about it, the more he wanted to teach his captors a lesson they wouldn't forget. And with surprise on his side, they were in for a nasty shock.

The boy handed over the knife and Garrick tucked it inside his boot.

'What are you going to do?'

'I'm going to ambush them inside the barn. Wait for me in the trees yonder,' Garrick said. 'Watch carefully. If anything goes wrong, ride for help. Can you do that?'

'I'd sooner hide in the barn with you.'

'I need you to stand watch. It's an important job.'

Dan looked unconvinced, but he finally agreed and Garrick squeezed back into his prison. Dan replaced the broken plank behind him. 'Be careful, my lord,' he whispered.

'I will. Try to stay awake.'

A snort greeted his words, then he heard the boy move off. Once back in his corner, he lay down in the straw with the manacle loose about his ankle. He was going to enjoy giving these rogues a taste of their own medicine. They deserved a little bit of terror, before he got his property back.

Dawn lightened the eastern sky, but it was still dark in the valley as Eleanor pulled back the barn door with shaking hands. If she had any sense she'd send Le Clere a note, tell him where to find his missing nephew and flee.

And they'd be out on the streets with no money and deeply in debt. No. Taking advantage of his attraction was the last arrow in her quiver. The fact that she found him equally attractive wasn't a bad thing either. It would make playing her part easier, perhaps even enjoyable, although thoroughly disgraceful. She shivered.

She touched her mask. If only she could keep it on. But she couldn't. He would have to know she was both Lady Moonlight and Ellie Brown. She'd have to tell him as much of the truth as she dared without actually admitting to her real identity. Once it was over, she'd disappear.

She took a deep breath and perched her hat on top of her boy's wig. It must look strange with her blue dimity gown, but she wanted to break the news gently.

Dust motes danced in the fingers of light poking through the knots and gaps in the walls. The Marquess lay on his back in the straw, his chest rising and falling as if he hadn't a care in the world. His lashes lay like dark fans above high olive cheekbones. So peaceful. His horse blew out a breath, a snort of disgust no doubt.

She shook his arm. 'My lord.'

He mumbled and opened his eyes, slowly gazing around.

'What is it? It's still the middle of the night,' he grumbled. 'The deuce.' He stared at up her, rather warily, she thought.

'My lord, you must listen, I—'

He sprang to his feet and grabbed her by the arm. She felt something cold and hard against her neck. A pistol.

'Cry out and you are dead,' he whispered.

The breath left her body in a terrified rush. He sounded angry enough to shoot her. Disaster. Her plan made no provision for this. She opened her mouth to speak and found her mouth drier than the well beside the barn. Her knees seemed to have lost all their strength.

'Where is he? Ben?' he asked.

His warm breath was hot in her ear, his arm a steel band around her waist. He brought the muzzle around to her face. 'Answer me, wench.'

She swallowed hard, managing to salvage some moisture for speech. 'He's gone.'

He squeezed her harder, crushing her ribs with his steely grip. 'When will he be back?'

'He left for good this time.'

She made no struggle as he propelled her towards the door.

'Let's hope he values your life,' he said with the pistol still pointed at her head. His body partly shielded by hers, he eased her out of the door. His heart knocked against her ribs, slow and steady, unlike hers, which seemed ready to leap from her chest. One false move on her part and she would find herself with a bullet to the brain. Not a preferred solution to her problems.

After a long pause, he thrust her away from him with such force she fell to her knees. Unmoving, she watched him check the vicinity of the barn.

Apparently satisfied, he returned to where she knelt, close to the spot where they had kissed the day before. He cast her a look of suspicion. 'He won't get far. When I catch him you'll both be up before the beak.'

He was going to cart her off to prison. She reached into the pocket of her skirt.

He levelled his pistol. 'Careful, wench.'

She froze. Her heart seemed to forget how to beat. 'I brought you something.'

One eyebrow went up. 'How sweet of you, my dear. A token of appreciation for helping you yesterday, no doubt.'

She opened her fingers. They shook and she steadied her wrist with her other hand. Beside the key in her palm lay his signet ring, a large solid circlet of gold mounted with heavy claws grasping the Beauworth shield. 'I was going to set you free. I hid the ring from Ben after you told me you wanted it back.'

The Marquess's lip curled. 'Admit it. You lost your nerve. Very clever of you to realise I would come after you for the ring. I suppose you expected me to forget the whole thing in exchange?'

This was not going according to plan. He clearly hadn't needed her to set him free and he accorded her only the worst of motives for returning his property. Even as it hurt, she acknowledged his right to think her despicable. She swallowed. What a fool she had been to risk everything on his seeming attraction, when a nobleman of his rank and physical beauty could have any woman he wanted.

She'd failed. Again. Moisture burned at the backs of her eyes. She sniffed. Whatever he decided now would be her punishment for letting William and Sissy down.

'Tears?' he said. 'You don't expect me to believe those are real, surely?' He sighed and took the ring from her hand. 'First, let's see who you are. Then we'll decide what comes next.' He grasped the edge of the mask and whipped it over her head in one swift movement. Her hat and wig fell to the ground. Her hair cascaded around her shoulders. Now he would know everything. Hot-faced, she lowered her head, hiding behind her hair's silky screen.

'No,' he said. 'It cannot be.'

A cool hand cupped her chin. He lifted her face, swept back the hair.

'Bloody hell. Ellie Brown?' He could not have looked more appalled to see Satan himself. 'There must be some mistake. This is some sort of trick.'

The disappointment in his expression took her aback. It was almost worse than his earlier disgust. Confused, she lowered her gaze, searching for the strength to follow through with her plan. 'It is me. I'm sorry, my lord.'

He reached out to touch her face as if he couldn't believe what he saw. 'Hell's teeth. You certainly fooled me finely. What game are you playing?'

For one mad moment she felt the urge to tell him the whole sordid story, to throw herself on his mercy. But she'd done that before, written to him asking him for more time to pay the mortgage without effect. No, far better to stick to her plan to bargain than beg for kindness. She dashed away tears that had somehow spilled over and took a deep breath. 'Ben was angry about what happened yesterday. He took all the money. Whatever will happen to Master William now?'

He blinked. 'Master William?'

'Lord Castlefield. He got into debt. The bailiffs came and threw us all out, because of the mortgage due on the estate. I was trying to raise money to help him, but it got out of hand.'

His glowered. 'More than out of hand, I would say, you little idiot. Why isn't this man taking care of his own debts?'

'He's away. Fighting in Spain.'

He cursed softly. 'Who holds the mortgage?'

She stared at him. How could he not know? Perhaps he just wanted to make her suffer. 'You do.'

His jaw dropped. 'Me?' He gave a harsh laugh. 'Don't tell me. You were going to use my money to pay me back? You really are one brazen hussy.'

If she didn't know better, she might have thought the glint in his eye was admiration. The straight line of his firm mouth and the hard set of his jaw said otherwise.

He looked down at the toe of his riding boots, scuffed and dirty, his thoughts hidden. 'Why come here today? Why didn't you cut your losses and run?' He frowned. 'Why not simply ask me for help without all this nonsense?'

'His lordship's lawyer wrote to you. You insisted the debt be paid or the house would be forfeit. When you said your uncle wouldn't pay the ransom, I thought of something else.' She winced as he narrowed his gaze on her face, his fingers playing with the strings of her mask.

'Well?' he prompted.

'I was going to offer to…' Heat spread from her face all the way to her feet. It had sounded so easy when she had gone over it in her mind. Now it sounded horrid. She swallowed what felt like a feather pillow stuck in her throat. 'To do whatever you wanted in exchange for the mortgage.' The words came out in a rush.

The thin black ribbons stilled. The silence lengthened. 'This Lord Castlefield must be very important to you.'

'Yes, he's—'

'Enough.' He squeezed his eyes shut briefly. 'I really don't want to hear the sordid details.' He stared down at the ring. 'I really have been seven kinds of a fool about you. I respected you, Ellie. Thought you were a very different kind of woman.' He shook his head. 'You and Ben must have enjoyed your little jokes at my expense.'

'I was desperate.'

He stilled. 'Desperate enough to offer yourself to me in exchange for this Lord Castlefield's debts.'

Spoken so softly, without emotion, it sounded dreadful. Her heart contracted, it grew small, and tight, all the joy and hope squeezed out of it as he laid out what she had become. 'Yes.'

'I'm not sure it's a compliment. How much does he owe?'

Her chest felt tight. 'A thousand pounds.' Her voice came out in a very small whisper.

'An expensive roll in the hay.' His gaze reflected some kind of cynical amusement. 'And for how long am I to receive the benefit of your services?'

Shame emblazoned her face. She closed her eyes briefly. What was one more nail in the coffin of her pride? In a panic, she picked a number at random. 'Three months. More if you want.'

Too much? Too little? She couldn't tell from his wooden expression.

'High priced indeed,' he said, his face bleak. He made a faint sound of disgust, then strode impatiently to the remains of the fire and stirred the ashes with the toe of his boot, clearly trying to make up his mind. The acrid smell of wood ash filled her nostrils as fine dust puffed up. 'I will let you know my decision tomorrow,' he said finally, without looking at her.

Clearly, he wasn't at all thrilled by her offer. No doubt he had plenty of beautiful women from whom to choose. Perhaps he wasn't as interested in her as she had thought. And that made her feel just a little…hurt. Which was ridiculous. At least he hadn't turned her down flat. Yet. 'Yes, my lord.'

He dropped the mask into the dead embers. 'How did you get here?'

'I walked.'

'Then I will take you home.' He put his fingers in his mouth and gave a shrill whistle. She jumped, her heart pounding. Who was he calling? Had he been playing some sort of cruel game? Toying with her the way he had during their duel? And now the constable would ride out to cart her off to prison.

Approaching hoof-beats had her spinning around in time to see a gawky blond lad emerge from the woods. The lad who'd been up on the box of the carriage the night of the robbery. He rode across the meadow in an ungainly gallop. So this was how her prisoner had escaped.

'Do you have any weapons on you?' the Marquess asked softly in her ear. She jerked away from him. 'No.'

'You won't mind if I check?'

She minded very much as his fingertips ran over her body. And even more when his large hands gently outlined the curve of her hip. She minded because her body responded with longing, whereas he looked completely unaffected, dispassionate. When he knelt before her, the tousled dark hair close to her stomach, and stroked between her thighs—gently, true, but missing not one inch of sensitised flesh—she minded so much that she felt dizzy and hot. Her breathing shortened, while her mind tried to assimilate the unnerving sensations on her skin.

He glanced up, an odd half-smile on his lips. 'I am glad you told the truth this once, wench.'

Her heart gave a painful squeeze. She wished she could tell him the truth about everything.

The boy drew his mount up close to the Marquess, staring at her open-mouthed.

'It's all right, lad,' the Marquess said. 'Return home and let Johnson know I will follow shortly.'

Knowing her face burned scarlet, Eleanor avoided the boy's curious glances by staring off into the distance. It wasn't until he had departed that she dared steal a glance at the grim man at her side.

He had said he would take her home. Did he mean that?

'Come. We will use my horse.'

He gestured her into the barn and readied his mare in silence. The ripple of muscle beneath his shirt as he worked reminded her of the strength she had seen in his arms on the previous day. Sculpted and bronzed, they'd been lovely. And his back had been broad and strong... and horribly scarred. She wished she hadn't seen that. It made her feel pity, when she wanted to feel practical, businesslike, unmoved by what would happen next.

With her wrist in a firm grip, he walked her and the horse outside and placed his hands about her waist.

They were warm and large, filling the hollow between her ribs and hips. He tossed her up on to his horse and climbed up behind her, pulling her on to his lap so she sat sideways across his thighs. She sat within the circle of his arms, wedged against his chest. Almost hysterical, still unable to believe how awry everything had gone, she held herself stiff and straight.

She ought to be flirting with him. Batting her eyelashes, charming him to do her bidding, but he seemed so remote, shc couldn't bring herself to try. He had his arms around her; she could feel the heat of his body against her back and yet she felt chilled. She'd hurt his pride. He'd as good as admitted it. After all, she was a woman and she had duped him finely. Not a good thing. Having grown up with two brothers, she knew how sensitive men were about thosc sorts of things.

Unable to bear the heavy silence any longer, she glanced up at his grim face. 'I truly am sorry for what I did. It was meant for the best. It was all I could think of to save my…lord.'

'Where is your sister?' he asked abruptly.

'I sent her to a relative.'

'I wish to hell you'd gone with her.'

She wished she'd seen it as an option. She shrugged. 'I needed the money.'

He leaned forwards, the hard wall of his chest pressing against her back, his warm breath tickling her ear, starting a series of tingles in other places she tried to ignore.

'Miss Brown,' he said, 'you are a reckless wench. Someone needs to curb your wild behaviour.'

'Someone like you?' she asked, and gasped at the hiss of his indrawn breath.

Silence was obviously the better part of valour, so she held her tongue for the rest of the way.

* * *

When they arrived at her door, the early morning sun was casting long shadows in the lane outside her cottage. Soon the rest of the village would be up and about. The Marquess set her down in the road and walked her up the path.

What to say under such awkward circumstances? 'Can I offer you tea, my lord?'

He hesitated, his brown eyes searching her face. He raised his hand and tipped up her chin. Her skin scorched where his fingers touched and she could not raise her gaze from his full mouth, as if her body yearned for the wicked sensations he engendered with his kisses. She held her breath. A delicious feeling of anticipation coursed through her veins. Her pulse raced. A shadow passed over his face. Regret? Longing? Or was it anger? It disappeared too fast to be sure.

He grasped her by the shoulders, turning her towards him, drawing her close. He touched his lips to hers. Her arms went around his neck. Her fingers twined in his silken hair. An instant surrender she could not control as he tasted her lips with infinite sweetness. A languor overtook her limbs.

He put her from him with an almost forced gentleness, as if he also fought some inner battle. Her arms felt bereft, her legs not exactly steady.

'I will come and see you tomorrow afternoon,' he said. He left without looking back. Eleanor went inside and bolted the door. She leaned against the old rough wood, a hand to her mouth. What had she done? She shivered. There had been no kindness in his face just now, no tenderness in his eyes. Just the heat of desire.

An answering heat flared in her body.

* * *

After bathing and changing his clothes, Garrick went down for breakfast and found his uncle already seated at the table with his usual two slices of toast.

Le Clere half-rose in his seat, relief warring with irritation for supremacy in his expression. 'Is it your idea to cause me an apoplexy, Garrick? I was ready to send out a search party if you hadn't returned this morning.'

The irony made Garrick want to smile. 'I rode over to Appleby's. Did you not get my message?'

His uncle cleared his throat. 'You did not say you'd be away so long.'

The sensation of being smothered returned to Garrick in full force. Memories of his boyhood. 'Well, here I am now,' he said cheerfully.

'You missed our meeting yesterday. I thought we had an agreement.'

'I apologise for that. I did look at the ledgers before I went. I wanted to ask you if I could look at the rent books when next we met.'

'Rent books?' Le Clere's eyes narrowed.

'Revenues have fallen. I wanted to see if the rent books gave any clue as to why. See which tenants are in trouble.'

His uncle frowned. 'They won't tell you much.' Garrick opened his mouth to argue. 'But why not?' his uncle said swiftly with a shrug. 'Matthews collects the rents. I'll ask him to bring them along, when he's finished making this month's rounds. How did you find the Applebys? All well?'

A rather swift change of topic, given how badly Le Clere had wanted him to take an interest in the estate. 'All in the pink of health, Uncle.' Fortunately for Garrick, they lived far enough away so that Le Clere was unlikely to run into them. Garrick pulled out a chair and sat down. 'They sent their regards.'

The butler bustled in with a freshly filled toast rack, poured coffee in Garrick's cup and left.

'I have a rather unusual request,' Garrick said, feeling a trickle of sweat run down the centre of his back.

Le Clere put down his paper with a genial smile. 'What can I do for you?'

'I understand that you…er, rather that we, have called in the mortgage on a property in Hampshire? Castlefield Place.'

Le Clere stiffened, his eyes narrowed, the expression in them piercing. 'What do you know about Castlefield?'

An oddly defensive response? Garrick maintained a relaxed expression. 'Not a great deal, although the name sounds vaguely familiar. You must know of it.'

Le Clere grunted.

'Ellie told me the son is unable to pay.'

'Ellie Brown?' An odd expression flickered across his face.

Blast. He hadn't meant to mention her by name, but since Le Clere made it his business to know every tenant on the estate, he would soon work it out. 'Yes, she was his servant.'

His uncle's eyes narrowed to slits. 'A servant, eh. Well, it's a straightforward foreclosure. What else did you want to know?'

Garrick's jaw tightened under his uncle's unblinking contemplation. 'I want you to forgive the mortgage and put the man back in dibs.'

'Is this some sort of jest?' Le Clere's laugh sounded incredulous. 'Do you know the size of the debt? The estate needs those funds to maintain your extravagant lifestyle.'

Garrick leaned forwards and locked eyes with his uncle. 'Are you telling me we are facing ruin? Is that why the servants have dwindled and Boxted is going to seed? You've never mentioned it before.'

Le Clere reared back. 'Damn it, Garrick. Is that all the gratitude I get for looking after your welfare? It's this bloody war of which you are so fond ruining everything. If you think you can do better, I encourage you to try.'

Struck with remorse at Le Clere's obvious distress, Garrick softened his voice. 'I didn't mean to criticise. You've worked harder than anyone for the estate, but my father would never have called in a loan if it meant throwing a friend's family out on the street and you know it.'

Le Clere sat silently for a moment, his expression pained, thoughts Garrick couldn't read racing over his usually bland face. A smile dawned and he visibly relaxed. Unaccountably, Garrick's hackles rose.

'Finally,' Le Clere said. 'I suppose I have Miss Brown to thank for you taking a real interest in Beauworth. While it is not exactly as I hoped, it is an interest none the less.' He leaned back, his lips pursed. 'I have a proposition for you. I will do exactly as you ask, against my better judgement, I might add. As your trustee, I could refuse, you know. In return, do something for me. Remain here at Beauworth. Devote yourself. Dally with this young hussy, if you must, but get yourself married and produce an heir.'

Garrick felt the room rock around him. 'I hadn't planned to marry for years.' If at all.

'Garrick, be reasonable. I must see you settled

before I relinquish control of the estate. It will ease my mind to know I did my duty, left everything properly ordered. It is what your father would have wished.'

He fought the guilt Le Clere invoked. 'It isn't what I want. Let Cousin Harry produce the next heir.'

Le Clere's eyes had a suspiciously moist glint. 'You are Beauworth. If you won't do it for me, do it for the family name.'

How could he fight such devotion? 'And the money?'

'It goes against the grain, my boy. The estate is owed that money.' He sighed. 'But Beauworth needs its Marquess far more. Do your duty and, if you still want it when the title is secure, you'll have your captaincy.'

Until he was of age, he could not access his funds without Le Clere's cooperation. And, damn it all, what was being asked of him was not unreasonable. 'I'll give you three months. That should be quite enough time to learn all I need to know about the estate. But no more talk of betrothals.'

Le Clere narrowed his eyes. 'What did Miss Brown offer in exchange? Her favours? Your women don't usually last more than three weeks.'

His skin crawled. How did Le Clere know so much? 'That is my business. I need a thousand pounds to pay off some of her pressing debts.'

His uncle blinked, clearly thunderstruck, but when he spoke his tone was soft and businesslike. 'Very well. Come back in two hours and I'll have it ready.'

Garrick supposed it could have been worse. And three months would be more than enough time for Ellie Brown. 'Thank you for being so understanding.'

'Dear boy, you forget, I, too, was young once.'

The oddly triumphant look on Le Clere's face disturbed something low in his gut. He pushed the feeling aside. Why would he quibble? His uncle had given him everything he requested. Although at a price.

The bigger question in his mind was what Ellie wanted.

Nervous and restless, Eleanor spent her morning tidying up the cottage and baking. Then she washed her hair and coiled it neatly at her nape. She dressed in her finest gown, a sprigged muslin, one of the few she'd brought from home. Whatever the outcome of his visit, she would behave with dignity.

A rap at the door. Her heart pounded. He was here. She smoothed her hair, took a deep, calming breath and opened the door.

He looked wonderful. Clean shaven, his hair carefully ordered *à la Brutus,* his dark blue coat snug on his powerful shoulders. Wonderful yet stern, his jaw set hard, his dark eyes watchful, as if he suspected her of treachery.

'My lord.' She curtsied low and gestured for him to enter.

'Good day, Miss Brown.'

His demeanour was so serious, her heart beat a warning of impending disaster. 'Please sit down, my lord. May I offer you some tea?'

'Thank you.' He took the wooden chair.

She felt his gaze upon her as she moved around the tiny kitchen, setting out teacups and a plate of cakes on the cloth-covered table. He appeared stiff and ill-at-ease. It must be bad news. She handed him his cup and perched on a stool.

He cleared his throat. 'Miss Brown, yesterday you made a proposal with respect to the relief of your employer's financial difficulties.'

'Yes, my lord.' Her voice sounded strained and tight. From the heat in her face she felt sure it must be crimson all the way to her hairline. She managed a smile. 'My lord, I believe that we discovered some warmer feelings for each other than mere acquaintance. Even though you did not recognise me in my other calling, I very much appreciated your kindness to me and my sister these past few days.' She was pleased to note that her voice barely shook.

He reached across and took her hand. Warmth travelled up her arm. His charming smile made an appearance and she knew everything would be all right.

'Ellie, I think you know that I found you enchanting the first day I met you in the village. I have continued to feel admiration for you since that day.' His serious expression returned. He placed a rolled document tied with a red ribbon and a package on the table between them. 'I was shocked when I realised your deception. I was rude. I honour you for your loyalty to your employer. I am returning the mortgage without further obligation. There is also enough money to help with the debts. You can choose to stay, or you can leave without recrimination.'

She gasped, not quite able to believe what she'd heard. He was letting her leave?

He rose, prowling to the window to gaze outside. Against the light, the profile of his cheekbone seemed to be cut from something harder than mere bone and flesh.

The hairs on the back of her neck prickled. This was a test. A trap. He was seeing if she would keep her word. If she didn't, he'd snatch up the papers and call their bargain off. Or was it something else? Something that made her stomach sink to her feet. She'd managed to disgust even a rake such as him. 'You don't want me.'

He swung around, his expression pained. 'Not true. I do not wish you to enter into an arrangement that is distasteful to you.'

Distasteful? It ought to be distasteful, given all it would mean. She ought to be snatching up the papers and running for her life. And yet something in his eyes froze her in place. Raw hunger swirled in the dark brown depths, tightly controlled, yes, but there all the same. Not the heat of desire, although that was there, too, but a bleak deep-seated loneliness as he waited to bid her farewell.

Her foolish heart ached to ease his hurt. A wild desire to dispel that look from his eyes pulled at her soul. She'd made a bargain. Arranged it so no one would know. It was only for three months, but perhaps given time…

'Go,' he said.

The harshness in his voice said if she accepted his generous offer, she would never see him again. Torn in two, she stared at the documents.

He turned away, clearly expecting her to leave.

Go now, the voice of sanity whispered. She didn't want to go.

Reckless Ellie, always too impulsive by half, crossed the room behind him and laid a hand on his arm. 'My lord, I would not have suggested it, if I did not wish it.'

He lowered his gaze to meet hers, and in those dark depths she saw a lightening of his spirit and felt glad. Then he pulled her close and brushed her lips with his, a hesitant questioning kiss as if he doubted her words. A sweet kiss. Her body thrilled to his touch, her traitorous heart picked up speed.

She leaned close and teased his lips with the tip of her tongue, something she had imagined doing in her dreams.

He groaned against her mouth

A rush of pleasure heated her body. Two days ago had been the first time she had felt a man's body, hard and strong against her own. And she'd liked it. She'd no idea, until then, that kisses created such internal conflagrations. And now she wanted more. He seemed equally inflamed by her bold responses. Crackling heat flickered between them like the electricity in the air before a storm.

He placed one hand behind her knees and one around her shoulders. He picked her up seemingly without effort and carried her into the bedroom, setting her on the edge of the small bed so that she faced him, her feet just off the floor, her knees touching his thigh. The intimacy sent heat to her cheeks.

He bent and kissed her mouth, a soft brush of his lips, back and forth, while his fingers worked on the fastenings of her gown. Little kisses rained down on her face, her lips and her neck. She shivered with pleasure. Her skin tingled wherever his lips touched. He pulled the pins from her hair. It fell around her shoulders, brushing against her cheeks, her neck. He ran his fingers through it, carrying it to his face and inhaling deeply.

'Lovely,' he murmured.

How easily she slipped down this path to dishonour, she thought as she reached for the buttons of his waistcoat. Was she really this wanton, or was it he only who tempted her into wickedness?

His sharp breath offered a reward for her boldness in the way her stomach clenched, as did the way he tore off his coat and helped her slip the waistcoat over his shoulders. He knelt and slipped her gown down to her waist, baring her stays and shift. He dipped his head to the exposed rise of her breasts and trailed butterfly kisses across skin so sensitive it shivered under his lips. Delicious torment. She moaned.

'You are beautiful.' The dark murmur as he gazed into her eyes sent waves of heat rushing to her core. There was more. She knew it in the way she wanted to touch and kiss and explore. Her fingers fumbled with the snowy white cravat at his throat and he chuckled. 'In a hurry, are you?' He dropped a kiss on her forehead, then unticd the knot at his throat and she pulled the muslin free. The buttons of his shirt came next. Finally she had her prize. Feeling exceedingly brave and very naughty, she placed her hand on his bare chest. His skin was soft, sprinkled with crisp brown curls and warm. Her fingers tasted his flesh, marvelling at the underlying muscle beneath the satiny softncss. She leaned forwards to kiss him on his breast the way he had kissed her. Again she heard his indrawn breath and hcr own little thrill. He liked her touch.

She drew back to see his expression. His eyes wore dark, almost black, his mouth curved in a sensual smile, his breathing as rapid her own. She rejoiced in her powers of seduction even as she trembled at the knowledge of her ruin.

He pulled her to her feet and turned her around. His movements were gentle, but swift and sure and very male. He pushed her gown to the floor and pulled impatiently at the ties of her undergarments until they, too, slid to her feet.

Oh, God. She was naked. She was a fallen woman. Heat consumed her. Embarrassment? Desire. She no longer knew as he parted her hair and kissed a delicious spot beneath her ear, one hand around her waist and his hips tight against her buttocks. His other hand caressed her breasts. The skin tingled, tightened. His thumb brushed across her nipples. They furled into tight little buds, an achingly irresistible sensation. Weakness invaded her bones. Only his grip prevented her from falling. He played with her breasts, stroking, kneading, teasing her nipples, till she thought she would go mad with the need to touch him.

Being married must be like this. The freedom to touch one's man. She'd never thought about that part of it. Exciting. Wonderful.

She leaned against his chest and reached up with her hands and stroked the back of his neck. She pulled his head down so she could kiss the side of his face. The stubble on his jaw rasped against her cheek. His musky cologne filled her senses. An intoxicating brew.

After this, she would not be the same person. All she had been taught in life to value would be gone. Another of her risky adventures. The last one.

She had never felt so alive or so scared.

Chapter Five

Her kiss, so tender on his cheek, cut through Garrick's lust. It hinted at affection. That she desired him was obvious. Her arousal was as strong as his, he could smell it, taste it on her skin, feel it in her physical responses. But there was unselfishness in her hesitant gentleness. The women he had known demanded satiation, as he had. It had always been about *taking pleasure*.

Ellie seemed to want to give. The intensity of tenderness she evoked in him threatened his defences, threatened his control. Pleasure. He had nothing else to give.

'Ellie, sweetheart,' he whispered. 'Turn around.'

She twisted in his arms, maintaining the contact of her lips with his face. Her breasts, nipples hard with desire, brushed against his arm, his ribs. Piercing longing ripped at his resolve. He bent his head and ravaged her mouth, plunged his tongue into the warm heat. He could taste her sweetness and smell her clean fresh fragrance, the hint of vanilla. She leaned against him, winding her arms around his neck, her fingers tracing a path through his hair.

He picked her up and laid her on the bed and her half-closed eyes watched him shyly. Her peeping gaze as he stripped off his shirt was more erotic than any bold stare. He wanted her so much his body trembled deep inside, as if every bone, muscle and sinew needed her for survival. He stopped undressing to kiss her, claimed her mouth, while her hands wandered his back in a light exploration that drove him wild with a need to make her forget her other man. Hands shaking, he rose and pulled off his boots and pantaloons. Her eyes widened as she took in his naked body. She looked away quickly, blushing. So she would play the maid to the end. God, how it inflamed him.

Golden hair spilling in abandon on to her shoulders and breasts, a small silver cross on a blue ribbon at her neck. He bent over her, kissing her cheek as chastely as a boy and she smiled. His chest ached sweetly as she draped her arms across his shoulders, encouraging him closer, but he held himself away, intent on his own exploration. His hands slid across her ribs, then around her waist, measuring the span. So fine, so tiny. He traced her navel with a fingertip, shaped the curve of her belly with his palm, until his hand reached her most private place. He combed through the crisp fair curls. She shivered and his shaft pulsed in response.

Garrick eased his hand between her elegant thighs, nudging them apart. A faint murmur of protest escaped her lips. The way she played the innocent was so unbelievably erotic. A delightfully sensual act designed to trap him in her web. His need surged rampant and urgent.

He stroked the velvet softness of her inner thighs, caressed her cleft and found it slippery with her moisture. For him. It felt like a gift from the gods. A treasure beyond compare. Her eyes drifted open on a moan. He smiled down into her passion-filled face, seeking the tiny nub of flesh, desiring her pleasure above all else. He circled his thumb. Her expression softened and her eyes glazed over, then she arched her back and cried out deep and guttural in her throat.

No virtuous games now, just her body responding to his touch in mindless ecstasy.

Her hands stroked his chest, his arms, his back. His skin tingled and his blood flared wherever her hands caressed. Sweet heavens, he needed to be inside her. He lowered his head and kissed her, tasting, plundering her soft welcoming mouth, sucking at her lips, drawing her tongue into his mouth as he kneed her legs wider. Slowly, he dipped the tip of his finger inside her wet, hot passage and found her ready. Hot blood roared through his veins.

Cradled by her body, her inner thighs a soft support for his hips, he lowered his mouth to her wonderful breasts. Tightly furled, her nipple rubbed against his lips as he kissed and licked the soft, tender flesh. Then he suckled. She moaned. His groin tightened. He lifted her hips, reached down and guided his rigid shaft to her entrance.

She stilled beneath him, her eyes wide in wonder and the pretence of fear. It drove him to the edge of madness and beyond. He eased into her warm wet flesh, rejoicing in her heat tight around him. So damned small. Almost too small. Deliciously resistant. He thought he would die of pleasure. He moved slowly. He knew how to prolong his partner's enjoyment, but now she struggled, deliberately exciting him beyond control, fuelling his masculine need for ascendancy.

He thrust his tongue into her mouth, gathered up her wrists and held them above her head, her breasts lifting.

He kissed and sucked each nipple while she squirmed beneath him. So damned sexy. He thrust his hips forwards and she cried out in genuine pain.

He froze. 'Bloody hell.' He stared down at her. 'Ellie?' She shook her head, her face shocked. His arms and body shuddered with the effort of holding still.

'Sweet Lord. Tell me this is not your first time.' His body screamed a furious protest. His mind refused to grapple with the truth.

She nodded and swallowed, obviously scared to death. He groaned. What was done was done. He stayed still inside her, gasping for air, summoning control. If he left her now, hurting and afraid, she might never recover. He had to bring her more than pain, but she was rigid beneath him. No longer aroused, just afraid and tight and tense. She wasn't pretending. He'd deflowered an innocent.

Hell and damnation. The realisation cut through him like terrible blades. He'd known. Deep down, he'd known. God damn it. The urge to strike out balled his fists.

He fought his rage, trembled with its force, beat it down until he could finally speak. 'I'm sorry,' he whispered. 'Trust me. I will try not to hurt you more. Sweetheart, kiss me.'

Her lovely mouth trembled. Tears welled in her eyes. Damn, they were joined together and he needed to gain her trust. He released her hands and, holding his torso completely still on his forearms, he lowered his mouth to hers. He placed tiny little kisses on each lip, barely more than a whisper. He could feel her warm breath on his throat, little gasps of terror.

His fault. He traced a path from her lips to her chin, across her throat. He nuzzled her neck, feeling her silky hair against his face, inhaling its light floral perfume. He ran his tongue around the edge of her ear and then softly probed the orifice. She shivered. She moved under him, he felt her arms encircle him. Felt her relax.

Sweat traced a cold path down the centre of his back as every muscle strained to hold his pounding need in check. He withdrew slowly, just a little, then slid forwards.

She lifted her hips, encouraging him now, welcoming him into her depths. Her courage humbled him. She was as brave as a warrior, and she was his.

'Ellie,' he groaned. 'Hold still, for God's sake.'

He heard her laugh low in her throat. 'I'm all right,' she whispered. She brought her legs around his waist. Unable to hold back, he thrust into her deeply, fiercely, and felt her rise to meet his every stroke.

She dug her fingers into his back. He welcomed the sting of pain and remembered to breathe.

Her heat engulfed him, making him forget all thoughts of restraint. He thrust faster, his body taking command. The storm built and swirled and raged and erupted in tearing, streaking light. Her back arched and she moaned sweetly and shuddered as she reached for heaven and found it. The edge of his abyss loomed close, hot and dark and welcoming. He withdrew from her body, spent his seed in the tangle of sheets and joined her on her downward spiral.

Panting, they lay together in heated bliss. He pulled her tight against his side, cradling her in the crook of his arm, stroking her until he was sure she slept.

Nom d'un nom. A virgin. If he had known, he would never have taken her. He shook his head in disbelief. Castlefield had not bedded her. Perhaps he scorned a mere servant, no matter that she had shown such love.

He couldn't help the feeling of triumph, even as he regretted her loss.

She'd given him, of all men, a treasure beyond price. He wanted to curl his body around her, shelter her from the world. The emotion tugged at a painful chord in the region of his heart. An emotion he couldn't afford.

He gazed down at her beautiful face, so young, so fragile in sleep. He brushed her silky hair away from her forehead and kissed each eyelid, with its sweep of fair lashes against fragile skin. Satisfied, he held her safe, then drifted off to sleep.

Shadows filled the room when Garrick opened his eyes. He stretched, feeling the wonderful pull of muscle from head to toe. None of the familiar feeling of panic of something urgent he needed to remember. Had he ever awoken feeling so utterly relaxed?

Ellie stirred. He rolled on his side, kissed her cheek, then her mouth, savoured the honeyed taste of his woman. 'Awake already, *chérie*?' he whispered. The wicked part of his body responded to the thought of her awake. Not a good idea, not when she'd be sore. And he was expected at the Court. He hung over the side of the bed and retrieved his watch, squinting at it in the fading light. Almost seven. 'I must hurry, if I want to be in time for dinner.'

Beside him, her body tensed.

He turned to face her, propped up on an elbow. 'What is it, sweet?'

Her gaze slid away. 'Nothing.'

In his experience, when a woman said nothing in that cool tone of voice it meant trouble. In the past he'd simply walked away, afraid to risk the heat of his anger. He didn't want to walk away from Ellie.

He tipped her chin with his hand and kissed her lips. They were as cold as ice and unresponsive. 'I'm expected. Surely you understand?'

Her lashes hid her eyes. 'Yes, my lord.'

'Call me Garrick. Ellie, I can't live here. What would your neighbours say? Besides, I have duties at Beauworth.' He'd promised his uncle and he would not go back on his word 'I will visit you every day.' He smiled. 'You won't be lonely, I promise.' He took her lips, kissed her long and hard, binding her to him, promising more. He felt the scorching heat spiralling around them, drawing them together, melting her against him.

For a moment, he surrendered to its power. More than anything, he wanted to stay, but he never went back on his word. He owed it to Beauworth and Le Clere to go home.

A week had passed. One of the most blissful Garrick had ever known. And he wanted Ellie to be happy, too. He'd thought of the perfect thing. So now with her at his side in the gig, he felt as nervous as a lad facing his first day at school. Ridiculous. And yet he hadn't felt this excited in years. Even the unpredictable weather had cooperated with a sunny summer day.

They turned on to the track winding to the barn where he'd been held captive. 'Where are we going?' The nervousness in her voice indicated she'd guessed their destination.

He kept his voice gruff. 'You'll see.'

Her body stiffened as if she expected some sort of trick. Perhaps he shouldn't tease, but he couldn't resist. She'd love his surprise. They turned through the gate. He tried to hold back his smile as her mouth dropped open at the sight of the two horses tied to the rail outside the barn.

'Oh,' she said. 'Mist.' She grabbed his arm. 'You remembered.'

'That you stabled him at Brown's farm? Yes.' He brought the horse to a halt and she leapt down without waiting for help. Skirts ankle high, she ran to the little white gelding, reaching out to him, petting his neck, murmuring soft words into his ear.

A huge warmth filled his chest, marred by a twinge of something small and mean. Jealousy for the damned horse? 'Struth. He must be losing his mind if he envied a bloody gelding.

Forcing a smile, he jumped down and strode to join her at the fence. 'Dan collected him this morning.'

'I never imagined you would do something like this.' Her laughter bubbled like champagne, even as her words cut through his joy and when she flung her arms around his neck and kissed his cheek, he forgave her careless dismissal and basked in her happiness. She could not have been more pleased than if he had brought her diamonds.

'Oh, I wish I had known, I would have worn my riding habit.'

'I can do better.' Garrick didn't try to hold back his smirk. He took her hand and led her into the barn. There, in a corner, was a suit of boy's clothes very much like those she had worn when they had fenced, and beside the pile, her sword leaning up against the wall.

She hugged him with abandon. 'I don't believe it.'

'Well, Miss Brown, first we ride, then we practise. I will teach you my sword trick, if you wish.'

Her face shone in the dim cool light. 'I do wish. Leave me, so I can change.'

Imperious and charmingly modest. A strange delightful mixture for a creature of passion and adventure.

Laughing, he tipped up her face with his knuckle. 'Do you need my help?'

'I'm used to doing for myself.'

Of course she was. Women of her ilk did not have maids to help them dress. Yet he would have liked to help her out of her clothes. Heat rushed to his groin. He could insist, of course. It was his right. But this was her day, and so he left and strode out into the sunshine where he paced in front of the barn, imagining her slipping out of her gown and into her other guise with increasingly lascivious thoughts.

When she emerged, her stride and the way she held herself reminded him what a great little actress she was, a woman who changed her persona with her clothes. Now, she was more boy than girl, swaggering in her form-hugging breeches with the sword belted at her waist and the cocked hat pulled down over her hair. The costume left nothing of her body to the imagination and the sight of luscious hips and thighs thickened his blood.

If he hadn't known how much she was looking forward to going for a ride, he might have pulled her down on to the grass where they'd kissed days before and teased her right out of her breeches. Instead, breathing hard, concentrating on the control he'd learned as a boy, he held his desire in check, merely nodding when she glanced from the horse to him.

In a flash, she mounted, a boy-like leap into the saddle, and urged the little white gelding into a gallop. Ah, but he would not let her get too far. He swung up on to Bess. The mare needed no urging to catch the fleeing pair. And when he came up on her, they rode side by side across the field. Not the sedate trot of an afternoon in Hyde Park, but a wild canter.

'A race,' she called out.

He grinned and dug in his heels. Bess easily out-stripped the smaller gelding.

He looked back to gloat. Damn her. She'd cut off at right angles. Headed straight for the field's low stone wall. His heart rose in his throat. She'd break her neck if she fell at that speed. He wheeled Bess around and followed. He roared a warning. The gelding took the wall with a playful little kick of rear hooves, clearing the coping with inches to spare.

Even as his heart swelled in admiration, Garrick wanted to take his crop to her backside. He wanted to shake her. Make her promise never to risk her life in that fashion again. He had to catch her first.

Never had he seen a woman ride so hard, better than many men he knew. Admiration outstripped anger as he watched the perfect harmony between horse and rider. She rode like a madwoman, but she knew her horse and by the time they were heading back to the barn, he'd forgiven her madcap dash. He laughed out loud when she raised a brow in question from beneath her cocked hat.

As they walked the horses cool, a feeling of content-ment washed through him. It was as if some great weight had gone from his shoulders, or some dark shadow had been erased from his soul. She made him feel…happy. A gift beyond price.

A happiness he didn't deserve, but would enjoy as long as it lasted.

'I'm starving,' he said.

'Me, too.'

'Lucky I thought to bring lunch.' He retrieved the hamper he'd left in the barn's cool interior and spread out a red-and-green plaid blanket on the grass overlooking the pond. She laid out the feast, small meat pasties in a feather-light crust, bread, cheese and fine red wine. Neither said much while they ate. It was good to see a woman eat with such gusto, unlike the ladies of his acquaintance in London, who picked at food as if it might be poison.

Crickets chirped a merry tune in the grass. A dove on the barn roof cooed softly. Appetite sated, Garrick stretched out, leaning on one elbow so he could watch her face. She sighed and, resting against his thigh, sipped her wine. 'Thank you for a most wonderful surprise,' she murmured.

The pleasure in her voice filled his heart with unaccustomed warmth. It burned like frozen fingers brought back to life. 'I'm glad it pleased you. Tell me, how on earth did you learn to ride and fight with a sword like a boy?'

She hesitated.

Would she lie? The warmth dwindled, but he tried to hold it fast. After all, he had his own dark secrets.

'I told you I was brought up with the Castlefield children,' she said. 'We spent a year or two in India. While travelling in some parts it was safer to dress the girls as boys. I took fencing and riding lessons with William…I mean, Lord Castlefield. I loved it. Sometimes I wished I'd been born a boy.'

William. Her familiarity with the man sent the heat of anger flooding to his brain even as he analysed her slight hesitations and carefully chosen words. No doubt about it. She was lying.

He kept his expression cool, detached. 'I envy you. I have never been outside England. The war with France made the Grand Tour impossible.' Not to mention his uncle's protectiveness.

She set down her half-full glass and stared at the rolling vista. 'It was the same for the oldest son, the heir. He hoped to go abroad once the war was over. He was killed in a carriage accident not long ago. Now William must return and take up the duties as heir. In a way, I'm glad.' Her voice caught. 'I hated thinking of him in danger.'

Garrick couldn't see her face, but he heard the note of deep longing in her voice. Clearly no matter what he did, she would prefer this man. Jealousy surged, twisted in his gut, knotted with a cold, hard lump of anger and bitterness. The thought of this other man wounded him in a way he hadn't expected, a way he'd never before experienced. He forced himself not to care. 'Is it your wish to go to him when he returns?' The hard edge in his voice told him he'd failed.

'Oh, no.' She sounded sincere, almost appalled.

More acting? And why would he care? His plans for the future didn't involve a woman. He eased away from her, rose to his feet and began packing away the remains of the picnic.

'One of your servants came to Castlefield, once,' she said, passing him her wineglass. 'He'd been in the same regiment as the old lord, and your father, I believe. A man named Piggot.'

His stomach lurched. The ground beneath his feet seemed to shift at the sound of a name he'd not heard in years. He stood stock-still. 'Piggot?'

'I can remember the Earl being quite upset after his visit, but he did not say why.' She rose to her feet and dusted off her breeches, her small hands patting the round curve of her derrière.

A tremor, so deep it did not disturb the surface of his flesh, quaked in his bones. Would Piggot have revealed the events surrounding his mother's death to Castlefield? Did the information that could destroy him lie in Castlefield's hands, awaiting imminent discovery? How Ellie would revile him if she learned the truth. And yet, in some dark corner of his soul lay a measure of relief at the thought of laying down a burden too heavy to bear.

Unseeing, he stared at the blanket in his hands.

'On guard.'

A sword point flickered in his face. He recoiled. 'What the deuce?'

She laughed, her eyes sparkling. She twirled her blade, then raised it in salute. 'You promised me a lesson.'

Sweat trickled off his brow and ran cold down his cheek. He let go a long breath and smiled. 'So I did.' He collected his weapon from the gig and took off his coat.

He bowed, then saluted. 'On guard.'

She took up her stance, lithe and alert. As their blades hissed together, he recalled her amazing skill. She'd been taught by a master. A worthy opponent, indeed, though she did not have the strength of wrist or the reach to best him. He demonstrated his technique of twisting a blade free of his opponent's hand. She grasped the theory quickly, but had trouble putting it into practice.

'It will work for you with a weaker opponent,' he said.

Clearly exhausted, the tip of her sword resting on the grass, she nodded and wiped her face on her shirtsleeve with a laugh. 'Enough, my lord. I can barely lift my arm.'

Her face was flushed, beads of sweat shone on her brow and her shirt was undone past what was decent. Delicious. Tantalising. His body quickened.

'Aye. It is time you changed, before my servant comes to retrieve the picnic, and he recognises you as the highwayman I kissed.' He led her into the barn.

Ellie tugged on his hand. 'Why did you kiss me that night? There was no legend, was there?'

He smiled at her frown. 'Because, like a fool I'd left my pistol in the coach.' And lucky it was he had. God, even now she might be dead.

'I was a fool to let you get so close. I'd not do so again.'

'There will not be a next time.' Cold fear struck his heart. He pressed her against him, the urge to keep her safe overwhelming. 'Will there?'

Against his arm, her spine stiffened. Her grey eyes cooled as she hid her thoughts. 'No. There is no reason for it any longer.'

He kissed her hard, trying to break through the barrier she'd put up. It worked. She melted against him and his blood grew thick and heavy with need.

'How do you do that?' His voice was low and husky with desire.

A laugh caught in her throat. 'I was going to ask you the same thing.'

He hoisted her into his arms, while she laughed and kicked. He put her down on the blanket amongst the straw, a lovely wild creature as comfortable in a barn as she was on a feather bed. An enigma. Perhaps that was the root of her attraction. She was unlike any other woman he'd known.

What was it about her that drove him to distraction? Perhaps not knowing how much of her was real and how much playacting held him enthralled. She'd been a virgin when she came to his bed, but there was nothing innocent about Lady Moonlight. Would he ever know the real woman behind the mask?

And if he did, would she disappoint? Was it better not to know?

She reached up and cupped his jaw in her small hand, dragging his face down to her lips with a saucy smile. Today, he had Lady Moonlight. God help him, he'd take whatever she felt free to give.

He wrestled with the buttons of her shirt while her lips were fastened to his, only breaking away to pull it over her head. When she did the same for him, he felt humbled. Honoured. He lay beside her, kissing her lips, her throat, the rise of her breast. Her nipples leapt to life under his tongue. Passion and adventure all rolled up in one unique woman.

While he nuzzled into her breasts to the sound of her delighted giggles, he unfastened her breeches, easing them over the curve of her hips. He caressed the soft skin of her buttocks and pressed her hard against his arousal.

She pushed him away. She laughed at his disappointment and, leaning forwards, nipped his shoulder with her teeth.

'Ouch!'

She slid slowly to her knees, her hands trailing down his chest and then his belly until they reached the waistband of his breeches. The white skin of her back melded into the roundness of her plump firm buttocks at its base. Groaning, he reached down and unpinned her silky golden hair so it flowed softly around her as she unbuttoned him and his shaft sprang free, rampant and ready. She kissed him, a quick shy brush of silky soft lips.

Mon Dieu, it felt good. A breath of pure pleasure hissed between his teeth. But he wanted more. He wanted to feel her soft curves against him. He lifted her to him and kissed her mouth. He plunged his tongue deep into her and felt her bold response.

'I need to be out of these clothes,' he whispered.

She cast him a shy smile of encouragement. He sat up and quickly stripped off his boots and breeches and turned to lay beside her. She gazed deeply into his eyes, seeking…what? Assurance. The passion in her smoky gaze drove blood from his brain to his groin.

He gathered her close, oblivious to everything except her warmth, her scent, the hint of vanilla. An honest, earthy scent. The sounds of desire from her throat while their mouths joined drove him wild with wanting. His fingers dipped into her moist, hot centre and he groaned. This was where he belonged. Somehow, he would make her forget her past.

He nudged his knee between her thighs and she, generous and yielding, let them fall open. He entered her and they became as one. He drove into her, thrusting again and again. Her gasps of excitement, the breath warm in his ear, her nails sharp points of wicked pain on his back and buttocks, drove him to new heights of desire.

The scent of her arousal filled his nostrils. Her cries, increasingly demanding, filled his ears.

So close. His own release threatened, demanded, tortured, tightened his groin until he thought he would explode. He clamped his jaw. Strained to bring her with him. Fought for control.

He shifted. Stroked her tight insides with his body, feeling the flutter and pull of her inner muscles goading him on. He reached between them, found the source of her pleasure, the swollen bud of her desire, and circled and rubbed, hard, fast.

'Oh God, Ellie, now.'

Her body clenched around his shaft, hot spasms against the sensitive head. He was going to die of pleasure. Not without her. Not alone.

Then she shattered. Crest after crest of heat and tight, clenching, muscles. In a panic, he withdrew, spilling his essence on her belly as he followed her into the surf. He collapsed on his side, grabbing his shirt to clean her skin. The scent of sweet-smelling straw and lovemaking in his nostrils, a harmony of breathing and slowing hearts, a paradise on earth. Blissful, sated, sweat cooling on exposed flesh, he gazed up into the ancient beams. If he stayed in England with her at his side, perhaps his inner demons could be vanquished.

With a smile, she nestled deeper in the crook of his arm, her straw-coloured hair trailing over her breasts like a silken veil. He ran a fingertip across her arm where it lay across her stomach, her hand resting on his hip. A beautiful, extraordinary woman.

His eyes drifted closed. When he came to and looked at her next she had turned on her back. His first thought was to kiss her awake and make love to her again. But tears were sliding from under her long, golden lashes and running down her face.

He reached out and captured a tear on his thumb and brought it to his lips. He tasted salt. What made her cry in her sleep? His stomach roiled as he forced his mind to recognise what his heart would not. She wasn't happy.

It was like a knife twisting in his chest, this sense of impending loss.

Yet perhaps it was as well. What if this thing inside him caused her harm? He'd never forgive himself.

Would he harm a woman he only wanted to protect?

The legends spoke of blind rage. He was almost sure he'd experienced it first-hand three times now, the sensation of control and memory slipping away. His gut churned.

Her eyes opened and she looked at him with a slight frown, as if she was trying to recall where she was, then her eyes cleared and she smiled.

'Why are you crying?' His voice sounded tight and hard.

'I didn't know I was.' Her laugh shook. She rubbed at her eyes with the back of her hand. 'A bad dream? I don't recall.'

A wave of guilt washed over him. He should have given her the money she needed and made her leave, instead of killing any dreams she must have of her noble patron.

He only wanted to give her happiness. In his selfishness, he had tried to win her heart, to make her want to stay, but if she cried for Castlefield after a day as perfect as this one, she'd never been his. Sadness rose up inside him, painful and dark.

He had spent years learning to control his deeper emotions, building a wall to keep out anything that might disturb his calm as a matter of survival. She had pierced that wall and he must make it whole again. He would tell her he was tired of her, send her away.

But not yet. Not today.

'Come, Dan will return soon. Let me help you dress.'

On the drive back to the village, Ellie rested her head on his shoulder, her body rocking against him with the horses' steady rhythm. Unconsciously he pulled her closer and she snuggled into him, nuzzling his neck. His heart felt tattered, torn to shreds, and he welcomed the pain.

They pulled up outside her front door. 'Goodnight, Ellie,' he whispered into her hair. He tipped her chin and brushed her lips with his thumb, aching for more.

'Goodnight, Garrick. Thank you for a wonderful day,' she murmured.

Tomorrow, he'd gather the strength of will to set her free. After all, she'd never been his to keep and a man with a stain on his soul didn't deserve happiness.

Chapter Six

Eleanor closed the door the moment the gig drove away. She busied herself preparing supper, trying not to think about the path she'd chosen and what it meant for her future.

He'd given her a beautiful day in idyllic surroundings and it hadn't been too hard to imagine herself spending the rest of her life with him. He was thoughtful, charming and fun. Most of all, when he made love to her, she forgot his reputation as a rake, forgot the duty she owed to her family, forgot she was ruined. It wouldn't matter how good he was to her, he could never marry her now.

Nor could anyone else.

And until their bargain was over, she must not let him steal her heart.

That foolish organ gave a funny little skip, a happy little hop in her chest. Too late, apparently.

She jabbed the fork into a slice of bread. What a fool. Each time she thought about bidding him goodbye, she cried. If she didn't take care she'd turn into a permanent watering pot. She'd always despised lachrymose females who complained about their lot in life. She'd made her bed and she'd lie on it, cheerfully, and think about the future when it arrived.

If she had a future. Drat it, there she went again.

She stared at the toast and jam she'd put on the plate, but there was no room in her stomach for food. Tea. She needed a nice cup of tea. In bed. And a book. She put the kettle on and changed into her nightdress and robe.

Her front door creaked open. Her spirits soared. Garrick had returned. She ran to greet him.

It wasn't Garrick outlined in the doorway, but a stranger. Large and threatening, with a wind-reddened face and heavy black brows above a red-veined, bulbous nose, he barged over the threshold. Oh, God. She must have forgotten to throw the bolt.

She backed away, her mouth dry and her heart beating loudly. While not tall, he was heavyset and could overpower her in an instant. Her stomach lurched as small black eyes ran down her body, eyebrows lifting. The worst thing about him was his grin, loose wet lips drawing back over broken yellow teeth beneath a greasy black moustache.

'Get out.' Her voice shook. She clasped her hands together, seeking strength. 'You have no right to be in here.'

'Now, now, my lady, don't get excited, I've come with a message from his lordship.'

'The Marquess of Beauworth?'

'The very same.'

Something jarred about his words. She gasped. He had called her my lady. Garrick knew? Her rapidly beating heart clogged her throat. She swallowed. 'Get out.'

He made no move.

She glanced around for a weapon. If only she had not left her sword at the barn.

The man closed the door with his heel, following step by step as she backed away. She daren't take her gaze from his face in case he attacked.

A weapon. She needed something heavy. She sidled into the bedroom, working her way to the brass candle-stick on the night table. Breathing steadily, clutching fast to her courage, she backed around the bed. The table nudged her back. Her fingers fumbled behind her and found cool metal.

She held up her other hand in a warning. 'No closer.'

He reached into his pocket. He must have a pistol or a knife. She had to act.

She grasped the candlestick firmly, hefting it in her hand where he could see it. 'Stay back or I will put a dint in your face so large your mother will never recognise you.'

His hand emerged with a small brown bottle. He laughed, an evil, sneering sound. 'Them's fighting words, my lady.' The sound of the front door opening sent a chill down her spine.

'Where the hell are you?' a male voice called.

More of them. Bile rose in her throat.

'In here, Sarg.'

She might be able to deal with one, but two? Dear God, what did they want? Her chest tightened, making it hard to breathe. 'There is money in the chest under the bed,' she croaked.

'I'll keep that in mind,' bulbous nose said. 'Later.'

The chill down her back turned to ice. She launched the candlestick at his head.

He knocked it aside with his arm. 'Ouch,' he bellowed. 'You little bitch!'

He lunged at her. She ducked under his arm. He caught a handful of her hair. Pain shot through her scalp. Eyes blurring, she twisted in his grip. Lashed at his groin with her bare foot and hit his thigh. She stumbled. He yanked her back by her hair. More pain. Her eyes streamed. She flailed at his face with her nails.

Arms grabbed her from behind, around her throat and waist. A belt buckle jammed into her back. The second man. Panic chilled her to the bone.

'I told you to wait.' His voice in her ear was low and angry. 'Where's the bottle, Caleb?'

''Ere, Sarg.'

A grinning Caleb held the small brown bottle to her lips. She recognised the smell. Laudanum. She clamped her mouth shut. The man behind pinched her nostrils. Hard. Painfully hard, while Caleb pressed the bottle against her lips. The fingers around her throat tightened. Arms crushed her ribs. Her lungs burned. Her head swam. Air. She needed air.

One quick breath. Turning her face, she opened her mouth. A bitter-tasting liquid flooded in. She swallowed. Managed a breath.

'More,' Sarg said.

More liquid. She struggled blindly. Her movements became weaker. Dizzy, she felt her limbs loosen. The triumphant leer of the man Caleb faded.

The cottage had an air of desolation. An emptiness. Garrick sensed it the moment he entered and still he called out, 'Ellie?' Silence.

He placed her sword and scabbard gently on the pine table. He'd thought she might want to keep it. He wandered into the bedroom, just to be sure. The bed was stripped, the clothes' press empty. She'd taken everything.

A hollow, sick feeling hit the pit of his stomach. Knowing how unhappy she was, he'd planned to send her home, rehearsed what he would say over and over, all the while hoping she might want to stay.

It was better this way. She'd gone of her own accord. Less painful. Then why did his chest ache? A small scrap of white poked out from under the bed and he picked it up. A minute square of lawn edged in fine lace. He pressed it to his nose. It smelled clean, fresh with traces of vanilla. Ellie. It was the only thing left. No note. Nothing to show she had ever lived here. He stuffed the handkerchief into his coat pocket and went back to the kitchen.

Barely conscious of his actions, he pulled a bottle of brandy and a tumbler from the dresser and set them on the table. He fought his bitter disappointment. Why not say goodbye? Had she found him so lacking?

He pulled out the plain ladder-back chair, turned its back against the scrubbed table and sat astride. Chin resting on his sleeve, he glared at the honey-coloured table top, as if it could provide an answer. Had she somehow seen the evil in him? She didn't lack for courage, but it was enough to send anyone running off into the night.

Bloody hell. Why couldn't he accept she loved Castlefield instead of trying to place the blame elsewhere? An urgent need to drink one glass after another and dull the pain tightened his gut. He reached for the bottle, astonished at the way his hand shook as he splashed liquid oblivion into the glass and on to the table. The pungent aroma stung the back of his throat, brought tears to his eyes. Oh, yes. Fool yourself about this, too. He smiled wryly. Tomorrow reality would stare him in the face, the way it did every day. He ought to be glad she'd gone, glad she'd never look at him in horror.

He buried his head in the crook of his arm. Rage, despair, roiling emotions he couldn't name, made his skin feel too tight, as if he might burst like an over-filled water-skin. With a muffled roar, he rose and lobbed the glass into the fireplace. It shattered with the sound of hail on a tile roof. Then silence. Brandy fumes hung in the air like the stink of an inn on a Saturday night.

What the hell good had that done, except waste perfectly good brandy? He picked up the bottle to put it away. The front door slammed back against the wall. Ellie?

Garrick turned, his heart beating hopefully against his ribs. Without warning, a blond, red-coated soldier lurched across the room and grabbed at his throat. Choking, he tore at the man's fingers.

'Where is she, you goddamned thrice-misbegotten whoreson?' the man yelled.

Even as his vision blackened around the edges, Garrick knew this man, 'Hadley?' His enemy.

A red wash coated his vision, rage running like liquid fire through his veins. He embraced it. Used its strength. He brought his arms up and around. Broke the other man's hold, shoved him backwards and raised his fists, longing to beat the furious face to a pulp.

'Not so fast, my lord.' The muzzle of a rifle pressed coldly against the back of Garrick's neck.

With his back to the door, Garrick had not seen the man enter, but he recognised the deep rumbling voice. He released his breath in a long, shuddering sigh, gaining control, clearing the red mists from his sight, tamping down the killing rage. 'Well, if it isn't Ben.'

'No, my lord. Martin Brown, at your service. Put up your weapons.'

Martin Brown, the relative she'd spoken of, was also Ben the highwayman? *Merde.* How many more lies had she told him?

Garrick lowered his fists.

Martin Brown withdrew his rifle and held it ready across his chest.

Hadley fixed his hard grey gaze on Garrick and repeated his question. 'Where is she?'

What the hell was going on? What did this man have to do with Ellie? No. This must be about some other woman. He racked his brain for possible contenders, women he'd forgotten, while he kept his face a blank slate. 'What are you doing here?'

Anger boiled up again, at Ellie, at himself, at this man from his past. He curled his lip and glanced down at the man's twisted right leg. 'Come for another beating, Hadley?' He shouldn't have said that. Hell, he'd always denied being Hadley's night-time attacker.

The other man reddened. 'Castlefield now.'

Garrick reeled. The breath left his body as if he'd been struck in the kidneys. This was Castlefield? 'But—'

'Haven't you done enough, you bastard? Did you have to take your revenge out on my sister?'

For a long moment Garrick's mind stuck on the word revenge, the old issue between them, the fight over a woman and the accusations hanging over him at school. The reason for Castlefield's halting gait. The second occasion he'd lost control and couldn't remember.

Finally, the word 'sister' forced its way to the surface. The floor beneath his feet seemed to tilt. 'Ellie is your sister?'

'Lady Eleanor Hadley, to you. My twin.'

His twin sister? He could only stare in stunned silence. Finally he found a shred of voice. 'She left.' His mind scrambled to make sense of what his ears were hearing. 'She must have gone home.'

Martin Brown shook his head. 'The bailiffs are gone, but no sign of her ladyship.'

A sense of dread filled his stomach. 'Then she went to her sister.' He refused to think about where else she might have gone.

'Damn you, Beauworth!' Castlefield choked out. 'If I find that one hair of her head has been harmed, I shall hold you fully responsible.' He drew his sword.

'Put up, my lord,' Martin Brown said sternly, his ruddy face grim. This time his rifle was pointed at the Earl. 'This was all her own doing. I did my best to stop her and when I could not, I did my best to protect her.' He nodded at Garrick. 'He became involved when we held up his coach and he followed us. She said she would set him free and go to Scotland.' He flushed. 'I had a feeling there was more to it. That was why I waited for your ship in Portsmouth. But if she's gone, she's gone to your aunt, or to her friend in Scotland. We should look for her there.'

Oh God, Ellie. What were you doing? He stared at her enraged brother. No wonder she'd longed for him to come home. The bastard had left her to face everything alone. Well, now he'd know the truth, because he wasn't fit to take care of her.

Garrick crossed his arms across his chest and stared down his nose at the other man. 'You were right to worry, Martin. She became my mistress to retrieve the mortgage and pay his debts.' He curled his lip as the other man squirmed. 'Not once did she tell me the truth.'

Horror etched on his features, Castlefield limped to the sofa and collapsed. He covered his face with his hands. 'Eleanor,' he moaned. 'Why?'

A wave of remorse washed away Garrick's anger. 'I'm sorry you had to find out this way, but you have only yourself to blame.'

Martin Brown assisted his young master to rise. 'Come, my lord, we have to find her and bring her home.'

Castlefield glared at Garrick. 'You despicable cur, taking advantage of a woman. My sister is worth two of you.'

What had he done? She'd been trying to save her brother, and Garrick had taken full advantage of the circumstances. Dear God. He'd ruined a noble-woman, taken her virtue. Were there no depths to which he would not sink? If only she'd told him who she was. Let him help her. *Nom d'un nom.* She'd lied rather than give him the chance to help because she didn't trust him.

He had to make it right. Offer her his name. It was all he could do. What he wanted to do. He felt a surge of hope. 'I will marry her, of course.' His voice sounded thick and hoarse.

In the doorway, Castlefield swung back around, granite eyes blazing, his pale skin flushed. 'Do you think I'd let her marry a cur like you?'

Cringing inside, Garrick somehow managed to keep his voice calm. 'It will be up to Ellie to decide.'

'Will it?' Castlefield's voice dropped to a whisper. 'When I tell her what you did to me, you know how she will answer. Eleanor will do my bidding in this. Say one thing to a soul about my sister and I swear I will kill you. Come near my family again and you will die.'

The bitterness in his voice rent Garrick's sympathy to shreds. 'Next time you find yourself in debt, don't leave your sister to rescue you.'

'Damn you to hell, Beauworth!' Castlefield

shouted, following Martin Brown out of the door and slamming it shut.

Hell looked inviting. Garrick sank on to the sofa. What a bloody mess. How could he not have seen what she was? Hell! He'd known she had secrets, but how could he have guessed she was a noblewoman? Liar. The signs had all been there—her conversation, her bearing, even her modesty and innocence. The selfish bastard in him hadn't wanted to see. He'd wanted the rogue, the woman in the mask, the woman he could not hurt.

He scrubbed his palm over his chin. She had no choice but to take his name. Castlefield would come to his senses, once he got over his anger. His heart lifted. In a way, it wasn't so bad.

'She's waking.' Shuffling footsteps crossed the room.

Eleanor turned her head towards the coarse female voice. Light sliced pain through her temples and she tried to swallow what felt like sand in her throat. The room spun like a child's top. Oh God, she was going to be sick. A basin appeared before her as if by magic. She vomited. Again and again.

Exhausted, she lay back, eyes shut. What was wrong with her? She'd never felt so ill in her life. Then she remembered. They'd dosed her with laudanum. After a few moments, she opened her eyes again and peered through a watery blur at four bare stone walls, a grimy window and flagstone floor. Where was she?

She struggled to rise. A dumpy old crone in black shoved her back against the pillow.

'Here, lovey,' the woman said. 'Drink. It'll 'ave you right as rain, it will.'

Feeling a glass against her lips, she gulped at the liquid. Bitter. Disgusting. Oh, no, more laudanum. 'Why are you doing this to me?'

'Rest, missie.'

'How long will she sleep?' A man's voice, low and harsh from across the room. Eleanor tried to raise her head to see. Too heavy. Too tired.

'A few hours.'

'Good. Keep the door locked. Caleb will keep watch.'

Caleb. A rush of fear engulfed her as she remembered the man's ugly face, the last person she'd seen before darkness sucked her down.

The next time she opened her eyes, she was alone. She felt better, stronger. The musty-smelling room remained steady. A chamber with crumbling plaster, and empty except for the cot on which she lay. A spyhole pierced the blackened wood door. Had they watched her sleep? She shivered. A blanket, rough to the touch, covered her nightgown and robe. Her skin crawled at the thought of those men with their hands on her in such flimsy attire.

Nausea rose in her throat. If she was sick, they would hear her. She swallowed.

'Is she awake?' Caleb's voice. Outside the door. A voice of nightmares. A voice she'd heard in vague dreams of being carried and shoved into a vehicle. Shuddering, she closed her eyes and lay still. She wasn't ready to face them. Not yet. Not until she felt stronger.

'Nah,' the woman replied, obviously peering through the hole in the door.

'Sarg will be back soon.'

'Aye. I'll make tea and wake her. He'll want her ready.'

Ready for what? There were noises, crockery rattling and footsteps. Eleanor imagined the woman moving around in the other room. The scraping of a chair being pushed back and heavier footfalls made her tense. Careful not to move, Eleanor opened her eyes a fraction.

'She's awake,' Caleb said. 'I know it.'

'Get away from there, you big lummox. You leave her to me, just like Sarg said. Get yourself back on guard or he'll have your guts for garters.'

'I've got a score to settle with the bitch for my arm,' Caleb growled. He clumped away and a door closed with a bang.

Barely clothed and a prisoner at their mercy. Her body trembled. Her heart raced. She couldn't breathe. They were going to kill her. She was going to die here in this horrid little hovel.

Ellie, calm down. Father's voice stilled her panic. Remember what he used to say? The reason many soldiers died was because they froze in fear and stopped thinking. Pull yourself together and you will be all right.

She hauled in a deep breath. Then another. Her heartbeat slowed. Her breathing evened out. She forced herself to listen to the sounds from the other room and was sitting up when the key turned in the lock and the woman entered with a tray.

'Where am I?' Eleanor said, looking down her nose at her female jailor. 'Who are you? What do you want with me?'

The woman set the tray on end of the bed and pulled her grey woollen shawl tight around her hunched shoulders. She looked like any woman you might see on the street in a village—black gown, grey hair scraped back, wisps escaping around her lined suntanned face. 'You'll get your answers soon enough, my lady. Now, drink your tea and eat something. You'll feel better.'

More drugs? Eleanor eyed the tray askance. Yet her stomach felt uncomfortably hollow. How long since she had eaten? 'What is the time?'

'Getting on for noon. You slept all day yesterday.'

She'd lost a whole day? Garrick would be worried. But how would he find her? 'You can't keep me here. The Marquess of Beauworth expects to find me at home.'

'Does he now?' The woman's smile was grim, but she didn't seem perturbed. 'Eat. Or go hungry.' She marched out and locked the door behind her.

Eleanor glanced at the tray. She needed strength for whatever they had in store for her, but not more laudanum. She carefully smelled the bread and the tea. Nothing obvious. Nor did she taste anything odd. She ate and drank her fill.

Feeling stronger, she strolled around her prison. The floor was cold and gritty under her bare feet, the air smelled of mould. Daylight struggled though a small window hung with dusty cobwebs high above her head. To see out, she would need to pull the cot beneath it and battle the spiders. She eyed the corners of the room. No doubt the horrid beasts lurked there, too. She shuddered and swallowed the urge to beg.

She peered through the peephole in the door into a kitchen much like the one in her own cottage, but not nearly as clean. From this angle, she had a view of an outer door and one end of the kitchen table.

The outside door swung open and a dark-haired burly man stepped in with an air of command.

'Is she awake?' this new man asked.

'Yes, Sarg.'

The man who'd grabbed her from behind. Her heart picked up speed. She retreated to sit on the cot. The door of her prison opened, admitting the newcomer. Eleanor clutched the collar of her robe tight.

'My lady, I hope you are feeling better?' Polite, well spoken, but not a gentleman. And he'd also addressed her as my lady. How did he know? Who was he? Her chest felt terribly tight as her heart drummed a warning. She gave him her haughtiest of stares. 'You have no right to keep me here against my will. I demand you release me, immediately.'

Sarg laughed softly. 'Very hoity-toity, my lady, and you a lightskirt and all.'

Eleanor gasped. Her face heated. 'How dare you? I am under the Marquess of Beauworth's protection.'

''Tis the Marquess bade us keep you here. Do as you're told and no harm will come to you.'

Her stomach dropped in a sickening rush. Garrick knew who she was? She couldn't believe it. Wouldn't. 'You lie, you cur.'

'Do I? His voice hardened. 'Your brother has Beauworth's property. And you are going to make sure it is returned.'

An odd sort of numbness enveloped her mind. It was as if she didn't want to feel the pain of the truth. For if this man knew her identity, then Garrick must know, too. How? Had she said something unwittingly? And why had he said nothing? Her stomach churned. She'd trusted him. Trusted his word that William was safe. Apparently Garrick, having enjoyed her favours, was striking out at her brother. But why? What on earth could he want? 'Lord Castlefield has nothing belonging to the Marquess.'

Caleb entered the room, grunting under the weight of a table and a wooden stool. 'Where do you want them, Sarg?'

Sarg pointed to the far side of the room under the window. 'There. Bring paper and quills.'

The man cast her a leering glance, then shambled out, only to return with writing implements. He set them on the table, all the while casting sly looks in her direction, seeming to peer right through her clothing. Revolting beast. If only she had a pistol or even her sword, she'd teach him a lesson in manners.

Sarg raised a brow. 'We brought your clothes, my lady. I will have Millie bring them to you, once you have written the letter to your brother.'

'My brother is abroad, fighting for his country.'

'Was abroad. His ship docked in Portsmouth three days since.'

She stifled a gasp with her hand. 'How do you know?'

'We've been watching.'

Someone had planned this very carefully. The realisation rolled up from her stomach, dark and sour and thick, like the winter fogs that slid up from a river. What could Garrick possibly want? 'I'm not writing anything to William.'

'Perhaps Caleb can change your mind.' The threat was delivered without a change of expression in the grim face staring down at her. Her heart missed a beat as Caleb grinned over Sarg's shoulder. She closed her eyes briefly. She couldn't suffer that man to touch her. 'Very well. I will write your letter.'

Caleb stomped out of the room.

At Sarg's gesture, she seated herself at the desk. The sheet of paper was blank. She glanced up in question.

'Write this,' Sarg said.

If you care to see me alive again, dearest William, please obey the bearers of this note. Only then will I remain, as I am now, unharmed. She signed, *Your sister, Lady Eleanor Hadley.*

She jumped when Sarg placed a calloused hand on her neck. She desperately wanted to jerk away. Instead, she held perfectly still. 'Don't touch me, you fiend.'

'Will your brother recognise this little trinket?' His finger looped under the ribbon around her neck.

'Yes.'

The man undid the clasp. Eleanor could not repress her shudder as his fingers touched her nape. The moment he drew the chain from her neck, she got up and moved away. He picked up the letter and left without a word. Caleb followed him out.

Drained, Eleanor sank on to the bed, her hands covering her face. This was all so dreadful. It seemed the Marquess had fooled her completely, taken her in. What could William have that was so important to him? The note told her nothing

What a fool she was, to be sure. Every step she took exploded in her face like a faulty pistol. Never again. She had learned her lesson. In future she would never interfere in things that were not her business. If she had a future.

Millie shuffled in. 'My lady, here are your clothes. Would you like help?'

The woman seemed genuinely regretful, far more kindly than the men. 'No, thank you. I am used to looking after myself.' Eleanor eyed the modest grey gown with longing. 'I would, however, appreciate something to cover the hole in the door.'

'Ye can use my apron.' The woman undid the tapes

and dropped it on the end of the bed. 'Just while ye dress.' She left.

After covering the peephole, and half-afraid that Caleb might decide to check on her progress, Eleanor dressed quickly. She tidied her hair, though without pins she could only leave it in a long braid down her back. Properly clothed, she felt a whole lot less exposed.

On the other side of the door, the woman moved around, humming softly to the sound of chopping and stirring. The revolting smell of boiling meat filled the air. Of Caleb and the man they called Sarg, she heard nothing.

The window offered her only hope of escape. Past the spiders. She shuddered. She had to try now, while they couldn't see in. She climbed up on the desk, pulled her sleeve down over her hand and swiped at nasty clinging webs. One floated against her face. Ugh. She brushed at it wildly. The table wobbled. She grabbed at the ledge. *Don't think about hairy bodies and long legs.* Gritting her teeth, her mouth dry, a lump in her throat, and her shaky breath loud in her ears, she peered outside.

Nothing but trees. No view. No landmarks. If she managed an escape, which way to go? It didn't matter. Anywhere would be better than here.

She pushed up on the sash. It refused to budge. She banged upwards with the heel of her hands. The rough wooden frame dug into her palms and the window shot up with a bang. A cobweb tickled her nose. She squeaked, yanked the window closed and jumped down. She tipped over the stool and smashed her plate on to the floor just as Millie and Caleb ran in.

'Oh, ho,' said Caleb, looking from the stool and the plate to her. 'There's that temper again. I'll tie you to the bed if you're going to start them sort of tricks.'

He loomed over her. Eleanor shrank away. 'I'm sorry. I won't do it again.'

'Aye. Well, you threw it down, you pick it up. Nay, Millie, do not help her. She better learn some manners right quick, or I will give her a lesson she won't forget.' His hand went to the belt at his waist.

Eleanor knelt swiftly and picked up the shards of pottery and crusts of bread. They watched her silently. She scooped them on to the tray and righted the stool.

Caleb pulled down the cloth that covered the peephole and ushered Millie out, leaving the door open. 'Break another platter, my lady, and you'll eat off the floor.'

Not until she was sure no one was watching her did Eleanor glance up at the window. Would they notice the lack of dust and cobwebs? She wiped her hands on her skirts with a grimace. After dark, she'd have to brave the spiders again. No choice. She must reach William before he paid her ransom. Then she'd decide what to do about Beauworth.

She recalled the words he'd spoken at the barn. *No abductor ever lets his victim live.* Had his charm been nothing but a ruse? Was he paying her back for what she had done as Lady Moonlight? Or did William really have something he wanted and she had let herself be fooled? Which meant somehow, he'd known who she was all along. Something squeezed in her chest. The horrid sensation of a heart in denial. But her heart was probably wrong.

'We need more wood for the fire.' Millie's announcement in the room beyond broke through her agitated thoughts.

'That's your job, woman. I'm guarding the prisoner,' Caleb said.

Millie cursed.

Through the open door, Eleanor watched Millie pick up a basket and head outside. Caleb remained sitting at the table, his half-closed eyes fixed on her. Her heart picked up speed. Now she knew how a mouse felt when faced by a cat. Finally, unable to stand the tension, she got up and closed the door. It swung back before she could step away.

'Leave it, wench,' Caleb said.

'Hoping I'll try to escape?'

He stepped threateningly over the threshold.

Damn. Why could she not keep her mouth shut?

Hand on the doorjamb, he raked her body with a hot greedy expression. She wanted to back away, to get as far from him as possible. Giving ground would be a fatal admission of weakness. She watched him warily.

Caleb smiled. His mottled skin flushed dark as he reached out to touch her. Calloused skin brushed her cheek. Sour breath filled her nostrils.

'Hands off, you oaf.'

He rocked back on his heels, clearly taken aback. He grabbed at the doorpost, unsteady on his feet. Drunk. 'Come on, pretty lady. Old Caleb only wants a little bit of what the Marquess 'ad.' He frowned. ''Twould be better if you gave it to me nice like, than if I 'as to take it.'

Every nerve in her body warned of danger. Flee or fight. Cunning was better. Eleanor smiled. 'Well…' She took a half-step forward.

His lips rolled back over his rotting teeth. She grasped the edge of the door and swung it with every ounce of strength. The corner hit the middle of his forehead with the crack of a hammer. His nose burst and blood spurted. He stood there staring, unblinking, unmoving, blood dripping off the ends of his moustache. She'd not hit him hard enough. She backed away. Now he'd come after her and she had nowhere to run.

His eyes glazed. He fell slowly backwards and crashed to the floor like a felled tree.

Oh, God, she was going to be sick. She had never in her life caused such damage to another human being. No time for regret. This would seal her fate if she didn't leave. She needed a weapon. A gun, or a knife. She dropped to her knees beside the unconscious man and feverishly searched his pockets. She found a pistol in one pocket and a dagger in the other. She ran for the door. Lifted the latch. Footsteps clattered on the flagstones outside.

Blast. She dodged back, hugging the wall behind the door. Her heart in her mouth, she cocked the pistol.

Chapter Seven

Something hammered against Garrick's skull.

'My lord!'

It wasn't in his head. There was someone at his door. 'Go 'way.' He could barely get the words through the fur lining of his mouth.

'Please, my lord. It's Dan.'

Garrick groaned and sat up. He was still wearing his shirt. The curtained room was dark and enough of the haze cleared from his head to wonder what time it was.

'My lord.' Nidd entered through the door to his dressing room. 'That lad says he needs to talk to you right bad.'

'Damn it all,' Garrick muttered. Couldn't a fellow get drunk in peace? If Uncle Duncan hadn't gone off to Portsmouth on business, he would have broached the old man yesterday, instead of a bottle of brandy. Now he had to face today with a bloody headache. 'All right, send him in. Nidd, can you find some of those miracle powders of yours?'

'Aye, master, right gladly.'

A few seconds after Nidd had left, Dan stood in front

of Garrick, his hat clutched in his hand, his face troubled. Bloody hell. Clearly the lad had been up to mischief. Garrick glared at him. 'What is it?'

'It's M-Miss Brown,' the boy stuttered.

Garrick narrowed his eyes. 'What about her?'

'I was having a drop of blue ruin on the quiet, like, late last night and I...' Dan gazed at his shuffling feet. Garrick had forbidden him to indulge the taste for gin he'd developed in childhood. 'I fell asleep in the loft. I woke up this morn when Mr Matthews rode in. His lordship came out to meet him.'

Good. Uncle Duncan was back. He must have returned after Garrick went to bed. He realised Dan was staring at him. 'Catch you, did they?'

'No, my lord. They were right under me. I couldn't help but hear what they said. I think Miss Brown is in some sort of trouble.'

Garrick straightened, the mists in his brain receding. 'You must be mistaken. Miss Brown left Boxted two days ago.'

The boy winced, but continued doggedly. 'Mr Matthews said something about a letter, but she was still sleeping. I didn't know what they meant. Then his lordship said it was kind of you, my lord, to hand them a weapon. It didn't make no sense.'

'Any sense.'

'Yes, my lord. Then Mr Matthews says for a lady she was a hellion and he looked forward to taming her. Then his lordship said no, that Mr Matthews was to leave the Marquess's ladybird alone. That's when I knew they meant Miss Brown, my lord, for I knows she's—'

Garrick scowled. Dan flushed to the roots of his hair. 'I didn't mean no disrespect, my lord.'

The boy had a screw loose. Unless Le Clere had some misguided notion of saving Garrick from himself. Hardly likely. Perhaps the boy had misheard. 'Did they say where Miss Brown was?' His voice creaked like an old door.

Dan curled into his shoulders, a picture of defiance underpinned with fear. 'I followed.'

'Followed who?'

'Mr Matthews, my lord. I couldn't hear no more, they walked away, but I got down from the loft and when I saw him ride away I followed. He went over by Standerstead, to a cottage.'

Utter nonsense. 'Did you see Miss Brown?'

'No, my lord, there was this big ugly cove standing outside. Looked to me like he was carrying a brace of pops as if he was guarding somethin'. Like them soldiers at Horse Guards.'

Garrick narrowed his eyes, cursing the fog in his brain. Dan had no reason to lie. It didn't make sense, but he had to be sure. 'What time was this?'

'Not long ago, an hour mebbe.'

'Can you find the place again?'

'Yes, my lord.'

'Good lad.' Garrick squeezed into his coat. 'Ask Nidd to hurry up with that powder, then meet me at the stables. Have Johnson saddle Bess.'

The boy touched his forelock and dashed off, looking exceedingly pleased with himself.

Garrick retrieved his duelling pistols from the case in his dressing room and shoved them into his waistband. He was struggling into his boots when Nidd arrived with the promised potion.

'Oh, my lord, look at you putting fingerprints all over them new Hessians.'

'Never mind that, Nidd. I'm off on some urgent business.' He tossed off the cloudy liquid and made a face at its bitter taste. 'Have you seen my uncle?'

'I understand he's busy in his study, my lord.'

'Good. No need to disturb him.'

Garrick reached the stables without seeing anyone at all, and found Dan standing in the yard holding a skittish Bess and the reins of the bag of bones he'd ridden before. Garrick shook his head. 'I'm sorry, Dan. Stable your horse and return to your duties. I will get there faster alone. Give me the directions.'

Dan's face dropped, but he complied.

For a city lad he had given very precise directions and Garrick had no trouble finding his way to the one approach leading to the cottage, a narrow cart track winding through the woods. The smell of smoke gave away its location. Garrick tied Bess to a blackthorn bush and surveyed the thatched half-timbered hovel. A wood-cutter's cottage. No sign of any guard. He crossed the clearing and strode up the flagstone path. No sound emanated from within. The door was ajar. He pushed it open.

A tub o' lard lay on his back on the stone floor, his face a bleeding pulp. What in hell's name had happened here?

Garrick crossed the room swiftly and knelt beside the injured man. He felt for a pulse. He swung around at a rustle behind him and stared from the barrel of a pistol to the rigid, white face of a very determined young woman.

He got to his feet and held out his hands, wariness and relief coursing through him. 'Ellie, you are here. Are you all right?' He hesitated and then bowed with a regretful smile. 'I mean, Lady Eleanor.'

'If I didn't know better, I might think you were pleased to see me.'

What the hell was she talking about? He stepped forwards. She waved her pistol. 'Stay back.'

'My lady, you seem to be in some danger. I think we should leave.'

Eleanor frowned. 'We? I think not. Where did you arrange to meet William?'

'Your brother? I made no such arrangement.'

She glared. 'Don't think to fool me again. Just tell me the meeting place.'

He recoiled, shocked by her obvious distrust. He kept his voice gentle. 'We have to leave before anyone comes, then we will talk.'

'*We* are not doing anything. Don't think me a fool. Your man here told me everything.' She levelled her pistol at his head. She backed towards the door. 'Don't make the mistake of thinking I don't know how to use this weapon, will you, Garrick? Make one move and you're a dead man.'

Clearly he was dealing with Lady Moonlight. 'As you wish. Go on your own. But go now.'

A shadow fell across the flagstones outside. He moved to get a better view. Her pistol followed him. Damnation. Matthews. With a gun in his hand and a smile on his face.

'Stay where you are, my lord,' she warned in a low voice.

Matthews's gun was levelled at her back. If he warned her, she would look. And she might die.

Garrick dived to the floor, rolling, yanking free a pistol. She kept her weapon trained on him. Garrick fired. Her shot came a second later. The burning, ripping pain of her bullet tore into his bicep. He reeled from the numbing force. Thank God she hadn't shot to kill.

She jerked around at a sound behind her. Face twisting in pain, Matthews shook his hand, blood trickling from his fingers, his pistol at his feet.

Garrick launched himself upright, staggered forwards, reversed his pistol and struck the steward behind the ear. He measured his length with a dull thud beside the first man.

'Go,' Garrick said. 'Get out of here. Take my horse. She's ten yards off to the right of the path. For God's sake, hurry.'

Eleanor pressed the back of her hand against her mouth. 'I shot you.'

'Never mind that.' Garrick bent to pick up Matthews's pistol. He forced it into her hand, relieving her of her discharged weapon. 'Run.' He pushed her ahead, urging her out the door and down the path. With one hand in the small of her back, he guided her to his horse.

A raucous shout came from behind. A woman running from the back of the cottage. They were done if she was armed. He kept going. His shoulder blades tensed, anticipating yet another bullet. More noise, ahead of them this time, a rider thundering down on them.

Garrick drew his second pistol. 'Keep going,' he shouted. 'I'll catch you up.' His left arm useless, he dropped to one knee and steadied his forearm on his thigh, ready to shoot the rider as he came in sight. He would only get one shot.

'My lord.' The rider turned his horse at the last moment. The blond curls were unmistakable. Dan? By thunder, the lad needed a good hiding if this was the way he followed orders. Garrick released his finger. 'You young idiot. I told you to stay at Beauworth.'

The boy stuck out his bottom lip.

'Never mind. Come on.' Garrick turned to follow Eleanor and almost tripped over her, crouching behind him with her weapon cocked and ready to fire. He cursed. Would no one obey anything he said?

She stared at him, a puzzled frown on her face. 'You don't really know anything about this, do you?'

If only that was completely true. 'We don't have time for talk. Move.' Grasping her arm, he guided her to Bess cropping at the grass. Dan leapt down, untied the reins and boosted Eleanor into the saddle. He helped Garrick to get up behind her, before remounting.

'Where to, my lord?' Dan asked, his eyes bright with excitement.

Good question.

'Brown's farm,' Ellie said. 'My horse is there.'

So, Lady Eleanor was taking charge. But since his head was spinning, it was just as well.

The Brown kitchen was like any other farmhouse kitchen in England: tiled floor, polished copper pots and hearth with a kettle steaming on a hook over a large brick fireplace. Or it would be, Garrick thought, had a Marquess not been sitting at the kitchen table with his shirt off while an apple-cheeked farmer's wife wielded a bowl of water and a bloody cloth.

The back door opened to admit a burly man of middle age with a craggy face. 'What's all this I hear from the lad in the stable about Beauworth needing help?' The man was a younger version of Martin Brown and, Garrick recalled, one of Beauworth's tenant farmers.

'His lordship had a bit of an accident. A fall from his horse,' Mrs Brown said.

'The lad said it were a bullet. Those highwaymen we've been hearing of, I'd wager.'

'Oh, my,' Mrs Brown said, her blue eyes widening.

Damn. They should have remembered Dan needed to know the story they had concocted for the farmer's wife.

Hands clasped at her waist, Ellie moved back to the table, whether seeking or offering protection Garrick couldn't tell, because her gaze was fixed on the farmer.

'The lad is mistaken,' she said firmly. 'Please, Mr Brown, do not concern yourself. We came only to fetch my horse. We will leave right away.'

Protection, then. It made Garrick want to smile, to pull her close and kiss her, but perhaps she'd change her mind about wanting to protect him, when she learned his secret.

John Brown scratched behind his ear and stared at Garrick's arm for a second or two. 'I'll send to Beauworth for the carriage.'

'No need,' Garrick said. 'It's nothing. I'll be back on my horse in no time at all.' He winked at Mrs Brown. 'Isn't that right?'

She batted her eyelashes. 'Yes, my lord.'

Brown touched his forelock. 'As you say, my lord. But we need to catch them villains. Terrorising decent folk they are. Mr Le Clere should be sent for. As magistrate, he'll know what to do.'

The irony of it struck Garrick hard. 'I'll bring it to my uncle's attention the moment I get home.'

'Aye. Well, you'll find me mucking out in the barn, if you needs me. That good-for-nothing cousin of mine has disappeared again.' He stomped out.

Mrs Brown continued her dabbing. 'It's just a graze, my lord,' she said. 'The men gets worse cuts at haying time.'

'I told you,' Garrick said to Ellie. She smiled absently. Damn it, they needed to talk about what had happened and then make some sort of plan to get her to safety.

'I'll just fetch a bit of liniment and we'll bandage you up,' Mrs Brown said. She bustled off into what must be the scullery.

'What do we do now?' Ellie asked.

'Now we have to get you back to your brother. He came looking for you at the cottage.'

If anything her face grew paler. 'You've met William?'

'Yes.'

'At the cottage?'

'Martin brought him.'

She winced. 'He knows, then. About us.' Her look of devastation pained him worse than the wound on his arm.

'Ellie, we'll be married right away. Everything will be all right.' He hoped.

Her lips tightened. She got up, taking the bowl of water to the sink under the window. He had the strangest feeling of loss, as if it wasn't mere feet, but miles she'd put between them.

She turned to face him, her back against the sink, her expression hidden by the light from the window behind her. 'What is going on, Garrick? Caleb, the man you found on the floor, said you arranged my abduction. Why?'

Garrick shot to his feet. 'Ellie, no. You can't possibly believe—'

Mrs Brown bustled back into the kitchen with a jar of something yellow and a roll of white bandage. The kindly woman must have sensed something amiss, because she hesitated, looking from one to the other. 'If you would sit down, your lordship, I'll have you better in a trice.'

'Thank you. You are a wonderful nurse.' He smiled at her.

She bridled like a young girl. 'Go on with you, my lord.' She waved her pot. 'Hold still now.' She removed the paper cover.

Garrick almost choked on the dreadful smell. 'By Gad, that stinks.'

The woman smeared a dollop on his arm and proceeded to wrap the bandage around it. 'We use this on the horses. Heals 'em up lovely, according to my John.'

She cut the end of the bandage with scissors and tied it off in a knot.

'Thank you.' Garrick reached for his shirt and pulled it on. He thrust his arms into his waistcoat and coat and knotted his cravat at his throat. 'Mrs Brown, I wonder if there is somewhere Lady Eleanor and I could converse for a moment or two?'

'Oh, yes, my lord. What was I thinking? Me keeping you here in the kitchen, with my parlour much more the thing. This way.'

She led the way to the front of the house, to a room full of highly polished chairs, their seats stuffed with horsehair and covered in plush. It reminded Garrick of a visit to his grandmother's house when he'd been a lad. 'Will this do, my lord?' Mrs Brown bobbed, all formality and humble apology now he looked more like himself.

'What a beautiful room,' Ellie said. 'Thank you.'

Mrs Brown beamed.

'Yes indeed,' Garrick said. 'A well-appointed chamber, and the view is very good.'

Mrs Brown smiled. 'I'll bring you that tea.' She left, closing the door.

'Good people,' Garrick said.

She nodded. 'They've been good to Martin, while he's been living and working here.' There were shadows in her eyes.

Garrick crossed to her side. 'Ellie, I had nothing to do with your imprisonment or the ransom. An overheard conversation between my uncle and Matthews led me to you.'

'Matthews?'

'The man I shot at the cottage.'

'Oh. They called him Sarg. He said—'

Anger clawed up his spine. 'I don't care what he said. I had nothing to do with it.'

She recoiled.

God, now she was afraid of him. He fought for calm. 'I would never do anything to hurt you, Ellie. I swear it.'

He held her gaze for a very long moment, saw acceptance slowly dawn on her face with a deep sense of relief.

'I didn't want to believe it,' she said softly. 'They made it sound true.' A sob caught in her throat. 'I should have known better than to think so ill of you. I'm sorry.'

He caught her to his chest and patted her shoulder. 'Please, *chérie,* don't cry. None of this is your fault.' He tipped her chin with his hand and his heart clenched at her tremulous smile. He brushed a wayward tear with his thumb and something welled in his throat. Tenderness. It didn't mix well with rage. It felt strange, confusing. He wanted both to comfort her and kill the men who had caused her harm. 'That's better.'

'Why did they blame you?' she asked.

He took her hand, kissed her small fingers briefly and gazed into her face. 'I think you should sit down.'

Gripping her hand as if it could anchor him to rational thought, he led her to the sofa. She sank on to the seat, clearly worried. He braced for the coming storm.

She gazed at up him, her eyes fearful. 'They said they wanted something from William.'

He wished he couldn't guess what they wanted. He wished her chance remark did not lead him into hell and he could deny all knowledge. He took a deep breath. 'Le Clere is behind your abduction. Without my knowledge, I promise. I believe it has something to do with Piggot's visit to your father.'

Silent, eyes wary, she stared at him. His palms felt suddenly damp. 'There was an accident. Years ago. My mother fell down the staircase at the Court. Piggot accused me. He said I pushed her deliberately. Then he fled.'

'Did you?' she asked.

He glanced down at their interlaced fingers. Dammit. He was avoiding her gaze and yet he didn't want to see her revulsion. 'I don't know.'

She pulled her hand away. 'How can you not know?'

'I can't remember.' He got up and went to the window. Looked out at the very fine view of English countryside, rolling hills, neat fields and woodland and saw only black-and-white tiles, black hair and white limbs sprawled...

'I remember nothing.' He glanced over his shoulder. She was watching him, her face serious, her eyes huge, her sweet lips pressed firmly together. 'Except her body on the floor at the bottom of the stairs, and Piggot, a footman, accusing me.' *He did it on purpose.* 'He disappeared. The other day you mentioned he visited your father. I can only assume he told him the tale. But unless you heard something, or your brother did, I can't understand my uncle's actions. Did you hear Piggot's story, Ellie?'

'No.' Her voice was a whisper, full of shock and horror. 'Did you…?'

He hadn't wanted to tell her like this, with so much at stake, and so much doubt in his heart. His voice grew thick and rough. 'I loved my mother. Adored her. I can't believe I would have hurt her, not deliberately. And yet…' He swallowed. 'The Le Clere blood carries a taint. Blind rage with the strength of several men. The blood of Norse berserkers shows up every generation or two. Good for battle. Not good around people. That's why Beauworths are always soldiers, not politicians.' He hated it. 'Uncle Duncan, my father's cousin, believes what happened to Mother was an accident.' He'd spoken the way adults pander to naughty children, leaving Garrick in doubt. 'I knew nothing of this disease until long after my mother died. Le Clere devoted his life to our family. He loves Beauworth. Far more than I. I think he is trying to protect me.'

'So you did not have anything to do with my abduction.'

What could he do to make her believe? 'I swear it. On my honour.'

'Then why would they say you did?'

'If they did it in my name, I suppose I am as guilty as they are.' He turned back to the view. 'There is only one way to end this nightmare. I have to go to the authorities and admit the truth.'

A light touch fell on his shoulder. He'd not heard her approach. Half-afraid of what he would see in her face, he turned and saw pity and the shimmer of tears. His heart cracked open and pain flooded in. The pain of guilt he'd held back for so many years.

'You really can't remember?' she murmured.

He shook his head.

'It must have been an accident,' she said.

Ellie. Sweet gentle Ellie. Even now she would give him the benefit of the doubt.

He forced a laugh, heard the bitterness. 'I don't need to remember. There was a witness.' He brushed the thought aside. 'The most important thing is to get you home safe. Then I will deal with my uncle.'

'But—'

A scratch at the door and Mrs Brown, her hands full of tray, entered. 'Here we are, at last. And look who came to see how you are, my lord. My John though it best to send word to the Court after all.'

Garrick's heart dropped to the floor as Le Clere stepped into the room behind Mrs Brown.

Ellie could not restrain her gasp.

'Why don't you all have a nice cup of tea before you set out?' the farmer's wife said with a beaming smile, placing the tray on the table in front of the sofa. 'There are some scones here and preserves and a nice dollop of cream.'

Ellie wanted to scream. While the sweet, well-meaning Mrs Brown chattered about cakes and set out plates and cups in front of her, she wanted to charge past the portly noble looking over the woman's shoulder with the sorrowful expression of a bloodhound.

Garrick stood pale and stiff, his hands clenched at his side. Why didn't he object, consign his uncle, or cousin, to the devil, if they weren't in league? This was a nightmare. At any moment she'd wake up in Castlefield and discover it had all been a horrible dream.

But it wasn't.

'That will be all, Mrs Brown,' Le Clere said, moving aside. Then Ellie saw the reason for Garrick's posture. Le Clere held a pistol. This really was too much. How many more men were going to hold her at pistol point today?

She started for the door, intending to follow Mrs Brown out.

'Don't move, Ellie,' Garrick said.

She darted a glance at him. It was two against one. If they rushed Le Clere, surely they could overpower him? His face a mask, Garrick shook his head, refusing her aid. Was he in this with his uncle, after all? Her stomach fell away, a sickening sensation.

'Well, well, isn't this pleasant,' Le Clere said in genial tones the moment Mrs Brown closed the door. 'And here I thought Matthews had lost the pair of you.'

'What the deuce do you think you are doing?' Garrick said tightly. 'This is Lady Eleanor Hadley.'

Eleanor let go of her breath. He knew his uncle better than she. Perhaps he thought he would listen to reason.

Le Clere raised a heavy black brow. 'I know.' He bowed. 'By now your brother should be in possession of your letter, and be following his instructions. The exchange will continue just as planned.'

'No,' Garrick said. 'I will not allow it.'

'You won't allow it?' Le Clere's face hardened. He no longer looked like a bloodhound, more like a bulldog. 'After everything I have done for this family? Either Lady Eleanor co-operates or she dies, as will every member of her family.'

Horrified, she stared first at Le Clere, then at Garrick, who paled.

'Uncle Duncan, what the hell have you done?' Garrick started forwards. 'This must cease now.'

Le Clere tightened his grip on his pistol and moved closer to Eleanor.

Garrick stopped short. 'Why are you doing this?' Garrick asked, his eyes intent. 'What does Castlefield have that is so important?'

'Sit down, Garrick,' Le Clere said mildly. 'We might as well have this conversation in a civilised manner. Perhaps, Lady Eleanor, you would be good enough to pour the tea?'

Back to kind elderly gentlemen. It was uncanny. A shiver ran down her spine. Garrick sat. She followed suit. With a sense of unreality, she poured each of them a cup of tea. Le Clere's pistol didn't waver as he took a sip from his cup.

Garrick refused tea. Eleanor poured a cup for herself. Perhaps if she threw it in his face...

'To answer your question, Garrick,' his uncle said, 'we need the letter Piggot left with this young lady's father and everything can go on as before.'

'Piggot left a letter?' Garrick squeezed his eyes shut as if the words caused him pain. 'How can you know?'

'He sent me word of a letter to be opened at his death,' Le Clere said. 'Do drink your tea, Lady Eleanor. And don't think about throwing it in my face. I can assure you a bullet travels faster than hot liquid.'

Eleanor put down her cup. 'It would be a waste of good tea.'

Garrick whipped his head around and gave her a hard, warning stare. Well, it had been a feeble idea, but she hoped he'd think of something better, and soon, or she'd be forced to give it a try. Perhaps the teapot would make a better missile.

Le Clere smiled. 'Very wise, Lady Eleanor.' He returned his attention to Garrick. 'Piggot warned what would happen if anything happened to him or his family. What I didn't know was the letter's location. I should have guessed he'd go to one of your father's army friends. When the man I hired finally tracked him down, Piggot was dying. It seems he wanted it all off his conscience and told his nurse the whole story. A few guineas later, and I knew exactly where to look.'

Garrick looked as if the walls of the farmhouse were folding in on him. 'You never told me any of this.' He looked genuinely shocked and horrified.

'Why did this all come to a head now?' Eleanor asked.

'The impending arrival of your brother made action imperative. He is bound to find the letter sooner or later. When he does, he will see it as his duty to bring it to the authorities. I could not allow that.' He sounded as if it was the most natural occurrence in the world.

Garrick leaned forwards, his face dark. 'Did you kill Piggot? Is there more blood on my hands I don't know about?' He was white beneath his tan, looking ill.

'Don't be foolish, my boy.' Le Clere almost chortled. 'What would that advantage? All the while he remained alive your secret was safe. Now the letter is to be opened. Fortunately your older brother died before he had time to go through your father's papers, Lady Eleanor. We needed more time to look.'

The words were like hot pebbles dropped on ice, the import fracturing the surface of her mind, the cracks spreading out, until the surface weakened and the stones fell through, sinking to the bottom with a threatening hiss. She gripped the fabric of the sofa, needing to feel something solid in her world. 'You killed Michael?'

'Let us say the timing was fortuitous,' Le Clere said.

'No!' The word seemed to be ripped from Garrick's chest. 'No,' he whispered. His fists clenched. The knuckles white.

'Control yourself, Garrick,' Le Clere said. 'Anyway, by foreclosing on the mortgage and forcing you out, I hoped to find it before the next brother returned to England. William, isn't it? Brave young man. Mentioned in dispatches more than once.'

A wave of fear rushed over her. William. She closed her eyes, as strength drained from her limbs like water running through her fingers. She wanted to collapse. To scream. But William's life was also in danger. She had to find a way to warn him.

She glanced at Garrick. He seemed frozen, his shoulders rigid, but his dark eyes blazed fury.

Unlike Le Clere, who looked calm, a relaxed, well-dressed gentleman taking afternoon tea, if it weren't for the evil hanging about him like a cloak. She repressed a shiver. She would not let him see how afraid he made her feel.

He leaned back in his chair, his face smug. 'I paid one of the bailiffs to search the house. He found nothing. Not even a safe.'

The room behind the panelling. Built in Tudor times as a priest hole. It would take a clever thief to find it.

'Ah,' Le Clere said, his gaze narrowed on her face, 'I see you know where it is.'

'Ellie,' Garrick said. 'Tell him nothing.'

Perhaps he'd let her guide him to it. Once at Castlefield, she'd be in familiar territory. It might give her an advantage. 'I've never seen this document, but my father did have a safe.'

Le Clere nodded. 'I would have found it given time,

but I made a mistake.' He looked at Garrick. 'I took advantage of Garrick's weakness for a certain young lady. I thought it would keep him at Beauworth.' He looked sorrowfully at the Marquess. 'We can solve all this right now, Garrick. Marry Lady Eleanor, get an heir and leave me as guardian. I'd be more than happy for you to go off and get yourself killed.'

The kind way he spoke the words made Eleanor's stomach heave. 'You are disgusting.'

'Despicable,' Garrick said. 'And the game is up.'

'Is it?' Le Clere rose to his feet. 'By now, Matthews should be outside with the carriage. All we have to do is meet your brother at the assigned place and everything will be all right.'

'I think not,' Ellie said with dawning fear. 'I know what he did.' She pointed at Garrick. He winced. A wry smile curved his lips and it wrenched at her heart that he did not deny it. How could she feel such a pang of sympathy when so much evil had been done in his name?

Le Clere pursed his lips, his head cocked on one side. 'You think anyone will pay any attention to the words of a jilted lover? Just do as you are told and you can return home safe and sound.'

He lied. Something in his face told her he would not leave any of them alive. Including William and Sissy. A cold wind seemed to brush across her shoulders and penetrate her bones. Fear. Deep and terrifying. She fought its numbing weight. 'You planned it all. The ship I invested in. The debt.'

Le Clere had the gall to laugh. 'Dear lady, your man of business works for me.'

'Jarvis?'

'The same.' The more this man said, the more she felt like a fly spinning around in one of those horrible sticky webs, and no matter how she struggled she would never get free.

Garrick must have sensed something similar because he leaned forwards, glaring at his uncle. 'I'll expose you. I'll go to the authorities the moment your back is turned.' He looked ready to spring at his uncle, his shoulders tense, his face a mask of fury.

Eleanor braced herself, ready to follow his lead.

'And Lady Eleanor will die,' Le Clere said softly. 'Now, or later. And it will be your fault.'

A hiss of breath left Garrick's lips. He sagged back against the cushions. 'Damn you.'

Mrs Brown stuck her head in the door. 'The carriage is here, my lord.'

Le Clere reached across the table and grabbed Eleanor by the arm. The pistol jammed against her ribs. 'I know you won't mind helping an old man out to his carriage, Lady Eleanor.'

If she resisted and Le Clere killed her, she would have no chance to warn William. She inhaled a shaky breath and rose to her feet.

Le Clere drew her close. 'Garrick, do go ahead. One misstep and Lady Eleanor will find a nasty hole in her stomach.'

Fury rolled off Garrick in dark waves. Lines bracketed his white-edged lips. The sinews in his neck stood out against his collar, his hands opening and closing as if he was ready to strangle his uncle. His eyes bored into Le Clere's for a long minute, as if he debated what to do, then his shoulders slumped and he walked ahead of them into the hallway.

Le Clere put an arm about her shoulders, let her feel the press of the weapon into her side, then urged her forwards. The front door stood open. In the farmyard beside the carriage, Matthews, a livid bruise on his temple and a bandage around the knuckles of his right hand, looked as if he would very much like to shoot someone.

Two horses were tied to the rear of the carriage and Caleb, his face a bloody ruin, glared at them from the box. She certainly didn't have any friends she could turn to for help among this lot. Not even Garrick, it seemed.

Of the helpful John Brown, there was no sign. Besides, what could a farmer do against his landlord? A movement in the barn, a flash of yellow. A slight figure peering out. Dan, no doubt. The poor lad could be of no help, either. No one could. The realisation sent a cold shiver down her spine.

Garrick climbed into the coach. Matthews followed him in. Then Le Clere shoved Ellie inside and climbed up behind. He pointed his pistol at her head. 'Tie their wrists at their backs, Matthews. We don't want any more problems.'

Blood pounding in his ears, vision hazed, Garrick stared at Le Clere. His father's cousin. A man he'd known all his life. His flesh and blood. Why had he never seen this side of Le Clere?

He had. Years ago. A faint memory of loud voices, his mother weeping. And later, when Garrick refused to admit pushing his mother down the stairs, the man had lost his temper and taken a cane to Garrick's back. Le Clere had changed after that, Garrick realised. Become his friend. His mentor. His kindly conscience, always reminding him what he'd done without coming out and saying it in words. In the close confines of the carriage, Le Clere's lust for power pervaded the air, rank and toxic.

The thought that Le Clere had done it on his behalf horrified him. Worse yet, Garrick wanted to kill him for what he'd done to Ellie.

The rope around his wrists bit into his flesh as he strained against them. He glared at the pair of them, Matthews and Le Clere, and smelled their blood in his nostrils. He wanted that blood on his hands. He pulled on the ropes binding him. But Matthews knew his work. The rage inside Garrick grew until he could see little more than their faces through a red mist.

Beside him, Eleanor sat rigid, watchful and coolly remote, when she should have been having a fit of the vapours after all she'd heard. Courage shone in her eyes, but how she must hate him now she knew what lay beneath his skin.

Control. He needed control or he'd be lost. He took slow, deep breaths. 'Where are we going?'

'You'll see,' Le Clere said.

He would. And when he did, he'd be ready to act. Surely he could outwit a man who had clearly lost his reason?

Chapter Eight

The carriage pulled to a halt. Garrick peered out. They were only a few yards into the lane beyond the farm. Matthews leaned over and tested first his ropes and then Ellie's. 'They won't be getting free in a hurry.'

'Good,' Le Clere said, and leaned forwards to open the door. Garrick's heart picked up speed.

His uncle laughed. 'Don't worry, Garrick. I'll be a few feet behind you all the way.' He stepped out, followed by Matthews. The two men mounted their horses, no doubt with a view of discussing their plans in private. The carriage set off once more.

Ellie stared out of the window, her shoulders stiff, her face white and her expression forlorn.

The rage in his gut unfurled like a dragon full of fire, heat rushed up from his belly. He took a deep breath. It wouldn't help. When she didn't say anything, he fished around for a way to break the silence. 'I'm sorry you got dragged into this.'

'I don't suppose you have a knife?'

He didn't like the way her gaze raked the interior of the coach. 'Please, Ellie, whatever you do, no heroics. Trust me to get you out of this and follow my lead.'

Nor did he like the way her determined chin came up in challenge. 'Do you have a plan?'

'I'll take advantage of whatever opportunity is offered.'

She curled her lip. 'An excellent plan.' She turned her head to gaze out of the window.

'Sarcasm won't help.' He huffed out a breath. 'Ellie, believe me, I won't let my uncle harm you.'

'He killed my brother. For you.' Her voice was husky. She turned her head slowly. The glitter of tears she'd tried to hide with harsh words cut a swathe through his heart. She'd been so brave up to now and to see her spirit leach away weighed heavy on his soul. Nor could he think of a word to say in his defence.

He couldn't afford to let himself feel her pain, because if he allowed the emotions through, the anger he held at bay would take over and he'd be nothing but a raging unthinking beast.

He stared out of the window. They were approaching the crossroads beyond the village. The place where the first Lady Moonlight had ended her life on the gibbet. With a wry twist of sick humour, he hoped it wasn't an omen.

The carriage halted behind a stone wall at the edge of the common where the villagers grazed a few sheep and a scrawny cow. Garrick watched Caleb take off at a run, a musket over his shoulder, heading for a ridge to the east where scattered boulders and gorse provided plenty of cover.

Matthews opened the door, blocking his view. 'Out you get. Ladies first, if you please.' He bowed.

Garrick thought about head-butting the man on his

way down the step, but saw Le Clere watching from a short distance off and could only watch in helpless fury as Matthews's hand clenched around Ellie's elbow. At the steward's nod, Garrick leapt down and glanced across the open tract of land to where Caleb had disappeared. The man had ducked out of sight.

A perfect place for an ambush.

Trust him? An admitted murderer? Ellie wanted to. He'd been naught but a child. Could such an act be the sign of some horrible disease, as Garrick seemed to believe, or simply an accident? It seemed incredible to believe he'd killed his mother on purpose. But both he and Le Clere seemed convinced of his guilt. And then he'd asked her to trust him.

Up to now, everything she'd done had turned out for the worst. Like a fool, she'd trusted Jarvis to guide her in the matters of business, and look where that had led. With William's life in the balance, the only person she dare trust was herself, and even there she didn't have a lot of faith.

Michael. A pain carved through her chest. Don't think about what had happened. Not now. Concentrate on what you need to do.

Her mind whirling in circles of indecision, she picked her way through the long grass to the wooden stile at Matthews's direction. Garrick followed.

'Wait here,' Matthews said. 'And don't try nothing funny. I'll be watching.' He marched back to Le Clere, who had remained with the carriage, scanning the surrounding countryside with a spyglass. Watching for William?

Should she run? Not with Matthews's shotgun pointed her way. If she wanted to escape, she'd need a distraction. She looked at Garrick. He seemed oblivious to the man and his weapon, gazing off into the distance with a faint smile on his face, as if he didn't have a care in the world.

He must have felt her gaze because he turned his head and raised a brow. 'I wish to hell you'd let your brother get himself out of his own financial difficulties. You might never have got involved in this at all.'

Was he bent on annoying her? 'If wishes were horses... And besides, they were not his financial problems. They were mine. I forged his signature.'

He groaned. 'I might have guessed.'

'Your Mr Jarvis said it was an opportunity of a lifetime.'

'He is not my Mr Jarvis. He works for the estate.'

'Your estate, my lord.'

'As trustee, Le Clere makes all the decisions until my twenty-fifth birthday.'

Well, that explained some of it. 'Not a wise choice for trustee.'

'He was like a brother to my father. I don't understand it.'

'He's protecting you.'

He sighed. 'I know. But he's far beyond the pale with this.'

'You could say that.'

'Squabbling is not going to help us.'

Her turn to raise a brow. 'What do you suggest?'

'We work together.'

She glanced up to find his eyes searching her face. Eyes full of bleakness, as if he guessed her doubts.

'All right,' she said.

Matthews was eyeing them suspiciously. 'What are you two lovebirds talking about?'

'None of your business, you cur,' Garrick said, glowering at the man from beneath lowered eyebrows.

'I could make it my business, your lordship,' Matthews said, clearly undeterred.

'Matthews!' Le Clere's voice held a warning.

Matthews closed his mouth like a fish on a hook, but the expression on his face threatened a future discussion, with fists.

Instead of blustering and squaring up like a contender at fisticuffs at a fair, Garrick should be focusing on their problem. She poked his ribs with an elbow.

Garrick watched his uncle direct Matthews to a position further along the wall. But where the hell was Caleb? And how many more men did Le Clere have up there? He scanned the rough terrain, with its clumps of gorse and shadowed folds.

A glint. A quick flash beside a rock he'd almost missed. And another, to the right. There were at least two of them. Garrick gauged the distance and the angle in relation to Matthews's position at the wall. Oh, yes, Le Clere had it all worked out very nicely. Whoever crossed the common would be caught by intersecting lines of fire.

They were running out of time and he couldn't find one weakness in Le Clere's strategy.

Garrick turned, casually leaning his elbows on the rough stone wall, reviewing the open ground. Not a scrap of cover, not even a clump of grass left by the hungry sheep.

A lone horseman walked his horse on to the far side of the common.

Le Clere strode over to Ellie. 'Your brother is right on time.'

The look of hope and joy on Ellie's face pierced Garrick's heart. What must it be like to have a family who cared the way she cared for her brother? What he had thought was caring, a bluff distant kindness, had turned to dross. His mother had loved him, he remembered dimly, but it hadn't served her well.

He had to reunite Ellie with her family.

The man on the other side of the common raised a hand to shield his eyes. Clever. With the sun in his eyes, he'd have trouble spotting the sharpshooters.

He must have seen the party gathered at the wall because he urged his horse into a walk. When he was in the centre of the open space, he stopped. Good.

'Where is my sister?' he yelled.

Le Clere thrust Eleanor through the gap in the wall, a pistol held to her temple. 'Come and get her.'

'William,' she yelled. 'Go back. It's a trap.'

Bloody hell. She'd caught them all by surprise.

Le Clere cursed and pulled her back behind the wall.

Castlefield remained where he was, tension in the set of his shoulders. The horse shifted uneasily.

'I ought to wring your neck,' Le Clere said.

Garrick felt like doing a bit of wringing himself. Or maybe not. Perhaps she'd given him the opening he needed. 'Leave her be. He won't come any closer. Not now. Withdraw and find another way to get the letter.'

Le Clere swore. 'No.' He put his glass to his eye. 'I've a good mind to… Bugger.'

Garrick straightened. 'What is it?'

'He didn't come alone. There are soldiers with him.'

Beside him, Ellie squinted across the field. She was starting to look hopeful. Garrick mentally groaned. What foolhardy idea would she take next into her head?

Le Clere pulled a knife from his belt and cut

Garrick's ropes. 'See for yourself.' He handed Garrick the glass.

Surprised, but not about to object, Garrick looked. There were two officers at the edge of the common behind Castlefield. Infantry. 'Men from his regiment by the look of it. Two of them.'

'A couple too many,' Le Clere growled.

'Beauworth,' Castlefield yelled, 'I want my sister.'

'Wait here,' Le Clere said to Garrick. 'One move in the wrong direction and the girl dies.'

There was cunning in his uncle's eyes. A sort of clever madness. Keeping that gaze locked with his, Garrick nodded.

Le Clere trotted off to join Matthews.

Her eyes full of shadows, her shoulders drooping, Ellie shivered. To see her so beaten down was more than he could bear. 'He won't harm you all the time your brother has the letter. I pray to God he hasn't opened it.'

'Or your neck is on the line.' The red flag of anger flew in her cheeks. The spirit he liked to see.

'Something like that.' If Castlefield had followed orders, then perhaps Le Clere could be convinced to let them go. It wouldn't be easy to convince him. Ellie knew too much. But without any solid proof…

Le Clere headed back in their direction and Garrick turned to face him.

Pistol steady on Eleanor, Le Clere handed him the knife. 'Set her free.'

What now? Garrick cut the ropes.

Le Clere retreated a step. 'Walk her to her brother, collect the document and return to me. No tricks or she dies. You can't escape, my men have every inch of the common covered. Are you clear?'

The scene played out in his mind. 'Absolutely.'

'And consider this, Garrick. By walking her out there, you are my accomplice. If anything goes wrong, you hang.'

Since if the contents of the letter were made known he'd hang anyway, it seemed a strange thing to say. 'Good point, Uncle. Thank you.'

Ellie stared at him, shock on her face. Well, he'd wanted to fool Le Clere and in accepting his defeat so meekly, he'd fooled her, too. The thought left a bitter taste in his mouth.

He helped her over the stile. 'Walk. Nice and steady.'

She tugged at her arm. 'Why are you helping him?'

He thrust her ahead of him. 'Keep walking.'

Only a few more feet and they'd be level with her brother. Castlefield's horse sidled. The man sawed at the reins, his face red.

Garrick raised his voice. 'Throw the letter on the ground. Be very careful, there are armed men behind us. One false move and I won't answer for what happens.'

Castlefield nodded. He pulled a packet from his saddlebag, a sealed document, and tossed it on the ground. The word Beauworth in black ink mocked Garrick from the ground. He kept going, pushing Ellie ahead. Eleanor gave him a startled look over her shoulder.

'Aim for the corner of the field. They cannot shoot you without hitting me.'

'Hey.' Castlefield cursed and brought his horse around.

'Hurry,' Garrick said.

Castlefield rode up alongside. 'What the devil are you playing at, Beauworth? Go back where you belong.'

'Ride ahead if you want to live.'

'Garrick!' Le Clere's bellow. Garrick did not turn.

Castlefield pulled his pistol. 'Get away from my sister. Or I'll kill you.'

'Don't be a fool,' Garrick said. 'I am the only thing between your sister and a bullet. Look out for yourself.'

'William, listen to him,' Ellie said.

Thank God she understood. Bright, bright woman, his Ellie. A ray of light in his dark, dark world.

A shot rang out; Castlefield's chestnut took off at a gallop.

'William,' she cried.

Garrick grabbed her arm. Stopped her from giving chase. Time was running out. Once Le Clere's men realised what he was doing, they'd shift position, if they hadn't already.

'Run,' he said. It was their only chance.

Her face pale, she lifted her skirts and took off at a steady clip. He breathed a sigh of relief and followed. A minute more and they'd gain the wall's protection.

'Hold your fire,' Le Clere shouted. The panic in his voice gave Garrick a moment of glee.

Another shot. Not Le Clere's men this time. A rifle. It came from ahead. Martin Brown, perhaps, trying to pick him off. Better he aim at Le Clere's men. Garrick glanced back. He couldn't see any sign of Caleb or Matthews or the other man he'd spotted. Perhaps they hadn't yet worked out what was happening.

More shots rang out. From all directions. A stinging sensation in his side. A tearing pain. His legs buckled. He stumbled on. The pain in his side sharpened. Keep moving. Keep between Ellie and them. The wall rose up like a grey mossy cliff. Hampered by her skirts, Ellie got stuck halfway over. Any moment another shot would find them. He pushed her over the top. Somehow he got a knee on the coping and fell to the ground on the other side. He lay gulping air and clutching his side.

He looked around for Ellie, found her bent double and panting. 'Are you all right?' he asked.

Gasping, she nodded. 'Did you see what happened to William?'

William. Always worried about her brother. He wanted to hit something. He reined in his anger. It was only right she should care for her brother. It was what real families did. 'His horse cleared the wall further down. I don't think he was hit.' He pushed to his feet.

Eleanor grabbed his arm, her face full of worry. 'Le Clere was right. You will be implicated in this. Go now, while you can. Save yourself. Take a ship to America.'

His heart soared. She cared about him, too. If it wasn't impossible, he would have sworn his vision blurred. He cupped her cheeks in his hands, capturing her storm-clouded gaze. 'Come with me.' He held his breath, hope a pale flame in a dark future. His heart drummed against his ribs.

She swallowed, her eyes glistened. Tears. Damn it. He'd made her cry. He'd no right to ask after what Le Clere had done in his name.

Before she could answer, Castlefield galloped up, pistol in hand. 'Stand back, Eleanor. I've got him in my sights. You're safe now.'

Glowering with righteous anger, the man who looked so like Ellie pointed his cocked pistol at Garrick's head. Strange he hadn't seen the similarity before. But Castlefield had been a chubby schoolboy the first time they met. Garrick curled his lip and held his hands clear of his sides. 'She's all yours, my friend. I'm done with her.'

Tears on her cheeks, Ellie put a hand to mouth. 'You should have gone when you had the chance,' she whispered.

Should he? Had he wanted to go without her? What would be the point?

Castlefield flung himself off his horse. 'I'll kill you for that.' Better a bullet than the noose.

Ellie stepped between them. 'William, he saved my life.'

'More likely he saw it as a way to save his own skin, the coward.'

Castlefield yanked off his cravat, swung Garrick around by the shoulder and pulled his arms behind him. Using the strip of fabric, he tied Garrick's wrists together. Garrick flinched as his ribs protested against the rough treatment.

Castlefield grunted approval. 'That will hold you until they put the chains on.'

Eleanor gasped. 'William, no!'

The heartbreak in her voice was like balm to Garrick's soul. He flashed her a grin. He didn't want her to think he was surprised by this turn of events.

Castlefield pushed him toward the two officers and a couple of farm labourers with a cart. 'My friends can't wait for the honour of escorting you and your pack of villains to prison.'

Eleanor's heart seemed to have been cut in two, her chest hurt so much. Garrick had looked so hopeful. If William hadn't arrived at that moment, what would she have said? Her breath stilled. She had the strangest feeling she would have said yes.

She stared after Garrick's tall, straight figure, so proud in his defeat. The pain intensified. Her eyes misted. She felt as if she might fly apart. She wrapped her arms around her stomach.

If only she didn't love the way he smiled at her as if

there was no one else in the world but the two of them, the way he teased and made her laugh, the way he held her, and the sensations he brought to life in her body.

Oh Lord. After all she knew of him, how could she feel this way?

A drop of something dark glistened on the ground at her feet. With a horrible premonition, she bent and touched it with a fingertip. Blood, sticky and red.

Garrick's wound must have opened. He needed a doctor. She hurried after the two men.

By the time she'd crossed the open ground, Garrick lay on the straw in a cart, a prisoner in his tumbrel, looking as calm as if he were out for a Sunday drive. Ellie trembled to see his lips looking bloodless and the skin on his cheeks ashen.

William, talking to Martin, didn't see her until she tugged on his arm. 'He's wounded. He needs a doctor.'

'Not now, Eleanor. There are more of these criminals to be rounded up.' He turned back to Martin. 'Follow them as best you can.'

'Yes, my lord.' Martin strode off as Caleb's unconscious body was thrown on to the cart beside Garrick.

She grabbed William's arm. 'Beauworth had nothing to do with my abduction.'

'The courts will decide innocence or guilt,' William said, and began walking away as if she was of no more importance than a bothersome insect.

'Damn you, William.' She ran after him. 'Give me your knife.' She snatched it from his belt. 'I can at least bandage the wound before he bleeds to death.'

William hunched a shoulder. 'Be careful. He's chained, but he's a dangerous man.'

'Not when he's half-dead,' she muttered. 'Where are you going?'

He stared across the common, his eyes narrowed. 'There's something I need to take care of. Wait here for me. I'll be back in a moment.' He marched toward the Beauworth carriage, his limp more pronounced than usual. Too much time on horseback, no doubt. He wouldn't welcome her suggesting he rest and arguing would keep her from Garrick.

She ran back and scrambled up on the cart. Once there, she slashed a strip from the bottom of her petticoat.

One eyebrow raised, his gaze on her ankle, Garrick smiled. 'Very nice.'

'Let me see where you are hurt.'

He lifted his hand from his side, revealing a sticky dark patch. 'A scratch,' he said.

A new wound. Oh, heavens. So much blood. 'I need to bind it.'

He frowned, his gaze flickering to Caleb. 'This is no place for a lady.'

'I'm Lady Moonlight, remember.'

He grinned at that.

She pulled his shirt free of his pantaloons and found a jagged tear below his ribs, blood oozing in a steady flow. She swallowed the urge to gag. 'I hope this is the last time today you are going to walk in front of a bullet.'

He chuckled, then winced with a hiss of breath through his teeth. 'Me, too.'

Panting, fearful, she pressed the wad against the gash. 'Hold this.' His fingers covered hers for a brief second, his skin chill. 'Thank you.' She glanced up to find gold flecks danced in his eyes and his lips curved in a smile, a smile she might never see again.

Her eyes blurred. Blinking, she pulled her hand

away, bound the second strip around his torso. Would it be enough?

He lifted a hand, touched her cheek. The ugly chain attached to the manacle encircling his wrist rattled. 'Now go.' He looked over at his companion. 'I don't want you here. Do you understand?'

The words hurt. But of course he didn't want her here. She'd rejected him.

He pushed forwards, as if he planned to get up. 'Leave now, Ellie.'

The labourer guarding the cart hefted his pitchfork. 'Miss?' he said. 'You shouldn't be up there.'

She didn't want to leave him like this, but if she didn't go, more bad things would happen. 'I'm leaving. Garrick, please, take care of yourself.'

He slumped back against the side of the cart and closed his eyes, pain etching deep lines around his mouth.

By the time she reached the ground, she was shaking so hard her legs wouldn't hold her. She leaned against the cart's wheel. A hand pulled on her shoulder. She jumped and whirled around.

'For God's sake, Len,' William said. He pulled a handkerchief from his pocket and wiped her face. 'You cannot be crying over that blackguard.'

She hadn't known she was crying. 'He needs a doctor. Please, William. You can't be so cruel.'

His lips flattened in a thin line, William stared into her face. 'You don't understand, Len. You don't know what he did, to us. To me.'

'It was his uncle.'

'No. It wasn't. There are things you don't know.' He let go of a long breath. 'We will discuss it later.'

'He needs a doctor.' She was beginning to wonder if

she had any other words. Never again, she swore silently. Never would she be anything but a model sister, if he would just get Garrick a doctor.

'All right. I'll see to it. But then enough until we get home.'

'Thank you.'

A young lieutenant approached leading a couple of horses. 'Lucky thing we accompanied you from Portsmouth, wouldn't you say, Wills?'

'Very lucky,' William said. He gestured to the cart. 'Can you escort that rubbish to Haverstock for me while we mop up here? Have a doctor sent to attend Beauworth the moment he is behind bars.'

The lieutenant snapped a salute. 'Certainly, sir.'

A few moments later the labourer was driving the wagon down the road, with the lieutenant in attendance.

Eleanor watched it go. There was nothing more she could do.

The steady sound of dripping water never ceased in this accursed place. Shivering, Garrick pulled the blanket tighter around his shoulders and leaned back against the wall. The damp of his cell pervaded every bone in his body. His teeth chattered uncontrollably if he let them. He clamped his jaw tight.

Out of respect for his rank, they'd put him in a private cell. As if it made any difference. Still, he'd glimpsed the condition of some of the other poor wretches who inhabited this filthy place and had no cause for complaint.

The hole in his side had been cleaned and his arm was on the mend thanks to Ellie insisting on a doctor. He'd cut a good strong figure on the gibbet, the doctor had said. Nothing like a little gallows humour to cheer a man up.

If they'd also caught Le Clere, he wouldn't feel quite so bitter. But what the man had done, he'd done in Garrick's name and the piper would be paid.

A sharp twist of regret squeezed his chest. He would have liked to marry Ellie.

Ellie. So dear and so brave. Right up to the last, she'd tried to save his worthless hide. He didn't blame her one bit for not wanting to fly with him. She deserved so much more. Though the thought of her with another man sent hot blood rushing to his head. Ah, well, soon he wouldn't have a head.

God, this place was really getting to him.

He did like thinking of her safe with her family, safe from Le Clere. It was the only thing making this stinking pit bearable. Not that he'd be here much longer. He swallowed. They'd take him to London for trial. A jury of his peers in the House of Lords. A chill ran down his spine.

He'd brought shame to the proud name of Beauworth. Harry, bluff, cheerful Cousin Harry would have to carry the burden. Good thing the man was well liked by his fellows. He'd make an excellent Marquess.

The noise of boots in the hallway echoed through the cells. Was this it? His heart picked up speed. He'd been expecting them all day, but deep in his heart he had hoped something would save him. If Piggot hadn't left the letter, he could have died honourably, serving his country in battle. No doubt his old enemy, Hadley, or Castlefield as he was now, would make sure he met a just end. Justice. The gods must be laughing their heads off at the irony of it all.

The footsteps drew closer. If only Eleanor had trusted him with the truth. His fist clenched. He slammed it into the wall, welcomed the jarring pain. He would never have ruined her. It was his one regret.

That and what he had done to his mother.

He smoothed his lank hair, and scratched at three days' worth of stubble. He must look like everyone's idea of a desperate killer.

The cell door opened. Letting the blanket fall, he pushed to his feet and held out his arms for his manacles. Thank God, they did not also chain him to the wall of his cell.

The warder ignored his outstretched hands. 'This way if you please, my lord.'

Stiff, joints aching, Garrick took a deep breath and straightened his spine. He followed the warder out of his cell and up the worn stone steps. This was it. A journey to London, a public humiliation and death.

At the head of the stairs the warder ushered him into a room. An office. For the first time in three days, Garrick felt some of the bone-chilling cold leave his body.

A man of medium height, middle-aged, grey at the temples, and his blue eyes twinkling, sat in one of two chairs in front of the desk. He rose at Garrick's entrance.

'My lord? Andrew Calder, at your service. I am your barrister.'

'I don't need a lawyer.' A guilty plea needed no argument.

'As to that, my lord, you are probably correct. However, Lord Dearborne asked me to meet you before your appearance.'

Dearborne was a local magistrate. He wasn't to be tried in the House? 'The trial is today?'

'No, my lord. You will be released today.'

Legs weak, Garrick dropped onto the other chair. 'I don't understand.'

'My lord, I have been asked by Lord Dearborne to

offer apologies for your wrongful arrest. You have been cleared of any involvement in the crime against Lady Eleanor Hadley. Caleb Trubbs has confessed the whole. His evidence proves you were a dupe in Le Clere's plans. Lady Eleanor herself confirmed his testimony.'

The room seemed to shift around him. At any moment he would awaken in his cold cell, lying on the filthy pallet, and discover he was hallucinating. It wouldn't be the first time. Usually it was Ellie who occupied his dreams.

The dapper little man continued to look at him with a kindly smile. Garrick began to believe. Slowly he felt his shoulders relax. Until he remembered. A bitter taste filled his mouth. 'There is another matter, Mr Calder. The death of the Marchioness of Beauworth, my mother.' He swallowed the dry lump in his throat as if the words would choke him.

Calder frowned. 'I know nothing of this matter.'

His hands gripped the chair arms, clinging to the only solid thing in the room. 'There was a letter. From an eye witness.'

Calder shook his head. 'There is no letter, my lord.'

'It was there.' Castlefield had dropped it at his feet. He'd seen it and so had Ellie.

'I have no reports of a letter, my lord.' Calder was beginning to sound just a little impatient, no doubt wondering why the prisoner wasn't leaping for joy. Garrick shook his head, trying to sort his jumbled thoughts into some sort of order. The letter had been there. Addressed to him. Lying among the sheep droppings on emerald grass. Something about it had puzzled him. And now it had disappeared.

This was his chance to confess. *Why admit to something you don't remember?* Ellie's words. He'd be confessing to something he didn't believe in his heart. Had never believed. The realisation dawned slowly. Before he said anything, he had to know for sure.

'Shall we go, my lord?' Calder said, rising to his feet. 'A carriage is waiting outside.' He coughed discreetly behind his hand. 'You might wish to, er…freshen up.'

Garrick looked down at himself, filthy, ragged and stinking. 'Yes. I would like that.' He stood up.

'Good. Lord Dearborne would be glad if you could call on him two days from now. At that time, you will be required to give a statement and the proper paperwork will be drawn up.'

'And Duncan Le Clere and Matthews?'

'The search continues.'

'I want to help.'

The lawyer grimaced. 'Leave it to the authorities, my lord. By all accounts Le Clere is a dangerous man.'

Only a Le Clere could deal with Duncan. But right now Garrick had something more important on his mind. A wife. His heart swelled. He would make things right for Ellie.

'Beauworth for Lady Eleanor.' He handed his card to the Castlefield butler. At least his voice sounded calm, despite his inner turbulence.

The butler ushered him into a saloon painted pale blue with white trim. Large windows overlooked an expanse of formal gardens. The house was a sprawling Tudor mansion, but this room occupied one of the newer wings. 'If you would wait here, I will see if her ladyship is at home.'

Why hadn't she replied to his letter of a week since? Unable to sit, he wandered the room. A room full of family treasures, Meissen china, paintings, statues. The clutter of generations of Earls and their families. Nothing like Beauworth, where few reminders remained of his parents. Le Clere had put them all away, even the portraits, supposedly out of respect for Garrick's feelings, but now he wondered if the old man hadn't tried to make him forget the happy part of his childhood.

He studied the portrait of a woman above the mantel. Eyes grey and clear like Eleanor's looked back at him from beneath a powdered wig. Eleanor's mother, no doubt. She seemed to smile down at him.

He swept her a bow. 'Lady Castlefield, you have a most beautiful daughter.'

'Garrick.'

He spun around.

She looked lovely, almost ethereal, in her white muslin gown. Tiny curls framed a face that seemed thinner and paler than he remembered. He could see no sign of Lady Moonlight in this very proper young lady, with her hands clasped at her waist in a dignified manner. This was Lady Eleanor.

In two strides he reached her, kissed each cool hand. 'Ellie.' He cupped her lovely face in his palms, brushed his mouth across her lips, losing himself in her taste as she parted to his questing tongue.

God, he'd missed her. He dropped his hands to her shoulders, enfolded her in his embrace. She arched into him. Kissing him with avid desperation, clutching at his shoulders. He cupped her buttocks, pulled her against his length, felt the stirring of his blood and sighed. His woman. He pulled back, smiling into her lovely face.

She bit her lip.

'What is it, sweet?' he asked, tipping her chin to look into her eyes.

They were shadowed, wary. His stomach plunged in a sickening rush. 'What is wrong?'

She pulled away, paced to the other side of the room before facing him. 'Why are you here?'

The ground felt unsteady beneath his feet. 'Didn't you receive my letter?'

Her eyes widened. 'Did you write, indeed?' She shook her head. 'I suppose William...' She made a small helpless gesture.

Suspicion writhed in his gut. 'I wrote to your brother for permission to pay my addresses to you. Didn't he tell you?'

'William is angry, disappointed in me.' She averted her face. 'I am fortunate he didn't turn me out.'

Turn her out? The heat of terrible rage flowed like lava in his veins. The accursed Le Clere temper gripped him in vice-like claws. His clenched fists shook with the effort to hold them at his sides and not strike out blindly.

He drew in a deep breath, forced his hands to unclench. 'Believe me, had I known who you were, I would never have offered you a *carte blanche*. I'm here to make it right as honour demands.'

'Honour?' She stiffened, drawing back. He felt as if he'd missed something important. He crossed the room to her side, took her hand in both of his, held tight so she could not pull away. He dropped to one knee and gazed into her face. 'Lady Eleanor Hadley, please do me the honour of becoming my wife. I will protect and cherish you all the days of my life. I swear, I will never cause you harm. Please, Ellie. Give me a chance.' He was begging and he didn't care.

Her eyes glittered with moisture. She pulled her hand free. 'You don't understand.'

He rose to his feet, paced away from her, then looked back, where she stood stiff and pale. She had never fully given herself to him and never freely. She'd only come to him because she'd needed money for her brother, but he'd been sure there was more between them than lust.

She swallowed. 'What about what you did?' The agony in her voice ripped through his heart. In her eyes, he saw fear.

Pain speared his heart. She knew him better than anyone. Did she sense the evil lurking in his blood? The thought filled him with a grief so deep, he didn't know how he remained standing. He forced himself to answer. 'You said it yourself. Why admit to something I don't recall?'

'What about what you did to William?' Her voice was a strangled whisper of pain. 'Do you deny that, too?'

A knot balled in his gut. He felt as if he'd entered a maze to discover all of the exits blocked and a monster breathing at his heels. 'Yes, I deny it. My friends vouched I never left the dorm.'

'Your friends.' Her lip curled. 'How very convenient. He bested you in a fight and everyone heard you swear your revenge. What kind of monster beats a boy in his bed? He wanted a cavalry regiment. Because of you he can't sit on a horse for more than an hour or two.'

She spun away. Left him standing mute, accused, trembling with rage and something deeper. Fear. Fear he was losing her.

She covered her face with her hands. 'Back then, he told us it was an accident. After all, men don't tell tales. If I had known, I never would have come to you. Never.'

'I didn't do it.'

She raised her gaze, the grey of her eyes fractured, as if something inside her had broken. 'Or do you simply not remember?'

The bitterness raked him like a cat-o'-nine tails. He hesitated. Oh God. His friends had said he never left his bed. But if he was honest, he really wasn't sure. Because he feared it might be true. He shrugged to hide the pain of her words stabbing his heart. 'I was asleep.'

'My older brother died for Beauworth's cause and once again William's dreams were shattered. He's angry, Garrick. He swears if I have any more to do with you, I will never see him or Sissy again. I can't let that happen.'

An iron band seemed to tighten around his chest. 'You care more for your sister than you do for me.' A painful truth entered his mind. 'You believe I did those things.'

Tears ran silently down her face. 'I don't know any more. I want to believe you. But…how?' She flung her arms wide. 'And besides, it doesn't matter what I believe. I promised Sissy I wouldn't leave her.'

Her tears ran and he couldn't think straight. Her family came first. She'd given up everything for the sake of her family. He'd ruined her and all she could think about was her sister. 'What about you? About your reputation?'

She stared at him, silent, sad, an island, a lonely rock, the tears drying on her face. 'No one else knows about us, unless you tell them,' she whispered.

She was ashamed of her time with him. And how could he blame her for keeping her word to a child? He felt as if someone had pitched him headlong into a bottomless well. He couldn't see a glimmer of light, or any way to climb out of the depths.

A bitter laugh rose in his throat. All those days in his cell, thinking about her, about her kisses, about the warmth in her eyes for him, were the dreams of a fool. He'd been nothing but a means to save her family. If she cared at all, she'd trust in his innocence.

You don't trust yourself, a small voice whispered in his head.

The sorrow in her face slid like arrows, wicked and barbed, between his ribs, tearing into his flesh, into his battered soul, releasing a monster of anger, a writhing twisting being with fangs bared and ready to strike.

'If you ever change your mind, Lady Eleanor,' he said softly, his lips drawing back in a caricature of a smile, 'you will need to tell me so on your knees. After all, you owe me the rest of my three months.'

Her soft gasp didn't ease his pain, nor did the glisten of moisture in her eyes. If anything, it made him feel like a wolf wounding a fawn and it was far too easy. None of this was her fault. He swung away, opened the door, pausing with his hand on the knob. God, he was a bastard. 'I apologise. I did not mean that. I truly wish you and your family well.'

How he left the room on his feet, he wasn't sure, because he seemed to be walking through chest-high water, wet and cold and sluggish. He felt older than England's green hills as he crossed the hallway.

A child ran down the stairs. She halted at the sight of him. 'Oh, it's Len's wicked Marquess.' She beamed and started towards him.

'Lady Sissy,' he said harshly, 'I bid you good day.'

He stormed out of the door to his carriage and Johnson set the horses in motion. As the carriage drew away, the truth seeped like bitter bile into his mind. She was right not to trust him.

Desolation, cold and empty, filled every corner of his being. She'd left him with nothing. Not even hope.

It was no more than he deserved.

Chapter Nine

London—May 1815

'Such a lovely girl, your sister,' Mrs Bixby said, touching Eleanor's arm. 'And so unaffected.'

Did the old bat mean Sissy enjoyed herself too much? William always said she did. Eleanor forced a smile. 'Thank you.' Cecelia certainly sparkled like a ruby among pale pearls. Her deep-rose gown showed her dark hair and eyes to splendid advantage as she laughed up at her partner in a cotillion. Did she stand out too much, as William said? Perhaps she should have worn white after all.

'She's a handful,' Aunt Marjory said on the other side of Mrs Bixby. 'Never know what harum-scarum thing she'll take next into her head.'

'Really, Aunt Marjory. It is simply high spirits,' Eleanor said. 'Nothing more.'

'She's a credit to you,' Mrs Bixby said.

Unlike herself, had Mrs Bixby known it, Sissy did indeed bring credit to the Hadley name. She was popular with her peers, also making their first Season, and the young gentlemen flocked around her without any sign of loose behaviour.

'Who is she dancing with now?' Aunt Marjory asked. The poor dear just couldn't keep up.

'Lord Danforth. Unexceptionable family,' Mrs Bixby said. 'He'd make a good catch, if he came up to scratch.'

'It is far too early to be thinking of marriage,' Eleanor said. Unless of course Sissy fell in love, which would be wonderful.

'Speaking of coming up to scratch,' Aunt Marjory said, 'I haven't seen Mr Westbridge this evening.'

'He is most likely in the card room,' Eleanor replied. 'He knows I will not dance.'

Mr Westbridge, a serious man in his middle years, asked Eleanor to marry him at least once a week. He refused to believe she would never change her mind. Wouldn't believe she was happy keeping house for William and Sissy.

Idly glancing around the room for another suitable partner for her sister, Eleanor's heart stumbled. Head and shoulders above the man at his side, hair the colour of chocolate and his olive skin startling among the pale English faces around him, stood Beauworth. After four years she recognised him in an instant. He looked broader, more assured and certainly sterner of eye. Older, of course. All that she saw in a second. Her heart steadied, but her breathing remained irregular. What changes would he see in her, if he knew her at all? She looked away, determined not to notice.

As if compelled by some unseen hand, her head turned to once more bring him into view. Time had taken its toll. Deep lines bracketed a far more sardonic mouth than she remembered. Lean and axe hard, his face offered no quarter as he gazed with dark and cool remoteness at the world. As dark as a Moor, he must have spent years beneath a harsh sun. The legends of his female conquests, his dissipation, his hedonistic lifestyle, whispered of in salacious detail in the salons of the *ton,* hung over him like a dark cloud. The ladies of the *ton* loved hearing of his exploits. At first, she'd felt pain, a sharp jealousy. As the years passed, it had reduced to a dull ache she could ignore most of the time. To be jealous of a man she'd sent away seemed impossibly selfish. The females in the room, young and old, eyed him with barely concealed fascination, while some of the men looked strained. He was, after all, a close friend of the Prince Regent and commanded their respect, if not their friendship.

In the brightly lit room, dressed in sombre black, he had the look of a living breathing shadow.

She shivered.

Perhaps she felt chilled by the cold half-smile with which the Marquess listened to his fair haired male companion. His gaze swept the room apparently without interest, moving swiftly and unerringly towards her corner.

Heart beating wildly, Eleanor lowered her gaze. Even if he did recognise her, he would surely not approach, not after what lay between them. Would he? Was that hope in her heart?

Dimly, she realised the set was ending. She started to rise, to go to her sister. Perhaps if she pleaded a headache, Sissy would leave. If not, perhaps she could leave her in Aunt Marjory's care.

'Lady Eleanor, a pleasure to meet you again.'

The deep voice with its trace of a French accent thrummed a chord low in her belly, a long-forgotten thrill. Trembling inside, she raised her head and gazed into brown eyes flecked with gold. Cold eyes. The charming smile she remembered curved his lips, his teeth flashing white. Yet he made her think of a predator, a panther, dark and sleek and hungry. He held out his hand.

Her throat dried. Heat rose in her face. Her heart pounded so hard she couldn't breathe. If she reacted like this to a simple greeting, people would talk. They would make guesses, gossip. She must not make a breath of scandal. She rested her fingertips on his pristine white gloves for no more than a second. 'Lord Beauworth.'

She turned in her seat to the ladies beside her. 'Aunt Marjory, Mrs Bixby, allow me to introduce the Marquess of Beauworth.'

'A pleasure.' Aunt Marjory gave him a speculative glance, assessing his worth and his lineage.

'My lord,' Mrs Bixby said, her eyes alive with curiosity and surprise.

'Ladies, a pleasure. May I have this dance, Lady Eleanor?' The words were no more than a polite murmur, but the slight quirk at the corner of his mouth issued a challenge.

Stunned to speechlessness, she could only stare. To feel his arms around her again would be wonderful, awful.

She never danced.

Mrs Bixby was nodding as if it was the most natural thing in the world. How would it look if she accepted? If she refused, would people think there was a reason and talk? Mrs Bixby loved to talk.

She inclined her head. 'Thank you, my lord.'

He brought her to her feet. Two layers of cotton separated their skin, yet she felt his touch as if their hands were naked. Did he notice the way her fingers trembled in his? Hopefully not.

The orchestra struck up a waltz. Of all things. Had he known? She glanced up at his face, thinking to cry off, but he gave her no chance, sweeping her into the steps of the dance, masterfully, gracefully, powerfully in command. He swung her around the floor in soft glides and elegant twirls. How strong his hand felt beneath hers. He guided her steps with the lightest of pressure, yet his hand was all she could feel. The room disappeared into a swirl of pastel and shimmering candles. She saw nothing but shoulders hugged by a black coat, a froth of white cravat above a pale cream waistcoat embellished with tiny forget-me-nots. The scent of his cologne filled her nostrils. The warmth of his body reached out to caress her skin, though he held her no closer than was proper.

Sissy, who had not yet received permission to waltz, stuck out her tongue as they passed.

'Your sister is as charming as ever,' the Marquess remarked. He sounded almost wistful, which must be her imagination.

'Her first Season,' she said. 'Lady Cecelia is a huge success.'

'I can see why. Are you also enjoying the Season?'

She glanced up, seeking assurance that this wasn't some sort of barb. He looked merely interested. He raised a brow.

'Seeing Sissy so happy, why would I not enjoy it?'

'Why not indeed? You look lovely.'

'Fustian,' she said. 'I look exactly what I am. A woman past her first blush of youth and firmly on the shelf.'

'Then perhaps I should rephrase my words. You look lovely to me.'

Her insides fluttered. An instant flare of arousal, her body crying out for completion. She swallowed her gasp of shock. The pink in her cheeks must have turned carmine, because her face was scalding. 'Why are you here? Why are you doing this?'

His hard mouth twitched at the corner, as if he guessed she spoke of her body's reaction, not his request to dance.

'I need to ask you something,' he said.

A twinge of disappointment pierced her heart. Had she expected he would seek her out for herself? If not expected, then hoped, perhaps? Against all reason. 'Then ask it and be done.'

A woman gliding by in emerald and gold turned her head to look at them. She must have heard the sharpness in Eleanor's tone.

Chagrined, Eleanor pinned a smile to her lips. He whirled her around the end of the floor, tucking her against his side, his strong arm at her waist in an almost lover-like embrace, then he turned her under his arm.

'Not here,' he murmured into her ear, his warm breath sending a shiver down her spine.

Breathless, she glanced up. 'I beg your pardon.'

'We can't talk here. Drive with me tomorrow afternoon.'

Not a request, a command. She stiffened. William would be furious if he knew she had danced with him. What would he say to her driving out? And yet she was tempted. Her heart was galloping like an out-of-control colt, all fits and starts and wobbly. 'And if I say no?'

The warm light in his gaze fled. 'Then I must seek my answer elsewhere.'

An undercurrent of something dark coloured his voice. Not a threat exactly, but then she saw he was looking at Sissy.

The dance drew to a close and he escorted her back to her chair. Mrs Bixby had departed, no doubt eager to regale her cronies with Beauworth's foray into the realms of respectable women. The news would cause a bit of a stir and some beating of matchmaking breasts, and Eleanor couldn't help feeling the tiniest bit triumphant.

'I'll call for you at four,' he said.

Blast. She'd hesitated too long. And besides, he knew very well she wasn't going to let him anywhere near her sister. 'I will be ready.'

With a bow to her aunt, he departed.

'Ready for what, dear?' Aunt Marjory asked.

Watching him make his way through the crowded room without effort, almost as if those before him cleared a path for a dangerous creature, she answered absently, 'He wants to take me driving tomorrow.'

'Oh, my dear. Such a handsome man. What will you wear?'

The Marquess disappeared from the room. Had he come tonight for the purpose of seeking her out? She felt breathless at the idea. And then horrified. Nonsense. He'd probably headed for the card room like most of the other gentlemen not on the marriage mart.

She turned to her aunt. 'I'm sorry, I missed what you said?'

'I think you should wear the celestial-blue morning gown you had made at the beginning of the Season.' Her aunt nodded as if the matter was settled.

It was a ridiculous gown. Not the sort of thing a woman past her prime should wear. The reason she had never taken it out of the press since it arrived. 'I'll think about it.' When she could think, when her heart settled into its normal comfortable rhythm and her gaze stopped searching the crowd for a tall dark figure. 'Aunt Marjory, where is Sissy?'

Her aunt pointed her fan. 'Dancing with Felton. The poor boy is quite besotted.'

Lord Felton was an honourable young gentleman who would not take advantage of Sissy's high spirits. Eleanor breathed a sigh of relief. The slightest hint of a scandal would bring William back to town in an instant. He'd been so distraught by what had happened four years ago he'd turned into a mother hen where his sisters were concerned, no matter how often she promised she'd sown all her wild oats.

Pulling his greatcoat close against the cool breeze, Garrick set out on foot from his house in St James's. At this late hour, there were few people on the street. A dank mist stinking of muddy river obscured all but the closest objects. He hunched deeper into his coat. If he hadn't promised Dan, he'd have preferred to down a bottle of brandy in his chamber and drown the memory of a pair of cool dove-grey eyes.

When he arrived, Dan grinned from ear to ear at the door of his small bachelor rooms off Piccadilly. 'I'd almost given you up, Major.' There was little of the old cockney left in Dan's speech.

'You'll get used to calling me Garrick one of these days, Dan.'

'No, my lord, it wouldn't be right.' Dan never made any pretence of being other than a man up from the gutter, no matter how high he rose or how highly his regiment sang his praises. It was all a source of wonder to the modest Lieutenant Dan Smith. 'Come in. Take your ease.'

Undernourished and small as a child, he now topped

five foot eight inches. His shoulders were broad and his expression open beneath his cropped blond hair. With his handsome face and bright blue eyes, he was as sought after by the ladies as Garrick himself. Too bad Dan was far too shy to take advantage of their lures.

Garrick settled into one of two armchairs by the fire and Dan poured a glass of whisky for him and a gin for himself.

'Did you see her?' Dan asked.

'I did.'

Dan looked ridiculously hopeful. 'And...'

'And...nothing. We met. We spoke. We danced and I left. I felt nothing, nor did she.'

'You danced?'

'Yes.' He did his best to sound bored, despite the jolt low in his gut.

'How did Lady Eleanor look?'

Garrick thought hard. She had looked...beautiful, womanly. Paler than he remembered, almost drab in the muted grey of her gown. She seemed restrained, as if she held her emotions in check, the lively spirit he'd admired replaced by severe English spinsterhood. And yet something had sparked between them when they had danced. Or had he imagined it, because he'd hoped to feel something? He closed his eyes briefly at the pang of something sharp in a place where he didn't have feelings at all. 'She looked well enough. A little older, I suppose.' He sipped at the fiery liquid. 'I had forgotten how stuffy these London parties are. What news do you hear?'

Always sympathetic to his moods, Dan let the subject go and grimaced. 'We expect to receive orders to leave at any moment. London will awake one morning and we will be gone.'

'I agree. The Duke will move swiftly once Cabinet makes up its mind. But their shilly-shallying will cost our men dearly.' The War Cabinet had bungled too many times to do any better now. Only Wellington's instincts had saved their bacon time and again in Spain.

'What about you?' Dan asked.

Only Dan would ask. No one else knew of his work for the Allies. Many suspected his loyalty even though they were careful not to show it, not when Prinny had admitted him to his closest circle. But the scavengers were circling. If one more person sighted him in France, things were going to get very difficult. But he trusted Dan with his life as he trusted no one else. 'I'm to go at the end of the week.'

Dan whistled through his teeth. 'That soon. You will take care.'

The only person who cared enough to worry. 'I will.'

'And after? When Bonaparte is back under lock and key?'

He never thought about after. He had never expected to live this long. He wouldn't come back to England. There was nothing for him here. 'Find another war? Hire myself out as a mercenary.'

Dan looked far from happy. 'And the other matter?'

'I asked her to drive out with me tomorrow.'

'And she agreed?' Hopeful had returned.

'She did.' He'd thought she would refuse. He shouldn't have threatened her, but she'd left him little choice.

'Will you tell her Le Clere has been seen in England?'

'I don't see the point. Not when we aren't sure. I plan to snare him before he gets anywhere near the Castle-field tribe. No more of this, Dan.' He smiled and reached across the space between them. He clinked his erstwhile tiger's glass. 'Here's to you and yours and may you come home safe.'

'And you and yours, my lord.'

Garrick swallowed the rest of his drink in one gulp. There was no one he called his. Not any longer.

He pushed the thought away and held out his glass for a refill. Better to take whatever pleasure life offered when it came along. Like a few hours of her company on the morrow, though he expected it would hold little in the way of delight for either of them.

In the end she did wear the blue gown. After all, one did not drive out with a gentlemen of Beauworth's standing looking like someone's governess, as Sissy had pronounced earlier with all the assurance of youth.

When Eleanor walked down the stairs a few minutes before the appointed time, she felt satisfied with her appearance. Her pulse beat a little too fast, her stomach was tied in a tight little knot that made breathing more difficult than usual, but the gown masked all of that. To the world, she looked cool and calm.

Sissy dashed out of the drawing room as she set foot on the last step. 'You look ravishing,' she said. 'I told you that gown was perfect. It makes your eyes look bluer.'

'Sissy, don't be a hoyden.'

'Hah.' Sissy's dark eyes sparkled. She brushed a tumble of chestnut curls back off her shoulder. 'Don't be such a stick in the mud.'

The case clock struck four. Someone rapped the knocker on the front door.

'Quick,' Sissy said. 'Into the drawing room. You don't want to look too eager.'

'Sissy.' Eleanor couldn't help laughing. Her sister

had certainly adopted all the niceties of a débutante in her first Season with alacrity and enthusiasm.

Eleanor allowed herself to be chivvied into the drawing room, while the butler hurried to open the front door.

'Very nice, dear,' Aunt Marjory said, glancing up from her embroidery.

'Thank you, Aunt.' What the old lady would say if she knew just how annoyed William would be was a whole other matter. By the time he learned of it, there would be nothing to discuss. Today she would answer Beauworth's questions and tell him not to bother her or her family again. If he had any sense of honour, he would abide by her wishes. And that would be that.

Her heart squeezed a little at the thought, but she ignored it, firmly.

She perched on a chair by the window.

'Not there, Eleanor,' Sissy said. 'The light obscures your face.' She frowned. 'And why are you wearing that horrid cap under that perfectly lovely chip straw as if you are an old maid?'

She was an old maid. 'Too late to do anything about it now,' she said calmly, although her heart thundered as the door opened and Beauworth entered.

If he could not see her features, she could see his very well indeed. Still handsome, but harsh, like granite carved by the wind, the furrows around his mouth and creases at the corners of his eyes deeply etched. Only a shadow of the young man she had known remained in his smile and the angle of his jaw, the wave of brown hair on his forehead.

He took Aunt Marjory's hand in his and murmured a suitable greeting. Then he moved on to Sissy.

She peeped up at him. 'I don't suppose you remember me?'

'The last time I saw you, you had soot on your nose,' he replied with a flash of his charming smile. Eleanor's stomach tumbled in a long slow roll. Would she never be able to see that smile without melting?

Sissy laughed. 'You are still Eleanor's wicked Marquess.'

'Sissy,' Eleanor said as Beauworth turned to her with a raised brow and one of those devastating smiles. She was going to be mush if this continued.

'What did you say, dear?' Aunt Marjory asked.

'Nothing,' Sissy said, with a blithe smile and a wink.

'Are you ready to leave, Lady Eleanor? Much as I delight in the company of your family, my horses do not like to be kept waiting.'

He took her hand and brought her to his feet. As he did so, his gaze searched her face. Seeking what? She lifted her chin and regarded him coolly. 'Indeed. I am quite ready, my lord.'

Sissy ran to the window. 'Oh, my,' she said. 'A high-perch phaeton. And matched chestnuts.'

'Come away from the window, dear,' Aunt Marjory said. 'Do take care with my niece, my lord. The thought of her up on those high things gives my heart palpitations.'

'Fear not, Miss Hadley,' the Marquess said. 'I will take care of Lady Eleanor's person as if it were my own.'

His velvet tones were like a caress on her skin. An insidious yearning filled her body. She managed a tight smile. 'I have no fear, my lord.'

'You never did.'

He was wrong, of course. She'd feared greatly for him all these years. But she could never show it.

He guided her out of the house and down the steps into the street.

Sissy was right, his equipage was high and dangerous. The horses, held by a groom, tossing their heads in the traces, were fresh, high-strung and beautifully matched. A team she'd love to drive, or she would have in her misspent youth.

While she didn't need his help, she allowed him to assist her up the steps. She sat on the seat and settled her skirts. The ground looked astonishingly far away and the slightest movement caused the coach body to sway on its swan-necked springs.

The Marquess went around the other side and climbed up beside her. He took the whip from its holder, catching the points deftly in his fingers and gathered up the ribbons in his other hand.

He glanced at her with a quizzical expression. 'Nervous, Lady Eleanor?'

'Certainly not,' she said. The fact that her heart seemed to be performing an endless drum roll against her ribs and had been since she awoke this morning had nothing to do with him. It was lack of sleep.

'Good. Then we will dispense with the services of the groom.' He raised his voice. 'Jeffers, spring 'em. You can walk home.'

Before Eleanor could protest against the breach of propriety, the liveried groom touched his hat, released the off-side leader's bridle and stepped back. The Marquess moved his equipage into the street and soon they were bowling down the quiet road at a clip.

'It is an open carriage, Ellie,' he said with the ghost of a laugh. 'I want our conversation to be private.'

Ruffled, she glared at him. 'We have nothing to say to each other of a private nature. And you should have asked me first.'

'Asking doesn't get me anywhere.'

Now what did he mean by that pithy little comment? Surely he wasn't referring to his disastrous proposal of marriage? And surely he wasn't going to ask her again? Her throat dried. A patter of hope ran through her heart.

'What did you want to ask me?' There, she sounded cool and collected.

He turned on to Piccadilly and headed toward Hyde Park. She admired his skill as he negotiated around a hackney coach stopped to pick up a fare and neatly avoided a brewer's dray coming the opposite way. He made it look easy, but the horses required all of his attention, so she sat quietly, content to enjoy being driven by a master, content to look at the hard-angled profile, the curl of his hair on his temple, the confident set of his shoulders. Her reckless gaze lingered on the firm line of his sensual mouth, the angle of his chin. He was still beautiful and very dangerous. She would not let him catch her unaware again and she'd already spoken to Sissy about keeping her distance.

They entered Hyde Park and started along Rotten Row. Because of the early hour, only a few carriages paraded their occupants.

'Now,' he said, 'I can concentrate on you, instead of these beasts.'

The thought of him concentrating on her made her breathless with longing. But it was not what he meant, surely it was not. She tried to ignore the trickle of hope sliding around in her stomach. She stared at the horses tossing their heads at every pedestrian they passed. 'What they really need is a good long run.'

'Should I have whisked you away to Brighton? I have the key to the Pavilion.'

The words were said with a teasing note, but she sensed an undertone of challenge, or perhaps a shadow of hope. She fought the very real urge to say yes, to kick over the traces she'd forced herself into these past years, the curb of propriety and duty.

'It was simply a comment.'

'Naturally,' he said.

'Well, here I am, all attention. What was so important that you must speak to me alone?' The words sounded sharper than she had intended, sharp enough to ensure her heart was not hanging on her sleeve like a flag.

The teasing light in his face disappeared and her foolish heart regretted the loss. 'You've changed, Ellie.'

'I'm older and wiser.'

'And none too happy, if I'm not mistaken.'

'My happiness is not your concern.' How could she ever be happy, hearing about his conquests, knowing other women were enjoying favours that could have been hers? And like a fool, she drank up every mention of his name because it brought him closer, when it was quite obvious he never thought of her at all. Until he wanted something.

'It could have been,' he said.

But she'd chosen. And she lived with the choice no matter how painful. 'Your question.'

'Quite honestly, I'm not sure how to ask.'

'Ask.' The torture of having him close, of hiding the warmth running beneath her skin, was a bit like trying to hide a fever. A fever with no cure.

'After you…after it was all over, Beauworth held no interest for me. I joined the army. Rumours circulated that I'd ruined a noblewoman.' The words were spoken calmly enough, but bitterness rang in his voice.

'I never spoke of what happened to anyone,' she said.

'Except your brother.'

She recoiled. 'Are you saying William blackened your name?'

'Yes.'

The flat statement knocked her off kilter. The carriage remained steady, but she felt as if she was being buffeted on all sides by a strong cold wind.

'There is something I want you to tell your brother.'

She could just see herself talking to William about Garrick. 'I—'

'Tell him it wasn't me who crippled him.'

The cold wind turned into an icy gale. She put a hand to her throat, felt the hard beating of her heart. 'What?'

'Your brother caught me exiting a window of the porter's lodging. He knew whose chamber it was and went off to report my despicable behaviour. I think he had some sort of boyish crush on the girl. Believe me, she wasn't the angel he thought.'

'Is that what happened? He never told me the full story.'

'He doesn't know the full story.'

He guided his team past a young gentleman in a phaeton who had stopped to greet some ladies on foot.

'Your brother hit me from behind. Stunned me. I called him a sneak and a tell-tale in front of his friends and threatened him with a sound thrashing.' He winced. 'I lost my temper. Later that night someone went to his room and beat him with a club as he slept.'

'He says it was you.'

His mouth tightened. 'I wasn't the only one punished. The porter was removed from his position, but someone forgot to retrieve his keys. Or perhaps he had an extra one. He'd lost far more than I. A month of waiting on the teachers' table doesn't warrant beating a man to within an inch of his life.' His voice was grim. 'Losing your livelihood might.'

Oh, God. And she'd believed William. She felt as if her heart might break. She stared at his profile. He looked unmoved. Completely unaffected. How could he be so cool, so icily calm, when he'd been so unjustly accused? Perhaps he no longer cared. 'And you have proof of this?'

He glanced at her with a cynical curve to his mouth. 'Still doubting me?'

'No. I was thinking of William. It will not be easy to change his mind after all these years.'

He nodded slowly. 'I found the daughter a year ago. Her father is dead and she's fallen pretty low, but she remembered me. She was happy to tell me the truth. She'd do so on the Bible and can point to the men who helped him. Ellie, more important than William, do you believe me?'

An odd bubble of joy filled her heart. The relief of knowing she'd been right about him all along seemed to take a heavy weight from her shoulders. 'Yes. I do. I wish I had known when—'

'So do I. Setting the record straight about your brother, however, wasn't my primary reason for wishing to have a private conversation.'

'Then what?'

'Cast your mind back to the day of the ransom. To Piggot's letter, if you will?'

They passed a barouche with an elderly woman and a pretty young lady. Garrick bowed an acknowledgement as they shot by.

She remembered too much about those days. But the letter? She frowned. 'William dropped it at your feet.'

'I left it there. Didn't want to give them a shot at you.'

He'd been brave that day, saving her life and William's. 'It was addressed to you. That is all I remember.'

His grip tightened on the reins as the horses started forwards. It was a few moments before he had them in hand again. 'Why?' he said.

'I beg your pardon?'

'Why was it addressed to me, the accused? And what happened to it?' While his expression remained calm, if a little grim, anger tinged his voice.

'I have no idea. I'm sorry.'

'I want that letter.'

What did this have to do with her? 'Le Clere must have picked it up during the mêlée.'

'Impossible. No. Someone else picked it up.'

'Who?'

He looked as her sideways. 'Who do you think?'

'If William had retrieved the letter, all he had to do was hand it over to the authorities and send you back to prison.' Her stomach dipped.

'Precisely. I want that letter, Ellie.'

The blood in her veins seemed to have been exchanged for melted snow. She took a breath. 'You think I have it.'

He didn't have to answer.

She did not have his stupid letter, but from the look on his face he wasn't going to believe a word she said. 'Why would you want it after all this time?'

His gloved hand tightened on the reins. 'Because it was addressed to me.'

'I don't have it.'

He sighed. An impatient male huff of breath. 'All right. Let me tell you what happened. You climbed aboard that cart and bandaged me up. For which I thank you. Then you walked back across that field and picked up the letter. Did you read it?'

She pressed her lips together.

'Answer me, Ellie. Did you read it?'

The man of ice from minutes before evaporated in the heat of his anger. And beneath the rage, she heard the cry of a small boy, afraid and hurt and very lonely. It made her feel sad. Hot prickles burned behind her eyes. Her heart felt wrenched into a thousand pieces. 'I do not have your letter. Even if I did, why dredge up history?'

He inhaled a long, slow breath and let it go. 'For the sake of my sanity. If you won't help me willingly, I will find the truth without your help.'

She reached out, put her hands on his forearm, felt the quiver of sinew and muscle as he steered the horses in a tight circle. 'Please, leave well alone. If anyone had the letter, they would have used it by now. Perhaps the wind blew it away.'

He shook her hand off, flicked his whip above his leader's head and set the team into a gallop.

'Slow down,' she said as they turned on to the Mall. He didn't seem to hear. Too busy driving to an inch, setting his team at impossibly narrow spaces with mere inches to spare, his face set like granite. He was angry, but he really had the wrong end of the stick.

It wasn't very many minutes before he set her down at her door. He didn't bother to escort her inside. He helped her climb down, then whipped up his horses and left her standing on the curb.

She nibbled at the tip of her glove, remembering those long-ago days. They'd all changed so much. Her, Garrick, William. Only Sissy remained the same.

She shivered.

Chapter Ten

Eleanor thought she might expire from lack of air. The Smithwicks's ballroom was far too small for the number of guests invited. She couldn't see the dance floor for the crowds as she squeezed her way back to her aunt from the withdrawing room.

She sat down. 'Where is Cecelia?'

'She was here a moment ago. Beauworth asked her to dance.'

Her heart jolted. 'Beauworth?'

'Mmm. Asked very prettily, too. Made her laugh.'

Why would Beauworth ask Sissy to dance? She didn't like the unpleasant little twinge in her stomach. She craned her neck to see around the group of friends clustered in front of her. 'I don't see her.'

I will find the truth without your help. That was what he had said. He had better not involve her sister in his plans. A chill breeze came out of nowhere, lifting the hairs on the back of her neck, a feeling of impending doom. 'I'll go and look for her.'

'She'll be back when the music stops,' Aunt Marjory

said. 'I've never heard it said Beauworth had a taste for misses in their first Season.'

He'd had a taste for one young miss. Years ago.

'I will be less than a moment,' she said. The air reeked of attar of roses, bay rum and hot bodies. Eleanor plied her fan, hoping to stir up enough air to give some respite from the heat as she strolled around the dance floor, twice. No sign of them. Nor were they anywhere else in the room. She was sure of it. She'd know if Garrick was present.

She headed for the doors, squeezing between tight knots of people trying to make themselves heard over the din.

Finally, she made it into the hallway. It was like going from Bedlam into a sanctuary. She took a breath. Where would they have gone? She would certainly have a word with Cecelia about disappearing without a chaperon. And Garrick would also get a piece of her mind.

Halfway along the corridor, she met a blond fresh-faced lieutenant in a dark green uniform coming the other way. He hesitated as she approached.

'Lady Eleanor?'

Eleanor frowned. He looked familiar, but she could not place him.

He smiled and bowed, his vivid blue eyes twinkling. 'Dan Smith, my lady.'

'Dan? Oh, my goodness, I would never have recognised you. A lieutenant, too. Congratulations.' He had been a bright young lad four years ago and the war had obviously given him a golden opportunity for advancement.

'My lord, the Marquess, put in a good word.' Dan spoke with pride and affection.

His words brought Eleanor back to her quest. 'Have you seen the Marquess and Lady Cecilia?'

'I believe they went into the drawing room. They have cards set out there. May I escort you?'

She smiled her agreement and took his arm. They walked along the brightly lit corridor, their footfalls making no sound on the thick Aubusson rug. Her heart knocked a protest at the thought of facing Garrick. She'd hoped to avoid him entirely.

The card room proved to be vacant except for a couple of elderly men playing whist. Dan looked around nonplussed. Disappointed, she turned to leave. The curtains rippled in the draught of an open window. She glanced at Dan. His expression tightened.

Before Eleanor could say anything, the young man strode to the curtain and drew it back, revealing an open French door. He stepped through. Eleanor followed on to the torch-lit balcony.

Sitting on a stone seat with her skirts above her calf, Sissy's stockinged foot rested on the bent knee of the gentleman kneeling before her. The Marquess, for that was who it was filling her pink satin slipper with champagne, glanced up with a wicked grin.

Eleanor's ribs squeezed tight. She could not hold back her gasp. 'Cecelia! What are you doing?'

Her face alight with laughter, the child looked up. 'Len? Isn't he the most ridiculous man alive?' She giggled. 'I think I'm going to lose my wager.'

She sounded foxed. They were on the brink of disaster. Scandal loomed a mere whisper away. Eleanor's lips felt tight, her jaw felt tight, her skin felt tight—if she took a breath, she might fly apart. She kept her voice low. 'And what did you wager, may I ask?'

'A kiss.'

Dan stiffened.

Even a commoner found this kind of behaviour appalling. She snatched the slipper from the Marquess and emptied its contents over the railing. 'Sissy, put this on, at once.'

As he rose to his feet, Garrick's mouth curled in a cynical smile. 'Good evening, Lady Eleanor.'

She ground her teeth, rather than throw the slipper at his head.

'Lady Cecilia,' Garrick said softly, 'I'm afraid your sister doesn't believe in the principle that one's word is one's bond, do you, my lady?'

A low blow, indeed, directed at her reneging on their bargain and far more painful than a slap to the face. Eleanor knew she must have gone red from the prickling heat in her cheeks and throat. Pretending not to hear, she pushed Cecilia's foot into her damp footwear and pulled her upright. 'Come back to the ballroom before anyone notices.'

'My lady,' Lieutenant Smith said, his voice low, full of concern. 'Might I suggest that if I escort Lady Cecilia and my lord takes your arm, it will look as though the four of us took a stroll?'

Eleanor glanced at him with gratitude 'You are very kind, Lieutenant Smith.'

'An outflanking manoeuvre, Dan?' The Marquess's voice from the shadows sounded dangerous. Then he gave a short laugh. 'I surrender. This time.'

Dan offered his hand to Cecilia and she looked up at him.

'Cecilia, this is Lieutenant Dan Smith,' Eleanor said.

'Lady Cecilia,' Lieutenant Smith murmured, his ears pink.

'Lieutenant, a pleasure.' Cecelia's smile was a little lopsided, but very sweet.

A slightly bemused expression on his face, the young man placed her outstretched hand on the green sleeve of his uniform.

Eleanor closed her eyes briefly. Heaven help them all. Cecilia was positively dangerous.

She ignored Garrick's glower and took his arm. 'How dare you?' she muttered.

He glanced down at her. 'I dare anything to get what I want, Lady Eleanor. As do you.'

A rush of heat flared in her face. 'You have no idea how much I regret what I did.'

His breathing changed, a slight hitch, and she had the sense she'd touched a nerve, yet when she glanced up, his expression was one of utter boredom.

'Promise me you will stay away from Sissy,' she said.

'Would you believe my promise?' he asked with a cynical smile.

She had no time to answer. They'd already entered the ballroom, where any chance word might be overheard. Whether he promised or not, she would make sure Sissy didn't come within ten feet of the Marquess of Beauworth in future.

A few heads turned in their direction as they traversed the room, but no buzz of conversation or sly whispers. Eleanor breathed a sigh of relief. Lieutenant Smith saw Sissy to her seat and bowed very properly. Eleanor took the chair on the other side of her aunt. 'Thank you, both,' she said, intending it for a dismissal.

'Do you not dance, Lieutenant?' Sissy asked.

Lieutenant Smith turned as red as a poppy. The Marquess, rot him, grinned wolfishly at his protégé's obvious discomfort. Eleanor wanted to bash him over the head with her reticule. She pretended not to notice.

'I do, my lady,' Lieutenant Smith said. 'I would be honoured if you would grant me a cotillion later this evening.'

The little minx grinned. 'I have one free after supper.'

Serious and courteous, the young soldier bowed. 'I will return then. Thank you.' He took the Marquess by the arm and led him away.

A considering expression on her face, Cecelia watched the angelic soldier and the dark rake depart, an odd combination to be sure. And the poor young lieutenant was no more suitable for Sissy than the Marquess of Beauworth.

Eleanor sighed. 'Really, Cecilia, what has got into you, going off alone with a well-known rake? You could be facing ruin right now. Not to mention it is shockingly rag-mannered to ask a man to dance.'

'You are a jealous old maid.'

It was unforgivably rude and hurtful, but Eleanor swallowed her pride. It was Garrick's fault Sissy had drunk too much champagne and there was no point in getting into an argument with her in a crowded ballroom. And besides, after playing mother to Sissy for so many years, she felt like an old spinster.

Her summer of madness with Garrick was the last time she'd felt truly young. It had been a wild and won-derful adventure and had led to nothing but pain. Not to mention the financial disaster she'd caused. No more adventures for her. She'd settled down. She was happy. Very happy. She sniffed into her handkerchief, blinked, then turned and entered a conversation between her aunt and the elderly widow beside her, just as she ought.

* * *

'What are you about letting her make a fool of herself with a man who comes straight from the stews?' William paced the floor in front of the table where she sat waiting to pour him a cup of tea.

It had been too much to hope that he would not hear the gossip and the guilt written on her face wasn't helping. She loved her twin dearly, but since inheriting the title he'd become one of the world's most intolerant men.

'William, dear, Lieutenant Smith is a brave and honourable young man. Everyone likes him, despite his lack of birth. He is but one man among many in Cecilia's court and I promise you she does not favour any one of them. You should be proud of her success.'

'I am proud of her,' he said. 'But, Eleanor, the man hangs on Beauworth's lips.' And that was the real reason for his anger. Dare she speak to him about Garrick? Her heart picked up speed.

'About Beauworth…'

His brow lowered.

She gulped a breath. 'I met him the other day.'

'I told him I would kill him if he came near you.'

'William, he has proof he was not the person who injured you.'

'Are you really so gullible? Stay away from that man. I don't want him near this house.'

She was unable to control the pain in her expression.

He sat down beside her. 'I'm sorry, Len. But if anything were to happen to Cecilia, I would never forgive myself.'

As he had never forgiven himself for what had happened to her. The reason she forgave him his ill humours.

He grimaced. 'Beauworth was seen in France, you know, but no one will come right out and accuse him to his face, even though he is half-French.' His lip curled. 'He curries favour with the Prince.'

'Rumour, William. Not fact.' She kept her face calm and her voice steady. 'William, there are other rumours about Beauworth, involving me. You didn't tell anyone, did you?'

'What do you think I am?'

He sounded defensive and he hadn't answered the question. Her heart sank. What had he done?

She handed him a white bone-china cup with a smile. 'You know, I always wondered what was in that letter Le Clere asked you to bring that day. Did you read it?'

He shifted in his seat, the cup rattling in the saucer. 'Of course not. Do you think I would have risked your life?'

Her heart softened at his obvious indignation and yet the way he sat sipping his tea, all stiff and uncomfortable, not meeting her gaze, stirred up a feeling that something wasn't right. 'And you didn't pick it up afterwards?'

'Eleanor, you are changing the subject. Make sure that young puppy Smith keeps within bounds and Beauworth does not enter this house and I'll say no more.'

It was he who had changed the subject, and he'd given in far too easily on the issue of Captain Smith. He was hiding something. Something to do with the letter? Surely not. What would it benefit him to keep Garrick's guilt a secret? Dash it all, now she would have to look for the letter. If only for her own peace of mind. She would send word to Martin. Ask him to look for it. As steward, he had access to all of William's papers. He wouldn't like it, but somehow she'd convince him to help her one last time.

She realised William was watching her, expecting some reaction to his generous surrender. She smiled. 'Thank you. Besides, I think the question will soon be moot. Lieutenant Smith expects to be called back to his regiment any day now. He thinks we will go to war again.'

His brow furrowed. 'No doubt about it.'

'Thank heavens you are out of it.'

'Damn it, Eleanor. I wish I could go. See the end of the little Corsican once and for all.' His expression betrayed an unusually boyish eagerness. A look she hadn't seen for years. Her stomach dipped.

'William, no! Think of me. Of Sissy. How would we go on if something happened to you? Your duty is here.'

He huffed out a breath. 'To be in at the end would be tremendous. If Michael hadn't died, I would have been there.'

'I wish he was still with us, too, but not if it meant you going to war again.'

He smiled at that, but still, frustration showed in the set of his shoulders and his pursed lips. He'd given up his military ambitions for the sake of the title, for his family, a sacrifice she knew he regretted deeply.

He set down his cup. 'I must be off. I am meeting with the fellows from my old regiment at Whites'.'

He rose awkwardly to his feet and kissed her cheek. 'Promise you will keep a close eye on Sissy?'

'Yes, William, I promise.' She walked with him to his carriage and waved him farewell. She sighed. He had his purpose, he would not shirk his duty, and she had hers, though what she would do when Sissy married, she couldn't imagine.

A footman approached her as she turned to re-enter the house. She didn't recognise the livery. 'Do you live here, miss?'

Lord, did he take her for a servant? She knew her gown was plain, but really. 'I do,' she said.

'Got a letter for one of the ladies of the house. Lady Sissy.' He thrust it in her face and ran off. Affronted, she watched him go.

She glanced down at the note, turned it over to see from whence it came. It was fastened with a red seal she recognised. Beauworth.

Her stomach sank. Why was Beauworth writing to Sissy? What mischief was he up to now? *I will find the truth without your help.* Was he trying to involve Sissy in his quest?

Feeling guilty, she took the letter and made her way to her chamber. Seated at her dressing table, she turned the paper over and over. It was addressed to Cecilia. She should not open it. But William trusted her to keep Sissy safe. If it was harmless, she would explain her motives. Sissy would be angry, but she would have to understand Eleanor meant it for the best.

Hand shaking, she cracked the seal. Bold words slashed across the page.

Meet me tonight after Midnight
At the corner of the Square. We will finish
Our wager, on my Honour.
Do not Fail me.
B.

That was all. No words of love, just a command. He must be very sure of himself. A surge of anger made her hot, followed swiftly by a cold feeling around her heart. Did he plan to seduce Sissy into helping him? To ruin her sister for his own selfish purposes?

She stared at the letter. It was lucky that the footman

had handed it to her instead of the butler, or she might never have discovered the plot. A careless mistake for a man like Garrick. She gazed down the street after the footman. A very careless mistake.

From inside his coach, Garrick watched the cloaked and hooded female figure pick her way along the footpath. The watch called midnight. Right on time. A streetlight on the corner revealed little but her height as she paused to glance around. He didn't have to see her face to recognise Ellie. He breathed a sigh of relief. After his escapade on the balcony had failed to flush her from cover, this was all he could think of to force her hand.

Lord knew what he'd have done if Lady Sissy had shown up instead. Given her a lecture and sent her home.

Still, he'd wondered whether Ellie retained any of the courage he'd loved in her, the reckless wench. A carriage rumbled past, cutting her off from view and he waited with baited breath for her to reappear. He bared his teeth as she stepped into the road.

Walking right into his trap.

He flung the carriage door open and leapt down to kiss her hand. Under the hood of her cloak she wore a hat with a veil.

'*Chérie,*' he whispered huskily, leaning close to her ear. Vanilla. Memories stirred. Seductive. Full of languor and heated flesh. They always did when he smelled that particular scent. Her small gloved fingers trembled in his hand. Nervous, then, afraid of what he might do when he discovered her ruse. And rightly so. If he was her brother, he'd lock her up. God. He'd love to lock her up in a room with him. But it wouldn't happen. Not when she learned of his treachery.

Without a word, she stepped into the carriage, settling into the corner.

He'd thought of every last detail, planned his strategy to an inch. The only wild card had been her. He leaned inside. 'I will drive, *chérie*. It is more discreet that way.' He didn't dare give her a chance to demand they turn back. He closed the door and climbed on to the box.

Startled, Eleanor made a lunge for the door. The carriage lurched into motion. Dash it. Why hadn't she noticed the lack of a driver? Too terrified by her own bravado to notice anything but his large form waiting in the dark. She hadn't expected him to leave her in the carriage alone with no chance for conversation.

She peered out of the window. Where on earth was he going? To his house? No, they had left St James's and were now heading out of town.

She stared at the trapdoor above her head. Should she knock to get his attention? Or wait until they arrived at their destination? Where was he taking her? Wherever it was, they'd be alone together. Despite her effort to remain calm, her heart picked up speed.

What if she was wrong about him? What if he lost the temper he feared? Things could go very ill.

After what felt like hours, but could not have been more than one, the carriage halted outside a small but elegant house, somewhere near Chelsea, she thought. She shrank into the shadows when he opened the door.

'Where are we?' She no longer felt quite so brave.

'Still veiled, sweet?' Garrick held out his hand. 'How very discreet. A good friend loaned me his love nest for the evening. I promise we shall not be disturbed.'

The announcement sparked her anger. Eleanor had heard hints of such places from the ladies of her acquaintance. Houses tucked away on the outskirts of town, where married men took their pleasure once they had fulfilled their duty as husbands. To think he would consider bringing her sister to a place like this. If that had been his plan.

She dredged up the words she'd practised at home, but before she could open her mouth he reached in, grasped her hand and tugged. 'Don't be shy, little one.'

Missing her footing on the step, she tumbled into his arms. Strong arms she remembered so well. His hand encircled her waist and he let her slide down his length before he set her on her feet. She shivered at the hot sensation of remembered bliss. How long since he had held her thus? A lifetime. The yearning she had buried deep returned with sharp vengeance.

He laughed at her gasp, his white teeth gleaming wickedly in the torchlight over the door. She was barely able to stand on legs as soft as warm butter; her heart beat a wild rhythm. Surely he heard it?

As if sensing her weakness, he swept her off her feet, picking her up as though she weighed no more than a child. If only he knew how she had longed to feel his arms around her again.

For one blissful, heavenly moment, she leaned her head against his shoulder, revelling in the oft-thought-of warm strength while he rang the bell. Oh Lord, someone would see them. She struggled and he set her down with a warm chuckle. 'Patience, woman.'

The door opened and, holding her elbow fast, he ushered her straight past a footman in dark green livery, into a small salon off the marbled and mirrored entrance hall.

From beneath her veil, she took stock of her surroundings. The dark green walls absorbed much of the light from the single candelabra. A brown velvet sofa guarded an intricately carved, white marble hearth. Beside it, a small round rosewood table held a bottle of champagne and two glasses. A thick white rug covered the floor in front of the fire. She could imagine him stretched out on that rug, caressing one of his women. Except the face of the wicked woman in her mind was hers. If her heart had raced before, now it galloped. Her skin warmed from head to toe.

Across the room, a door led to an adjoining chamber.

He stood behind her, his hands at the hollow of her waist as he nuzzled her nape.

Delicious shivers raced down her spine. The years rolled away and she ached to lean against him, to let him carry her away into bliss. 'My lord,' she said firmly.

His lips stilled. He drew back.

She turned and threw back her hood and the veil. 'You and I need to talk.'

He smiled. All white teeth and little humour. A wolf inspecting his prey. His gaze travelled from her head to her feet in a slow appraising look that made her feel hot and cold by turn.

'Well, well, here you are, just as I expected.'

'Of course you did. You had your footman hand me the note. You didn't think I'd see it and not open it, did you?'

He looked a little stunned, but she had to hand it to him, he recovered quickly. 'Aah, *chérie,* I knew you'd do anything to protect your sister. Even this.' He bent his head and pressed his lips against her mouth, hard, demanding, ravishing. His tongue traced the seam of her lips and rivers of fire raced along her veins to burst into flame at her core. Her heartbeat drummed. She stood stiffly, resisting him with every fibre of her being.

He lifted his head. 'You resist me now, but you won't. You never could.'

'Any more than you could resist me?' she said, only too aware of the breathiness of her voice. 'Garrick, I don't have your letter. I swear it on my honour.'

His face fell. He spun away, anger and disappointment writ large on his face along with belief.

'I think William does,' she said to his stiff back. 'He went back across the field, while I was in the cart. He must have protected you all these years, for my sake.'

He turned back. 'William?' He lifted his hands from his sides, his shoulders rising. 'It makes no sense. I'd swear he'd do anything to pay me back. Unless...' His expression turned to horror. 'Oh God. It could not be that.'

He strode for the window and stared into the dark.

'What? Tell me. You are scaring me.'

He turned his head and met her eyes, his gaze clear, but his expression shuttered as if he was afraid she might see too much. 'What if that letter exonerates me?'

'I don't understand.'

'Why would he keep it hidden, if it proves my guilt? Think, Ellie. He hates me.'

William wouldn't. He couldn't.

Garrick must have seen the denial in her face because his mouth twisted in a wry smile and his eyes held pain. 'You always believe the worst of me and the best of him. Get me that letter and you will never hear from me again.'

He offered it like a bribe. Was that what he thought she wanted? 'What if it proves your guilt? What then?'

Agony blazed in his eyes. 'It is not your business,' he said harshly. 'I want that letter before I leave for France.'

She froze. 'France?'

'Where else would I go? The beloved emperor returns.' Bitterness charged his voice, gave it a hard edge.

'Are you telling me you are a traitor?'

'I'm telling you nothing.'

Fear constricted her throat. 'And once you have the letter, I will never see or hear from you again.'

He swallowed. 'I swear it.'

Her heart ached as if it had been pounded by a hammer. He truly believed she didn't care. And if he went to France, he would be lost to her forever. Even the little flicker of hope she carried deep in her heart would go out. 'Garrick—'

'Don't say another word.' He grabbed her cloak, tossed it to her, turning away as if he couldn't bear to look at her. 'Just find the letter.'

She clutched the soft fabric in her arms, struggling to comprehend his anger. 'You hate me.'

He turned slowly. Two strides took him to her side. He gripped her shoulders. 'How could I hate you? You saved my life, remember?'

A mistake, Garrick thought. Touching her, feeling her skin beneath his fingers. Seeing the flare of longing in her eyes, knowing the depths of her passion. It made letting her go all the more difficult. He'd been wrong to think he could seduce her all over again and feel nothing.

She reached up with her other hand, smoothing his hair back from his forehead—a gentle, intimate caress.

'I've missed you,' she said. 'Did you ever think of me?'

He bit back the words in his heart: *I never stop thinking of you, wanting you, looking for you.* He dared not admit it. She'd find a way to use it against him. And still he wanted her, body and soul. As if without her he was incomplete, insubstantial, a wraith, walking through life on the outside looking in.

Struggling for control, he breathed deep and stepped back. 'Ready to go?'

'Must we?'

Anger at her naïvety sparked a brush fire in his veins. 'What did you want to do? Reminisce about old times? There is only one reason a man brings a woman to a place like this. If you don't go now, I can't promise nothing will happen.'

'Oh. I see.'

Damnation, she looked hopeful and it was all the encouragement his raging desire needed.

He caught her wrist and pulled her close. He fastened his mouth to hers, ravaging, demanding. And she kissed him back, arching against him, her mouth fervent, insistent. Four long years of loneliness rolled away as if they'd never been. Her kisses, the feel of her against him, was as familiar to him as his own face in the mirror. Perhaps more so, for his face had changed as she had not.

In a wonder that felt almost reverent, he lifted his head to look into her face and found her eyes heavy-lidded with desire and with an expression of such abandon, it sent him beyond the edge of reason. Groaning with passion so intense his body shook, he swept her up into his arms.

'Chérie,' he whispered as he entered the bedroom lit only by a fire. He set her down gently on her feet next to the bed covered in snowy white linens.

She reached up to twine her arms around his neck, her fingers running through the waves of hair that fell over his collar.

He pulled her hairpins free, letting her hair fall in a golden river around her face and over her shoulders. He grasped a handful of it and held it to his face. He inhaled deeply. The unique scent of her. '*Ma mie, je t'adore.* It is the colour of spun gold and soft like silk.' It was part of his memory.

Then his hands were behind her, expertly unfastening her gown, as he carefully placed tiny, fluttering kisses on her face. She whimpered, a sound so small, but so filled with longing, it stole his breath and any shred of reason he had left. Her hands shaped the curve of his shoulders, then grazed his chest, caressing, stroking, as if they remembered.

A moment later, she was pulling urgently at the buttons of his coat. He stopped unbuttoning her gown to allow her to push his jacket over his shoulders and shrugged it off. He tugged at his cravat till it, too, followed his coat to the floor. Feverish, on fire, he undid the top few buttons of his shirt and pulled it over his head. He heard the intake of her breath and drew in a hissing breath of his own as she pressed her lips to his chest.

He placed his hand beneath her chin, desperate to feel her mouth on his lips and as he crushed her close, her back arched, her hips hard against his thigh. His heart drummed so hard he thought his ribs would crack.

She wanted him. Always in this, he had her trust.

'Turn around, *mignonette,*' he whispered into her mouth. 'I need you out of this gown.'

Eleanor did not want to let him go, to lose his heat, the feel of his skin under her fingers in case she lost her nerve. It was dreadfully wrong, but this would be their last time together. He seemed to sense her need for his touch, for even as he pulled at the tapes he kept one arm around her waist, pressing her buttocks against his thighs, his erection evident. An illicit thrill clenched between her legs. Rough and fast, he pulled her dress down over her arms and her hips to the floor. The brush of cool air sent shivers down her spine, and her knees trembled. The stays went next, tossed aside, and she turned to face him, smiling, clad only in a fine white-lawn chemise, silk stockings and slippers.

In the warm flicker of firelight, he loomed over her, tall, dark eyes licked with golden flame. Her gaze drifted down his lean body, fixed on a white indentation on his shoulder. Her gaze travelled over his chest, the dark curling patch of hair around his flat male nipples, a line running down his ridged hard belly. His muscles were taut as he held himself tense, a dangerous wild animal ready to spring, ready to devour and she longed to be tasted. Another scar zig-zagged across his side, ragged and badly puckered, a blasphemy in such masculine beauty. Her gaze flew to his face as she remembered. She touched it gently, for this was her fault.

He grasped her fingers and brought them to his lips, never taking his gaze from her face.

He smiled then, warm, open and wicked. The smile she loved. This was no ravening beast to be feared. This was her own wicked Marquess, his full mouth soft, his eyes gilded with longing. She slid her arms around his shoulders and he picked her up and deposited her upon the bed.

She was just as Garrick remembered, just as he had seen her every day in his mind. He always denied any thoughts of her at all. Now she was his for the taking and he exulted.

Nothing else mattered.

Not France, not England, and not his quest for truth.

He leaned over her, gently stroking her breasts, down the soft plane of her belly, measuring her slender waist, his hands remembering the silken feel of her skin on his palms, the sweet rounded curve of breast, the valley between ribs and flare of hip. Slender, yet luscious.

She reached for him, pulling him towards her. She'd always been a bold, sensual wanton beneath the prim-and-proper miss. His body tightened, urging him on. He smiled down at her.

She frowned as if uncertain and touched his lips. Would she change her mind? Dear God, he prayed not, yet he waited. She grasped his shoulders, pulled herself up to kiss his mouth.

He closed his eyes in brief thanks. 'Give me a moment, *chérie*.' He sat on the edge of the bed and dragged off his boots, hurrying, half-afraid she'd change her mind, stripping out of his pantaloons.

He turned to find her watching. His member pulsed at the touch of her gaze. His groin felt heavy and full. Placing one hand on each side of her head, he covered her body with his. Skin of satin, soft yielding flesh, welcoming warmth. His woman.

His breath left him in a long sigh and he plundered her mouth with his tongue, savoured the sweetness, triumphed in the way her tongue tangled with his, giving him pleasure, the way her body cradled him, her eyes glazed with desire. Then, with only the gentlest of pressure, he slid his knee between her thighs.

She opened to him, sweetly, honestly.

Desire writ strong in smoky eyes, she smiled and his

heart cracked asunder at the sweet curve of her lips. This she wanted. His body. His pleasuring. Her hands wandered his arms, his shoulders, his torso, encouraging, urging. And this he would give.

He thrust into her, hard, deep. Tight and hot and wet, her body welcomed him home. Her moan of pleasure drove his own pleasure to heights he'd forgotten all these long years.

He groaned, and captured her mouth.

The feel of his body within her and the touch of his mouth on hers made Eleanor feel alive for the first time in years. Time returned to when she'd been happiest, if only she'd recognised it.

He was wrong about why she had come to him tonight, though she hardly dared admit it to herself. Taking Sissy's place had been the fulfilment of a purely selfish need to spend one more night in his arms, taking joy for herself one last time.

Each movement of his body sent glorious sensations rippling beneath her skin. His tongue teased her lips, filled her mouth and she succumbed to the heat and the fire. Conscious thought became impossible as, hot and moist, his mouth licked and nibbled at her jaw, her throat and finally the rise of her breasts.

And she panted for more, as he lingered in the valley between her breasts, nuzzling and kissing the sensitised skin. With a whimper, she grasped his hair, brought his mouth to peaks tingling with anticipation.

He licked one, then the other. Circling his tongue around each hardened nub, nibbling, promising bliss, until she thought she might go mad. At last, his mouth, hot as fire, closed around her nipple. He suckled.

Sweet agony. Back arched, her hips rose off the bed.

He slid deeper inside her, tormenting her, as she sought her release.

And he held her there, between bliss and torture, driving her higher, tightening the connection between them, yet never letting her reach the precipice, where bliss awaited in silken black depths.

'Garrick,' she moaned, 'please.'

Supported by arms knotted with muscle and sinew, he lifted his head, eyes molten and heavy as he gazed into her face. She clenched her inner muscles around his flesh as he'd taught her so many years ago. A growl of hunger rumbled up from his chest, and then his hips drove him into her, hard and fast, almost furious, his lips drawn back in a feral snarl.

Yes. Hard and fast, and very good. She clung to his shoulders, feeling his heat, his skin slippery, rising up to meet each forward thrust.

He tilted his pelvis, the base of his shaft grinding against the sweet place between her legs.

Every nerve tightened, until she thought she must break. Agony twisted his features as he stared into his own abyss. 'Now, Ellie.' The plea in his rough voice tipped her over the edge. She shattered.

A tide of heat rushed outwards, turning her limbs to molten lead. She lay gasping for breath and he slipped out of her body and, shuddering, spilled his seed into the sheets, then stretched beside her and pulled her into the crook of his arm.

Even as she lay, blissful, warm, panting for breath, a faint tinge of bitterness twisted her heart. Even in the heat of passion he'd been in control, where she'd been completely abandoned, thoroughly wanton.

She turned her head to look at him and he brushed her lips with his mouth, a brief caress, as soft as a butterfly wing. 'Rest, sweetheart,' he murmured, pillowing her head on his shoulder.

Was it minutes or hours later when she opened her eyes? Held fast in the circle of his arm, her cheek on his warm chest, his breath tickling the lock of hair on her forehead, she watched fire weave patterns on his skin, gleam on the arc of his cheekbone, shadow the hollows of cheek and throat.

The scent of his musky cologne filled her nostrils. Tenderness seeped into her heart, the trickle building into a stream, then a river, perhaps even an ocean, it felt so vast. She raised her head and kissed his jaw, the stubble rough against her lips. He was lovely in sleep, relaxed, his deep, even breaths stretching the muscles of his chest, which might have been carved from marble if it weren't for the dark sworls of hair.

She drank in his well-remembered features. The hard planes of his lean cheeks, the firm, sensual lips. The face she saw each night in her dreams was softer, more boyish. This hard new face had character, determination, and perhaps even shades of cruelty.

The thought shimmered through her body, frightening and exciting. Impulsively, she pressed her lips against his. If only she could tell him what she'd locked in her heart. Too late. Unless she went down on her knees.

He tensed, his eyelids snapping open, his gaze at once alert. His vision focused and he huffed out a breath. 'It's you.'

'Yes. Me.' Her heart twisted. Had he hoped for someone else? No matter. Tonight he was hers alone. And because she could, she kissed him again. And his hand came up to catch her nape, to angle her head and he deepened the kiss. He rolled on his back, bringing her with him, drawing her up on to his body.

His strong muscled body. His burgeoning erection. A thrill shot though her core as she felt him harden. Perhaps she could show him how well she remembered, with her hands, her lips, her body.

She traced the seam of his mouth and when his lips parted, she swept his mouth, teasing his tongue with hers, tasting. He grunted, a low guttural sound of approval, and sucked. Ripples of pleasure rushed outward from low in her belly.

God help her, the man knew her too well.

Thoroughly aroused, she rocked her hips in small circles against his groin.

'I want to be inside you,' he said, raising his shoulders, reaching down, using his hand to press the head of his erection against her mons. 'Now. Lift up.'

'Not yet,' she said, her voice huskier than she had ever heard it.

'Heaven forefend, woman, do you want to kill me?' He dropped his head back on the pillow.

Smiling, she claimed his lips in a swift kiss. 'Only a little.' She kissed his forehead, his nose, the hollows of his cheeks, the hard line of his jaw. He squirmed and hissed in a breath when she explored the depths of his ear with her tongue, salty and bitter, and very sensual.

His hands gripped her buttocks, large and firm, squeezing gently. He ground his hips against hers with a groan.

'Let me inside you.'

'Hush, let me play a while.'

Shifting to her side, she pressed her lips to his throat, wandered lower, across his shoulders, to his chest, the springy curls rough, the flesh beneath hot and salty and musky. She ran her palms over his flat male nipples and they puckered and hardened. Next she traced the plane of his belly; muscles beneath tanned skin rippled like waves on an ocean, as they tensed beneath her mouth. Too shy, too young, to do more than peek at him before, now the strength and the beauty of his body left her in awe.

'God. Ellie. Don't stop.'

She glanced up at his face. His eyes were closed, his jaw clenched, his expression one of agony.

She took pity on him and her hand found the hard, hot length of his erection. Watching his face, she wrapped her fingers around him, then squeezed.

His eyes opened wide. 'Harder.'

'Won't it hurt?'

'God, no.'

Taking him at his word, she squeezed and he moaned and took her hand in his, showing her how to stroke, from tip to base and back without releasing the pressure.

The tip darkened, while the shaft hardened and pulsed against her palm. 'Oh, my.'

A small drop of moisture glistened in the tiny slit at the tip. She licked it away. Salty, warm, musky.

His hips shot off the bed. He grabbed her around the waist, lifting her over him. 'Enough.' It sounded more like a growl than a word.

A shudder of pleasure held her enthralled and instinctively she straddled his hips, somewhat like mounting a horse astride, except her naked female flesh pressed against his hard penis and the heartbeat beneath his skin matched her own little pulses. The rough hair on his leg grazed her inner thighs. Quite wicked and absolutely tantalising.

Lifting her with one hand under her bottom, he

guided himself inside her body. Rigid and hot, he stretched her. She slid down the delicious intrusion. Hands about her hips, fingers digging into the swell of her buttocks, he helped her set a tantalising rhythm. Definitely like riding a horse, but far more enjoyable as the friction brought new and delightful sensations. If it were not for the tension in his face and the corded muscle and sinew in his large powerful body, she might have thought him submissive to her command of their lovemaking. Hers to do with as she willed.

Would that it were true. The wicked thought thrilled her to the core.

Wanting his touch, she brought his hand to her breasts. He curled his fingertips into her flesh, weighing, massaging, shaping to fit his palms. He caressed her nipples with his thumbs, strumming them, bringing them to life in aching little bursts of pleasure. At each downward stroke of her hips, his pelvis rose to meet her, pressing himself deeper into her heat, but leaving her to set the pace.

He lifted his head and suckled, hard. The thrill shot all the way to her centre. Little quivers, deep earthquakes of passion drove her to find completion. Her body hummed with tension. 'Garrick.'

'Let go, darling.'

He touched where they joined, at the sensitive spot above where he entered her body, pressing and circling with his thumb. A sensation like nothing else, pleasure and sweet, sweet pain, unbearable.

'Oh, yes,' she said. The tension inside her vibrated, the breaking point just out of reach.

'Harder?'

'Faster.'

By increasing the tempo, he brought her to new

heights. The world narrowed to one arching stretch of pleasure.

She flew apart. Burst in glorious quivers of delicious pleasure. He groaned and withdrew, spilling his seed into the sheets while her own shudders went on and on.

He rolled on his side and kissed her forehead, the corner of her mouth, her throat, a delicate brush of his lips against her breast.

'You were glorious,' he said. 'Thank you.'

She lay in his arms with her skin cooling and tears a blink away. Loss of what might have been as real as the death of a loved one.

'Your hunger was great,' he said into her hair.

Before, he had always been the driving force in their lovemaking.

'Yes,' she whispered. 'It…has been a long time. But not for you, I think.' She couldn't help the little knife of jealousy.

'You have an itch. You scratch it.'

An itch. Well, she should have expected no more. 'William always said you were an unprincipled wretch.'

'William.' He rolled away, flung the sheet back and stood up, his bare flanks lean and muscled. She repressed an urge to lean out and caress the lovely firm rounded flesh.

'I did offer marriage,' he said. 'You chose otherwise.' He shrugged, a lift of broad shoulders. 'You would have had my name, my title. What more did you want?'

A declaration of love? Would it have made any difference? She'd made so many wrong decisions that summer, caused untold harm. Now was not the time to open old wounds. And yet he deserved an answer. She swallowed. 'I could not abandon my sister.'

His back stiffened, then he picked his shirt up from the floor and pulled it over his head. 'Admit it. You were afraid.' He continued to dress, his focus entirely on his articles of clothing, as if her answer made no difference.

She slipped out of her side of the bed. She drew on her chemise and tied the bow at the neck. 'Afraid?'

He turned to look over his shoulder. 'Of me. Of what I might do.'

'It wasn't like that.' She struggled with the laces of her stays at her back. 'I made a promise.'

'And so you made your choice. And here you are once more, the sacrificial lamb.' He strolled to the mirror over the mantel and in swift, sure movements tied his cravat. 'What about you, Ellie? When will you choose you?' He laughed, a short mirthless crack. 'Please. Don't answer. I don't want to know. Just get the letter and you can forget me, and go back to your safe little life.'

He had changed. She really didn't know him any longer. But he was right about her life. It was little. And it was all she had left. 'Take me home.'

Garrick glanced at the clock. A flash of concern crossed his face. 'Yes, you should leave now. My friend will be home soon.'

He hurried her into the sitting room, picking up her cloak, shoving her bonnet and veil into her hand, clearly wishing her gone. She'd lost him. So quickly. She could see it in his distant expression. Her heart sank.

What had she expected? That he would renew his offer of marriage after a brief encounter? He was using her to get what he wanted, the way she had used him. Mayhap, it served her right.

He opened the door and she followed him out of the chamber.

In the hallway, a footman was in the process of opening the front door.

Garrick cursed under his breath as a rather bosky young gentleman and a scantily dressed woman stepped over the threshold. He handed his cane to the waiting lackey.

Ellie gasped and pulled up her hood.

'Morning, Beauworth,' he said, grinning beneath his fair moustache. 'Finished gambling a bit early. Pleasant night, I assume?' His glance shifted to Ellie and he bowed unsteadily. 'Lady Eleanor.'

Her stomach dropped away in a rush. Once more, impetuosity had led her to ruin and this time she'd well and truly stepped over the brink.

She lifted her chin. 'Lord Goring.'

Chapter Eleven

W hat had she done? Alone in the carriage, Eleanor
wanted to bang her head against a wall or throw
herself beneath the rumbling wheels. Years she'd
spent making sure not a breath of scandal besmirched
her name. And now this.

Impetuosity.

It had got her into trouble in her youth and here she
was again, acting without thinking. Only this time her reputation would never recover. A little hot rush of something
naughty sang in her veins. Since she was ruined, why not
go the whole hog and finish out her bargain with Garrick?
The mere idea of it made her feel hot and breathless.

Oh, yes, and ruin Sissy's chances of making a good
marriage. She couldn't do it. She'd have to retire to the
country in disgrace. She struck the cushioned seat with
her fist. Idiot.

After swearing she'd never do anything rash again,
here she was, a fallen woman. And it was all her own
doing.

When the carriage pulled up to her front door,
Garrick helped her down and escorted her up the steps

without a word. She scrabbled in her reticule for the key.

'What the devil!' William's voice from behind her.

Heart tripping, Eleanor whirled around. Garrick's hand gripped her elbow, whether for support or to stop her from fleeing she couldn't be sure.

William bounded out of a hackney carriage wearing a scarlet uniform. Open-mouthed, shocked, confused, Eleanor watched him toss a handful of coins at the driver and limp across the footpath to stand at the bottom of the steps.

He glared up at Garrick. 'You bastard.' His voice sounded choked.

'I believe my lineage is as impeccable as yours.' Garrick moved closer to her as William's scowl deepened. 'Len, for God's sake, get inside before someone sees you.'

'It's too late,' she said, surprised how calm she sounded, how matter of fact, in the face of his rage.

Garrick's eyebrows shot up. He looked startled, even a little impressed. Had he expected her to lie?

William turned to Garrick. 'You'll meet me for this. In an hour in Green Park. It's all the time I have before I leave.'

Dread curdled her stomach. 'William, why are you in uniform?'

His lip curled. 'Because my country needs all the help she can get with traitors like this in our midst.'

'William, you can't. You have duties, responsibilities.'

His cheeks flamed. 'So do you, but you don't let them stop you.' He swung back to Garrick, his hand on his sabre hilt. 'Name your seconds, sir, or be named for a coward.'

Garrick looked down his nose. 'You've waited a

long time for this, haven't you, Castlefield? It's true what they say, then—revenge is best served cold.'

Eleanor grabbed her brother's arm. 'William, no! I went with him willingly.'

'Damn it, Len. Why?'

Garrick's smiled, cruel, taunting. 'Because she wanted some fun for a change.'

William lunged at him, fists flying. Garrick blocked his wild blows, captured his wrist.

Eleanor wormed her way between them.

'Stop it! It's bad enough that you might be killed by the French, but to risk death in a duel is nonsense. I have no virtue to defend.'

'A man who sends a woman to fight his battles is unlikely to fall victim to a French bullet,' Garrick said, releasing William's hand and stepping back.

William's face drained of colour. 'A traitor like you is more likely to shoot a man in the back.'

Eleanor had the hysterical urge to laugh. They were like male dogs, stiff-legged, hackles raised, circling each other. The two men that she loved most in the world hated each other.

William pushed her towards the door. 'You and Sissy are going home. Go inside and pack. I'll decide what to do when I return, but believe me, if this gets out, you will never again be accepted by the *ton*. Let us hope your behaviour hasn't ruined Sissy. As for you, you cur, damned well name your seconds.'

'It will be my pleasure,' Garrick said with a feral smile.

'No!' She clutched at William. 'I will not allow you to fight a duel over me.'

Garrick looked down at her, a glimmer of something strange in his eyes—yearning, or devilment? 'If you want to put a stop to this, marry me.'

She gaped at him.

'You will never come near this family again if you marry this murdering, traitorous cur,' William said.

Garrick stood silent, his face a mask.

William looked equally grim.

The painful truth kicked her in the stomach like a flying hoof, sending her heart into a runaway gallop. She couldn't breathe. She couldn't move. This was her last chance.

'Yes,' she said. 'I will.'

Face blank, Garrick stared at her. She'd called his bluff. He hadn't meant it. He was posturing, taunting William.

'Len.' William's voice was hoarse. 'Don't make it any worse, for God's sake.'

'I think it's best, William.'

He turned his back. 'Go, then, and be damned to the pair of you.'

'Garrick wants Piggot's letter,' she said.

His shoulders shook, but he did not turn around. 'He can go to hell.'

'Let me say goodbye to Sissy, then.'

'Leave, Eleanor. Now.'

Eleanor stumbled down the steps, held up by Garrick's strong arm.

'Ellie, don't let him see you cry,' he whispered fiercely in her ear. She pulled herself upright and held her head high.

'That's my brave Lady Moonlight,' he said softly as he handed her back into his coach.

Beside Garrick, in front of the altar of St Mary's in the City of London, Eleanor's heart seemed determined to make a quick escape. Was it fear or joy making it beat so hard? Perhaps both. Behind them stood Lieutenant Dan Smith, Joshua Nidd and Johnson the coachman, and rows of empty pews. Eleanor wore the gown she'd worn the previous evening.

The vicar perused the special licence. 'Everything seems in order.'

The sound of the church door opening interrupted the hushed solemnity. Garrick signalled impatiently for the man to go on, but Dan held up a restraining hand. Boot heels echoing, the young officer walked back to greet the latecomer.

Curious, Eleanor turned. A slight figure in a peach gown and green spencer hurried up the aisle on the Lieutenant's arm.

'Cecilia?'

'What the deuce?' Garrick said, looking beyond her, as if expecting someone else.

Cecilia brushed a dark curl off her shoulder. 'William forbade me to come. I left as soon as he went out.' She handed Eleanor a bouquet of silk flowers. 'I thought you might need these.' She looked accusingly at Garrick, who merely raised a dark arching eyebrow and turned back to the minister.

To Eleanor, the next few minutes passed in a blur, but throughout the ceremony she clung to Garrick, her lifeline in a storm-tossed sea while the necessary words were spoken.

He, on the other hand, seemed preoccupied, impatient for the conclusion, speaking his words crisply and clearly, tensing when she spoke hers. Considerate, and gentle when he kissed her, bland as he received the well wishes of those present, even generous as he hugged Cecilia and called her his *chère* sister, he clearly wished it over. Was he already regretting his hasty offer?

Eleanor had a strange sense of foreboding, when she should have been happy.

The moment the vicar sprinkled sand on their signatures in the register, Garrick hurried her down the aisle with his hand in the small of her back, almost pushing her into the carriage when she would have lingered with Sissy at the steps.

He turned to clasp the Lieutenant's hand. Garrick clapped a hand to the young man's shoulder. A look of regret passed between them. This was more than just a casual parting. The thought stuck her like a blow.

Garrick was leaving. Despite their marriage he was still going to France. And soon. Her stomach roiled as if the lifeline had snapped and all hope of rescue was disappearing into the distance. Somehow she had to stop him.

'Take Lady Cecelia home, Dan,' Garrick ordered, then climbed into the carriage.

Married. Garrick eyed his lovely wife on the opposite carriage seat. She smiled at him tentatively. He wanted to smile back, to pull her on to his lap, to bury his face in her hair and inhale her sweet perfume, when what he must do was get ready to leave. And he was going to have to tell her.

The carriage pulled up outside the door to Beauworth House. 'Here we are,' he said to fill the awkward silence when they'd never been short of conversation.

He handed his bride down. His bride? The beautiful English rose he'd thought he'd lost. But she'd married him to save her brother and her reputation. Would she constantly remind him of her sacrifice, or would she be content? If they never learned the truth about his mother's death, would she fear him? Hell, if she didn't she'd be a fool.

And yet she'd married him. Trusted him with her body and soul. He felt humbled and very afraid.

She peeked up at him, looking more nervous than she'd been last night, when she ought to have been terrified witless. A need to protect cut a swathe through his determination to remain uninvolved. He swept her up in his arms, bearing his burden with pride. It was what bridegrooms were supposed to do on their wedding day. He liked the way she clung around his neck, the weight of her, the curve of her waist, the bend of her knee, the glimpse of slender ankles when he glanced down to mount the steps to his open front door.

'This is your home now,' he said, putting her down when he wanted to keep her in his arms and run straight upstairs. 'Order it as you will.'

He stepped away while the butler relieved her of her outer raiment, the damned cloak she'd worn the night before, and beneath it the pale blue gown. He'd like to see her dressed in nothing but satins and silks in shades of gold and sapphire. Hell, he'd like to see her naked.

'Dinner is served, my lord,' the butler said.

'No point in waiting,' Garrick said. 'Unless you feel the need to freshen up.'

She shook her head.

'Good.' He held out his arm. He escorted her into the panelled dining room, with its twenty-foot table and two places set at one end.

'Will Lieutenant Smith not be joining us?' she asked, hesitantly.

The tiny hesitation scoured his heart. He could not allow her to wound him again, not with all that was at stake. 'Afraid to be alone with me, Ellie? Do you think I will devour you instead of the meal?'

At that she smiled, a glorious lightening of her beautiful face, and the band around his chest eased.

'Of course not,' she said. The butler placed several platters on the table, filled their glasses with red wine, then retreated to stand silent at the wall.

Garrick filled her plate with slices of roast duck, an assortment of vegetables and a slice of beef pie. They addressed themselves to the dinner. Or rather she pushed the food around on her plate, while he drank wine. After ten minutes of utter silence, he waved the butler away. The door closed softly behind him.

'What is the matter, Ellie?'

She bit her bottom lip, then raised her gaze to his face, her eyes swirling with shadows. 'I hope you don't regret...' she waved her fork as if words failed her '...this. Us.' A tinge of colour stained her cheekbones.

What had he hoped for? A declaration that her marriage to him was more than a saving of face? He leaned back, keeping his voice cool. 'To be honest with you, I had not thought of marriage at all. My life is already full.'

She responded with a lift of her chin. Proud and heartbreakingly vulnerable. He found himself wanting to kiss her. But he wasn't going to humble himself before the one woman with the power to bring him to his knees. Not again.

'Then I do hope I won't be in the way,' she said in bright, brittle tones. 'After all, it is no business of a wife's what a man does for entertainment.' She inspected the fruit centrepiece, as if expecting maggots to crawl out of it. 'I do not ask you to change.'

Bloody hell. So this is how she thought they would go on. 'How understanding, *ma belle mie.*'

Her eyes flashed, but she presented an innocent

smile. 'I assume, of course, that I shall have the same level of freedom.'

So, she would once more cross swords with him. This was more the Ellie he knew, rather than the crushed little figure who had stood at his side in church. But he didn't have time for games. 'Not at all.'

Her hand gripped her knife, as if she contemplated thrusting it into his anatomy. Then her shoulders relaxed and she smiled as if butter wouldn't melt in her mouth, the little witch. 'La, sir, shouldn't what is sauce for the gander be also sauce for the goose?'

His back teeth ground together. He knew her little games too well. She thought to keep him in England with threats of infidelity. God, he'd always admired her spirit, but in this she'd be disillusioned. He forced a smile and inclined his head. 'I see.'

Her disappointment, her hurt, flashed in her eyes, quickly hidden. It was wicked of him to be pleased, but then she should know better than to play her tricks off on him.

He pushed to his feet and moved to stand behind her. 'Perhaps I need to remind you that you are mine, *chérie.*' He placed his hands under her elbows, bringing her to her feet, unreasonably pleased when she didn't resist. He kicked the chair out of the way and spun her around to face him. Her gaze searched his face. Looking for what? His surrender? If he had any sense, he'd put her across his knee and spank her bottom. Lust flared at the thought.

Her eyes widened as if she had read his thoughts. He thought he might drown in their brilliant silver depths.

He had his orders. Dover tonight, France in the morning. In the time he had available, he wanted her settled and secure, even if he could not ease her fears.

He didn't want her throwing herself at another man in a fit of rebellion.

He bent his head and kissed her lips. She stiffened and he smiled. She would not resist him for long, she never did. He kissed her gently, a whispering brush of lips, a flicker of tongue. Her breathing shortened to little gasps, her hand came to his shoulder, she pressed her mouth against his and parted her lips. Oh, yes. His woman. His love.

He picked her up, so light, a creature of air and light and liquid silver who would slip through his fingers if he wasn't careful. He carried her upstairs to his bed. He did not know where his next meal was coming from once he left here, but the next hour would be food for his soul. And he would feast.

Overwhelmed by languor, Eleanor barely realised he was out of bed and dressing. Their lovemaking had been wild, almost desperate. Its intensity had left her limp and replete. Her eyes slid open as she heard movement beyond the bed.

He wore his usual black and his face looked bleak, as if he faced an unpleasant duty. Her heart sank. He was leaving. If the threat of her cuckolding him was not enough to keep him at her side, perhaps another weapon would work.

She smiled and reached out. 'It is too early. Come back to bed.'

'I didn't mean to disturb you.' He leaned over her and kissed her almost absently. 'I will return.' He moved towards the door.

'It is dark.' Panic laced her voice, but she didn't care. 'Stay until morning at least.'

'I'm sorry.' He turned the handle.

He did sound sorry. A small victory. 'You are going to France, aren't you?' she said, her voice rising, sounding shrill to her own ears. 'It is true what they say? You have changed your allegiance?'

He didn't look at her. Just opened the door. Finally he spoke in flat tones. 'I will not tolerate another man in your bed, Eleanor. If you so much as look at a man, I will kill him. You do understand, don't you?'

He shut the door behind him.

A hysterical laugh escaped her. She pressed the back of her hand to her mouth. As if she would ever want anyone else. How little he understood. Less than a day married and he'd left.

The tightness in her chest made it hard to breathe. If he really was a spy and he was caught, he would be shot.

A tear slipped over her lower lashes and made its way down her cheek. She swiped it away.

No, she would not believe such a thing of him. Betraying his country was dishonourable, and whatever Garrick was, he had never been that.

Wherever he was going, he had to return, because she hadn't said goodbye.

Waiting in the drawing room for Sissy to call as usual, Eleanor pressed her hand flat to her stomach. She still could not believe it. She and Garrick has made a baby on their final night together. After all the years of assuming she would never marry, she was going to be a mother. How she longed for Garrick to share her joy.

A contentment filled her, the thought of the future a bright shining horizon. Her and Garrick and their babe.

This news would bring him home now the war was over. Napoleon was finally defeated at Waterloo. All the reports spoke of a great victory.

Nidd knocked on the door. 'Lady Hadley,' he announced in solemn tones, as if Sissy did not arrive at the same time every day. Bless her, she'd ignored William's admonition to stay away and had visited almost daily these past few weeks.

'Have the papers arrived yet, Nidd?' Sissy asked with a jaunty smile.

Poor old Nidd could not resist her. 'I'll bring them directly, my lady.' He scuttled away.

'Len, don't think of getting up,' Sissy said, leaning over her. 'You need to be careful in your condition.'

'I'm not an invalid,' Eleanor said, kissing the soft cheek presented at her level.

A moment later, Nidd returned with a freshly ironed newspaper. '*The Times,* my lady,' Nidd said, offering it to Eleanor.

Sissy whisked it out of his hand. 'Thank you.'

'Will that be all, my lady?' Nidd asked.

'Tea, please, Nidd. And cake. And perhaps some of those cucumber sandwiches Cook makes.' The butler disappeared.

'Good Lord, Len, it is barely ten o'clock. You can't have finished breakfast more than an hour ago.'

'I feel nauseous if I don't eat,' Eleanor said.

'Oh, poor you. It must be simply dreadful.'

Eleanor smiled at her sister. 'No. It is wonderful.'

With much rattling and cursing, Sissy opened the paper. Everyone in London was doing it. Looking at the endless lists of the fallen. There was not a family among the *ton* who had not lost a brother, a son or a close friend.

Dark head bent over the paper, Sissy ran her finger down the columns of names. Her finger stopped its downward course a few lines down. She looked away, blinking, as if trying to clear her sight.

Eleanor snatched the sheet from her hand.

'Captain Lord Castlefield,' she read slowly. 'Missing.'

Sissy flung herself at Eleanor's chest, hugged her tight. 'Missing. It says missing, not dead.'

Eleanor took a deep breath, tried to keep the shake from her voice. 'He might well be wounded and not yet recognised.' Surely she would know if her twin was dead? A breath seemed to catch on a lump in her throat. So many of those listed as missing at the beginning of the week had more recently been reported among the dead. And what about Garrick? There had been no word. No information about those killed or wounded on the French side.

'I will write to Captain Smith,' Cecilia said, her eyes glistening with tears. 'He will search the hospitals.' She ran to the writing table.

Dan Smith, now a captain, had sent word immediately after the battle by way of a friend ordered to London with dispatches.

'Good idea,' Eleanor said, though why Captain Smith, so vilified by her brother, would feel obligated to seek him out wasn't clear. And what if he found him dead? She gulped a painful breath. 'Cecilia, we must prepare for the worst.'

Sissy looked up from sharpening her pen. 'No. William is all right. He has to be. And your Marquess, too.'

Eleanor swallowed what felt like a handful of pins. 'I am sure you are right.'

If that was so, why hadn't she heard? She held her hands to her waist for a second. Would his child ever see its father?

A week later, Sissy dashed into her drawing room, laughing and crying at once and waving a letter. 'He's safe! Oh, Len, William is safe. I received a letter from him this morning. He was unconscious for a while, but is recovered now. Captain Smith found him in a field hospital with other men from his regiment. They were at Hougoumont. Here, see for yourself.' She pressed the crumpled paper into Eleanor's hand.

Relief washed through her in a torrent. As Eleanor read William's letter, tears stole down her face, for his last lines touched her deeply.

Tell Len I send my love. I have had a great deal of time to think, lying here in hospital, with so many other good and brave fellows dying around me. I could not have borne it if I had left this world without a chance to beg her forgiveness. I have enclosed a letter for her eyes only.

'See,' Cecilia said triumphantly, 'I knew he could not be angry at you forever.' Four years had felt like a lifetime. 'Did you see where he mentioned Captain Smith? Not a word of censure. In fact, he says he's a good sort of chap and very brave. Oh, Len, everything is going to be all right.'

William sounded like a changed man. Eleanor smiled at her sister through her tears. 'I do hope so,' she whispered. 'Sissy, is there another letter for me?'

'Oh, yes, I'm so sorry, I almost forgot.' She pulled out a fold of paper from her reticule. While Sissy once more pored over the part of William's letter that spoke of Captain Smith, Eleanor went to the window where the light was better. Fingers trembling, she broke the seal. Her heart felt too large for her chest. William had forgiven her.

My Dearest Len,

I am sorry to be the bearer of bad tidings, but I feel it is my duty. One of the men who died here yesterday told me he saw Beauworth just before the battle started.

He had been captured by a company of Dutch. He was being held at their headquarters. No doubt, by now he has been executed.

A pain spasmed in her chest. She clutched her throat. Her vision blurred. She couldn't breathe. The paper shook so hard, she couldn't make out the words. She wiped her eyes with her handkerchief and forced herself to read on.

I am so sorry. But I feel obliged to unload my burdens and tell the truth at last. Beauworth was innocent of any crime against his mother. Le Clere was her murderer. I have Piggot's letter in my safe at Castlefield explaining it all. I picked it up and read it the day of the ransom and have kept it ever since. Dishonourable, I know.

When I read of his exoneration, I couldn't stand to think of him getting away with what he did to you. And, God help me, to me. Though I now know the truth of that, too, from young Smith. I can only blame it on some sort of madness. It has haunted me every day since. Part of the reason I returned to my regiment. A sort of atonement, I think.

To my shame, I believe my vengeful actions drove Beauworth into the arms of the French. I can only beg your forgiveness. I pray you will find it in your heart, though I cannot blame you if you turn away.

No matter what, I will take care of you always, if you will allow. Your loving brother, William.

Eleanor stared at the paper. Garrick. Dead. What William had done paled in comparison. The tears that had flowed so freely at the miraculous news of William's survival dried on her cheeks. Her mind seemed numb. The words *shot as a spy* reverberated like an echo in an empty vessel. He would never see his child.

Outside, the sun shone brightly on the garden in the centre of the square; inside, the house seemed to be full of fog. She couldn't see or feel, or hear. She wasn't even sure she was breathing. She didn't want to breathe.

Her eyes burned. She'd sent her man off to war and never once told him she loved him.

'What did William say?' Somehow Sissy's voice reached through the void. She held out the paper without looking at Sissy's face. If she saw sympathy, she might start to scream.

Her grip was so tight on the paper, Sissy had to force open her fingers.

'Oh, no!' Sissy's cry of anguish came from a great distance, then the floor shifted and a strange darkness descended. It was fitting that the world should be dark, she thought, as she watched the floor come up to meet her.

The months were passing and Eleanor moved through her life like a stranger. Only the child growing in her body held any real interest. This morning, as usual, she sat in her drawing room, waiting for Sissy to call and see how she did. No doubt Sissy would report on her progress to William, whose last letter had been full of news of Paris under the allied army of occupation. He had sounded cheerful and anxious to return home as soon as Wellington agreed to release him from his duties. While their reconciliation by letter had been wonderful, many things remained unsaid between them. It would be good to finally clear the air once he returned home.

Nidd knocked at the door. 'My lady?'

'Yes, Nidd, what is it?' She spoke gently. The old Yorkshire man looked thinner and more like a skeleton than ever. The loss of the Marquess had been difficult for all of the Beauworth servants.

'There's a man at the servants' door, said he was sent by Captain Smith to help Johnson in the stables. Is it all right if I give him your permission?'

This was the third unemployed soldier Dan Smith had sent. Starving men who had served with the Marquess in the Peninsula. Dan had insisted Garrick would want her to help them. Eleanor trusted Captain Smith, but she had found the other two men rather frightening. They were large and rough and clearly not used to serving in a gentleman's establishment. Once or twice she had found them lounging around in doorways or outside the stables with seemingly nothing to do.

'Perhaps I will speak to him first.' She followed him back to the kitchen.

Slouched against the doorpost, Garrick had to hold himself back when Ellie entered the kitchen. Would she know him, disguised as he was? He'd spent the last four days perfecting his disguise while his men, with Dan's help, infiltrated her house.

God, he'd missed her. She looked pale. Too thin, despite her blooming body. He longed to put his arms around her, hold her close, feel that soft body melding with his, run his hand over the soft swell of her belly full with their child. His child. Months he'd been without her, praying she'd wait for him. Thoughts of her had kept him alive during some of the worst days of his life.

Forcing himself to play his part, he pushed away from the wall. 'Look busy. 'Ere comes 'er ladyship,' he said in a hoarse voice straight from London's gutters.

'Let's have a little more respect from you, my lad,' Nidd said. 'This is the Marchioness of Beauworth. Bill Dodds, my lady.'

Garrick gave her a sloppy salute and kept his gaze fixed on the floor, his shoulders hunched. The patch he wore over one eye covered most of one side of his face and obscured his vision. The growth on his chin formed a straggling beard and his hair, cut short by Dan, he knew showed patches of white skin.

God, he hoped she wouldn't know him. It would ruin all his plans. He shambled across the room and made an awkward bow.

'Captain Smith suggests you help in the stables. What knowledge have you of horses?' She sounded tense, almost afraid. He didn't blame her. He cut a dreadful appearance.

He kept his one eye fixed on the cap he twisted in hands he'd roughened by working in the stables at Horse Guards. 'I looked after 'orses for the cavalry, yer ladyship.'

'You are fit enough for these tasks?' She gazed at his leg, which he favoured, giving an impression of an injury and reducing his height by leaning heavily on his hip.

'Aye, milady.'

She peered at his face, as if looking for someone she knew.

Dammit. For all his efforts, Ellie was going to see straight through the filth. God, he loved this woman.

He coughed, a harsh, chest-racking sound that bent him double. He hawked and looked around for somewhere to spit and decided on the sink.

With a grimace, she turned her face away. He hated that his ploy had succeeded so well she would not look at him. But he kept on coughing.

'Very well, report to Mr Johnson,' she said.

He breathed a sigh of relief. Le Clere might strike at any moment, but he would have to go through Garrick and his men to get to Ellie.

Without glancing at her face, he touched his forelock and shuffled out of the door. He sensed her staring at his back. He'd have to be very careful around his clever wife.

Chapter Twelve

A day or so later the weather turned fine and Eleanor decided to drive out in her carriage. She was a little surprised to see the scruffy Dodds on the driver's box when she stepped out of the door. She frowned. 'Where is Johnson?'

''E's got a touch of the rumytism, milady,' the shabby Bill Dodds explained.

Strangely, Johnson had spoken highly of Dodds's competence, despite her initial misgivings, and so she had left things alone. 'Well, Dodds, if you are going to drive my carriage, I would appreciate it if you would borrow Johnson's coat.'

'Er, yes, milady. Thing is, it don't fit.'

Eleanor grimaced. The man was far taller than Johnson, despite his slouch, and broader across the shoulders. 'Wait here.'

She returned with the oldest of Garrick's greatcoats. 'See if this fits.'

It could have been made for the man, she thought, as he shrugged himself into it.

'Thank you, milady. Right kind o' ye.' He grinned,

a flash of white teeth through the thick beard. A strange sense of recognition flooded through her. He turned away quickly, fiddling with the reins.

She was imagining things. Every tall man with dark hair on the street made her heart jump. She had stopped running after them, but her heart still gave a hopeful little lurch.

She stepped into the carriage. The horses trotted sedately through the traffic under the firm control of Bill Dodds and it wasn't long before they turned into Hyde Park. It was too early for the *ton* to be much in evidence. Some fresh air and a spot of exercise would do her good. Tired of the way everyone, from Sissy to Nidd, fussed because she was increasing, she longed for a rest from their anxious faces and solicitous words.

She tapped the overhead door with the handle of her parasol. It opened. 'Pull over, Dodds. I'm going to walk.'

'I don' know, milady. Better if'n you stay with the carriage.'

'Oh, for goodness' sake. Are you going to start now?'

He muttered an apology and stopped the carriage. He helped her down and stepped back quickly. There was something almost guilty about the way he refused to meet her gaze. She shook off her discomfort. The man was competent, that was all that mattered.

'I will be back within a half-hour. Feel free to walk the horses if needed.'

She was aware of the gleaming dark eye that followed her as she strolled away. She should not have been so fierce. It was their respect for the Marquess making them all so attentive. Given the rumours about Garrick, she was grateful for that respect.

Her spleen relieved by a brisk walk, she sat down on a stone seat beside the lake and watched the ducks dabble. She would bring the baby here. Garrick would have approved.

What would he have thought, had he known she was with child? Would he have left for France? She couldn't help a wry little smile, because she didn't doubt it for a moment. But she did wish she'd found the courage to tell him her true feelings. If they'd had more time, they might have rediscovered the joy they'd shared so briefly. In time, perhaps she would have found in him the handsome Marquess with warm brown eyes and wicked smile with whom she had fallen in love.

She would never know.

The pain in her chest rose into her throat in a hot, hard lump. Damn. She blinked back the watery veil obliterating the view.

''Scuse me, miss' She gazed through the mist at the urchin standing in front of her. The boy seemed ill-at-ease and out of breath. 'You the Marchingness of Bosworth?'

She frowned. 'What of it, child?'

'I got a 'portant message. But yer gotta promise not to tell.' The ragamuffin shifted from foot to foot as if on the verge of flight.

Her heart picked up speed. She desperately tried to quell the rush of hope. It was foolish to hope. And yet she'd received no official confirmation of Garrick's death and it was always there, catching her unawares, like a candle that refused to be snuffed. 'I promise.'

''Ere.' The boy flung a dirty scrap of paper at her and dashed away.

Eleanor uncrumpled the paper. A bold scrawl emblazoned the page.

Meet me tonight after Midnight
at the corner of the Square.
B.

B. meaning Beauworth? It would be like Garrick to issue such a command. Who else could it be? Garrick was alive. Hands shaking, she stared at the note. She pressed it to her lips, inhaled the scent of ink. Her eyes burned and blurred. What? Crying? Now was not the time for tears. Think. He must be in danger if he couldn't come openly to his house. So she would go to him.

She tucked the note into her reticule. Alive. She leapt to her feet, her heart so light it could have carried her away on a breeze.

What would she wear? What would she say? Would he ask her to go with him? She headed back for her carriage and home. Would he be happy about their child? No matter what his circumstances, she would go with him this time. Even if it meant flight to the ends of the earth, if he asked. She pushed a surge of fear aside. When she reached the carriage, Dodds had a strange look on his face. If she'd hadn't known better, she might have thought it was utter relief.

The rest of the day passed far too slowly, the clock's hands creeping minute by minute until she thought her head would burst. After dinner, she went upstairs to her chamber, and after sending her maid away, changed into a practical walking gown, dressing her hair in a simple knot. If they were going to be on the run, the less fuss the better. Since he'd not asked her to bring anything, she decided not to pack a valise in case there wasn't room. On the other hand, he might be in need of money, so she stuffed her reticule with bills. What else? She paced in front of the hearth. A weapon?

She ran to the dressing room and opened her trunk to find the only thing she'd kept from her madcap youth in the bottom. Her sword.

She drew it part way from the scabbard. The blade caught the light of her candle with a wicked glint. As instructed by her father, she'd cleaned it and oiled it faithfully at regular intervals. Father had been right. You never knew when a sword might come in useful.

A woman with a sword wasn't exactly a common sight. She rummaged through her clothes' press and found a thick woollen cloak. She wrapped the sword and scabbard in the folds of the cloak and stood in front of her mirror. If she carried it like so, tucked under her arm parallel with her body beneath the cloak, it should pass unnoticed. After all, no one expected a woman to carry such a weapon.

Unable to think of anything else, she sat down to wait.

It was the most horrid hour she'd ever spent, but finally the clock on the mantel chimed twelve and she slipped downstairs and opened the front door, feeling a little bit like Cinderella. Garrick was waiting. She hugged the thought close.

What if he took her with him tonight? Sissy and William might never know what had become of her. It didn't bear thinking about. She took a deep breath.

Deal with one problem at a time. First she had to see Garrick. Find out what was happening. Her palms damp and her heart racing, she stepped out of the house and into the dark street.

Dark shadows loomed between the houses and beneath the trees in the middle of the square, but nothing seemed out of the ordinary. Her footsteps a light tap on the flagstones, the scent of coal fires in her nostrils, she stepped out briskly.

'Who's that?' Garrick, lounging against the side of the house, prodded his companion.

'I dunno. One the maids, I 'spose. The little saucy one, most likely. She slips out sometimes to visit her fella.'

'She ought to be careful, walking the streets at this time of night.' Garrick limped out on to the footpath, careful to avoid the light cast by the streetlamp. The maid paused at the curb, then crossed the street under a light. His breath hissed between his teeth. 'What the devil? Fetch my horse. Now.'

He dashed to the other side of the street, maintaining his halting gait and staying close to the park's iron railings where the shadows were deepest. He turned the corner of the square in time to see the woman step into a waiting hackney. The driver whipped up the horses as soon as the door closed.

Gut in a knot, he ran back. Abandoning stealth in favour of speed, he shouted orders as he ran for his horse. 'You, follow me. You, take this message to the Captain. Damn the woman. And damn Le Clere.'

The faces of his men looked tense as they hurried to do his bidding.

* * *

When the horses drew up at an inn somewhere near Hampstead Heath, Eleanor thought, she opened the door and jumped down.

The driver clambered down and waved her towards the entrance of a small, mean-looking place with moss-covered thatch and grimy windows. 'After you, my lady.'

The voice struck a chord of memory and she stared at his face. A face she only saw in her nightmares. 'Matthews?'

'I didn't think you would recognise me, my lady, after all this time.' He grinned.

A sick feeling churned in her stomach. Why would Matthews be helping Garrick? She hesitated. No. She would not turn away again. There must be some reasonable explanation.

'Where is my husband?'

'In there.' He jerked his head at the open door of the inn.

Eleanor strode into the taproom with Matthews close behind. The room was empty and Eleanor turned to him with raised brows, only to find the man holding a pistol. She stepped back. 'What does this mean?'

'It means, my lady,' said a hoarse voice from behind her, 'you have very kindly assisted me in my quest.'

She turned slowly and took stock of the man who had entered the room through another door. He was old and so bent over he was forced to look sideways up at her. Deep lines etched his heavily jowelled face below a shock of pure white hair.

Eleanor had never seen him before. 'Where is the Marquess?'

'Dead.'

Eleanor's knees weakened. The room seemed to

spin. She clung to the back of a chair. 'No! I received a note.'

'Oh, yes. A note. *Meet me tonight after Midnight at the corner of the Square.*' The old man cackled. The sound pierced her heart like knives.

'Really, my lady, do you think my traitorous nephew would be foolish enough to walk into England for you, even if he lived? British spies watch you every minute in case he returns. You didn't tell anyone where you were going, did you?' He glanced at the other man. 'Matthews, you are sure you were not followed?'

'No, sir, nary a sign or a peep.'

This twisted gnome was Duncan Le Clere. She recognised his cold eyes. Her heart beat became erratic. He'd tricked her. Garrick was dead. An ache spread through her chest. Cruel man to raise her hopes, then shatter them with a single word. She wanted to curl into a ball. To shut out the world. To let the darkness dancing at the edge of her vision descend. But she couldn't, for the sake of the child. Garrick's babe.

'Why?' she whispered, her voice breaking.

'Please be seated, my lady.' He waved towards one of the chairs. 'You carry his child, do you not?'

Eleanor put one hand protectively over her belly and held her ground. 'What concern is it of yours?'

'I want it. And I want a certain letter only you can get for me.'

The whole thing became clear. What a fool she'd been. She should have guessed. 'I see.'

His piercing dark eyes glittered like the eyes of a snake laid out on a rock watching a rabbit. She felt very much like a rabbit. 'You know, don't you?' he said.

She would not show her fear. 'That it proves you a

murderer? Yes.' He cocked his head on one side, his mouth twisting. Clearly the wrong thing to say. 'You cannot keep me against my will.'

'Can I not? You will be well looked after until the birth of the child. If you fail to produce an heir, there is a woman standing by with a male replacement. But you won't. Le Cleres always beget boys.'

His voice was so cold, so rational, she had no trouble believing he meant every word, mad as they sounded. She couldn't breathe. It was as if something was wrapped around her chest and was slowly squeezing all the air from her lungs. She felt dizzy. What a fool to walk into his trap. She had to do something. Her hand clenched around the scabbard hidden in the folds of her cloak. What could a sword do against a pistol? Perhaps something, if the right moment came along. She'd have to be patient. The safety of her babe depended on not making another mistake.

Le Clere grinned. 'Do what I tell you and who knows, I might let you live.' He withdrew a pistol from his pocket and cocked it. 'Matthews, have one of the men take the hackney back to London. There must be no trace. Then bring the coach around and let me know when you are ready. I will not be thwarted this time. I will have the heir in my control and this time he will be obedient.'

A shudder of horror crept down her back. Clenching the scabbard, she held herself rigid, aloof, waiting her moment.

Matthews left to do his bidding and Le Clere grinned up at Eleanor. 'You see, my lady, I amassed quite a fortune from Beauworth during the war, but Garrick managed to upset my plans.' His laugh was harsh and sounded more than a little crazed. 'I moved all my money to the Continent.' The old man's voice lowered to a mutter. 'France is ruined. I am ruined.'

The door opened with a soft click. He raised his voice, but didn't turn around. 'But what we did before, we can do again, isn't that right, Matthews?'

The door swung back. 'I'm afraid, Le Clere, that Matthews is otherwise detained.'

'Garrick.' Eleanor reeled at the sound of her husband's voice. It was really Garrick, looking like Dodds, without the patch and the limp. A sob of joy rose in her throat. She started forwards, wanting the feel of his arms around her, wanting to touch him to be certain it wasn't her imagination playing tricks.

'Hold,' Le Clere said, grabbing her. He hooked an arm around her throat. He pressed his pistol against her temple.

Garrick cursed.

Eleanor could not take her gaze from his dear face. Garrick had come home. Tears ran down her face. He was alive.

'Well, nephew,' Le Clere said with a sneer, 'I heard you were dead.'

Garrick nodded, his face grim, the lines beside his mouth deepening. 'I knew it would bring you out of whatever hole you had crawled into. I must say, though, I would never have recognised you.'

'An unlucky bullet the day you betrayed me. It hit my spine. I have not walked upright since. I should never have let you take her across the field.'

From the wild look in the old man's eye, Garrick judged him capable of anything, even the murder of an innocent woman. There was no doubt in his mind. Le Clere was quite mad.

'Drop your weapon and kneel down, Garrick.'

He should have waited for Dan, but his fears for Ellie had scrambled his wits. 'Go to hell.'

Le Clere's lips drew back in the grimace of a smile and he jammed the pistol harder against Eleanor's temple. Her repressed gasp told Garrick he'd hurt her. No more. He'd done her far too much ill already. He threw the pistol to one side and, with one hand on the arm of the chair, sank to his knees, praying his men would arrive soon.

'That's so much better.' Le Clere's grin was sly. 'I hate looking up at anyone.'

'Let her go. Your quarrel is with me.'

'But you don't understand, Garrick, she is with child. Your heir.'

He kept his face blank, despite the roar of blood in his ears. 'I know. So?'

'Sadly, you were spoiled by the time you came under my authority. I had thought that without your mother's influence, you would settle down. Hence, I disposed of her. But you proved uncontrollable. This newest addition to the Beauworth family will learn obedience. This one will know his master.'

By his own admission, this man had killed his mother. Anger raged inside him like a beast that refused to be chained. His vision narrowed. All he could see was Le Clere's leering face. He clenched his fists, ready to launch himself forwards.

Ellie. He was pointing the pistol at Ellie. Garrick took a deep breath. Then another until the beast subsided. He would not risk Ellie's life to satisfy his lust for blood.

Le Clere, watching him closely, nodded. 'Thought better of it, eh, Garrick? You always were a coward.' He shifted his aim to Garrick. 'You always tried to save your own neck. Well, it won't work this time, dear boy.'

Garrick gritted his teeth and fought for control. If he could just get Le Clere further away from Ellie, he could give the signal to his men. 'I'm not your dear boy. I never was.'

'True.' The old man grimaced. 'I must say I was shocked when I heard of your activities in France.'

Ellie fiddled with her cloak, as if looking for somewhere to lay it down.

Garrick's hackles rose. He kept his face blank and glared at his uncle. 'You know nothing of my activities.'

'No? I heard secrets exchanged hands. I sold a few myself. Had to recoup my losses somehow. Not that the bastards paid me very much.'

Ellie leaned against the back of a sofa, her free hand fussing with the cloak's folds, which looked strangely stiff. A long, dark object fell to the floor. Oh, no. She couldn't have.

'I, on the other hand, made a fortune,' Garrick said, watching his wife from the corner of his eye.

The old man leered. 'And it will all be mine.'

As Ellie shifted, Garrick blinked at the flash of steel she let him see. Blood buzzed in his ears. Damn her. If she missed, someone was going to die.

There was no stopping her, he could see it in her face. And she trusted him to follow her lead. He glared at Le Clere and made as if to rise.

The old man tightened his grip on the pistol. 'Are you so ready to die?'

Ellie let the cloak drop, the blade clutched in her fist behind the sofa. A sword against a pistol. Utter madness. But she'd done it before.

He needed to keep Le Clere looking his way. 'You whoreson. You won't get away with this.'

Le Clere took aim. 'Now then, Garrick, such language in the presence of a lady.' He sounded almost jocular.

Garrick got a firm grip on the chair. 'She is not the lady you think her.' His voice was hoarse, hating the thought of the pain she'd endure.

Le Clere grinned. 'I guessed as much.'

One quick step. Her arm came up. The hilt arced. The pistol discharged into the ceiling with a puff of smoke, a deafening roar and a rain of plaster. She threw the sword, hilt first, to Garrick.

He plucked the weapon from the air. 'She's Lady Moonlight.' He pricked Le Clere's throat before he could so much as blink, watching the trickle of blood run down his neck with supreme satisfaction.

The door sprang open. His men charged through. Ellie looked terrified. She backed against the wall, her gaze fixed on him. She must think they were Le Clere's men.

Dan clambered in through the window, pistol at the ready, his expression furious. He pointed his pistol at Le Clere and the old man put up an arm to shield his face.

'Why the hell didn't you wait?' Dan said.

'Give me a moment.' Garrick crossed the room to where Ellie stood rigid, unsure whether to kiss her or to shake her for taking such a risk. Neither seemed appropriate from the fearful expression on her face.

'You idiot,' he said instead. He lifted her hand, pulled off her cotton glove and looked at her bloody palm. 'You were lucky. I don't think you will need stitches.' He tied it up with his handkerchief.

'I'm all right, or I will be, when you tell me what is going on,' she croaked. 'Who are these men?'

Some of the men were speaking French. After what his uncle had said, no wonder she looked horrified.

'Not all Frenchmen are loyal to Napoleon. I'm sorry, *chérie,* I can't talk now. Some of Le Clere's henchmen are still on the loose. Captain Smith will see you get home.'

He turned to survey the room. Le Clere was already handcuffed. Matthews had been dragged in. But until he saw Le Clere safely to prison he would not feel easy.

'Dan,' he called out, 'take Lady Beauworth home.'

And that was it. Numb, reeling, not sure what to make of what was happening, Eleanor watched him stride coldly away. It was as if what was happening in the room gave him the excuse he needed to pull away, to keep her at a distance.

A moment later, Dan was at her side. 'I have a carriage waiting outside, my lady.'

Eleanor glanced across the room to where Garrick was issuing orders in French.

Not Napoleon's men. Was this the truth, or had Le Clere been right? Was it simply a smokescreen to ensure her compliance? And how did Captain Smith come to be involved?

The captain urged her forwards, supporting her around her shoulders, leading her to the waiting carriage. One of the recent additions to her stables jumped down from the box and opened the door. Now Garrick had accomplished his goal, heard Le Clere's admission of guilt, would he regret being trapped into marriage? He must have known about their child and yet he'd stayed away.

Which would be worse? Finding out he was a traitor, or losing him?

Captain Smith handed her into the coach and gave orders to the driver in a low voice, then he returned to speak to her through the window.

'You are quite safe now, my lady. You will be taken home.'

'But what about Garrick?' She sounded pathetic, she knew she did, but she did not care.

'He will come to you as soon as he can, he gives his word.'

His word. He gives his word. It was all that sustained her on the long drive home.

Chapter Thirteen

The case clock announced five in the morning and Eleanor pulled back the edge of the drawing-room drapes. No word from Garrick. She rubbed her arms, trying to maintain some warmth in her limbs. The fire in the hearth had died long ago.

If he was not a traitor to England, he would have revealed his presence instead of skulking in her stables for weeks on end. Or would he? She still found it hard to believe he would betray his country. Nevertheless, she had sent the scullery maid back to bed when she had come to light the fire just a few minutes ago. She didn't want the servants seeing him and talking.

If he came.

She heard a noise in the entrance hall and ran to see. Garrick was already climbing the stairs. He turned when he heard the drawing-room door open.

He had changed his clothes. His hair was still impossibly short, but the scruffy beard was gone and she had no trouble recognising her husband.

'Ellie, I didn't expect to find you awake.' He spoke

softly and came back down to her, putting his hands on her shoulders.

'You expected me to sleep?' She pushed him away.

'I thought we would talk tomorrow.' A gentle smile curved his lips, his gaze dropping to her stomach. 'You need your rest.'

'Will you be here tomorrow? For months, you let me think you were dead.' Her voice caught in her throat and she swallowed hard. 'I have to know why.'

His expression filled with doubt, then he nodded. He took her hand and led her back into the drawing room.

'It's cold in here,' he said, looking at the empty grate. 'No wonder your hands are like ice.' He sat opposite her and leaned back negligently. 'What would you like to know?'

There it was again, the withdrawal. The feeling he didn't want her involved in his life. 'Everything. Start with tonight.'

He made a sound of disgust. 'Tonight was almost a disaster. I had sworn to bring Le Clere to justice for his part in what he did to you. He admitted it all to the magistrate just now. How he made me believe I killed my mother. How he drained the estate year by year after her death.'

'The man was evil.'

He looked up as if surprised at her vehemence, then returned his gaze to the empty fire.

'I knew Le Clere would never give up, not once he heard you were with child and I was dead. I used you as bait.' He paused, as if expecting a reaction. When she said nothing, he went on.

'I persuaded Dan to get me and my men into this house so I could be close to you.' He chuckled slightly. 'I thought you had recognised me that first day, and I thanked my lucky stars for that evil cough left over from the Dutch prison. I have never seen such a look of disgust as on your face.'

He glowered. 'I almost missed you when you slipped out tonight. We had no idea you'd had contact with him. It must have been during that damnable walk in the park. I couldn't leave the horses.' He looked at her for confirmation and she nodded. 'If I hadn't known that walk of yours, the determined tilt of your chin, I might not have guessed who you were tonight.'

He frowned. 'You risked my child.' He brushed his knuckles down the line of her jaw. 'I would have been at *pointe non plus* right now if you had not stopped under the light.'

Guilt clenched her stomach. He was right. She had risked their child. She hadn't given it a thought. All she could think of was Garrick. She should have known something was wrong. Impetuosity always had been her downfall. 'Thank God you did know it was me.'

His eyebrow flew up.

'But Garrick, Le Clere said you sold secrets to the French. And those men?' The catch in her voice betrayed her efforts to appear calm. 'Who were they?'

'The two men Dan placed here are from my old regiment. Known as "sweeps", they do all of the army's dirty work. Reconnoitring, spying, cleaning up the messes left by the redcoats. The Frenchmen are friends of mine. They followed Le Clere from France and had the inn surrounded before we arrived. I thought I could handle Le Clere alone. They were waiting outside for a signal from me.'

His mouth quirked up in the cynical smile she had realised he used to hide his feelings. 'It was very nearly a bullet in my brain that brought them in on us.'

She couldn't prevent a shudder.

He looked at her as if surprised. 'Would you have cared, *mignonette?*'

'How can you ask? How did you come to be involved with these men? Frenchmen, Garrick.'

He hesitated, his eyes shuttered against her. Her heart sank. What web of lies would he spin?

'*Chérie,*' he answered, soft and low, 'these are not my secrets to tell.'

'I am your wife. If you can't trust me, there is no more to be said.' She started to rise.

'What then, *ma perle*? Will you send me away again?' He sounded bitter.

It was hopeless. She began to move away, but his low voice continued and she sank back down. He was staring at the hearth as if seeing events unfolding in the cold ashes.

'I bought a commission in a regiment after I saw you at Castlefield, as you probably know. The Ninety-Fifth. It's not one of the most glamorous regiments and the work is dangerous. It suited my mood.'

He leaned forwards, elbows on his knees. 'You know what I feared I had done.'

'You are innocent. William has the letter. I'm so sorry.'

'I know. Sissy told Dan and he told me.'

She thought he'd be pleased, but it seemed to make him sadder, more remote as if he was already lost to her. Could she blame him? After all, she had trapped him in a marriage he didn't want. She wanted to reached out, but didn't dare, kept her hands clenched in her lap.

'You saw Le Clere. That blood runs in my veins.' He looked sickened. 'I hoped I would be killed and end the damned curse. Indeed, when I first joined the regiment I cared so little for my own safety, men called me the mad Marquess.' He smiled, but there was no joy in it, just bleak satisfaction.

She shivered.

'I liked army life. The danger kept my mind off other things.'

'What things?' It was foolish to ask, and she couldn't keep the hope out of her voice.

He glanced up. 'You.' It was said so simply, without anger or accusation, that she felt his pain. She forced herself to remain still, much as she wanted to kneel at his feet and beg forgiveness.

Once more he sat silent and gathered his thoughts, staring into the past. Finally, he continued in the same low tone.

'Then the rumours started. I'd ruined a virtuous lady. Beaten a youth to within an inch of his life. They were muttered behind my back, and sometimes hinted at to my face. Slowly, my friends among my brother officers dwindled away. They believed it. No smoke without fire, eh, *chérie*?'

She winced. He would never forgive William for starting those rumours or her for believing them. How could he? If only she'd trusted her heart. 'Go on.'

'During that time my French background came to the attention of a certain man on the general's staff. You will forgive me if I do not give you his name. The fact that I had little care for my own personal safety also suited his plans. Briefly, I was recruited as a spy, but not by the French.' He smiled grimly. 'For England. I was honoured to be chosen. It was, and is, a very important task. But it has some drawbacks.' He laughed softly.

Wishing she could comfort him, Eleanor reached out. He saw her hand, but didn't take it, keeping his gaze fixed on the fireplace as if he couldn't bear to look at her face.

'It was the hardest thing I ever had to do…almost.' He gave her a look of such raw agony, she knew instinctively he was referring to the day he had walked away from Castlefield Hall. Her heart shrank painfully small. She felt his hurt with pain of her own. The pain of regret.

'I sold out. Complained I'd been passed over for promotion.' He shook his head. 'My fellow officers suspected me of more cowardice. All but Dan, poor lad, cut me dead.' This time his smile was warm.

'I became a malcontent. Half-French, bitter at England and highly placed. The perfect material for use by England's enemy. Unfortunately, I was seen in France by a captured English officer. More rumours made the rounds. Not a bad thing as a smokescreen, but if I became a pariah, I would lose my usefulness to the French. We arranged for the Prince of Wales to befriend me—after all, who would speak out against Prinny's closest companion without proof? The French were delighted with the development. The Prince thought it a great joke. Able to move freely in France, I rallied the few remaining loyalists. Some of whom you saw tonight. I still hold the rank of Major in the British army. Not that it will ever be acknowledged.'

That hurt him. She could hear it in his voice. 'Garrick, I—'

He winced and held up his hand, his face stark, his eyes clouded by inner storms. 'As a spy, I had access to many resources, here and abroad. I discovered your brother was the source of the rumours about what I had done to you. It didn't come as a surprise. I was just glad he never let fall your name. For that I would have been forced to take his life.'

The chill determination in his face sent a shiver down her back.

He took a deep breath, as if forcing himself to go on. 'Over the years, I thought about the letter's disappearance.' He laughed, a bitter, self-disparaging sound. 'I'm such a bloody romantic, I thought you'd tried to save my worthless skin by hiding it.'

She should have trusted him as her heart had demanded. Her vision blurred. 'I wish I'd thought of it.' Her voice caught.

He looked up. 'Ellie, don't, please. Let me finish. With Napoleon imprisoned on Elba, I thought the war was over. It was time to put my personal affairs in order.'

'But why were you so set on recovering the letter, if you thought it proved your guilt?'

This was the moment Garrick had feared most. He could not draw back. He had committed to telling her everything.

He hung his head. He'd thought revenge would ease the pain. All it had done was make things worse between him and Ellie.

'I sought you out with the express purpose of finding the letter and accusing your brother of protecting a murderer.' He could not stay his short, hard laugh. 'I would get my punishment, and he'd go to jail. The perfect Le Clere revenge. I knew your brother would accept the blame rather than see you punished.' Bile rose in his throat as he heard himself utter the words. He forced himself to continue.

'Everything William did, he did to protect his

family. But that wasn't good enough for me. I wanted him to suffer because he took you from me, even if it hurt you, too.'

She laid her hand on his. He stared at her small bandaged fingers resting on his large tanned hand. He had almost been the cause of her death tonight, her and the babe. Only her courage and wit had saved the day.

He put a hand on top of hers, encasing the cold, icy skin. Thank God she didn't pull away in disgust. Somehow feeling her hand beneath his gave him the courage to go on. He smoothed it gently.

'I even went so far as to involve your sister, pretending I would ruin her, to lure you in. I used you. When you agreed to marry me, I couldn't believe it.' He closed his eyes and shook his head. 'It was hell on earth. I had my orders. I had to be back in France the next day. Yet I couldn't resist. It was all I ever wanted. You. A family...' His voice broke. 'I never meant to give you a child. Before I met you, I intended never to marry. To never pass on the Le Clere curse. You trusted me and I let you down.' A lump in his throat made further speech impossible.

The truth lay between them, ugly and raw. Now she knew he was just as bad as Le Clere. Worse. She knew he'd planned her beloved twin's downfall.

She didn't move or speak, just stared at him with her grey eyes huge in her pale oval face. The face he saw every night in his dreams.

'I'm sorry,' he said softly. 'I'll not force you to stay with me. I am not fit for human company. All I ask is a role with our child. That somehow we find a way not to destroy another life with bitterness and hate.'

He could not look at her. He heard her get up. She would leave now. He would not beg her to stay. He'd begged once before and she had sent him away. And rightly so. It was for the best.

The silence between them seemed endless.

The rustle of silks as she knelt beside him whispered of hope. 'I don't believe in curses.'

Ah, Ellie—even now she would try to take his part. He could not let her be fooled. '*Chérie,* the Le Clere tempers are legendary, it shows up in history books.'

Ellie couldn't bear the sorrow-edged guilt in his voice, the defeated slump of his shoulders. 'Name one person you have hurt in a rage. Yes, you have a temper. But so do I. And like everyone else you control it.'

He lifted his gaze to her face, his eyes wide. 'Don't be blind, Ellie. Look what Le Clere did to your older brother, to my mother. Looked what I planned for your brother.'

'Le Clere is a bad man. But he did nothing in a rage. He planned it. All of it. And he made you, a small boy, believe you were evil.' She shook her head. 'You had every right to be angry at William, but you never followed through with your plans. Think back, Garrick. Even when you had me at your mercy, when you discovered I was Lady Moonlight, you were furious. But you did nothing but help me. You were kind to me.'

'That was different, *chérie.* I had other plans for you.'

The words struck a chord low in her belly and with it came flutters of desire, sparks of heat. She thought she might go up in flames. She fought to keep her voice full of reason, not passion. 'People get angry and they do exactly what you do. They control it.'

The crease between his brows deepened. 'Not always. I once came very close to murdering a man.' His fists clenched. 'I don't know what would have happened if I hadn't been stopped. It was what decided me to join the army.'

The starkness in his expression cut her to the quick. She had the feeling that if she showed the slightest doubt, he would leave, that she would never see him again. She had never feared him. Not for one moment. 'Tell me what happened.'

His lips thinned. 'I caught him beating a child. I lost all reason and attacked in a blind rage.'

'This man, he was a scrawny fellow, begging for mercy while you attacked him, I suppose.'

'God, no. He was a bruiser. Could have killed the boy with one blow. It took two fellows to hold him down after Harry pulled me off.'

'Fisticuffs, then, between two equals. It sounds as if he deserved a taste of his own medicine. And yet you didn't kill him.'

'Don't make light of it, Ellie. What if I hurt you? Or our child? How can I know for certain? You are better off without me.'

Her heart gave a little leap. Was this the reason for his withdrawal? Not his anger at being forced into marriage?

'I know,' she said firmly. She put a hand under his chin, drew his gaze up to meet hers. 'I know you. I trust you.'

A smile dawned slowly. A smile full of hope as well as love. A smile that made her stomach tumble and her heart leap. 'So, you are willing to take a chance on me?'

'Of course.' She put her heart and her soul into the words. 'I love you.'

He leaned forwards and nibbled her neck. 'Are you sure?'

The flutters tightened into yearning and arousal.

'Absolutely certain.' She punched his shoulder. 'Take me to bed.'

'Ouch!' He leapt up. 'No more of this abuse, beloved. And no more sitting in this freezing room. You have a child to consider. My child.' The pride in his voice, and the joy in his face, sent a sweet pang to her heart.

He gazed into her eyes. 'I know a place where you and I could be warm together. Will you come with me, my one and only love?' He held out his hand and stood, hesitant, waiting for her reply.

Eleanor's eyes misted. His love. At last he had called her his love.

'Oh, Garrick. If only I had said yes, instead of sending you away, none of this would have happened.' She blinked and swallowed the sob that threatened to choke her. 'I was a coward. Afraid of making another mistake.'

He reached out and touched her cheek, catching, with his finger, one of the wayward tears. 'You are the most courageous woman I know.'

So many things had got in the way of their love, her pride as well as his, but even as that regretful thought saddened her, a new enlightenment followed.

He would never be the wicked careless young man she had fallen for that summer so long ago, but it was this man, this battle-weary, hard man who now had the courage to bare his heart whom she loved. He was her own true love and the man she and her child needed, and in this man she was truly blessed.

She opened her arms. 'Oh, Garrick, I love you so much, I always have. When I thought you were dead, if it hadn't been for the child I would have died, too.'

'Thank God for that, then,' he said hoarsely. 'Come with me, Ellie, wherever life takes us from this day forth.' He enfolded her in his arms.

'Yes, my love,' she whispered against his lips.

He crushed her to him and kissed her mouth, the beat of his heart a rapid tattoo against her ribs. She melted against him and heard his deep sigh of relief as he picked her up and started for the staircase.

'Welcome home, my wicked Marquess,' she whispered.

* * * * *

The Gamekeeper's Lady

ANN LETHBRIDGE

This book is dedicated to my husband,
and my hero, Keith.

Chapter One

London—1816

Lord Robert Deveril Mountford propped himself up on his elbow in his bed. He brushed aside Maggie, Lady Caldwell's waterfall of chestnut curls and kissed her creamy shoulder. 'Two weeks from now?'

Dark eyes sparkling, she cast him a dazzling smile. 'Evil one. Can't you fit me in any sooner?'

'Sorry. I'm going out of town for a few days. Hunting.'

'Furred, feathered or female?' She stood up, slipped her chemise over her head and reached for her stays.

He slapped her plump little bottom. 'Whatever comes along, naturally.' Pleasantly sated, he yawned and stretched.

Maggie sighed. 'It is time you settled down, you know.'

Robert tensed. 'Not you, too.' He leaned across to lace her stays, then pulled the silky stockings off the blue canopy over the bed and tossed them at her.

She sat to pull them over her shapely legs. 'Why not? There are all kinds of nice young things available. Take my niece. She has a reasonable dowry and her family is good quality.'

A sense of foreboding gathered like a snowball rolling downhill, larger and colder with each passing moment. It wasn't the first time one of his women had tried to inveigle herself or a member of her family into the ducal tribe, but he hadn't expected it from this one. He had thought he and Maggie were having too much fun to let familial obligations intrude.

He didn't want a wife cramping his lifestyle, even if the ducal allowance provided enough for two, which it didn't.

Dress on, Maggie went to the mirror and patted her unruly curls. 'Just look at this mess. Caldwell will never believe I was at Lady Jeffries's for tea.' She gathered the scattered pins from the floor and tried to bring some order to her tresses.

Naked, he rose to his feet and stood behind her. Her eyes widened in the glass, the heat of desire returning.

He picked up the hairbrush, all at once disturbingly anxious for her to be gone. 'Let me.' With a few firm strokes, he tamed the luxuriant brown mane, twisted it into a neat knot at the back of her head, pinned it and teased out a few curls around her face. 'Will that do?'

A lovely lush woman still in her prime and wasted on her old husband, she turned and laughed up at him. 'My maid doesn't arrange it half as well. If you ever need a position as a lady's maid, I will be pleased to provide a recommendation.'

He gazed at her beautiful face, then brushed her lips with his mouth. 'Thank you. For everything.'

He liked Maggie. Too bad she had to bring up the subject of marriage. He bent to retrieve her shoes and she sat on the stool. As he put them on her small feet, he caressed her calf one last time. A faint sense of regret washed through him. Too faint.

She sighed and ran her fingers through his hair.

The clock in the hall struck four.

'Oh, botheration,' she said, jumping to her feet. She took another quick peek in the glass. 'I think I will pass muster.' Her trill of laughter rang around the room.

He stood up with a wry smile. Maggie always maintained such good spirits. She never indulged in tantrums or fits of jealousy about his other women. She'd been the perfect liaison. Until now.

He'd send a token tomorrow, a discreet little diamond pin with a carefully worded message. No fool, Maggie. She'd understand.

She reached up and cupped his cheek with her palm. 'One of these days some beautiful young thing is going to capture that wicked heart of yours and you'll be lost to me and all the other naughty ladies of the *ton*, mark my words.'

Too bad she couldn't leave well enough alone. He caught her fingers and pressed them to his lips. 'What? Be tied to just one woman when there are so many to enjoy?'

'You are a bad man,' she said. 'And I adore you.'

She whirled around in a rustle of skirts, a cloud of rose perfume and sex. She opened the door and dashed down the stairs to her waiting carriage.

Yes, Robert thought, he would miss her a great deal. Now whom did he have waiting in the wings to fill his Tuesday afternoons? A knotty, but interesting problem. The new opera dancer at Covent Garden had thrown him a lure last week. A curvy little armful with come-hither eyes. And yet, somehow, the thought of the chase didn't stir his blood.

It wouldn't be much of a chase. Perhaps he should look around a little more. Looking was half the fun.

He whistled under his breath as he readied himself for an evening at White's.

Kent—1816

It was almost perfect. Wasn't it? She just wished she could be sure. In the library's rapidly fading daylight, Frederica Bracewell narrowed her eyes and compared her second drawing of a sparrow to the one in the book. The first one she'd attempted was awful. A five-year-old would have done better. Drawn with her right hand. She sighed. It didn't matter how hard she tried, right-handed she was hopeless.

Devil's spawn. An echo of Cook's harsh voice hissed in her ear. Good-for-naught bastard. She rubbed her chilled hands together and held the second drawing up to the light. It was the best thing she'd done. But was it good enough?

The door opened behind her. She jumped to her feet. Heat rushed to her hairline. Heart beating hard, she turned, hiding the drawings with her body.

'Only me, miss,' Snively, the Wynchwood butler, said. A big man, with a shock of white hair and a fierce bulldog face, but his brown eyes twinkled as he carried a taper carefully across the room and lit the wall sconces.

Her heart settled back into a comfortable rhythm.

'I didn't realise you were working in here this afternoon or I would have had William light the fire,' the butler said.

'I'm not c-c-cold,' she said, smiling at one of her few allies at Wynchwood. She didn't want him losing his position by lighting unnecessary fires.

She picked up her rag with a wince. She'd completed

very little of her assigned task: dusting the books. Uncle Mortimer would not be pleased.

In passing, Snively glanced at the pictures on the table. 'This one is good,' he said, pointing at the second one. 'It looks ready to fly away. People pay for pictures like that.'

'Do you think so?'

'I do.' Snively's face hardened. 'You ought to have proper lessons instead of copying from books. You've a talent.'

Always so supportive. Sometimes she imagined the starchy butler was her father. It might have been better if he was. Who knew what kind of low man the Wynchwood Whore had bedded.

'It is not s-seemly for a woman to d-draw for money,' she said quietly, 'but I would love to go to Italy and see the great art of Europe. Perhaps even s-study with a drawing teacher.'

His mouth became a thin straight line. 'So you should.'

'Lord Wynchwood would never hear of it. It would be far too expensive.'

Snively frowned. 'If you'll excuse me saying so the wages you've saved his lordship by serving as housekeeper these past many years would pay for a dozen trips to Italy.'

'Only my uncle's generosity keeps me here, Mr Snively. He could just as easily have left me at the workhouse.'

He glowered. 'Your turn will come, miss. You mark my words. It will.'

She'd never heard the butler so vehement. She glanced over her shoulder at the door. 'I beg you not to say anything to my uncle about these.' She gestured at the drawings.

'I wouldn't dream of it, miss. You keep it up. One day your talent will be recognised. I can promise it.'

She smiled. 'You are such a d-dear man.'

The library door slammed back.

Frederica jumped. Her heart leaped into her throat. 'Uncle M-M-Mortimer.' The words came out in a horrible rush.

The imperturbable Snively slid the book over her drawings and turned around with his usual hauteur. 'Good evening, Lord Wynchwood.'

Uncle Mortimer, his wig awry on his head, his cheeks puce, marched in. 'Nothing better to do than pass the time with servants, Frederica? Next you'll be hobnobbing with the stable boy, the way your mother did.'

Beside her Snively drew himself up straighter.

She trembled. She hated arguments. 'N-n-n—'

'No?' the old man snapped. 'Then Snively is a figment of my imagination, is he?'

'My lord,' Snively said in outraged accents, 'I was lighting the candles, as I always do at this time. I found Miss Bracewell dusting the books and stopped to help.'

'I'm not chastising you, Snively. My niece is the one I need to keep in check.' Frederica wasn't surprised at her uncle's about face. A butler of Snively's calibre was hard to come by these days.

'S-s-s—' she started.

'Sorry? You are always sorry. It is not good enough.' He frowned. 'Didn't you hear me ringing?'

She took a quick breath. 'N-no, Uncle. You asked me to d-d-dust the books in here. I d-d-did not hear your bell.'

'Well, listen better, gel. I've some receipts to be copied into the account book. I want them all finished by supper time.'

Frederica hid her shudder. Hours of copying numbers into columns and rows. Trying to make them neat and tidy while not permitted to use anything but her right hand. Her shoulders slumped. 'Yes, Uncle.'

'Come along. Come along, don't dilly dally. It is cold in

here. My lungs cannot stand the chill. Snively, send word to Cook to send tea to my study.'

Snively bowed. 'Don't worry, miss, I'll return everything to its proper place.

He meant he'd put her drawings in her room. If Mortimer found she'd been wasting her time drawing, he'd probably lock her in her chamber for a week. Which might not be so bad, she reflected as she hurried out of the room. She threw the butler a conspiratorial smile.

Without Snively and her impossible dream of travelling to Italy and learning from a real artist, her life would be truly unbearable.

Refreshed and relaxed after his afternoon with Maggie, Robert strolled through the front door of White's and handed his coat and hat to the porter. 'Lord Radthorn here yet, O'Malley?'

The beefy red-haired man blinked owlishly. 'No, Lord Tonbridge.'

Robert didn't bother to correct the fool. It never did any good. Only close family, friends and the odd woman could ever tell him and Charlie apart.

He took the stairs up to the great subscription room two at a time. The dark-panelled room buzzed with conversation and laughter despite the youth of the evening.

A group of gentlemen crowded around a faro table, the game in full swing. Guineas and vowels were heaped at the banker's elbow—Viscount Lullington, a fair-haired Englishman with thin aristocratic features whom many of the ladies adored. He had a Midas touch with gambling and women. Only Robert had ever bested him on either count—something that did not please the dandified viscount. But that wasn't the reason for the bad blood between them. It went a whole lot deeper. As deep as a sword blade.

The one Robert had put through his arm dueling for the favours of a woman. Robert glanced around the panelled room. No sign of Radthorn amongst the crowd, but a glance at his fob watch revealed he'd arrived a few minutes earlier than their appointed time. He drifted towards the faro table.

'Who is in the soup?' he asked Colonel Whittaker as he took in the play.

'Some protégé of Lullington's,' Wittaker muttered without turning. 'The young fool just bet his curricle and team.'

Lullington smoothed his dark blond hair back from his high forehead, his intense blue gaze sweeping the players at the table. A clever man, Lullington, his fashionable air a draw for unwary young men with too much money in their pockets.

Too bad the man had chosen tonight to play here.

As if sensing Robert's scrutiny, Lullington glanced up and their gazes locked. His lip curled. Slowly, he laid his cards face down on the green baize table.

'Mountford?' Lullington never confused him with his twin. 'How did you get into a gentleman's club?' he lisped.

Robert recoiled. 'What did you say?'

The viscount's lids lowered a fraction. He shook his head. 'You never did have a scrap of honour.'

All conversation ceased.

The hairs on the back of Robert's neck rose. Fury coursed through his veins. He lunged forwards. 'You'll meet me on Primrose Hill in the morning for that slur. Name your seconds.'

The young sprig to Lullington's right stared opened mouthed.

'Gad, the cur speaks. Does it think because it is sired by a duke, it can mix with gentlemen?'

An odd rumble of agreement ran around the room.

Robert felt as if he'd been kicked in the chest. 'What the deuce are you talking about?'

Lullington's lip lifted in a sneer. 'Unlike you, I would never sully a lady's reputation in public.'

Robert felt heat travel up the back of his neck. So that's what this was all about. Lullington's cousin, the little bitch. He should have guessed the clever viscount would use the incident to his advantage. 'The woman you speak of is no lady,' he said scornfully. 'As you well know.'

'Dishonourable bastard,' Wittaker said, turning his back.

'No,' Lullington said softly, triumph filling his voice. 'Mountford is right not to bandy the lady's name around in this club. Mountford, I find the colour of your waistcoat objectionable. Please remove it from our presence at once. None of us wants to see it here again.'

One by one each man near Robert turned, until Robert stood alone, an island in a sea of bent backs. Some of these men were his friends. He'd gone to school with them, drunk and gambled with them, whored with them, and not a single one of them would meet his eye.

One or two of them were the husbands of unfaithful wives. The triumph in their eyes as they turned away told its own story.

Good God! They'd decided to send him to Coventry, because he'd refused to marry a scheming little bitch.

The only man who remained looking his way was Lullington, who lifted his quizzing glass as if he had spotted a fly on rotten meat.

'It is a lie and you know it,' Robert said.

'Cheeky bastard,' Pettigrew said.

'Oh, it's cheeky all right.' Lullington's lisp seemed more pronounced than usual. He gave a mocking laugh like splintering glass. 'It remains. Pettigrew, will you have O'Malley throw this rubbish out, or shall I?'

One of the men—Pettigrew, Robert assumed—left the room, no doubt to do the viscount's bidding. Robert stood his ground, forced reason into his tone. 'I didn't touch the girl.' Damn. If he said any more, he'd be playing right into Lullington's hands.

Ambleforth, round and red about the gills, a man Robert had known at Eton, shuffled closer. He caught sight of Lullington's glass swivelling towards him and stopped, shaking his head. ''Fore God, Mountford,' he uttered in hoarse tones. 'Go, before you make it any worse.'

Worse. Heat flooded his body, sweat trickled down his back. How could this nightmare be worse? Lullington had turned every man in the room against him for a crime he hadn't committed. The girl had brought it on herself.

'If you'll just step outside, my lord?' O'Malley grasped his elbow. 'We don't want no unpleasantness, now does we?'

Robert yanked his arm away. 'Take your greasy paws off me.' He swung around to leave.

'Thank God,' Lullington said into the heavy silence. 'The air in here was becoming quite foul. Did you hear gall of the fellow? Actually had the nerve to challenge me. I wouldn't let him lick my boots.'

A ripple of uncomfortable laughter followed Robert down the stairs. He clamped his jaw shut hard. He wanted to ram his fist through Lullington's sneering mouth, or bury his sword, hilt deep, in the man's chest.

He certainly wasn't going to marry Lullington's scheming little cousin to please them. Charlie was the only one with the power to get him out of this predicament.

He snatched his hat from O'Malley and stormed out onto the street, almost colliding with someone on the way in. He opened his mouth to apologise, then realized it was Radthorn. He reached out and pressed a hand on his friend's shoulder. 'John, thank God.'

'Mountford?' Embarrassment flashed across John's handsome face. 'You're here?'

What the devil? 'We had an appointment, remember?' Robert dropped his hand. Had John joined the rest of them in sending him to Coventry? It certainly seemed so.

'Damn you,' he said. The curse made him feel only marginally better as he barrelled up St James's Street.

Charlie was his only hope, because the duke had long ago washed his hands of his dissolute second son.

Mountford House was no different from all the other narrowly sedate houses on Grosvenor Square. A spinster on a picnic couldn't be more externally discreet and so seething with internal passions. These days Robert only visited the Mountford London abode in Father's absence. He might not have visited then, if it weren't for Mother. He certainly didn't visit Charlie who grew more like Father every day, only interested in his estates and the title and the name.

The door swung open. Robert ignored the butler's hand outstretched for his hat and coat. 'Is Tonbridge home?'

'Yes, Lord Robert. In his room.'

'Thank you, Grimshaw.'

He took the stairs two at a time and barged into Charlie's chamber. A room with all the pomp and circumstance required for the heir to a dukedom, it was large enough to hold a small ball. The ducal coat of arms emblazoned the scarlet drapery and every piece of furniture. It always struck Robert as regally oppressive. Charlie took it as his due.

Charlie, Charles Henry Beltane Mountford, named for Kings and Princes, the Marquis of Tonbridge and the next Duke of Stantford, neatly dressed, his cravat pristine, his jacket without a crease, sat at his desk, writing.

He looked up when Robert closed the door. 'I've been expecting you,' he said coolly.

Robert rocked back on his heels. 'You knew? You bastard. Why the hell didn't you give me some warning?'

Charlie's mouth flattened. 'I sent word to your lodging. My man missed you.'

Robert ran a glance over his older brother. It was like looking into a distorted mirror. He saw his own brown eyes and dark brown hair, his square-jawed face and the cleft in the chin that made shaving a chore. He saw his own body, tall and lean, with long legs and large hands and feet, but he hated the rest of what he saw. The weary eyes. The lines around his mouth. He looked like their father.

He looked like a man who had given up the joy of life for duty and honour.

'I need a loan so I can pay the girl off. With enough of a dowry, she'll soon find a husband willing to hold his nose and that will be an end to it.'

Charlie tipped his head back and squeezed his eyes shut for a second. 'I'm sorry, Robin. I don't have that kind of money.'

'Ask Father for a loan. He never refuses you anything.'

'It's all over town. Do you think he won't know why I'm asking for such a large sum?'

'Tell him it's a gambling debt.'

Charlie shook his head. 'You play, you pay. You know the rules. It's time you settled down, anyway. Take some responsibility. Father will think the better of you for it.'

Robert clenched his fists at his side in an effort not to smash his fist in Charlie's face. He took a deep breath.

'What the hell, Charlie—do you think I'm going to marry a girl who was prepared to sacrifice her reputation for the chance of becoming a duchess? I did you a favour.'

Charlie's gaze hardened. 'Don't bother. I don't need your kind of favours.'

'What if it had been you she'd lured into the library? Would you have married her, knowing she trapped you?'

Charlie curled his lip. 'Come on, Robin, we both know there isn't a female alive who can lure you if you don't want to go. But if it had been me, I would have offered for her immediately. It would be my duty to the family name.'

Robert swallowed the bile rising in his throat. 'I won't be blackmailed into wedding a scheming little baggage.'

'Marriage wouldn't hurt you one bit.'

A sick feeling roiled around in Robert's gut. 'I'm not getting married to a woman who wanted my brother.'

Charlie looked at him coldly over the rim of his brandy glass. 'Then you shouldn't have kissed her.'

'Damn it.' Robert felt like howling. 'She kissed me.'

'You've been going to hell for years. Marriage will do you good. It will please Father.'

Robert's gaze narrowed. He suddenly saw it all. The glimmer of regret in Charlie's eyes gave him away. 'You have already discussed this with Father. This is a common front, isn't it?' He balled his fists. 'I ought to beat you to a pulp. How dare you and Father play with my life?'

Charlie's mouth tightened. 'No, Robert. You did this all by yourself. Even though I agree with you, it was her bloody fault, you ought to offer for the girl or you'll leave great blot on the family name.'

'That's all you bloody well care about these days.'

'It's my job.'

They used to be friends. Now they were worse than

strangers. Because Charlie disapproved of everything Robert did.

Robert stared at his older brother. Older by five minutes. Three hundred seconds that gave Charlie everything and left Robert with a small monthly allowance courtesy of his father. And because he'd thought to do his brother a favour, thought it might restore their old easy fun-loving companionship, he'd been cast adrift on a sea of the last thing he wanted: matrimony.

Hot fury roiled in his gut, spurted through his veins, ran in molten rivers until his vision blazed red. 'No. I won't do it. Not for Father and not for you. She made her bed, let her lie on it.'

'Don't be a fool. Lullington won't forget this. You'll never be able to show your face in town again.'

'I'm a Mountford. With Father's support...'

Charlie shook his head. 'He's furious.'

Bloody hell. Cast out from society, perhaps for all time? It wouldn't be the first time the *ton* had discarded one of their own. Robert felt sick. 'He'll come around. He has to. Mother will make him see reason.'

'Never at a loss, are you, Robin?' Charlie frowned. 'But I won't have you upsetting our mother. I'll talk to Father. Convince him somehow. It's going to cost a lot of money and if I do this you have to swear to mend your ways.'

Ice filled Robert's veins. He wanted to smack the disapproving look off his brother's face. 'What makes you a saint?'

Charlie gave him a pained look. 'I'm not.'

'I don't suppose you could lend me a pony until quarter day. I've some debts pressing.' Inwardly, he groaned. At least one of which was Lullington's. Not to mention a diamond pin to present to Maggie.

'Damn it, Robert.' He got up and went to a chest in the

corner. He unlocked it and pulled out a leather purse. 'Fifty guineas. If that's not enough I can give you a draft for up to a thousand. But that's all.'

'A thousand?' Robert whistled. 'You really are dibs in tune.'

'I don't have time to spend it.' He looked weary, weighed down. Robert didn't envy him his position of heir one little bit.

Sure his problems were solved, Robert grinned. 'You need a holiday from all this.' He waved a hand at the cluttered desk. 'Want to exchange places again?'

'You will not,' a voice thundered. 'And nor will you give him any money.'

Father. Robert whipped his head around. The brown-eyed silver-haired gentleman framed in the doorway in sartorial splendour glared as Robert rose to his feet. Rigid with anger and pride, Alfred, his Grace the Duke of Stantford, locked his gaze on Charlie. 'He has brought dishonour to our name. He is no longer welcome in my house.'

Robert felt the blood drain from his face, from his whole body. He couldn't draw breath as the words echoed in his head. While he and Father didn't always see eye to eye, he'd never expected this.

Charlie's eyes widened. 'Father, it is not entirely Robert's fault.'

Mealy-mouthed support at best, but then that was Charlie these days. 'The woman—'

'Enough,' Father roared. 'I heard you. You are not satisfied with being a parasite on this family, a dissolute wastrel and a libertine. No. It's not enough that you drag our name through the mud. You want your brother's title.'

The taste of ashes filled Robert's mouth. 'Your Grace, no,' he choked out, 'it was a jest.'

Stantford's lip curled, but beneath the bluster he seemed

to age from sixty to a hundred in the space a heartbeat. In his eyes, Robert saw fear.

'You think I don't know what you are about?' the old man whispered. 'An identical brother? I always knew you'd be trouble. You almost succeeded in getting him killed once, but I won't let it happen again.'

Nausea rolled in Robert's gut. The room spun as pain seared his heart. 'I would never harm my brother.'

'Father,' Charlie said. 'I wanted to join the army. I convinced Robert to take my place.'

The duke's lip curled. 'I expected he needed a lot of convincing.'

'No, I didn't,' Robert said. 'I thought it was a great lark. How would I know what a mess Waterloo would be? Napoleon was a defeated general.'

They'd all thought that and Charlie, desperate to join the army from the time he could talk, saw it as a chance to fulfil his dream despite Father's refusal.

Robert had avoided the family while he played at being Charlie for weeks before Waterloo. Had a grand old time. Until he'd felt Charlie's physical pain in his own body. He'd known something was wrong. But when the lists came out announcing Robert Mountford's death and the family started to grieve, they thought he'd gone mad. He'd insisted on going to the site of the battle. When he finally found Charlie, one of the many robbed of his clothes and out of his head in a fever, the truth had to come out. After that, Father had refused to have anything to do with Robert. Until today.

'You are not my son,' the duke said.

Charlie stared at Father. 'No,' he whispered. 'You are going too far. I won't let you do this. Robert will marry the girl. Won't you?'

Reeling, Robert almost said yes. His spine stiffened. He would not be blackmailed, forced into a mould by his father or anyone else, especially not Miss Penelope Frisken. 'No. I did not seduce her and I won't accept the blame.'

'You idiot,' Charlie hissed.

'I want that cur out of my house,' the duke commanded. 'I won't see the name of Mountford blackened any further by this wastrel. He'll sponge on me no longer.'

Sponge. Was that how he saw it? Without his allowance, he wouldn't be able to pay his debts. Any of them. He had debts of honour due on quarter day, as well as several tradesmen expecting their due. He'd gone a little deeper than he should have this month, but then he'd expected to come about. And there was always his allowance.

'You can't do this.'

His father glared. 'Watch me.'

A horrid suspicion crept into his mind. Was this Lullington's plan all along? He was clever enough. Devious enough.

How else had the information about what had happened at White's reached the duke so quickly? Now Father had the perfect opportunity to be rid of the cuckoo in his nest.

He'd always been inclined to laugh off matters others thought important, but when Charlie had almost died on the battlefield at Waterloo, he knew he should have thought it out a bit more carefully. He never expected this as the end result, though, and he wasn't going to beg forgiveness for something he hadn't done.

His stomach churned. He gulped down his bile and drew himself up straight. His face impassive, he stared at his rigid father. 'As you wish, your Grace. You will never have to set eyes on me again, but first I would like a few minutes alone with Lord Tonbridge.'

The duke didn't glance in Robert's direction, addressing himself only to Charlie. 'There's nothing for him here. No one is giving him money. I mean that, Tonbridge. Tell him to be out of my house in five minutes or I will have him horsewhipped.' He wheeled around and shut the door behind him.

Charlie fixed his tortured gaze on Robert's face. 'I'll talk to him. I had no idea his anger went so deep.'

Robert tried to smile. 'If you try to defend me, it will only make things worse. He's suspicious enough. He'll think I have some hold on you. Don't worry about me. I'll manage.'

'How?'

'I'll find work.'

At that Charlie cracked a painful laugh. 'What will you do? Find a woman to employ your services in bed?'

Robert's hand curled into a fist. He smiled, though it made his cheeks ache. 'Well now, there is an idea. Any thoughts of who? Your betrothed, perhaps?'

Colour stained Charlie's cheekbones. 'Damn it, Robert, I was joking.'

'Not funny.' Because it came too close to the truth. He'd prided himself on those skills. Bragged of them. He stared down at the monogrammed carpet and then back up into his brother's face. 'You don't think I planned to take the title?'

'Of course not,' Charlie said, his voice thick, 'but damn it. I should never have gone.'

'I'd better be off.' Robert straightened his shoulders.

Charlie held out the bag of guineas. 'Take this, you'll need it.'

Pride stiffened his shoulders. 'No. I'll do this without any help. And when the creditors come to call, tell them they'll have their money in due course.'

Charlie gave him a diffident smile. 'Stay in touch. I'll let you know when it is safe to return. I'll pay off the girl. Find her a husband.'

Even as Charlie spoke Robert realized the truth. 'Nothing you can do will satisfy Lullington and his cronies. I'm done for here. Father is right. My leaving is the only way to save the family honour.' A lump formed in his throat, making his voice stupidly husky. 'Take care of yourself, brother. And take care of Mama and the children.'

An expression of panic entered Charlie's eyes, gone before Robert could be sure. 'I don't want you to go.'

Puzzled, Robert stared at him. Charlie had always been the confident one. Never wanting any help from Robert. In fact, since Waterloo, he'd grown ever more distant.

Wishful thinking. It was the sort of pro-forma thing family members said on parting. He grinned. 'I'd better go before the grooms arrived with the whips.' Just saying it made his skin crawl.

Charlie looked sick. 'He wouldn't. He's angry, but I'm sure he will change his mind after reflection.'

They both knew their father well enough to know he was incapable of mind-changing.

Robert clapped his brother on the shoulder. The lump seemed to swell. He swallowed hard. 'Charlie, try to have a bit more fun. You don't want to end up like Father.'

Charlie looked at him blankly.

Robert let go a shaky breath. He'd tried. 'When I'm settled, I'll drop you a note,' he said thickly, his chest full, his eyes ridiculously misted.

He strode for the door and hurtled down the stairs, before he cried like a baby.

Out on the street, he looked back at a house now closed to him for ever. Father had always acted as if he wished Robert had never been born. Now he'd found a way to make it true.

He turned away. One foot planted in front of the other on the flagstones he barely saw, heading for the Albany. Each indrawn breath burned the back of his throat. He felt like a boy again pushed aside in favour of his brother. Well, he was a boy no longer. He was his own man, with nothing but the clothes on his back. Without an income from the estate, he couldn't even afford his lodgings.

All these years, he'd taken his position for granted, never saved, never invested. He'd simply lived life to the full. Now it seemed the piper had to be paid or the birds had come home to roost, whichever appropriate homily applied. What the hell was he to do? How would he pay his debts?

Ask Maggie for help? Charlie's question roared in his ear. No. He would not be a kept man. The thought of servicing any woman for money made him shudder. If he did that he might just as well marry Penelope. And he might have, if she hadn't been so horrified when she realised he wasn't Charlie.

Father would scratch his name out of the family annals altogether if he turned into a cicisbeo. A kept man.

It would be like dying, only worse because it would be as if he never existed. The thought brought him close to shattering in a thousand pieces on the pavement. The green iron railings at his side became a lifeline in a world pitching like a dinghy in a storm. He clutched at it blindly. The metal bit cold into his palm. He stared at his bare hand. Where the hell had he left his gloves?

Gloves? Who the hell cared about gloves? He started to laugh, throwing back his head and letting tears of mirth run down his face.

An old gentleman with a cane walking towards him swerved aside and crossed the street at a run.

Hilarity subsided and despair washed over him at the speed of a tidal bore. He'd never felt so alone in his life.

God damn it. He would not lie down meekly.

He didn't need a dukedom to make a success of his life.

Chapter Two

Kent—1819

She wouldn't. She couldn't.

The words beat time to Frederica's heartbeat. Pippin's hooves picked up the rhythm and pounded it into hard-packed earth. The trees at the edge of her vision flung it back.

The damp earthy smell of leaf mould filled her nostrils. Usually, she loved the dark scent. It spoke of winter and frost and warm fires. Today it smelled of decay.

She couldn't. She wouldn't.

She would not wed Simon the slug. Not if her uncle begged her for the next ten years.

The ground softened as they rode through a clearing. Pippin's flying hooves threw clods of mud against the walls of a dilapidated cottage hunched in the lee of the trees until a tunnel of low-hanging hazels on the other side seemed to swallow them whole. Frederica slowed Pippin to a walk, fearful of tree roots.

At the river bank, she drew the horse up. Her secret place. The one spot on the Wynchwood estate where she could be assured of peace and quiet and the freedom to think. A narrow stretch of soft green moss curled over the bank where the River Wynch carved a perfect arc in black loam. The trees on both sides of the water hugged close.

Barely ankle deep in summer, the winter flood rushed angrily a few inches below the bank, swirling and twisting around the deep pool in the crook of its elbow. Downstream, beyond Wynchwood Place's ornamental lake, the river widened and turned listless, but here it ran fast, its tempo matching her mood.

Breathless, cheeks stinging from the wind, she dismounted. Pippin dipped his head to slake his thirst. Satisfied he was content to nibble on the sedges at the water's edge, she let his reins dangle and strolled a short way upstream. She stared into the ripples and swoops of impatient water, seeking answers.

No one could force her to wed Simon. Could they?

The casual mention of the plan by her uncle at breakfast had left her dumbfounded. And dumb. And by the time she had regained the use of her tongue, Uncle Mortimer had locked himself in his study.

Did Simon know of this new turn of events? He'd never liked her. Barely could bring himself to speak to her when they did meet. It had to be a hum. Some bee in Uncle's bonnet. Didn't it?

If it wasn't, they'd have to tie her in chains, hand and foot, blindfold her, gag her and even then she would never agree to marry her bacon-brained cousin.

A small green frog, its froggy legs scissor-kicking against the current, aimed for the overhanging bank beneath her feet. She leaned over to watch it land.

'What the devil do you think you are doing?'

The deep voice jolted through her. Her foot slipped. She was going—

Large hands caught her arms, lifted her, swung her around and set her on her feet.

Heart racing, mouth dry, she spun about, coming face to face with a broad, naked chest, the bronzed skin covered in dark crisp curls and banded by sculpted muscle.

The breath rushed from her lungs. Swallowing hard, she backed up a couple of steps and took in the dark savage gipsy of a man with hands on lean hips watching her from dark narrowed eyes. Hair the colour of burnt umber, shaded with streaks of ochre, fell to a pair of brawny shoulders. His hard slash of a mouth in his angular square-jawed face looked as if it had tasted of the world and found it bitter.

Fierce. Wild. Masculine. Intimidating. All these words shot through her mind.

And frighteningly handsome.

A tall rough-looking man, with the body of a Greek god and the face of a fallen angel.

Heat spread out from her belly. Desire.

A shiver ran down her spine. Her heart hammered. Her tongue felt huge and unwieldy. 'Wh-who are you?' Damn her stutter.

Arrogant, controlled and powerful, he folded strong bare forearms over his lovely wide chest. He looked her up and down, assessing, without a flicker of a muscle in his impassive face. A dark questioning eyebrow went up. 'I might ask the same of you,' he said, his voice a deep low growl she felt low in her stomach.

She clutched at the skirts of her old brown gown to hide the tremble in her hands and inhaled a deep breath. Every fibre of her being concentrated on speaking her next words without hesitation, without showing weakness. 'I am Lord Wynchwood's niece. I have every right to be here.' Panting with effort, she released the remainder of her breath.

He took a step towards her. Instinctively, she shrank

back. He halted, palms held out. 'For God's sake, you'll end up in the river.'

The exasperation in his tone and expression did more to ease her fears than soft words would have done. She glared at him. 'Of c-course I w-won't.'

He backed up several paces. 'Then move clear of the edge.'

Since he had ruined the solitude, shattered any hope for quiet contemplation, she might as well leave. Head high, she strode past him, carefully keeping beyond his arm's length, and caught up Pippin's reins. Prickles ran hot and painful down her back as if his dark gaze still grazed her skin. She couldn't resist glancing over her shoulder.

He'd remained statue-still like some ancient Celtic warrior, bold and hard and simmering like a storm about to rage. A terrifyingly handsome man and thoroughly annoyed, though what he had to be annoyed about she couldn't think.

How would he look if he smiled?

The thought surprised her utterly. 'Wh-who are you, s-sir? W-what are you doing in these woods?'

'Robert Deveril, milady. Assistant gamekeeper. I live in the cottage yonder.' He hesitated, pressed his lips together as if holding back something on the tip of his tongue. She knew the feeling only too well. Except for her, it was because it was easier to say nothing.

And yet after a moment, he continued, 'I thought your horse had bolted the way you tore past my house, but I see I was mistaken. Forgive me, milady.'

Suntanned fingers touched his forelock in a reluctant gesture of servility. If anything, he looked more arrogant than before. He pivoted and strode towards the path with long lithe strides.

'Y-your h-house?' A recollection of flying dirt striking

something hollow filled her mind. No wonder he'd been surprised and come to see what was happening. Heat flashed upwards from her chest to the roots of her hair. 'P-p-p—' *Oh, tongue, don't fail me now.* She forced in a breath. 'Mr D-Deveril,' she called out.

He halted, then turned to face her, looking less than happy. 'Milady?'

'I apologise.'

He frowned.

'It w-w-will not h-happen again.' Mortified at her inability to express even the simplest of sentences when off-kilter, she turned to her mount. It wasn't until the cinches on Pippin's saddle disappeared in a blur that she realised she was close to crying and wasn't sure why, unless it was frustration and the realisation of just how inconsiderate she'd been.

'Let me help you, milady.'

At the sound of his deep, rich, oh-so-easy words, she almost swallowed her tongue. 'G g go away,' she managed.

Clinging to Pippin's saddle, she turned her head. A good two feet away, he waited, calmly watching her, the anger still there, but contained, like that of the panther she'd once seen in a cage. Beautiful. And dangerous.

Yet she wasn't afraid. She just didn't want to look like a fool in front of this man.

'Look,' he said reasonably, 'I'm sorry I scared you. I thought you were in trouble when I saw you teetering on the brink. The rains have made the bank treacherous.'

'I'm a g-good s-s-swimmer.' She tried a smile.

'It's no jesting matter. No doubt you'd expect me to pull you out.'

Simon's face swam before her eyes like a pudgy Banquo's ghost. 'I'd prefer you didn't bother.'

His eyes gleamed. Amusement? 'My, you are in high ropes.'

He was laughing at her. He saw her as a joke. A wordless fool. He was so perfect and she couldn't string two words together. A spurt of resentment shot through her veins. 'This was m-my p-place. You have s-spoiled it.' She gulped in a supply of air. Her stutter was out of control. At any moment she'd been speechless. A dummy. For the second time today. 'G-good d-day, sir.'

His face blanched beneath his tan as if somehow she'd stabbed him and the blood had drained away. His hands fell to his sides, large hands that bunched into fists, knuckles gleaming white. 'I beg your pardon, my lady.'

An apology he scorned. She could see that in his expression.

She grabbed for Pippin's reins. Tried to pull herself up. The horse sidled. *No, Pippin. Don't do this now.* 'Shhh,' she whispered.

A strong calloused hand grabbed the bridle beside her cheek. Her heart leapt into her throat at the size of it. Afraid her heart might jump right out of her mouth, she drew back.

'You'll scare him,' she warned.

He murmured something. Pippin, the traitor, stilled. Deveril lifted the saddle flap and adjusted the cinch. He cocked a superior brow. 'You were saying?'

There it was, the arrogance of man. She breathed in slowly. 'F-for an assistant gamekeeper you are very haughty.'

'Once more I find the need to apologise.' A rueful grin curved his finely moulded lips.

Breathtaking. Heartstopping. A smile so dangerous ought to be against the law. Her anger whisked away as if borne aloft by the breeze tossing the branches above their heads. All she could do was stare at his lovely mouth. She inhaled a shaky breath. 'N-no. I was n-n…' She swallowed, then closed her eyes, surprised when he didn't finish the word. 'I was not very polite. I am sorry.'

He bowed his head in gentlemanly acknowledgement. 'Can I help you mount, my lady?'

Since when did assistant gamekeepers have elegant manners and glorious bodies? Every time he spoke, her knees felt strangely weak and she just wanted to stand and look at him. He made her want things young ladies were not supposed to think about. She wanted to touch him. Trace the curve of muscle and the cords of sinew. Feel their warmth.

And he wanted to help her onto her horse. 'Thank you, Mr R-Robert Deveril.'

His eyes widened. 'I must apologise for my earlier abruptness. I thought you an interloper.'

'I had not heard the cottage was let.' She frowned. She'd barely stumbled on her words. 'We d-d-don't have an assistant gamekeeper.'

'I started on Monday.'

No one ever told her anything. 'This is a lovely spot.' She glanced around, drinking it in with a sense of sadness. She wouldn't be able to come here any more.

'Aye, it is. Even at this time of year.' Slivers of amber danced in his dark eyes like unspent laughter. He really was outstandingly beautiful, despite the day's growth of beard. Or maybe because of it.

'You are not from this part of the country, are you?' she asked.

An eyebrow flicked up. He smiled again, another swift curve of his mouth, instantly repressed, but still her skin went all hot and prickly. 'I'm from the west. Dorset way.'

His accent had changed, broadened. He thought to trick

her, but she always noticed every word, every inflection, in other people's voices. How could she not? This man hailed from London, and had been educated well, of that she was certain. She mentally shrugged. It mattered little to her where he came from. She prepared to mount.

'Allow me,' he said.

He bent and linked his hands, then cast her a frowning look. 'Don't let me keep you from this place, milady. I shan't disturb you again.'

A furnace seemed to engulf her face. 'Th-thank you. And it is not my lady, just plain Miss Bracewell.' She caught herself lifting her chin and tucked it back in.

His head tilted to one side as if considering her words, then his gaze slid away. 'Yes, miss.'

She placed one booted foot in his cupped hands and he tossed her up without effort.

Tall and broad, straight and grand beside the horse, he planted his feet in the soft earth like a solid English oak. A man she would love to draw.

Naked.

The wicked thought trickled heaviness to the dark, secret place she tried never to notice. Little flutters made her shift in the saddle. Wanton urges. The kind that led a woman into trouble. Her gaze drank him in. Her heart sank. Was it any wonder she felt this way, when Slimy Simon loomed in her future? 'Good day, Mr Deveril.'

She wheeled Pippin around.

She couldn't help looking back one last time. He raised a hand in farewell. Her heart gave a sweet little lurch, which once more set her stomach dancing.

The horse broke into a trot and plunged into the trees. Robert could hear the sound of twigs snapping even as, utterly bemused, he followed in its wake. By the time he reached the clearing, the spirited gelding and its rider had disappeared.

A strange little thing, this Miss Wynchwood. In her drab brown clothing, she reminded him of some wild woodland creature ready to run at a sound. Certainly no beauty—her eyes were too large, the colour changing with her thoughts from the bluish-grey of clouds to the grey-green of a wind-swept ocean. Her tragic mouth took up far too much of her pixie face.

He'd wanted to kiss that mouth and make it tremble with desire instead of fear. He'd longed to release the tightly coiled hair at her nape and see it fall around her face. Pulled back, it did nothing to improve her looks. And yet she was oddly alluring.

Her style of conversation left much to be desired, though. Short and sharp and rude. Clearly a spoiled rich miss who needed a lesson in manners. Her Grace would not have tolerated such abruptness from one of Robert's sisters.

A dull stab of pain caught him off guard. Hades. Even now thoughts of home sneaked unwanted into his mind. He stared at the mud splattering the door of his cottage. What a reckless little cross-patch to ride at such speed through the woods. He groaned. And quite likely to report him to Lord Wynchwood for taking her to task.

Damnation. What the hell had he said?

He'd been terrified she'd fall in the river, furious at her carelessness. He'd spoken harshly. He'd made her angry.

Angry and woman did not mix well.

He shouldered his way into the hut he called home and kicked the door shut. Damn, it was cold, but at least he had a roof over his head. He sorted through his bedclothes on the cot against the wall, found his jacket and shrugged into the coarse fabric. He stirred the embers to get the fire going and hung the kettle on the crane. He'd been making tea moments before running outside because he thought the walls were collapsing. Moments before he'd ripped into the girl whose family owned these woods like a duke's son instead of a servant. He'd been scathing when he should have thanked her for the honour her horse's hooves had paid to his dwelling, or at least kept his tongue behind his teeth.

Such a small, fragile thing making all that rumpus. A good wind and she'd blow away. And when he boosted her on to her horse, she'd weighed no more than a child. Her eyes, though, had looked at him in the way of a woman. And his body had responded with interest. He cursed.

This was the best position he'd found in over two years and he'd be a fool to lose it because of a slip of a girl.

He stabbed the fire. Sparks flew. His nostrils filled with the scent of ashes. If he wasn't mistaken, once he'd cooled down, he'd treated her the way he treated his sisters, with amused tolerance. No wonder she'd been annoyed. No doubt he'd be apologising tomorrow. Unless she had him turned off.

Blast. For the first time he'd found a place with a chance for advancement and enough wages to start paying off some of his debts and he'd scolded his employer's niece.

Would he never come to terms with his new position in life?

He poured boiling water into the teapot and took it to the table set with a supper of bread and cheese. He cut a hunk of bread and skewered it with his knife. He took a bite and munched it slowly.

If there was a next time, he'd be more careful. He'd remember his place.

Chapter Three

'There you are, Miss Frederica.' The butler, Mr Snively, emerged from the shadows at the bottom of the staircase. He gave her a small smile. 'I thought I better warn you, Lord Wynchwood is asking for you. He is in his study.'

Frederica winced. 'Thank you, S-Snively. What is his current m-mood?'

Snively's muddy eyes twinkled, but there was sadness in them too. 'He's seems a little irritated, miss. Not his normal sunny self.' He winked.

She almost laughed. 'It's probably his g-gout.'

'Yes, miss.'

'And the w-weather. And the state of the Funds.'

'Yes, miss. And I gather he's lost his glasses.'

She grinned. 'Again. I'll go to him the moment I am changed.'

Snively shook his head and the wrinkles in his bulldog face seemed to deepen. 'No point, miss, he knows you took Pippin.'

Dash it all. One of the grooms must have reported her hasty departure. She sighed. 'I'll go right away. Thank you, Snively.'

He looked inclined to speak, then pressed his lips together.

'Is there s-something else?'

'His lordship received a letter from a London lawyer yesterday. It seems to have put him in a bit of a fuss. Made him fidgety.' Snively sounded worried. 'I wondered if he said anything about it?'

Uncle Mortimer was always fidgety. She stripped off her gloves and bonnet and handed them to him. 'Perhaps Mr Simon Bracewell is in need of funds again. Or perhaps it is merely excitement over my p-pending nuptials.'

Snively's dropping jaw was more than satisfying. He looked as horrified as she felt. He recovered quickly, smoothing his face into its customary bland butler's mask. But his flinty eyes told a different story. 'Is it appropriate to offer my congratulations?'

'N-not really.' All the frustration she'd felt when Uncle Mortimer made the announcement swept over her. 'I'm to m-marry my cousin S-Simon.' After years of him indicating he wished she wasn't part of his family at all.

His eyes widened. His mouth grew grim. 'Oh, no.'

She took a huge breath. 'Precisely.' Unable to bring herself to attempt another word, she headed for the study to see what Great-Uncle Mortimer wanted. Steps dragging, she traversed the brown runner covering a strip of ancient flagstones. This part of Wynchwood Hall always struck a chill on her skin as if damp clung to the walls like slime on a stagnant pond.

A quick breath, a light knock on the study door and she strode in.

Great-Uncle Mortimer sat in a wing chair beside the fire, a shawl around his shoulders, his feet immersed in a white china bowl full of steaming water and a mustard plaster on his chest.

In his old-fashioned wig, his nose pink from a cold and his short-sighted eyes peering over his spectacles at the letter in his hand, he looked more like a mole than usual.

He glanced up and shoved the paper down the side of the chair. Was that the lawyer's letter to which Snively referred? Or another letter from Simon begging for funds?

'Shut the door, girl. Do you want me to perish of the ague?'

She whisked the door shut and winced as the curtains at the windows rippled.

'The draught,' he moaned.

'Sorry, Uncle.'

'I don't know what it is about you, girl. Dashing about the countryside, leaving doors open on ailing relatives. You are supposed to make yourself useful, not overset my nerves. Have you learned nothing?'

He put a hand up to forestall her defence. 'What sort of start sent you racing off this morning? I needed you here.'

Of all her so-called relatives, she liked her uncle the best since he rarely had enough energy to notice her existence.

'I d-don't—'

'Don't know? You must know.'

She gulped in a deep breath. 'I don't want to marry S-S—'

'Simon. And that's the reason you dashed off on Pippin?'

She nodded.

'Ridiculous.' He leaned his head against the chair back and closed his eyes as if gathering strength. 'I am old. I need to know that my affairs are in order. Simon has kindly offered to alleviate me of one of my worries. It is the perfect solution. You do not have to get along, you just have to do your duty and give him a son. Surely you would like a house and children of your own, would you not?'

A dream for most normal women, the image sent a chill down her spine. 'No.'

'There is no alternative.'

'I can s-support myself.'

His bushy eyebrows shot up and he opened his eyes. 'How? Good God, you can scarcely string two words together.'

Heat rushed up to her hairline. Anger. 'I d-draw. Art.' Even as she said the words, she knew her mistake.

His face darkened. He sat up straight. 'What respectable woman earns money from daubing?' He made it sound like she had proposed selling her body.

'I'm not r-respectable.'

He narrowed his eyes. 'You have been brought up to be respectable. You will not bring shame on this family.'

Like your mother. Like the Wynchwood Whore. He didn't say it, but she could see he was thinking it by the tight set to his mouth and the jut of his jaw.

Dare she tell him about the drawings she'd already sold? Prove she could manage by herself? The money she earned would give her an independence. Barely. What if he prevented her from completing the last pictures of the series? It would void her contract, a contract she'd signed pretending to be a man. She sealed the words behind her firmly closed lips. Not that he ever let her finish a sentence.

'And another thing,' he said. 'No more excursions on Pippin. There is too much to do around this house.'

She stared at him. 'W-what things?'

'Simon is bringing guests for the ball. There will be hunting, entertainments, things like that to arrange. I will need your help.'

Horror rose up like a lump in her throat. 'G-guests?'

'Yes. The ball will also serve as your come out.'

A rush of blood to her head made her feel dizzy. 'A come out?'

Mortimer tugged his shawl closer about his shoulders. 'Don't look surprised. Anyone would think this family treated you badly. It is high time you entered society if you are going to be Simon's wife. We can hope no one remembers your mother any more.'

'I d-d-d—'

Mortimer thumped the arm of his chair with a clenched fist. 'Enough,' he yelled. He lowered his voice. 'Damn it. Any other girl your age would be in alt at so generous an offer. Make an effort, girl. Why, you are practically on the shelf.'

'I w w w—'

'Will.'

Breathe in. Breathe out. 'Won't. I don't want a husband.' A husband would ruin all her hopes for the future.

The red in Mortimer's face darkened to puce and his ears flushed vermillion. He reminded her of an angry sunset, the kind that heralded a storm. His bushy grey brows drew together over his pitted nose. 'I am the head of this family and I say you will obey me or face the consequences.'

Did he think she feared a diet of bread and water or isolation in her room? 'I—'

'No more arguments, Frederica. It is decided. I have only your best interests in mind. I have clearly allowed you far too much liberty if your head is full of such nonsense. Art, indeed. Where did you ever get such a notion?'

'I...' Oh, what was the point? She didn't really know where the notion came from anyway.

'What you need to do, girl, is learn to make yourself useful. Find my glasses. I know I had them here earlier.' He poked around in the folds of his robe.

Frederica stifled a sigh. 'Uncle.'

He looked up. She pointed to her nose and he put a hand up to his face. 'Ah. There they are. Now run along and prepare for our guests. Hurry up before you add a headache to my ills.'

Mortimer pressed one gnarled hand against his poultice and closed his eyes. 'Ask Snively for more hot water on your way out.'

Dismissed, Frederica lowered her gaze and dropped a respectful curtsy. 'Yes, Uncle.'

She turned and left swiftly, before he found some other task for her to do. It was no good fighting the stubborn man head on. And Snively was right, he was unusually crotchety. And this idea of his to marry her to Simon was strange to say the least. He'd never expressed a jot of interest in her future before. Perhaps age was catching up to him.

As she headed for the butler's pantry to deliver her message, her mind twisted and turned, seeking an escape. She would not marry a man she despised as much as he scorned her.

Simon was the key, she realised. He would never agree to this scheme.

And to top it all off, she was to attend a ball? With strangers, people who might know of her mother. People who would expect her to make conversation. And dance. Never once had she danced in public. She'd probably fall flat on her face.

For a moment, she wasn't sure which was worse: the thought of marriage or the thought of a room full of strangers.

A shudder ran down her spine. Of the two, it had to be Simon. Simon didn't have a soul. He'd crush hers with his inanity.

* * *

Robert shouldered his shotgun, the brace of hares dangling from its muzzle. Fresh meat for dinner. His mouth watered.

He strode down Gallows Hill, mud heavy on his boots, the countryside unfolding in mist-draped valleys and leafless tree-crested hills. The late-afternoon air chilled the back of his throat and reached frigid fingers smelling of decayed vegetation into his lungs.

On the hill behind him, the rooks were settling back among the treetops with harsh cries. He whistled blithely, unusually content at the prospect of stew instead of bread and cheese, or the rations of salt beef provided by his employer.

Perhaps he'd request a recipe for dumplings from Wynchwood's cook next time he arrived in her kitchen with a plump pheasant for his lordship's dinner. A wry smile twisted his lips. How the mighty were fallen.

A sudden sense of loss made his stomach fall away. The whistle died on his lips. Damn it. He would not sink into self-pity. Live for the moment and plan for the future must be his motto or he would go mad.

He slogged on down the hill, unable to recapture his lighter mood. At the bottom, he took the overgrown track alongside the river, pushing aside brambles and scuffing through damp leaves. Without vegetables his stew would be a sorry affair. Perhaps instead of going up to the house in the morning for a list of the cook's requirements from the local village, he'd go now. She might have some vegetables to spare.

The trees thinned at the edge of the clearing. Stew. He could almost smell it.

Robert stopped short at the sight of a hunched figure perched on an old stump a little way from his cottage, her brown bonnet and brown wool cloak blending into the carpet of withered beech leaves. He knew her at once, even though she had her back to him and her head bowed over something on her lap. Miss Bracewell.

Hades. It seemed she'd taken him up on his invitation to return whenever she liked.

He inhaled a slow breath. This time he would not scare her. This time he would be polite. Polite and, damn it, suitably humble, since no word had come back to him about yesterday's disastrous encounter.

He'd not had the courage to ask Weatherby about her either. If something had been said, he didn't want to remind the old curmudgeon.

He circled around, thinking to come at her head on. A twig cracked under his boot. He cursed under his breath.

She leaped to her feet and whirled around. Sheets of paper fluttered around her, landing like snowflakes amid the dry leaves.

Large and grey-green, her eyes mirrored shock. Another emotion flickered away before he could guess its import. Strange when he rarely had trouble reading a woman's thoughts. It left him feeling on edge. Out of his element.

He touched his hat. 'Good day, Miss Bracewell.'

An expression of revulsion crossed her face.

It took him aback. Women usually looked at him with favour. Had he upset her so much? And if so, why was she back?

The focus of her horrified gaze remained fixed above his right shoulder. On his dinner, not on him. Not that he wasn't the stuff of nightmares, with his worn jacket and fustian trousers mired with the blood of his catch. He'd gutted them up on the hill, preferring leaving the offal for scavengers rather than bury it near his hut. He put the gun and its grisly pennant on the ground at his feet with an apologetic shrug.

Her breast rose and fell in a deep breath. 'Mr Deveril.'

Recalling his mistakes of the day before, he snatched his cap off his head and lowered his gaze. 'Yes, miss. I am sorry if I disturbed you.' One of her fallen papers had landed near his foot. He retrieved it. His jaw slackened at a glimpse of a drawing of his own likeness, jacketless, shabby, unkempt, disreputable.

Shock held him transfixed.

She leaped forwards and snatched it from his hand. At a crouching run, she scuttled about picking up the rest of the sheets. Each time he reached for one, she plucked it from beneath his hand, allowing only fractured glimpses of squirrels in their natural setting.

All the sheets picked up, she stood with the untidy bundle of papers clutched against her chest as if fearing he might make a grab for them, staring at him as if he had two heads and four eyes. Obviously she found his presence disturbing.

Her wariness gnawed at his gut like a rat feeding on bone. He quelled the urge to deny meaning her harm. She should be afraid out here alone in the woods without a chaperon.

Glancing down for his rifle, he saw scattered charcoal and the upturned wooden box beside the stump. He crouched, righted the box and scooped up the charcoals. He dropped them into the box. A glint caught his eye—a fine gold chain snaking amongst the leaves. He picked it up, dangled it from his fingers.

'It's mine,' she said in her strangled breathy voice.

Without looking at her, he felt heat rise from his neck to the roots of his hair. Did she think he would steal it? He let it fall into the box amongst the dusty broken black sticks.

'I b-broke it,' she said in the same forced rush of words.

He glanced at her.

She tucked the messy pile of paper between two board covers and tied the string. 'I caught it on a branch on my way here.' She offered him a conciliatory smile.

He blinked, startled by the sudden change in her expression. She looked witchy, oddly alluring, almost beautiful in a vulnerable way. He pulled himself together. 'What are you doing here?' He sounded sullen, ungracious, when he'd meant to sound jocular. He half-expected her to take to her heels in terror.

This woman had him all at sea.

But she didn't run, she merely tilted her head to one side as if thinking about what to say.

'L-looking for squirrels.' She tapped her portfolio.

And she'd picked this clearing when hundreds of other places would do. What was she up to? He gestured to the stump. 'Don't let me disturb you.'

'N-no. I was finished. The light is fading. Too many shadows.'

A true artist would care about the quality of the light. And the drawings he'd seen were excellent. Most ladies liked to draw, but her pictures seemed different. The squirrels had life.

Perhaps her artistic bent was what made her seem different. Awkward, with her utterance of short, sharp and direct sentences, yet likeable. A reason not to encourage her to return.

'May I help you mount your horse?' He glanced around for the gelding.

She bit her lip. A faint, rosy hue tinted her pale, high cheekbones. 'I w-walked.'

Robert frowned. Riding in the woods was risky enough,

but a young female walking alone in the forest with the sun going down he could not like.

'I'll drop my dinner off inside and walk you back to Wynchwood.'

'P-please, don't trouble. I know the way.'

'It's no trouble, miss. It's my duty to my employer to see you home safe.'

In his past life, he would have insisted on his honour and charmed the girl. His mouth twisted. As far as his new world knew, he had neither honour nor charm.

A protest formed on her lips, but he continued as if he hadn't noticed. 'I have to go up to the house before supper to collect an order from Mrs Doncaster.'

Her glance flicked to the pile of fur. A shudder shook her delicate frame. It reminded him of shudders of pleasure. Heated his blood. Stirred his body.

Unwanted responses.

Furious at himself, he glowered at her. 'Do you not eat meat, Miss Wynchwood?' Damn, that was hardly concilia-tory. Hardly servile. He wanted to curse. Instead, he bent, picked up his haul and strode for his front door.

'Y-yes,' she said.

He swung around. 'What?'

'I eat m-m-m—' she closed her eyes, a sweep of long brown lashes on fine cheekbones for a second '—eat meat—' her serious gaze rested on his face '—but I prefer it cooked.' She smiled. A curve of rosy lips and flash of small white teeth.

Devastatingly lovely.

What the deuce? Was he so pathetically lonely that a smile from a slip of a girl brought a ray of light to his dreary day? And she wasn't as young as he'd thought the first time he saw her. She was one of those females who retained an aura of youth, like Caro Lamb. It was something in the way they observed the world with a child-like joy, he'd always thought, as if everything was new and wonderful.

It made them seem terribly young. And vulnerable.

Another reason for her to stay away from a man jaded by life.

He glanced up at the pink-streaked sky between the black branches overhead. 'I'll be but a moment and we'll be on our way.' Shielding her view of the carcasses with his body, he dived inside his hut. He hung the hares from a nail by the hearth and stowed his shotgun under his cot out of sight. Swiftly, he stripped off his boots and soiled clothing, grabbing for his cleanest shirt and trousers. He had the sense that if he lingered a moment too long she'd be off like a startled fawn. Then he'd be forced to follow her home. She might not take kindly to being stalked.

To his relief when he got outside, she was still standing where he left her, staring into the distance as if lost in some distant world, the battered portfolio still clutched to her chest.

He picked up the box of charcoal from the stump. 'Are you ready?'

She jumped.

Damn it. What made her so nervous?

'Yes,' she said.

'After you, miss.'

Then suddenly she turned and walked in front of him. The hem of her brown cloak rustled the dry brown leaves alongside the track. For the niece of a nobleman, her clothes were sadly lacking. Perhaps she chose them to blend with her surroundings when drawing from nature.

She spun around to face him, walking backwards with cheeks pink and eyes bright. 'There was something I wanted to ask you.'

Of course there was. No female would arrive at his door

without an ulterior motive. In the past it usually involved hot nights and cool sheets. But not this one. She was far too innocent for such games. He waited for her to speak.

'Do you hunt a great d-d—' Her colour deepened. 'A lot?' she finished.

She stumbled over a root. He reached out to catch her arm. She righted herself, flinching from his touch with a noise in her throat that sounded like a cross between a sob and a laugh. Her eyes weren't laughing. Unless he mistook her reaction, she looked thoroughly mortified.

He resisted the urge to offer comfort.

Damn it. Why did he even care? She was one of his employer's family members. Even walking with her could be misconstrued. But he didn't want her to trip again. He didn't want her hurt.

God help him.

He caught her up, and she turned to walk forwards at his side.

'Do you?' She peered at him from beneath the brim of her plain brown bonnet with the expression of a mischievous elf. His hackles went up. Instincts honed by years of pleasing women. She definitely wanted something. He felt it in his gut. Curiosity rose in his breast. He forced himself to tamp it down. 'It is all according to Mr Weatherby's orders and what Cook requests for his lordship's table. Most of my work relates to keeping down vermin.'

'You hunt foxes?'

'Gentlemen hunt foxes.' He couldn't prevent the bitter edge to his tone. 'I trap them and keep track of their dens so the hunt can have a good day of sport.' There, that last sounded more pragmatic.

'Is there a den nearby?'

They left the woods and followed the river bank, the same path he'd walked earlier. 'There are a couple. One up on Gallows Hill. Another in the five-acre field down yonder.' He pointed toward the village of Swanlea.

Her eyes glistened with excitement. An overwhelming urge to ask why stuck in his throat. He had no right questioning his betters.

'Badgers?'

Great God, this girl was a strange one. 'Stay away from them, miss. They're dangerous and mean. We hunt them with dogs.'

The light went out of her face a moment before she dropped her gaze. He felt as if he'd crushed a delicate plant beneath his boot heel. Good thing, too, if it kept her away from the sett not far from his dwelling.

'I've never seen one,' she murmured.

'They come out only in the evening. Usually after dark.'

Once more he had the sense he had disappointed her, but why the strange urge to make amends? If she disliked him, so much the better. He held his tongue.

The path joined the rutted lane that led to the village in one direction, and over the bridge to the back entrance of Wynchwood Place in the other. The way to the mansion used by such as he. The lower orders.

He scowled at the encroaching thought.

Off in the distance, on a natural rise in the land, the solid shape of the mansion looked over green lawns and formal gardens. A house of plain red brick with a red-tile roof adorned by tall chimneypots. Nothing like the grandeur of the ducal estates, but a pleasant enough English gentleman's country house.

Their footsteps clattered with hollow echoes on the slats of the wooden bridge. At the midpoint she halted and looked over the handrail into the murky depths of the River

Wynch. 'When I was young, my cousin, Mr Bracewell, told me a troll lived under this bridge. I was terrified.'

She glanced over her shoulder at him, a tentative smile on her lips. A vision of his sister Lizzie, her eyes full of teasing, her dark curls clustered around her heart-shaped face, flowed into his mind. A river of memories, each one etched in the acid of bitterness. Mother. The children. And Charlie before he got too serious to make good company. The acid burned up from his gut and into his throat. He clenched his jaw against the wave of longing. He bunched his fists to hold it at bay.

Slowly he became aware of her shocked stare, of the fear lurking in the depths of strange turquoise eyes. 'L-listen to me ch-chattering. You want to get h-home to your d-d— meal.'

Fear of him had turned her speech into a nightmare of difficulty. He saw it in her face and in the tremble of her overlarge mouth. He was such a dolt.

Before he could utter a word, she snatched the box from his hand and fled like a rabbit seeking the safety of a burrow.

Hades. The past had a tendency to intrude at the most inopportune moments. He thought he had it under control and then the floodgates of regret for his dissolute past released a torrent emotion. Silently he cursed. Now he'd spend more hours wondering whether she'd report him to her uncle or Weatherby. The girl was a menace. Whatever else he did, he needed to avoid her as if she had a case of the measles.

For all his misgivings, he followed her discreetly, making sure she arrived at the door safely. As any right-thinking man would, he told himself. Especially with so fragile a creature wandering around as if no one cared what she did or where she went.

While she didn't look back, he knew she was aware of his presence from the way she maintained her awkward half-run, half-trot. Her ugly brown skirts caught at her ankles and her bonnet ribbons fluttered. A little brown sparrow with broken wings.

The thought hurt.

Perhaps she now thought him a rabid dog? A good thing, surely. Hopefully she thought him terrifying enough to keep away from his cottage. He ought to be glad instead of wanting to apologise. Again.

At the entrance to the courtyard, she cut across the lawn. He frowned. What the devil was she up to now? Instead of entering through the front door, she was creeping through the shrubbery toward a side door. Well, well, Miss Bracewell was apparently playing truant. The little minx was nothing but trouble.

She slipped inside the house and he continued around the back of the house to the kitchen door, passing through the neat rows of root vegetables and assorted herbs in the kitchen garden. Mrs Doncaster knew her stuff and Robert had been doing his best to pick her brains, with the idea of planting his own garden in the spring.

The scullery door stood open and, removing his cap, Robert entered and made his way down the narrow stone passage into the old-fashioned winter kitchen.

Mrs Doncaster, her face red beneath her mobcap and her black skirts as wide as she was high, looked up from the hearth at the sound of his footfall. A leg of mutton hung over the glowing embers, the juices collecting in a pan beneath and the scent of fresh bread filled the warm air. Robert's stomach growled.

'Young Rob,' she said with a frown. ''Tis too busy I am to be feeding you tonight.'

Robert smiled. 'No, indeed, mistress. Mr Weatherby

is sending me to town tomorrow—is there anything you need?'

'Wait a bit and I'll make you up a list.'

Wincing inwardly, he forced himself to ask his question. 'I'm also in dire need of some carrots if you've any to spare, and a few herbs for my stew.'

'Oh, aye. Caught yerself some game, did you?' She tucked a damp grey strand of hair under her cap. 'Maisie.' Her shriek echoed off the rafters. Robert stifled the urge to cover his ears.

The plump Maisie, a girl of about sixteen with knowing black eyes, emerged from the scullery. 'Yes, mum?' When she spied Robert, her round freckled face beamed. 'Good day to you, Mr Deveril.'

'Fetch Robert some sage and rosemary and put up a basket of carrots and parsnips, there's a good girl,' the cook said.

Maisie brushed against him on the way to the pantry. They both knew what her sideways smile offered, had been offering since the day he arrived. She wasn't his sort. Far too young and far too witless. And the warning from Weatherby that his lordship would insist on his servants marrying if there was a hint of goin's-on, as the old countryman put it, had ensured Robert wouldn't stray. He edged into a corner out of Cook's way.

'Saucy hussy, that one,' Mrs Doncaster said, swiping at her hot brow.

'Do you need more coal?' Robert asked, pointing at the empty scuttle beside the blackened hearth.

'You're a good lad, to be sure,' she said with a nod. 'You thinks about what's needed. You got a good head on your shoulders. I can see why Weatherby thinks so highly of you already. Take a candle.'

Praise from the cook? And Weatherby? His efforts

seemed to be paying off. More reason to make sure he didn't put a foot wrong. Hefting the black iron bucket, Robert made his way through a low door and down the stairs. The coal cellar sat on one side of the narrow passage, the wine cellar on the other.

Helping the cook had paid off in spades, or rather in vegetables and the odd loaf of fresh bread, but he wanted far more than that. He needed the respect and trust of his new peers if he was going to get ahead.

He tied a neckerchief over the lower part of his face. Dust rose in choking clouds, settling on his shoulders and in his hair as he shovelled the coal up from the mountain beneath the trapdoor through which the coalman deposited the contents of his sacks. Removing the kerchief, Robert ducked out of the cellar and heaved the scuttle back up the wooden flight.

'Set it by the hearth,' the cook instructed. 'Wash up in the bowl by the door.'

Robert washed his hands and face in the chilly water and dried them off on a grubby towel hung nearby. He'd wash properly at home.

'Drat that girl,' Mrs. Dorset said. 'I need her to turn the spit while I finish this pastry.'

'I'll do it.' Robert made his way around the wooden table and grasped the iron handle. It took some effort to turn. How poor Maisie managed he couldn't imagine.

The aroma of the meat sent moisture flooding in his mouth. God. He hadn't tasted a roast for months.

'Slower, young Rob,' the cook said, her rolling pin flying over the floured pastry.

He grinned and complied. 'I met Miss Bracewell in the garden on my way in,' he said casually, hoping to glean a little more insight into the troublesome lass. 'Is she the only relative to the master?'

The cook's cheerful mouth pursed as if she'd eaten a quince. 'The devil's spawn, that one. You want to stay well clear of her.'

The venom in her voice rendered Robert speechless and...angry. He kept his tone non-committal. 'She seemed like a pleasant enough young lady. Not that she said much more than good day.'

'I likes her,' Maisie said, returning with basket in hand. 'She opened the door when I had me hands full once.'

'Goes to show she's not a proper lady,' the cook said and sent Robert a sharp stare. 'A blot on the good name of Bracewell, she is. Her and her mother. My poor Lord Wynchwood is a saint for taking her in. Mark my words, it'll do him no good.'

'What—?' Robert started to ask.

'Mrs Doncaster.' The butler's stern tones boomed through the kitchen.

Robert jumped guiltily. Old Snively was a tartar and no mistake. All the servants feared the gimlet-eyed old vulture. A smile never touched his lips and his sharp eyes missed not the smallest fault according to the house servants.

Snively's cold gaze rested on Robert's face. 'Gossiping with the outside staff, Mrs Doncaster?'

Robert felt heat scald his cheeks. Arrogant bugger. Who did the butler think he was? Robert gritted his teeth, held his body rigid and kept turning the spit, lowering his gaze from the piercing stare. This man had the power to have him dismissed on a word, and from the gleam in his eye the stiff-rumped bastard wasn't done.

'If you've no work to keep you occupied, Deveril,' Snively said, 'perhaps Mr Weatherby can do without an assistant after all.'

'I'm here to fetch a list for tomorrow, Mr Snively,' Robert said.

'Now see here, Snively,' Mrs Doncaster put in, clearly ruffled, 'if you kept that good-for-nothing footman William at his duty, I wouldn't need Rob's help, would I? Fetched the coal up, he did. Without it, his lordship would be waiting for his dinner.'

Snively fixed her with a haughty stare. 'Planning, Mrs Doncaster. The key to good organisation. If you had William bring up enough coal for the entire day, you wouldn't need to call him from his other duties.'

'Ho,' Mrs Doncaster said, elbows akimbo. 'Planning, is it? Am I to turn my kitchen into a coal yard?'

It was like watching a boxing match threatening to spill over into the crowd, but Robert had no wish to become embroiled. It was more than his job was worth. It didn't help that the old bugger was right, he had no business coming here this evening.

Across the room, Maisie had her lips folded inside her teeth as if to stop any unruly words escaping. Robert knew just how she felt. The portly, stiff-necked Snively was terrifying. Mrs Doncaster's bravery left him in awe.

'Planning,' Snively repeated and swept out of the kitchen.

'Hmmph,' Cook grumbled. 'Johnny-come-lately. Thinks just because he worked in London, he can lord it over the rest of us who's been here all our lives. Hmmph. His back's up because he heard what we was saying. Always jumps to defend her, he does.'

The butler rose a notch in Robert's estimation. 'I'll be on my way now Maisie's back.'

'Yes. Go.' Mrs Doncaster, still in high dudgeon, waved him away.

Holding out the basket, Maisie lifted a corner of the cloth covering its contents. 'I've put a nice bit of ham in there for your breakfast,' she whispered with a wink, then trundled off to her spit.

A cold chill seemed to clutch his very soul with icy fingers. They were all at it. Handing him food, putting him under an obligation. One day, by God, he would repay their charity. Somehow he'd find the means.

More debts to pay.

He pulled his cap on and made his way out into the growing dusk. 'Spawn of Satan'? What the hell had Mrs Doncaster meant? And why the hell had he bristled?

Chapter Four

'Bring the light closer, Frederica, for goodness' sake—how can I read in the dark?'

Frederica rose from her chair and moved the candlestick on the tea table two inches closer to her uncle.

Looking up from the most recent missive from Simon, Mortimer peered over his spectacles at her. 'That's better.' He coughed into his ever-ready handkerchief.

Frederica handed him his tea. She hated tea in the drawing room. A senseless torture for someone who had not the slightest chance of making polite conversation under the best of circumstances. Which made her almost easy conversations with Mr Deveril all the stranger.

'You s-said you needed to talk to me about something, Uncle?' She needed to get back her drawings of squirrels. She hadn't yet decided which ones to colour.

'Is everything prepared for Simon's visit?'

Inwardly she groaned. 'Yes, Uncle.' She took a deep slow breath. 'I've asked Snively to have the sheets for the guests' rooms aired and instructed him to hire help from the village for the day of the ball.'

He glanced down at the letter in his hand. 'Radthorn is bringing guests, too, I gather. They will stay at the Grange with him. The ball is going to be far grander than usual. Simon has raised a concern.'

Hurry up and get to the point. She tried to look interested.

Uncle Mortimer lifted his glasses and rubbed at his eyes. 'He worries you have nothing appropriate to wear. That you won't be up to snuff. In short, he says you need dresses. Gowns and such. Kickshaws. He also says you need a chaperon, someone to keep an eye on you.'

Oh, no. Frederica's body stiffened bowstring tight. Vibrations ran up and down her spine as if at any moment she would snap in two. A chaperon would interfere with all her plans. 'I d-d-d—' Inhale.

'Do.' Uncle Mortimer shifted in his seat. 'Simon is right, you run around the estate like a veritable hoyden. Look at the way you ran off yesterday.' He shook his head. 'Do you even know how to dance?'

'Simon showed me some country dances.' Sort of. 'Mrs Felton in the village has my m-measurements and can make me up a gown or two, but I d-don't n-need someone watching over me. I'm almost five and twenty.'

Uncle Mortimer scratched at the papery skin on the back of his hand, a dry rasp in the quiet. A deep furrow formed between his brows. 'Simon said there must be waltzing.'

She gulped, panic robbing her of words. All of this sounded as if Simon had every intention of submitting to Mortimer's demands. Because he needed money, no doubt. She felt a constriction in her throat.

Breathe. 'I've n-never attended the T-Twelfth Night ball before—why this time?'

Uncle Mortimer stared at her for a long time. He seemed to be struggling with some inner emotion. 'Dear child. You cannot wed a man like Simon without at least learning some of the niceties. Given your…your impediment, I would have thought you would be eager to oblige. I am going to a great deal of expense and trouble, you know.'

He sounded kind when she'd never heard him sound anything but impatient. He was trying to make her feel guilty. 'I'd be h-happy s-single.'

'We are your family. You are our responsibility. Simon is generously shouldering the burden. You must do your part.'

'Simon must know I'll never be a fitting wife. After all, I'm m-my mother's daughter.'

A knobby hand pounded on the chair arm. Uncle Mortimer's tea slopped in the saucer. 'Enough. You will do as I say.' As if the burst of anger had used up all his energy, he sagged back in his chair and covered his face with one hand.

Frederica took the teacup from her uncle's limp grasp. 'Surely we can d-do without a chaperon.'

'No,' he whispered. 'Lady Radthorn has agreed. It will be done.'

Could this nightmare get any worse? 'Lady Radthorn?' Frederica had seen the old lady in the village. She looked very high in the instep. Not the kind of person who would take kindly to a noblewoman's by-blow sired by no one knew who, but everyone assumed the worst.

'No arguments. Lady Radthorn has arranged for the seamstress to attend you at her house tomorrow. You will need a costume for the ball. Several morning and evening gowns and a riding habit. The bills will be sent to me.'

Frederica felt her eyes widen as the list grew. 'It sounds d-dreadfully expensive.'

Uncle Mortimer's jaw worked for a moment. He swallowed. 'Nothing is too much to ensure that you have the bronze to make you worthy of Simon.' He closed his eyes and gave a weak wave. 'No more discussion. All these years I have paid for your keep, your education, the food in your stomach with never a word of thanks, ungrateful child. You will do as you are told.'

Selfish. Ungrateful. The words squeezed the breath from her chest like a press-yard stone placed on a prisoner's chest to extract a confession. Was someone like her wrong to want more than the promise of a roof over her head?

It all came back to her mother's shame. The Wynchwood Whore. She'd only ever heard it said once as a child, by Mrs Doncaster. Frederica had turned the words over in her mind with a child's morbid curiosity, and later with a degree of hatred, not because of what her mother was, she had realised, but because she'd left Frederica to reap the punishment.

The sins of the father will be visited upon their children. Who knew what her father's sins actually might be? For all she knew, her father could be a highwayman. Or worse, according to the servants' gossip.

Well, this child wasn't going to wait around for the visitation. She had her own plans. And they were about to bear fruit. In the meantime she'd do well not to arouse her uncle's suspicions. 'As you request, Uncle,' she murmured. 'If you d-don't n-need anything else, I w-would like to retire.'

He didn't open his eyes. Frederica didn't think she'd be closing hers for most of the night. She was going to finish her drawings and be up early to catch a fox on his way home. The quicker she got her drawings done, the sooner she could get paid. If she was going to escape this marriage, time was of the essence.

In the hour before dawn, normally quiet clocks marked time like drums. The ancient timbers on the stairs squawked a protest beneath Frederica's feet. She halted, listening. No one stirred. It only sounded loud because the rest of the house was so quiet.

Reaching the side door, she slid back the bolt and winced at the ear-splitting shriek of metal against metal. Eyes closed, ears straining, she waited. No cry of alarm. She let her breath go, pulled up her hood and slipped out into the crisp morning air.

To the east, a faint grey tinge on the horizon hinted at morning. Ankle deep in swirling mist, she stole along the verge at the edge of the drive. Her portfolio under her arm and her box of pencils clutched in her hand, she breathed in the damp scent of the country, grass, fallen leaves, smoke from banked fires. Somewhere in the distance a cockerel crowed.

Thank goodness there was no snow to reveal her excursion.

Once clear of Wynchwood's windows, she strode along the lane, her steps long and free. Gallows Hill rose up stark against the skyline. Its crown of four pines and the blasted oak, a twisted blackened wreck, could be seen for miles, she'd been told. She left the lane and cut across the meadow at the bottom of the hill, then followed a well-worn sheep track up the steep hillside.

By the time she reached the top her breath rasped in her throat, her calves ached and the sky had lightened to the colour of pewter. Across the valley, the mist levelled the landscape into a grey ocean bristling with the spars of sunken trees.

She stopped to catch her breath and looked around. Bare rocks littered the plateau as if tossed there by some long-ago giant. Among the blanket of brown pine needles she found what she sought: a narrow tunnel dug in soft earth partially hidden by a fallen tree limb. Where should she sit for the best view?

She had read about the habits of the foxes in one of Uncle Mortimer's books on hunting. Her best chance of seeing one was at daybreak near the den. Hopefully she wasn't too late.

A spot off the animal's beaten track seemed the best idea for watching. A broom bush, one of the few patches of green at this time of year, offered what looked like the best cover. From there, the light wind would carry her scent away from the den.

She pushed into the greenery and sank down cross-legged. Carefully, she drew out a sheet of parchment and one of her precious lead pencils. Pencils were expensive and she eked them out the way a starving man rationed crusts of bread, but knowing this might be her only chance to observe the creature from life, she'd chosen it over charcoal, which tended to smudge.

As the minutes passed, she settled into perfect stillness, gradually absorbing the sounds of the awakening morning, cows lowing for the milkmaid on a nearby farm, the call of rooks above Bluebell Woods.

Someone whistling and stomping up the hill.

Oh, no! She looked over her shoulder…at Mr Deveril striding over the brow of the hill, a gun on his shoulder, traps dangling from one hand. He was making straight for the fox's den with long, lithe strides. Blast. He'd scare off the fox. She put down her paper and rose to her feet, gesturing to him to leave.

He stopped, stock still, and stared.

Go away, she mouthed.

He dropped the traps and started to run. Towards her. The idiot.

She shooed him back with her arms.

He ran faster, his boots scattering pine needles.

She felt like screaming. He'd ruined everything. Any self-respecting fox would be long gone by now and no doubt Mr Deveril would have him shot long before her next opportunity to come up here. Drat. She would need to find another den and right when she didn't need a delay.

She bent to pack up her stuff.

'Are you all right?' he asked, stopping short of the shrubbery. His massive shoulders in a brown fustian jacket blocked her view of the sky as his chest rose and fell from exertion. Lovely, beautiful man. She had the sudden desire to snatch up her pencil and draw. Him.

A dangerous notion. 'I would have been perfectly all right had you stayed away,' she muttered, pushing through the scratchy branches.

He frowned. 'You waved me over. I thought you must have had an accident. Fallen from your horse.'

'I walked.' As if it mattered how she got here.

'All the way up here?'

'An early morning stroll. For my health.'

His expression of disbelief said it all and his gaze dropped to the portfolio beneath her arm. 'You came up here to draw the fox?' He sounded disapproving, dismissive, just like everyone else.

'Not possible since you decided to gallop over here like a runaway carthorse.'

A muscle in his jaw flickered. His lips twitched. Amber danced in his eyes. Was he laughing? It certainly looked like it. She found herself wanting to smile, despite her disappointment.

'You looked as if you were trying to get my attention. I didn't realise you were here on a drawing expedition.'

'What else would I be doing up here? I had hoped to

draw it, b-before you k-killed it.' She marched past him and headed downhill.

'Wait,' he commanded, deep and resonant.

How dare he order her about? She forged on.

'Miss Bracewell,' he called out. 'There is a better place from which to watch.'

She twisted to look back at him.

He stared at her silently, challenging her to return, looking like a dark angel with the grey sky behind and the dark pines above. A tempting dark angel. Her heart speeded up. She hunched deeper into her cloak. 'W-Where?' Now she sounded like a sulky child. What was it about this man that made her behave so badly? Apart from his physical beauty, that was, which would affect any warm-blooded woman.

'You would have missed him from there.'

'Oh?'

'I can show you, if you wish?'

'You said him? Is it a male?'

He smiled and her knees almost gave out as he transformed into a Greek god with a simple curve of his mouth. 'The dog fox. Aye. This tunnel is his escape route. The front door is yonder.' He nodded toward the blasted oak. 'I've seen him go in three times this week.'

The country accent missing from his earlier speech returned. She hesitated, her mind clamouring a warning even as her eyes worshipped the fierce beauty of his carved features. She longed to draw the character and darkness in his face and the athletic grace of his body. Not a clumsy attempt from memory, but from the flesh. Heat crawled up her face.

His smile disappeared. 'As you wish, miss,' he said, clearly taking her silence as refusal.

'I will.'

A brow winged up and he tilted his head. 'You mean, yes?'

She nodded, her head bobbing as if her neck had turned into a spring.

'This way, then, miss, if you please.'

She followed him to a knobby protrusion of rocks beside the blackened tree.

'There,' he murmured, pointing at the ground a few feet away.

Nothing. Then the darker black of a hole took shape among the shadows. 'I see it.' She tore off the portfolio's ribbon.

'Sit here,' he said, a large, warm hand catching her elbow, steering her to another pile of rocks. Sparks seemed to shoot up her arm, as if he'd touched a lightning bolt and transmitted its energy to her through his fingers.

Her mouth dried. A man of his ilk shouldn't be touching her at all.

Was this how her mother had felt with the lower orders? Entranced. Breathless. Hot all over. She could quite see why one might want to experience it again. And more.

Somehow she sank down in the place he suggested and saw with amazement that the rock on which she perched formed a comfortable backrest and screened her from the opening to the fox's den, except for a narrow slit between two rocks.

'Oh,' she said. 'This is perfect.'

'I aim to please,' he replied with a flash of a grin.

The breath in her chest left her mouth in a besotted rush. The man should not smile. It was fatal. And, from the broadening smile, he knew it.

He sank to his haunches beside her, his back against the rock on which she sat, his shoulder touching her skirts. He sat and stretched out legs which seemed to go on for ever and terminated in sturdy brown boots covered in mud. The rough fabric of his trousers clung to his thighs in a most revealing manner, suggestive of hard muscle and power.

In the confined space between the boulders, his shoulders hemmed her in. Trapped her. His steady, even breathing filled her ears, warmth radiated from him and the smell of bay drifted on the still air, instilling a strong desire to inhale his manly scent. From the corner of her eye she admired the black curl of hair on the bronzed skin of his strong column of a neck and the way it skimmed the collar of his coarse linen shirt. Once more her pulse galloped out of control.

Oh, yes, he would make an excellent subject. She had never drawn a man from life, but this one had an air of natural nobility for all his lowly station. Intangible to the eye, it radiated off him like an aura. No other man of her acquaintance had such elegant male beauty. Particularly not Simon.

But would she have the skill to do him justice? It would mean spending hours in his company—his naked company—if she was to work in the classical style she longed to emulate. Any decent art school in Italy would want to see more than drawings of birds and wildlife to accept her as a serious artist. If her portfolio presented a study of him, and if it was any good…

Would he even be willing? Perhaps if she offered to pay him? She didn't have much money, but she had some.

He glanced at her with a raised brow.

Heat suffused her face. What would he think of her, if she asked him to pose in the nude?

'Tired of waiting?' he asked.

She shook her head. 'Do you know why they call this Gallows Hill?' she choked out over the pounding of her heart.

'No.'

'They hung the last highwayman in the district here. Mad Jack Kilgrew. Apparently, he took to the roads when he wasn't allowed to marry the girl he loved.' She knew she was gabbling, but she couldn't stop. And since she didn't have the nerve to broach what was on her mind, she just kept going. 'They say all the local ladies were in love with him because he was so handsome and only ever stole kisses—the reason the menfolk hanged him out of hand.'

'Romantic claptrap,' he muttered.

She laughed. 'No. It is true. He stopped Mrs D-Dempster, the baker's wife, when she was a girl.'

'A man can't live on kisses,' he said.

'Well, he did. Along with the money he stole from their husbands.' She shivered. 'They say you can hear the rattle of the g-gibbet on the anniversary of his death.'

He grinned. 'You've been reading too much Mrs Radcliffe.'

The fatal grin again. She could not hold back an answering smile. For a long moment they said nothing. His gaze dropped to her lips and stayed there.

A heart-quickening tension gripped every nerve in her body. The small space between them seemed to shrink and she was certain his breath brushed her cheek. A shiver slid across her shoulders, something sweetly painful tugged at her heart. A longing to be held.

She'd felt nothing like it since childhood. She swallowed.

He jerked back as if he, too, resisted the strange pull. 'The fox will be along any moment now, if he's coming.' His voice sounded harsh, his breathing rushed, but his expression seemed quite blank as he stared ahead as if completely oblivious to what had just happened between them.

Nothing had happened.

She must have imagined the sense of connection. How could she feel such a thing for a man she'd met only a few times? But he was unlike anyone she had ever met. Handsome and arrogant, and occasionally humble. Well educated, too. He even knew about Mrs Radcliffe. Fascinating. And obviously very dangerous to her senses.

He touched her arm. 'Look,' he said in a soft whisper.

Pencil poised, she stared at the sleek red creature trotting into her field of vision. His bush hung straight to the ground, his shiny black nose tested the air and his ears pricked and twitched in every direction.

With held breath, she sketched his shape. Focused, imprinted the colours on her mind, even as her hand caught his outline, the shadow of muscle, lean flanks, the curve of his head. Attitude, intense and watchful—not fearful, though. Eyes bright, searching, body sleek, softened by reddish fur.

Apparently satisfied, the fox trotted the last few feet and, after one glance around his domain, disappeared into his lair.

Frederica didn't stop drawing. The image firmly in her mind's eye, she captured the narrow hips and deep chest, the tufted ears and pointy muzzle, the white flashes on chest and paws.

Finally, she stopped and rolled her shoulders.

'Did you see him for long enough?' he murmured.

She jumped. She'd forgotten his presence. 'Yes.'

'You draw with your left hand.'

The devil's spawn. She waited for him to cross his fingers to ward off evil spirits the way some of the other servants did. She should have used her right hand as she'd been taught by hours of rapped knuckles. But then the picture would be stilted. Useless. Tears welled unbidden to her eyes.

How could she have let him see her shame? She never let anyone watch her draw. She transferred the pencil to her other hand. 'I—I—'

His hand, large and warm, strong and brown from hours outdoors, covered hers. 'My older brother is left-handed.'

She glanced up at his face and found his expression frighteningly bleak. 'Y-you h-have a b-b—' she swallowed and took a deep breath '—brother?'

'Yes. I have two brothers and three sisters.'

'How lucky you are. Do they live near?'

She winced at his short, hard laugh. 'I don't know about lucky. They live in London most of the time.' He shrugged. 'What about you? Do you have any siblings?'

How had she allowed the conversation to get on to the topic of families? Had he really not heard the gossip about her mother, or was he looking for more salacious details? 'I never knew my parents.'

The small breath of wind lifted a strand of dark hair at his crown in the most appealing way. 'An orphan, then. I'm sorry,' he said softly.

'You forgot your Somerset accent again, Mr Deveril.'

He pushed to his feet, unfolding his long lean body and stretched his back. 'So I did, Miss Bracewell. So I did.'

'Why pretend?'

'Weatherby wouldn't have hired a man educated above his station.'

The words rang true, but she sensed they hid more than they told. Clearly he was not about to reveal any secrets to her. With a feeling of disappointment, of an opportunity missed, she packed up her drawing materials. It really was time to go or she would be late for breakfast.

She held up her portfolio. 'Th-thank you for this. I presume it was my last opportunity to see him at all?'

His gaze followed hers to the tools of his trade, the

fierce metal traps and the gun. He inclined his head. 'I expect so.'

She nodded. 'Good day, Mr Deveril.' Great way to convince him to let him sit for her as a model: accuse him of murder.

She'd have to do better than that if she wanted to escape her fate with Simon. And she'd have to have a little more courage.

Chapter Five

The gamekeeper's office beside the stables smelled of old fur, manure and oil. A small lantern on a rickety table provided enough light for the task of cleaning his lordship's shotguns before daylight would send Weatherby and Robert out into the fields.

'Did ye catch the fox on Gallows Hill yesterday, young Rob?' the gamekeeper asked in his creaking voice.

Until yesterday, Robert had never balked at culling Reynard's population. Cunning and sly, their raiding of henhouses and other fowl made them unpopular vermin. Caught in its natural setting by an artist who seemed almost as wild as the creatures she brought alive on paper, the dog fox had looked magnificent.

The far-seeing hazel eyes on the other side of the table required an honest answer.

'No, sir. I don't think that'un's raiding Lord Wynchwood's chickens, after all. The only bones I saw were voles and rabbits.'

'Hmmph.' Weatherby stared down the barrel of the shotgun, then picked up his ramrod. 'Still, it's a fox.'

'The most likely culprit lives by the river,' Robert continued. 'I've set traps.'

'Make no mistake, Lord Wynchwood wants to see a brush, lad. It's results what counts with our master.'

And it was the creatures who counted with the young lady of the house. The thought of her knowing he'd killed the creature she'd drawn so lovingly made him feel sick. He was a soft-hearted fool. She'd got her drawing, made a damned fine job of it, too. She didn't need the animal as well. Yet the sadness in her eyes had caused him to forget his duty to his employer. He'd risked his position for gratitude in a pair of ocean-coloured eyes. He must have lost his mind.

'He'll have his brush,' Robert muttered. 'I'll check the traps later.' Robert placed the gleaming weapon in the rack on the wall. 'Do you have any instructions for today?'

'Hares, if you can get 'em, and trout, for his lordship's table.'

Robert nodded. 'By the way, I noticed a break in the hedge down by the river—might be the way our poacher is getting in. Shall I have it fixed?'

'I don't know how I managed before you came along,' Weatherby said.

Robert nodded his thanks and picked up his far-inferior shotgun to the one he'd cleaned for his lordship. 'Is there anything you'd like for your pot, Mr Weatherby?'

'Not today, lad. The missus exchanged a brace of pheasant for a nice bit of pork. I reckon it will do us for a couple of days.'

Roasted pork. Robert could almost taste it.

'What you need, lad, is a wife.' Weatherby groaned to his feet and shouldered his own gun. 'You'd get a proper dinner.'

Robert couldn't imagine anything worse. What woman

would want to share this hard life of his? Not the kind of woman he'd want. But celibacy didn't appeal much either. Perhaps he'd snuggle up to the barmaid at the Bull and Mouth this evening. She seemed like a cheerful sort, and willing, from the gleam in her eye.

Weatherby gave him a dig with his elbow on the way to the door. 'How about our Maisie? She's taken quite a shine to ye.'

He repressed a shudder. As a kitchen wench, Maisie was a fine lass, but not one to whom he could bear to be shackled.

'I'm not looking for a wife until I'm better set up. I'd best be off, sir, if I'm to get all of this done before dark and catch his lordship's fox.'

Weatherby grunted. 'Right-ho. Talking of getting established, I heard of a position for a head gamekeeper opening up in Norfolk. Small place, mostly water birds. Might be a good start. I'd miss you here, but you've a talent for the work.'

Hard work did pay off. For the first time in his life Robert felt truly appreciated. He couldn't stop the grin spreading over his face. 'Thank you, Mr Weatherby. I'd appreciate your recommendation.'

'Ah. Time to thank me, if you get the job. We'll see, lad. We'll see.' He stomped out of the door. For Robert, hard on his heels, the chill winter day suddenly seemed a great deal brighter.

Out in the courtyard, he toyed with the idea of stopping by the kitchen and asking Maisie to deliver the book he'd dug out of his meagre store to Miss Bracewell. Charlie had purchased it for him when he'd expressed an interest in helping with the ducal estates. It hadn't taken Father long to veto the idea. The estates were not his concern.

For some reason he'd kept the book.

Miss Bracewell would find it helpful in locating the animals she liked to draw—assuming she'd accept a gift from someone like him. The thought cut off his breath. Servants, particularly Maisie, loved gossip. He'd be giving them grist for their mills if he did something so stupid. He patted his pocket. He'd better keep it for when he could give it to her privately.

If the young lady stayed true to her habits, he'd see her somewhere on the Wynchwood estate in the next few days.

Later that evening, Robert strode back from the Bull and Mouth with a foul wind driving needle-sharp rain up under his hat into his face. Trickles of water ran down inside his collar. Not that he cared much. The glasses of heavy wet he'd sunk with a group of jolly companions prevented the cold from penetrating too deep. Hardworking men they were, who enjoyed a tall tale. And he'd told a few of his own to uproarious laughter. Especially those about some of his adventures with the ladies. Embellished a bit. And no names mentioned.

He'd enjoyed himself.

He frowned, not quite sure why he was heading home in the rain soaked through to the skin instead of being tucked up cosily in a warm bed with the saucy barmaid. Cheery though she was, he just hadn't fancied her. Too many images of Miss Bracewell swimming around in his head. Lascivious images brought on by too much beer.

He lifted his head to get his bearings. Rain ran down his face, but he was so wet already it didn't make a scrap of difference.

A little unsteadily, he plunged forwards. 'Steady, Robin, or you'll end on your backside.' He got back into his stride, sure he was going in the right direction.

The evening had reminded him of the first time he and Charlie had ventured to the tavern near one of the ducal estates. They'd got rollicking, barely able to hold each other up on the way home, singing and laughing fit to burst.

In those days, he and Charlie had been inseparable. He missed that closeness. He missed his family. He even missed Father. They'd be at Meadowbrook now for the Christmas season.

Oh, no. No thinking about that, Robin. Not tonight.

Keep it sweet and light. That was the trick. What *was* the song they learned from the barmaid? How had it gone?

He stopped. Thinking. No. Couldn't remember.

He started walking again, the mud sucking at his boots as he staggered forwards. A tree stepped out in front of him. He bowed. 'Beg your pardon.'

Careful, Robert. You aren't that bosky. Just a little warm.

He picked up his pace. Became aware of a tune hummed under his breath. That was it. He raised his voice.

Last night young Nancy laid sleeping,
And into her bedroom young Johnny went a-creeping,
With his long fol-the-riddle-i-do right down to his knee.

'Bloody rude.' He chuckled.

He knew one bedroom he'd like to creep into in the middle of the night with his fol-the-riddle-i-do, and it wasn't the barmaid's at the Bull.

And it wasn't going to happen.

A shame, though. He didn't know how he'd kept his hands off her up on the hill yesterday. A bit of a surprise, since he'd never been attracted to innocents. She was the kind of female men married, whereas he preferred high flyers or a merry widow. The lass was good at her drawings, though. Odd sort of occupation for a gently bred girl. It would all come to an end when she found herself married and raising a passel of children.

A husband with the right to caress her slender body, to palm her small breasts, to stroke those boyishly slim hips.

Desire jolted through him, hardening his body, quickening his blood.

What the hell was her family thinking, allowing her to roam the estate without an escort? A prime target for men like him. Or, worse yet, men without a shred of honour. They were out there. She would be an easy target.

What the hell. It wasn't his business what the wench did. He had his work and his prospects to worry about and that was enough for any man. He picked up the next verse.

He said: Lonely Nancy, may I come to bed you,
She smiled and replied, John you'll undo me,
With your long fol-the-riddle-i-do right down to your knee.

That wasn't going to happen. He was likely going to be spending a great many nights alone. He shivered at a sudden chill running down his spine.

He stopped dead, his mouth open at the sight of a shadow huddled against his front door.

The shadow rose like a wraith. 'Mr Deveril?'

'Miss Bracewell?' Well, how about that. He just had to think about her and she appeared—or was it a beer-induced vision?

He shook his head to clear his sight.

She lifted a hand. 'I need your help.'

He knew the kind of help he wanted to provide and it involved helping her between his sheets. He wrestled his evil thought to the ground and his body under control. 'At this time of night? Are you mad?'

Her eyes looked huge in the light of the lantern. 'I'm sorry. I'll go.'

'Good Lord, how long have you been waiting?'

'I d-didn't expect you to be out.'

If he had one scrap of sense, a smidgeon of honour, he would turn her around and send her straight home. And let her freeze to the bone? A few minutes while she warmed up wouldn't hurt. He might a libertine, but he wasn't a debaucher of innocents, no matter how badly they behaved.

'Come inside before you catch your death of cold.' He grabbed her elbow. Beneath his fingers, he felt a shudder rack her fragile body. He cursed under his breath and urged her through the door. It took only moments to coax the banked fire into a crackling blaze with a fresh log. A sudden gust down the chimney blew smoke into his face. He coughed.

She laughed, a low smoky chuckle, and his body tightened at the seductive sound.

He shook his head. 'Did no one ever tell you it's not appropriate to visit a man in his house alone, late at night?' He tossed another log on the fire and poked at the embers. 'Why are you here?'

No answer. The door latch clicked. He leaped forwards and caught the door before she opened it enough to slip out. A blade of cold air cut through the room.

Rigid, she stared at the rough wood inches from her nose. 'I apologise for m-my intrusion. R-release the door.'

The raw hurt in her voice tore at his defences. He enfolded her fine-boned fingers in his. Ice cold. 'Come back to the fire. I'm sorry if I sounded harsh—my concern is for your reputation.'

She snatched her hand out of his.

'Is it not mine to r-r—' she took a ragged breath '—risk?' Despite the defiance in her gaze, she let him lead her back to the glow of the fire.

He shrugged. 'Then think about my position.'

Her shoulders slumped. She raised her lashes, eyes dark with regret and something else he couldn't make out. He could not read this woman. It was an odd feeling when most of them had been an open book.

Her soft mouth trembled. 'I am s-sorry. You are right. I should not have troubled you.'

Right now, looking into those fathomless eyes through the muzz of alcohol with heat from the fire warming his body, he didn't care about his job or her reputation. He desperately wanted to chase away the shadows in her face and see her smile.

'Apology accepted. Sit closer to the fire.' With hands that shook only slightly, he undid the strings of her oilskin cloak and tossed it aside. Beneath it she was as dry as a bone.

The grateful curve of her lips tempted him more than he dared admit. He cupped her face in his hands, small and chill and buttery soft to his work-roughened skin. The muscles in her jaw flickered against his palms. All he had to do was bend his head and claim those lushly formed lips.

A brush of his mouth against hers, a taste of heaven, one little sip.

Trust shone from her eyes.

The dregs of his conscience pierced his beer-soaked mind. Inwardly he groaned and dropped his hands to her shoulders and nudged her away.

Even the glow from the fire could not hide her blush. So pretty. So innocently knowing. So arousing.

He forced himself to turn away. He stripped off his coat and hung it behind the door.

'You are soaked through,' she said, sounding surprised. 'Did you not wear your oilskins?'

'It wasn't raining when I left.' He wasn't going to tell her this coat was all he had. He retrieved a towel from the dresser and rubbed at his hair.

She was frowning. 'You really ought to get out of those wet clothes. You could catch an ague.'

He'd have been out of his clothes and under his covers the moment he walked in the door if she'd not been standing on his doorstep. He'd like to be under his covers with her.

'Why did you come here, Miss Bracewell? You said you wanted to ask me something.'

'I did. But I think perhaps I was mistaken.'

Women. Now he'd have to charm it out of her.

A shiver ran down his spine. Despite the fire, the cold was creeping into his bones. She was right. He did need to get out of these clothes. He couldn't afford to get sick. And even if he was going to take her home immediately, he should at least start out dry. 'Turn your back.'

Her little gasp reminded him that it was not his place to issue orders.

'Please,' he said. 'I am going to change and, short of going outside, there is nowhere to do it but here.'

'Oh,' she said. 'Come closer to the fire.' She moved away from the hearth and faced the corner near the dresser. She looked like a child being punished for some naughtiness.

He couldn't help smiling. She was naughty coming out here. He ought to smack her sweet little bottom. Damn. He did not need thoughts like that right now.

His glance fell on the brown-paper-wrapped parcel on the dresser top. He'd set it there before he went out.

He turned his back and set to work on the buttons of his vest with numbed fingers. 'That package is for you.'

'For me?' She sounded astonished. And pleased. Almost as if she'd never before received a gift. What did she think was in there, a diamond necklace?

He scowled. His days of giving gifts of jewellery were long past. 'Open it.'

Another shiver hit him. The effects of the ale were wearing off rapidly. He edged closer to the fire, stripped off the waistcoat, stripped off his neckerchief and shirt.

The sound of paper tearing was followed by a gasp. 'Oh. It's a book.' She sounded just as pleased as if it was diamonds.

'I thought you might find it useful. It has information about foxes and badgers. Their habits and habitats.'

'Won't you need the book? For your work?'

'Mr Weatherby is teaching me all I need to know.'

A feeling invaded his chest. A feeling he had not felt in a very long time. Happiness. Because she was pleased. And something more. Something he wouldn't acknowledge, not with this young woman who didn't have a subtle bone in her body. She was just too vulnerable for a man like him.

Damn. Between her and the beer he was so confused he didn't know what he was thinking. Then don't think. Get changed and get her home.

He shed his boots and stockings and peeled his trousers off. He scrubbed at his damp skin, focusing on nothing but getting dry.

Frederica listened to the sounds behind her. A man undressing. The rustle of cloth. The thump of boots. The sound of a towel plied vigorously. The urge to watch battled with modesty. Her mouth dried. Her heart fluttered in her chest. Warmth flooded her skin.

Just one little peek.

He'd asked her to turn her back, to respect his privacy. She wasn't going to betray his trust. But she did want to draw him and had promised herself she would pluck up the courage to ask.

She drew in a quick breath. 'Will you sit for me?'

'What?' His voice was deep and very dark and laced with danger.

She started to turn.

'Hold!' The word was harsh.

She heard him move across the room. Away from her. Away from the fire.

She huffed out a breath. 'I've always wanted to draw a person. In the flesh. I came to ask you if you would sit as a model.'

She heard a swoosh of fabric and turned to find him wrapped neck to toe in the quilt from the cot. Disappointment washed through her. How wicked she was, to be longing to ogle a naked male.

It wasn't just about drawing. It was him. The desire to look at him made all the more tantalising because of the glimpses she'd already seen.

No wonder he wore a disgusted expression. He must think her completely wanton.

'Do you have any idea what people would say if they found you drawing me naked?' he asked.

Well, that wasn't a no, was it? 'I-I don't care what they say. I want to be an artist. One day I want to go to Italy. Take lessons from a master. Right now, I am using what I have to hand.'

'Using?'

Now he sounded angry.

She waved an impatient hand. 'Not you. I meant squirrels and foxes.' She hesitated. If she told him and he betrayed her, it would ruin all her plans. Like everyone else, he wasn't taking her art seriously. So galling. Why couldn't anyone respect what she wanted to do? She inhaled a shaky breath. 'I am being paid. For local animals. For a book about British fauna.'

He raised a quizzical brow and sat down on the bed. 'Are you now?'

Was he laughing at her? His face was perfectly serious, but there was that slight curl to his mouth. If she could see his eyes, she would know, but they were in shadow. She moved closer, clasping her hands. 'I know it sounds strange. I know women artists aren't thought well of here, but on the Continent there are several who are famous. I just want to know if I have talent. Drawing the human body from life is the greatest test. You have a beautiful body. You make a perfect male subject. I am willing to pay for your services.'

He stiffened. His brows lowered. His grip clutched the quilt.

He was going to refuse. Somehow he'd been insulted by her admiration. 'I cannot pay much,' she said quickly. 'Say a shilling an hour.' She was gabbling. She couldn't seem to stop. 'It would be enough buy an oilskin,' she added with a pointed glance at his sodden coat on the nail in the back of the door.

His expression as he gazed at her was unfathomable. 'You are a strange young woman.'

Did he see that as a good thing or as something bad? Somewhat encouraged, she let go the breath she'd been eking out in little gasps as she spoke. 'Will you? Please?'

He looked at her for a long moment. 'Does it mean so much to you that you'd risk your reputation?'

'Yes,' she said, nodding her head hard. 'Yes, it does.' And besides, she had no reputation worth worrying about. She was surprised he didn't know.

'When?' he asked.

A shudder gripped her chest. Her throat tightened. This would decide her fate. 'Now. Tonight.'

'Now?'

'You are already undressed.'

At that he laughed. A laugh from deep in his chest. It rolled over her like a summer's day breeze, promising good things to come. She grinned back.

His laughter slowly subsided, though his smile remained. 'A bird in the hand, is it, Miss Bracewell?'

'Frederica,' she said. 'Please, call me Frederica.'

'Frederica,' he murmured. 'An unusual name for an unusual girl. I'm all yours.'

Her wicked insides did a pleasurable little dance of excitement.

He meant for drawing, she pointed out crossly.

Chapter Six

She strode around the room, narrowing her eyes. She wanted to capture him as she saw him, glorious, beautiful, dangerous. A brooding Greek god.

'Move the cot closer to the fire, please,' she said.

He flung the end of the quilt over his shoulder, making him look rather like a Roman senator, and dragged the cot across the room. 'There?'

'More at an angle, so the light falls across its length.'

He shifted one end into the room.

'Yes. That's good.' She moved the table with the lantern closer. She frowned at the way the light fell and the shadows it created. 'The light isn't high enough.'

'Here.' Stretching to his full height, the curves of his biceps carved deeper by shadows, he hung the lantern from a nail on the beam above his head.

She swallowed and found her mouth dry. Anticipation. Anxiety. 'Thank you.' Heat rushed to her face. 'Now take the qu-quilt off and stretch out.'

He shrugged. 'Your wish is my command.' He planted his feet wide. The fabric fell to the ground. It was a bit like watching the unveiling of a masterpiece, only better, because he was warm flesh and blood.

Nothing she'd seen in pictures or sculptures had prepared her for such a sight as this, though. Firelight played across the curves of his muscled shoulders and arms. Shadows and light sculpted his broad chest in a way an artist would weep to emulate. His physique was a perfect triangle, far better than da Vinci's *Vitruvian Man* with wide shoulders tapering to narrow hips. Muscle rippled across his stomach with its line of dark hair drawing her eye to the nest of dark curls between his thighs and his magnificent male member, darker in colour than she'd expected, and larger.

He looked lovely.

Desire pooled in her loins. Breathless and hot, she glanced up at his face.

A sinew flickered in his tight jaw. 'Where do you want me?'

Clearly he'd seen her ogling as if she'd never seen a man before. She hadn't. Not in the flesh. Not alive and vital. She opened her mouth to apologise.

No. She was an artist, she needed to inspect her model. But she had better start behaving like an artist and get down to work, or he might change his mind.

She drew in a deep shaky breath. 'Reclining, I think. Raised on your elbow, one knee up.'

He moved to straighten the covers.

'No. Leave them tumbled. They will make a nice contrast to your clean lines.'

He raised a brow, but stretched out and posed as she had requested, one hand covering his private parts. Her vision did not include modesty. This male was meant for pride and arrogance. 'The other hand draped over your knee, please.'

He complied and glanced along his length. 'I'm not

...o find myself in a caricature in Ackerman's sho
...dow, am I?'

'Ackerman's?'

'In the Strand in London. They sell salacious prints as well as views of London.'

'You sound familiar with them.'

He stared at her; his eyes became unreadable, his expression blank. Not the expression she wanted on his face. 'I have heard of them.'

'Well, I am not drawing anything salacious, nor do I plan to sell this work. I simply want it for my portfolio.' And perhaps to treasure as a memory once she left.

The picture he presented was good, but not quite right. Too formal, too tense. Ignoring the pleasurable little clenches of her body when her fingers encountered warm skin and sinew, she adjusted his arm so his wrist rested on his knee and his hand fell relaxed. She pushed and pulled at his supporting arm, until he looked like a Roman at a feast. She raised his chin a fraction so the lantern fell full on the planes of his face and threw shadows on his neck. She stepped back. And lost her breath.

Oh, God. He was lovely.

'If you keep staring at me like that,' he said with a half-smile, 'you are going to have quite a different effect on some of my parts.'

Her face flamed. 'I'm not looking at you like anything. I'm simply posing you to get the best of the light. But keep that smile.'

'Can I ask you to hurry?' he said. 'We do not have all night.'

Brought back to reality in a flood of anxiety in case he changed his mind, she picked up her papers and pencils from the table and set to work. Her stomach clenched.

What if she couldn't? What if her lines and curves showed nothing but the outer shell of the man?

Her wrist seized in a knot and her fingers trembled. She forced herself to begin with his head. Slowly the flow of lines across the paper settled her heartbeat and her fluttering stomach as she focused on form and shape and play of light and shadow across skin and bone and muscle.

'Where did you learn to draw?' he asked.

'From the books in my uncle's library. When he wasn't looking.'

He raised a brow at that. He probably thought her wicked. Mentally, she shrugged. He was probably right. With a mother like hers it wouldn't come as a surprise to anyone. And her father might have been a whole lot worse if the gossip she'd heard came anywhere close to the truth.

Or perhaps he was the one who'd bequeathed her a love of art? Hardly likely, given the low company her mother kept.

She focused on her flying fingers. 'Did you always want to be a gamekeeper?'

He spoke slowly as if picking his words. His expression reverted to blank and his accent to west country. 'I grew up on the estate of a great nobleman. I liked the work.'

He did not say which nobleman, clearly preferring to keep his origins a secret when most would be only too eager to speak of their high connections. Was that it? Was he, like her, the unwanted bastard of some noble house? The question was poised on the tip of her tongue, but something held it back. His guarded air. His frown. Already his attitude had changed from relaxed to tense.

Another skill needed by a portrait painter. The ability to set a subject at ease. *Find a less sensitive topic*. She jerked her chin towards the table, to the book he had given her. 'Where does your brother live?'

'I have no idea.' His face grew hard, his eyes shuttered. Were there no safe topics for this man?

She let some time elapse, worked on his shoulders, the line of his neck, before trying again. 'Where did you g-go this evening.'

'To the Bull.' The muscles in his face relaxed.

'Oh. What kind of drink do you prefer?'

'Brandy.' His answer came swiftly, then he shot her a sharp look. 'And ale.'

While he answered her questions, she sketched his hand in rough on a separate piece of paper. It would take too long to complete now. Fingers were hard. She moved on to his feet. Large feet at the end of long well-formed legs. 'Do you dance?'

'I do, when required.'

'What kind of dances?'

'Country dances, cotillions, waltzes.'

'Waltzes? You know how to waltz?' She stopped drawing and looked at him.

His mouth thinned as if he thought he had said too much. He took a breath and deliberately eased his jaw. 'Do you like to dance?'

She wrinkled her nose. 'I'm not sure.'

'All ladies love dancing,' he scoffed as if challenging her indecision. 'For me it was always a means to an end.' His expression darkened to that of a brooding angel staring into the depths of hell. An expression that brooked no further questions. And fired her artist's imagination.

Perfect. While he lost himself in his own thoughts her pencil flew.

A long time later she became aware of his gaze on her face.

'Almost done,' she said, looking down at her sketch. The

lantern above his head flickered and died. 'Oh, we need more oil.'

'That was the last of it,' he said, his tone resigned. 'I have one or two candles in the dresser.'

Guilt washed through her. Absorbed in her work, she had forgotten all about him as a person. No, not true. She had never been so aware of any individual in her life; her senses were awash with his mood, his physical presence, and, while she worked, he became part of her, intrinsic to her being, as if they were one.

And as a result she had used up all his oil. She would beg some from Snively and bring it to him tomorrow.

Stretching her back and rolling her shoulders, she felt the pull of muscles. He must also be stiff from remaining still for so long. 'I am finished.'

'Good,' he said.

Her gaze flew to his face. No longer brooding, it exuded determination. And he had not asked to see the work. Afraid he might find it hopeless, perhaps, and not want to lie?

Frederica stared at the paper in the light from the candle on the table, at his face, his body, and saw the likeness and more. The drawing resonated with his dark persona, a simmer of anger beneath the outward calm. It was the best thing she'd ever done. At least she thought so. It still needed work. When she got back to her room and daylight she would touch it up from the memory branded on her brain.

Sadness sat like a rock in the pit of her stomach. She often felt that way when she completed a work. But this felt worse—a sort of emptiness, because he'd been kind and she would one day leave and never see him again. There weren't many kind people in her life.

'I suppose I should go,' she said in a hoarse breathless voice.

He looked at her sharply. 'I'll walk you.'

'Oh, no. I wouldn't like you to go out in the rain again. I'll be perfectly fine.' She got up and packed up her papers and pencils.

He got up, came around the table and grasped her shoulders in his big strong hands. Hands she would later draw, while she remembered their pressure on her skin and the flesh beneath. 'Don't be stubborn.'

She looked up at him. At the worry in his face. At the firm set to his lips. Earlier, she had thought he might kiss her. But he'd pushed her away. He didn't find her attractive. Of course he didn't. A man like him would have his choice of women. And he would not choose a plain, skinny female like her.

But he wasn't completely immune. Of that she was sure. There had been too much heat in his gaze when he'd stared at her earlier.

He must have thought she was awfully bold coming here at night. Wanton. Like her mother.

Prickles of shame ran across her shoulders. 'When we were children, S-Simon said my speech was enough to put any man off.'

'Whoever this Simon is, he's an idiot,' he said harshly.

He strode across the room, gloriously naked. She watched him avariciously, like a miser might watch his pile of gold glint in the firelight. He moved with a grace and an economy of movement one didn't expect from such a large man. It was like watching a sonnet, muscle and sinew moving in perfect harmony.

She wanted to draw him crouched at the fire, the warm glow bronzing his skin and casting shadows over muscles and sharp angles. She wanted to draw him with the flicker of the candle making his dark axe-like features seem almost satanic as he set the candles on the rough-hewn table.

She wanted to touch him.

He opened the lid of a battered chest in the corner.

She came up behind him. "He is a sort of cousin."

He glanced over his shoulder. 'Sort of?'

'We are distant relations.' As in on the other side of the proverbial blanket. Didn't he know? She was sure the servants gossiped about it. She looked down into the chest. It held a couple of neatly folded shirts, trousers and some woollen stockings.

Unable to resist, she ran a fingertip over his shoulder blade and down the knobby protrusions of his spine as she visualised the skeleton beneath, the supporting ribs, the narrow hip bones…

He froze, mid-movement, the trousers in his hand.

She snatched her hand back as he whirled around. His eyes blazed anger, or some equally dangerous emotion that left her breathless and trembling like the aspens in Wynch-wood churchyard.

He closed his eyes as if in pain. 'Innocent, gently bred females do not go around running their hands over naked men.' He pulled on the trousers, the fabric hiding his beautiful body from her hungry gaze.

He cursed. 'Any men. What do you think your family would say?'

'I'm no innocent. And I don't care what Uncle Mortimer thinks.' She had tried for years to make him think well of her, to no avail. And now he was going to marry her off to Simon.

'Not innocent?' he scoffed, but there was a glimmer of hope in his expression, like a small boy eying a biscuit barrel.

With a mother like hers, how could she be innocent? She certainly wasn't ignorant. A book by a woman of pleasure and caricatures by Thomas Rowlandson found hidden in her uncle's library, both deliciously explicit, had stirred illicit sensations in her body, just as his nearness induced the ache of arousal.

'W-would you like to find out?' Her words came out in a breathy rush, too eager, too desperate.

'No,' he said.

'Because you don't find me attractive.'

He half-groaned, half-laughed. 'Not that. Definitely not that. I've had too much to drink. You've got your drawing and I don't want to lose my job.'

'I would never tell anyone.'

'You are a naughty little puss. Do you know that? A temptress.' His lips brushed her ear, her throat, her collarbone, sending shivers down her spine, tightening her nipples. 'Leave now, before I take you at your word.'

Shivers turned to rivers of molten metal in her blood. Her heart beat so hard, she could not draw breath. She turned to face him, to look into his eyes, but his thoughts were hidden by shadows cast by the fire. 'I don't want to go. I want to kiss you.'

Heat flared in his eyes. 'One kiss, then,' he murmured seductively.

Weak with anticipation, she lifted her chin and closed her eyes. Nothing happened.

She opened her eyes.

He raised a brow. 'You said you wanted to kiss me.'

The raised brow and the glimmer of laughter in his eyes said he thought she wouldn't dare. Her breath stuck in her throat. Was he right? She had no experience kissing a man.

But she had seen the pictures. She leaned forwards and brushed her mouth against his firm lips. He didn't move. She placed her hands on his broad shoulders, feeling sinew and bone beneath her palms, along with growing heat. She touched her tongue to the seam of his lips.

He opened his mouth. Her insides clenched more powerfully than anything she had experienced during her imaginings. His hands slid up her back, drawing her closer. Lips, warm and soft, moved over hers with persuasive pressure. Her lips parted in response.

'Oh, yes, sweetheart,' he murmured against her mouth. He licked her lower lip. A delicious thrill trickled down her spine. See, she did know. It was in her blood. She slid her hands around his neck, ran her fingers through his hair.

He angled his head, his mouth moving and coaxing and teasing. Chills shivered through her body, leaving her weak. She parted her lips to his teasing tongue and she clung to him, panting against his wonderful mouth.

He pulled away. 'God, give me strength.'

Ragged breaths shaking her frame, she watched him rub his palms on his thighs and realised his breathing was equally fast. 'That is all you want?'

He half-laughed, half-groaned. 'What I want and what I can take are very different.'

While she didn't know exactly what she wanted, she knew they had been heading in the right direction during their kiss, and that it was just the beginning. When she worked on a sketch, each pencil stroke brought the design closer to completion. Heavenly perfection, if done well, a disaster if one misplaced a line. In the art of kissing, he was her master, and it seemed he was not prepared to complete this work.

'You find me lacking?'

'You little fool. I'm doing this for your sake. You are a lady. I'm…nothing. You will only ruin yourself.' The words seemed torn from him, regretful, as if he truly did not want to stop.

A sense of empowerment glowed within her, drove her to reckless abandon. She was, after all, the bastard daughter of the Wynchwood Whore. 'I am already ruined.'

Ruined? The word was a siren song to Robert's beleaguered senses. He'd meant to frighten her off. Scare her silly. Instead, he'd found himself battling the demon of self-control. Was this what the cook meant by devil's spawn? That this child-woman really was not the innocent she seemed? Was she his kind of woman after all? The kind who enjoyed casual, carefree encounters? The kind who had sampled others before him?

His brain, still hazy with drink and clouded by lust, was partly hopeful and partly angered at the thought of another man with his hands on her delicate body.

'Kiss me, R-Robert, please.'

Did she have any idea how alluring he found her little hesitation when she said his name? God, he hoped not, or he was lost.

He pulled her slight frame against him, cradled her in his arms, her hips against his groin, her small hands curled on his chest. It felt right. Too right. More than he deserved.

His heart sang when she lifted her face to him, her full lips begging to be kissed.

He couldn't look at her enough. It was as if he needed to absorb her into his skin, into the empty place in his chest that had been cold and hard and now felt soft and warm and full of longing.

She stroked his jaw. He hadn't shaved. He captured her fine-boned fingers, kissed the palm of her hand, her wrist, the inside of her elbow, felt her shiver of desire in the deepest fibre of his being.

Heaven could not be more blissful.

He caressed her back. Her neck above her woollen gown felt like silk. Exquisitely soft.

He slipped one hand under her knees and lifted her. Arms around his neck, she snuggled against his shoulder as if she belonged there. He buried his face in her hair, inhaled her unique scent. Intoxicated, he carried her to his cot where he lay her down. She gazed up at him, then raised her hands above her head, seemingly submissive, yet her sea-green and mysterious eyes held a glint of a dare.

Desire flamed in his body. Out of control, and yet control it he must. He swallowed a growl of frustration and knelt beside the bed. She captured his hand, kissed the knuckles one by one, her moist tongue lapping at his skin like a cat, tasting him.

'Lie down with me, R-Robert.' Her husky voice grazed the most sensitive parts of his body.

Desire, heat, lust, pooled in his loins. 'Are you sure?' He ground out the question from a throat so tight it hurt to speak. Even as the words left his mouth, in some deep part of him he dreaded her reply, whichever it was.

'Yes.'

His body demanded it, even as his brain advised caution. Damn caution. He'd given her every chance to leave. She understood exactly what she was doing. He dipped his head to taste of her mouth, to savour her honeyed sweetness with his tongue, and lost his senses.

Light, fluttering, teasing, her hands roamed his back, smoothed his shoulders, explored his chest and arms and set his skin on fire.

His tongue swept her mouth, his palm found her high, small breast beneath her bodice. The nipple pearled against his palm, begging for his mouth, his tongue.

She moaned when he squeezed her beautiful soft flesh. Her tongue flickered over his lips, then plunged into his mouth.

Hard as a rock, he wanted to ravage her, fill her with

his essence, cover her with his scent, brand her as his own, possess her body and spirit. Dear God. No woman had ever brought him to such a state of mindless passion.

Where now was his legendary control? He hauled in a deep breath. She deserved more than a hurried engagement of the flesh, no matter how much he wanted to sheathe himself inside her heat.

Slow. Steady. Focus on her needs, her desires. He inhaled. With each deep breath, his heartbeat eased to a manageable level and control slid back into his grasp. He trailed kisses across her jaw, and soaked up her sigh of pleasure. He brushed his lips across the hollow of her throat and tasted the rapid pulse beat with his tongue.

Her thighs fell apart as if her limbs were now his to command. He licked the rise of flesh above her stays. He grazed her nipple through her chemise, then blew on the damp fabric. She shuddered and her hips bucked beneath him.

'Slowly, love,' he whispered. He caressed her ribs. Front closing stays, thank God. He untied the bow at her bosom. Firelight gilded her elfin face and threw mystic shadows across her face. A woodland sprite, a magical being who filled him with tenderness.

Between kisses on her lips and cheek and chin, he unlaced her ties. Finally loose, he tossed the stays away and eased her chemise upwards over a beautifully turned knee, exposed her thigh, where he pressed little kisses all the way to her hip. He shuddered on an indrawn breath at the sight of her pale brown nest of curls.

Intending to reassure, he glanced at her with a smile and found her watching him, her eyes full of firelight, her chest rising and falling, her body tense as if she might flee.

'May I remove your chemise?' he asked.

She nodded and bit her lip.

Despite his body's protest, he paused. 'Are you sure?'

Again she nodded, her gaze drifting down his body. 'Are you?'

'Oh, yes, my sweet. Very sure.' He drew the filmy fabric over her head and gazed in awe at her loveliness. A tiny waist hollowed beneath ribs he could count, his gaze lingered on peach-sized breasts with skin so translucent the blue veins shone beneath. He swallowed and let his gaze wander her elegant length, springy curls at the juncture of her thighs, already bedewed with her moisture, just waiting for him, strong legs that would wrap his hips when finally he rode her to bliss.

The grey woollen stockings held up by sturdy garters hid her calves and feet from view. He ran his forefinger under one stocking top and smiled at her. 'These too must go.'

The hiss of her indrawn breath tightened his balls. He almost lunged at her as desire clawed at his vitals. Not yet. Hand shaking, he rolled the garter down her leg and off, then tugged on the stocking until it slipped down her leg, inch by inch. He kissed each and every bit of beautiful skin thus exposed until he reached her toes.

Before he could say her nay, she stripped off the other stocking and tossed it aside.

Naked, she lay back. Her voracious gaze roved his body. The tip of her tongue moistened her lips. A shudder ran through him.

'Take off your trousers,' she said.

It was only fair. He stripped them off, grateful to be free of the confinement; his erection rose hard against his belly.

'Oh, my,' she whispered. 'It is lovely like this.' She reached out and touched the head of his shaft.

It jerked in response.

'Oh.'

He groaned. 'Any more of that and I will disgrace myself.'

'Then hurry up.'

'Demanding, aren't we?' In any other woman, he would have hated that demand. From her, it made his heart swell. 'Then I must obey, my lady.'

Careful not to crush her delicate form, he covered her with his body, took her lips in a kiss that demanded attention and heard her moans with deep satisfaction.

He caressed her, and kissed her breasts. She kissed him back, licked his ear, nibbled at his neck, her thighs open, her hips arching up begging for his attention. 'Soon, little one,' he crooned.

He stroked her hips, her swell of thigh, and suckled at her breast, until she became wild, her small fists beating at his shoulders, demanding what she wanted. Finally, he allowed himself to enter her body, to stroke the pulsing inner flesh with his shaft, to bring her to the height of passion, where he called on all of his skill with his hands and mouth to keep her trembling at the brink.

'Please, R Robert,' she moaned.

Raging desire ran rivers through his blood. He could not hold back any longer. He drove deep into her warm depths, pounding into her in fierce possession. He couldn't hold back, couldn't stop. God, if she didn't reach her climax… He shifted his weight, found the little nubbin of her pleasure, circled his thumb.

She shuddered, moaned his name, shattered around his shaft.

He wanted to die inside her.

Some small scrap of sense exerted itself and he pulled free, shuddering to a finish on her belly while she lay boneless beneath him.

He cleaned her up with a corner of the quilt and pulled her into his arms.

What the hell had just happened? One second he'd been in control, the next he'd been a raging animal. He pulled the quilt over her sleeping form, glancing down into her pale face, still blissful.

This was what she'd come for, of course. Not the drawing. Like all the other women in his life, he'd seen it in her eyes. And he'd not been able to turn her away, despite his good intentions. He'd have been a lot less susceptible if he hadn't been celibate for nigh on two years. He'd never been without a woman for so long since he'd first discovered sex at the age of fifteen.

No excuses, Robert. Apparently, Father was right. He was nothing but a dissolute wastrel. He'd risked everything for a few moments of satiation and the warmth of woman's arms.

He felt like the worst kind of cur. He'd wanted to protect her, but he'd been unable to protect her from himself. This must not happen again.

On a slow, pulsing tide, Frederica's spirit returned to her body. For long moments she floated on the heat of passion, listening to her heart, hearing his breathing slow, his hand warm about her shoulders and hip. For the first time in her life, she felt as if she had drifted into a harbour, safe from all the storms of her existence. How much time had elapsed? Hours, minutes? She had no idea. She only knew she wanted to remain here, cradled in his arms for ever.

Yet it could not be. Following her destiny required leaving England.

The breathing at her side was not the deep measured rhythm of sleep, just a steady rise and fall. She glanced up to find him watching her, his expression unreadable.

'I thought you were awake,' he said, his voice rumbling in his wide chest against her ear. 'I must get you home before you are missed.'

Conscious of her nakedness beneath his steady gaze, she sat up and pulled on her shift. He helped her with her stays and began fastening her gown.

He looked at her with eyes so bleak she shivered.

'I'll see you to the bridge,' he said. 'I won't come any farther, in case we are seen from the house. And whatever you do, promise you won't let anyone see that drawing.'

'I won't. I'll bring you the money for the sitting as soon as—'

'No. I don't want your money. Consider it another gift.' He pressed the book into her hands, opened the door and looked at her coldly. 'Do not come here any more.'

The words sounded as chill to her ear as the sleet felt on her face.

Chapter Seven

The next morning, Frederica set the portrait on an easel. She'd risen early to draw in the hands, and changed the cot into a roman divan and the rough blanket into a dark velvet throw.

In her eyes, he looked gorgeous. She shifted the easel to catch the north light and squinted at the drawing, trying to view it with dispassion, when all she could think about was his hands on her body and the beautiful, terrible passion.

Had she captured the spirit of the man?

A scratch at the door. She jerked around, standing in front of the picture as Snively stepped in. 'Good morning, miss.' He raised a brow at the easel.

'G-good morning, Snively. W-what can I do for you?'

'A letter came from Dr Travis.'

'Oh, good.' She stepped forwards to take it, then stopped. 'Er…would you put it on the desk?'

'Certainly, miss. I hope it is good news.'

'So do I,' she said with an embarrassed smile, wishing he would go.

'Should be a nice little nest egg when all's said and done.'

She'd told Snively about her contract with the doctor. She hadn't wanted the letters ending up on her uncle's desk to be opened without her knowledge. Snively, as usual, had been more than happy to help.

'As soon as I get the fox finished...' she nodded at the drawings on the desk '...he'll send the final payment.'

The butler set the letter down right next to the rough draft of Robert's hands. He leaned to his left, looking over her shoulder. 'Nice. Does him justice.'

Heat flooded her face. 'I drew it from imagination.'

'The kind of imagination that brings you home at three in the morning.'

She gasped.

'Don't worry. I won't tell anyone, but be careful of that young man, miss. He's not all he seems.'

Her heart sank. 'What do you mean?'

'It's just a feeling, miss. But you've trusted me before to put you right, so this is my advice. You've got through things pretty well up to now. Don't do anything rash. Your birthday is coming up. Your majority. Everything will seem much clearer then.'

'How?'

He tugged at his cravat. 'I can't say, miss. It's this feeling I have.'

'The same feeling you have about Mr Deveril.'

He glanced at the picture. 'No. That's a different feeling altogether.' His craggy face shifted into the small smile he sometimes gave her. 'It's very good, that picture, but you better not let anyone else see it.'

'On that I will take your advice, Mr Snively.'

'On the other too, I hope, miss.' He bowed and departed with his usual dignity.

Frederica pressed her hands to her hot cheeks. How could she have been so careless? She whisked the easel into the corner and turned it to face the wall. She covered it with an old shawl.

Dear old Snively, never one to get in a flap. And she could rely on him to keep quiet about what he'd seen, but if one of the other servants had walked in and seen the picture, there would have been a horrible fuss.

Could he have guessed just by looking at her that things had gone much further than her drawing Robert's picture? Did she look different?

She felt different. More like a woman. For a while, she'd felt desirable too. Their lovemaking had been so utterly wonderful. To her.

'Don't come here again.' He'd sounded weary.

Perhaps she'd disappointed him in some way. That must be it. Before they'd made love, they had been friends. Now, it seemed, they were nothing. He couldn't wait to be rid of her. When they walked home through the woods, he'd said not a word.

And he'd refused to accept any money. Did he consider she'd paid him with her favours? A rather horrid thought. It sounded like something her mother would do.

Or was it something much more mundane? Did he fear she'd betray him to her uncle? Well, she wouldn't. Never.

Frederica picked up the letter from the desk. Her hand shook as she read Dr Travis's words. He wrote first of his delight with the drawings received so far. He was happy to accept them for his book.

Her heart seemed to stop in her chest. He liked her work. It was going to be published. In a book. Dreams did come true. Even if they could not be published in her own name.

He noted that the first instalment bank draft awaited her, or rather waited for a Mr Smith, at the publisher's office in London. The second instalment would be paid on publication.

Her excitement subsided. It might take months for publication. She'd understood the final and much larger payment would be due on delivery of the last of the pictures. Without all of the money right away she wouldn't have enough to leave Wynchwood.

She picked up a pen and dipped it in the ink. Slowly and carefully, she pointed out that this was not how she had understood his offer. If she provided everything he asked for on time, should he not be equally as timely?

Feeling rather bold, she sanded the letter and folded it. She'd have to await his answer, before making her own plans. Another delay.

And then there was the matter of her unwanted chaperon. The meeting with Lady Radthorn this morning. No doubt the dowager countess would find her a dreadful disappointment. Too thin. Too plain. The thought of trying on gowns in front of the elegant lady made her stomach churn.

Nothing too expensive, Uncle Mortimer had begged, even as Frederica had begged him to let her cry off from the ball. Not even her lack of knowledge of the waltz had changed his mind. Just sit it out, he'd advised. Tell anyone who asks that I do not approve of such scandalous cavorting.

Scandalous cavorting, like her mother. They'd be shocked if they knew she'd been doing a bit of scandalous cavorting of her own. After all, *a bad apple never falls far from the tree,* Uncle Mortimer always said. She glanced down at the letters, her key to leaving the tree far behind. Carefully, she tucked the doctor's letter into her clothes press and her reply in her pocket.

Until the doctor's answer came, she had a role to play. Uncle Mortimer must not suspect a thing, which meant facing Lady Radthorn.

There was one good thing, though. On her way through the village, she could post her reply to Dr Travis.

Stomach fluttering as if it might fly off by itself, Frederica followed the Radthorn butler's directions into an impressive drawing room full of family portraits and gilt furniture.

An elegantly gowned middle-aged woman with grey dusting her pale gold hair and a warm smile creasing her patrician face held out her hands. 'There you are, Miss Bracewell, and right on time, too. I like promptness in a young gel.'

Frederica didn't know she had an option but to be on time. She took a deep breath and made her curtsy. 'Good morning, my lady.' Good. No hesitations.

As she raised her gaze, she saw that Lady Radthorn was regarding her with narrowed eyes and slightly pursed lips.

'Curtsy is good,' the elderly lady murmured. 'Gown is dreadful.' She cocked her head to one side. 'Looks nothing like her mother.'

Frederica's jaw dropped. This woman knew her mother? 'I b-beg your pardon.'

'Oh, la, did I say that aloud? John, my grandson, is quite sure I have reached my dotage when I do that.' She laughed, a bright tinkling sound in the spacious room. 'Would you like tea? Of course you would. And besides, I want to take a look at your comportment. Nothing like serving tea to separate a lady from a hobbledehoy, I always say.'

Lady Radthorn glided to the bell pull and gave it a swift tug. 'Do sit down, my dear. My word, you look terrified. I assure you I have not sharpened my teeth this morning.'

Was that a joke? It was hard to tell with such a grandam. Sure her knees were knocking, Frederica crossed the room beneath the critical gaze and perched on the sofa indicated by the lady's imperious gesture.

The dowager countess took the chair opposite. 'Now I look at you more closely, I see you have your mother's lovely skin.' She touched her own lined face. 'Poets wrote odes to her complexion.'

Frederica's heart thudded uncomfortably in her chest, questions stuck in her throat, like a fishbone gone down the wrong way. She swallowed hard. 'You knew my mother?' She had a sick feeling in the pit of her stomach. It was all very well hearing vague rumours from servants and dire warnings from Uncle Mortimer, but the thought of someone actually knowing the person felt like opening Pandora's Box. She wished fervently she hadn't asked.

'Gloria came out the same year as my oldest son.' She smiled sadly. 'My poor John.' She gazed off into the distance, lost in the past. Everyone in the neighbourhood knew that the loss of her son and his wife to influenza had been a huge blow. The current Lord Radthorn had inherited the title as a minor. But that had been years ago.

Frederica shifted in her seat. 'I'm sorry.'

Lady Radthorn blinked as if clearing her sight. 'So foolish. What is past cannot be undone.'

Were all those of Lady Radthorn's generation prone to quote little homilies? Uncle Mortimer spouted them upon every occasion. She clasped her hands in her lap and tried to look calm. 'True. Some topics are better avoided.'

The dowager looked at her askance. 'What do you mean?'

Heat licked at Frederica's cheeks. Oh, why had she said anything at all? 'The topic of my mother. The Wynchwood Whore.'

Lady Radthorn clapped her hands to her ears. 'Child!

Such language! Where did you hear such a thing?' She sounded horrified. And disgusted.

It might be one way to do away with an unwanted chaperon. Make her think she was utterly beyond the pale. 'It is the truth, is it not? The reason why no one in the family mentions her name?'

'I'm appalled.'

Good. Perhaps she'd send her home.

But Lady Radthorn clearly felt the need to say more. 'Oh, I'll admit it was all an embarrassment. But your mother was not...well, not what you said.'

Frederica stared at her open mouthed. Her heart gave a painful squeeze of longing. A yearning to know her mother and not feel ashamed.

It could not be true. The elderly lady was simply being kind, trying to make Frederica feel better. Her mother's wickedness had been drummed into her for too long for it to be sloughed off as a matter of degree. Her voice shook as she spoke. 'She had a child out of wedlock. I'm a b—'

'Lud, child, say not another word.'

Frederica snapped her mouth shut. Now she would be sent home in disgrace.

Lady Radthorn pulled out a lacy handkerchief and dabbed at the corners of her eyes. 'What is Wynchwood thinking, letting you believe this poison? Your mother married Viscount Endersley.'

The world seemed to spin as if she'd just stepped off a merry-go-round. 'My father is a viscount?'

Lady Radthorn coloured. Someone tapped at the door. Lady Radthorn pressed her finger to her lips.

Her mother was married? The stories she'd heard told of a young woman who bedded men on a whim, no matter their origin. A wicked woman.

Just as she, Frederica, had bedded Robert, because she

couldn't seem to stop it from happening. Because she was wicked. Like her mother.

Her hands were clenched so hard, her nails dug into her palms. She opened her fingers and resisted the temptation to wipe them on her skirts while the butler methodically deposited a silver tray loaded with a teapot, pretty china cups and a plate of iced cakes on the table in front of her chair. She wanted to scream at him to go.

She needed to hear the whole story.

'Thank you, Creedy. That is all,' Lady Radthorn said. 'We are expecting Mrs Phillips shortly. Have Digby help her in with her swatches and fabrics.'

'Yes, my lady.' He bowed and left.

'Where were we?'

'A v-viscount.'

'Ah, Endersley. Gloria married the old gentleman under duress.'

'Old?'

The dowager nodded. 'His only son died unexpectedly and he desperately needed an heir. Gloria had been in and out of love with several young men during her first Season. Her father was in despair, thinking she would never settle on one. Then rumour had it she'd fallen hard for someone he absolutely refused to countenance.'

'Like a coachman? Or a criminal?' Or an assistant gamekeeper.

'Well, as to that, I couldn't say. There were rumours.' Lady Radthorn frowned. 'All the gentlemen adored her and if they knew this man's identity, they never said. Gentlemen are like that. But your grandfather, Wynchwood, saw Viscount Endersley's suit as the answer to a prayer. He was rich, you see, and as usual the Bracewells were balanced at the edge of financial disaster. He bore the expense of your mother's come-out with the idea she would catch a wealthy man. It was her duty to save them.'

'So she was forced to marry Endersley?'

'Nobility marries for duty,' the dowager countess pronounced. 'If one is fortunate, as I was, love grows after a time. If not...' she shrugged '...one endures.' She let go a sigh. 'Gloria was not the enduring kind, I'm afraid. Endersley knew the child she carried wasn't his when you were born three months early.'

'I was born in wedlock?' She could scarcely believe it. All these years she'd been lectured about her place in life. Lowest of the low. Fortunate the family hadn't cast her off.

'Few men will accept another man's love-child as their own. Endersley put the word out that the child Gloria bore was stillborn.'

They'd said she'd died? She felt sick. 'And my mother agreed?'

'Gloria was in no case to agree to anything. Milk fever, you know. It killed her soon after you were born.'

Well, at least that part of the story matched what she knew about her mother. Everyone at Wynchwood saw it as justice for her wicked ways. 'I don't know why they didn't drop me off at an orphanage.'

Lady Radthorn's brow crinkled. 'I wondered about that myself, to be honest. My guess is Endersley paid the financially strapped Wynchwood off on condition he keep you. As a sort of punishment. It would have been like him to exact some sort of payment. Or Wynchwood might have done it for Gloria. He loved the gel. He was deeply saddened by his daughter's passing. Went into a complete decline. When he died, the title passed to Mortimer, a distant cousin of his, along with your guardianship.'

The thought of her grandfather grieving for her mother

was a shock. It gave Frederica an odd sensation in her chest to think that someone actually cared for her mother. It made her feel a little less of an outcast.

'If Endersley was not my father, who is?'

The dowager's wince made Frederica's heart clench. 'No one knows.' Lady Radford shook her head. 'Gloria couldn't have been more than eighteen when they announced her betrothal.' Her old eyes misted. 'It really wasn't fair. She rebelled. Said she was going to enjoy herself while she could. Things were different in those days. More free and easy. My son John said there was talk in the clubs. Masquerades at Ranelagh. Footmen. Even a highwayman. It seemed unlikely, but who can say.'

Criminals and servants? No wonder she'd earned the horrid sobriquet from her family. Nor had she given a thought to the result. An unwanted child. 'She was wicked.'

'Spoiled, I think. Too adored. I always thought her too finicky to have an affair with a man who was not a gentleman.'

Robert was a gentleman for all his rough ways. It was possible for a man to be of low birth and gentlemanly. Could her mother have fallen for that kind of man? Or was she completely wanton as Uncle Mortimer said?

She desperately wanted to believe Lady Radthorn, but feared Uncle Mortimer, a member of the family, was more likely to be privy to the truth.

The dowager countess was looking at her sadly, as if she felt sympathy for her mother, which was really rather sweet.

Frederica sat a little straighter in her chair, felt a little less guilty about who she was. An odd feeling filled her chest. 'Thank you,' she said. And she meant it. 'You've answered questions I never dared ask.'

'And added some too, I'll warrant,' the old lady said kindly.

Not added, just increased her curiosity and dread. Who was her real father?

The widow tucked her handkerchief away and smiled. 'And now it seems your family has decided to let bygones be bygones and bring you out. You know, I never had a daughter and here you are, attending your first ball, and I am to bring you up to scratch. We are going to have such fun spending your uncle's blunt. Now, young lady, serve the tea—we have a great deal to do before the seamstress arrives.'

Frederica poured milk into both cups.

'Ah,' Lady Radthorn said, 'a very good start.'

The next hour proved less arduous than Frederica expected despite Lady Radthorn's constant verbal stream of instructions.

'Now to deportment,' Lady Radthorn announced after the butler retired with the tea tray. 'Let me see you walk across the room.'

It wasn't her walking that would cause her trouble, it was her speech, though Lady Radthorn hadn't said a word about her hesitations. The thought of talking to a herd of strangers made her quake in her shoes.

None the less, Frederica rose and walked to the window through which she had an excellent view of the park's formal gardens. They seemed to stretch for miles. If only she could be out there, instead of in here, even if the grey lining to the large fluffy clouds did portend rain.

'Straighten your shoulders, Miss Bracewell. Keep your chin up. Breeding shows in every step. Walk as if you are floating on air, not tramping through a field.'

On air? She felt like she was sinking into a quagmire. Still, who could resist Lady Radthorn?

'Turn,' the doughty lady said. 'No, no. Not like that. As if you had a book on your head. Try again.'

Frederica did.

'Much better, gel. You've your mother's grace if nothing else.'

The compliment almost sent her to her knees.

Her taskmaster tsked. 'Now you are sagging again. Straighten your spine. Imagine a chord from the top of your head to the ceiling and it is too short. Glide, gel. Glide. As if you were waltzing. You do know how to waltz, or course.'

Oh, God. More evidence of her lack of breeding. 'I d-d-d—'

'Do.' Lady Radthorn flicked her fingers. 'Of course you do. All young ladies do these days. Wait until you see John, my grandson. He is a wonderful dancer.'

Another knock at the door diverted Lady Radthorn's attention and cut off Frederica's words.

'Mrs Phillips is here, my lady,' the butler said.

'Show her in at once.' Lady Radthorn rubbed her blue-veined hands together. 'Now we will truly enjoy ourselves.'

And they did, much to Frederica's astonishment. But who would not be charmed by the array of muslins and laces brought by the seamstress? Best of all, the two ladies consulted Frederica about each item selected, often praising her taste and sense of style. She put it down to her artist's eye, though she didn't say that to the two women.

Informed of the urgency, Mrs Phillips had brought several ready-made gowns from which to choose with the idea of altering them to fit. The riding habit was to be made new, as well as an evening gown.

'Do you think you can manage all of that in three days, Mrs Phillips?' Lady Radthorn asked, leaning against the sofa back and fanning her face.

The bird-like Scottish lady smiled. 'Oh, I think so, your ladyship. I'll gain some help from a couple of lasses I know.' She turned to Frederica. 'And it is pleasure, I assure you, to dress such a lovely young lady.'

Frederica's heart jumped. Lovely? Not possible. It must be flattery because they'd spent so much money. Although Robert could not have found her completely unattractive or he wouldn't have... Oh, heavens. If Lady Radford guessed at the direction of her thoughts, she'd probably dismiss her as worse than her mother and toss her out on her ear. She didn't want that. She liked the dowager countess. She was the first person who had taken any real interest in her, apart from Robert. She'd do anything to keep her friendship.

'Thank you, Mrs Phillips,' she said. 'There is one thing we haven't yet discussed.'

'Nonsense,' Lady Radthorn said. She counted off on her fingers. 'Three morning dresses, two afternoon dresses, a pelisse, an evening gown and a riding habit.' She frowned at Frederica. 'That was all your uncle asked for.'

'The m-masked ball?' Frederica said.

'Oh, my,' Mrs Phillips said, her eyes widening. 'That's right. A costume. Oh, mercy.'

'Masked?' Lady Radthorn said. 'What flummery.'

Frederica wanted to giggle at her disparaging tone. 'Simon requested it.' She rather liked the idea of pretending to be someone else for one night.

'Well,' Mrs Phillips said, 'if the young lady is wanting to go as Mary Queen of Scots or some mythical beast, I truly will not have time to make all of these other things as well. A poor body can only do so much, your ladyship.'

'Let me think,' Lady Radthorn said. 'I dressed once

as Guinevere, and Radthorn was Arthur. All that metal clanking around quite gave me a headache.'

'I had thought of something less complicated,' Frederica said. 'Perhaps a Roman lady. It needs no more than a long length of white sheeting.'

'Too plain,' Lady Radthorn said, narrowing her eyes on Frederica as if she was an exotic weed that had shown up in a bouquet. 'But, yes, something simple. Something to show off your delicate skin and lovely figure.'

There was that word *lovely* again. Frederica felt heat in her cheeks and a bubble of something pleasant in her chest, as if life suddenly held a great deal of promise. Was this part of Uncle Mortimer's plot? Woo her with gowns and balls, so she would go like a lamb to the slaughter?

'What about Titania?' Mrs Phillips said. 'From *A Midsummer Night's Dream*. A wisp or two of fabric, some wings and daisy crown. Sure, I could do that in an hour or two.'

A wisp of fabric? Frederica shivered. 'I prefer the sheeting.'

'Nonsense. My word, gel, it is the very thing. Caroline Lamb would have eaten her heart out for curves like yours. Titania it is.'

'I—'

'I'll hear no more from you, miss.' Lady Radthorn laid the back of her hand against her high forehead. 'I am exhausted. Ring the bell for Creedy and a footman to help Mrs Phillips out and then take yourself off.'

When Frederica didn't move, she sat up. 'No arguments. Go along, child. Come back tomorrow and we will continue our lessons.'

In short order, Frederica found herself bundled out of the house and into her uncle's waiting carriage.

She collapsed against the squabs. Titania. And she had

hoped to spend the ball hiding out in a corner, avoiding Simon. She would have to hide if all they gave her was a wisp of fabric. And Lady Radthorn thought she knew how to waltz.

There was one person she trusted who knew how, but he had forbidden her to call.

For Robert, the New Year had come and gone with barely a mention. The next day, collar turned up against the wind, he walked to Wynchwood. The faint grey of dawn was already dimming the stars to the east. He'd grown to love the peace of the early mornings, but today he felt tired. Once again, thoughts of Frederica had kept him tossing and turning on his cot and now if he didn't hurry he'd be late. Damn the girl for plaguing his nights. The lost look she'd given him when he told her not to come back had been a hard bed mate, particularly when all he'd wanted to do was pull her close and offer comfort.

As well as seek his own.

He should never have drunk so much.

Damnation, he should never have dallied with the girl, innocent or no. But he just couldn't resist, could he? A wastrel, Father had called him. Dissolute. Perhaps the reason it hurt so much was because he'd been right.

Making love to her had been incredible, but he still couldn't believe he'd jeopardised his position here at Wynchwood for the fulfilment of transient lust. From now on, he must ignore her, or better yet frighten her off.

The trouble with that plan was that she seemed hard to scare. He'd thought she'd run a mile when he called her bluff, but she'd accepted his challenge and he'd forgotten his intentions in the pleasure of her arms.

Never again.

The decision lay on his chest, cold and hard, as he

strode across the stable yard where the impending visit
of London gentry had already made its impact by way of
freshly washed cobbles and repaired stable doors.

Young Bracewell had not been part of his circle of
friends, thank God, so there should not be anyone in the
party of guests he knew well. For added security, he'd let
his beard grow for the past couple of days.

He knocked on Weatherby's office door and ducked
inside at the gruff permission to enter.

A lantern on the bench relieved the gloom and gave
Weatherby's weatherbeaten face a rather saturnine cast.
'I'd almost given you up, Deveril,' the old man growled.
'Did you catch our poacher?'

'I think I scared him off when I removed his traps last
week. It was likely some poor sod from the village adding
a bit of meat to his cooking pot.'

'You are too soft-hearted, my lad. It's his lordship's game
they're stealing. If you find him, you'll deal with him.'

Robert nodded obediently. *If I find him.*

'Ah, well, these are the plans for the guests' hunt. Think
you can handle it?' Weatherby handed Robert a map and
gestured him to take a chair.

Robert pored over the map. Weatherby intended to draw
out the fox from Gallows Hill and give the hunters a fair
run. So Miss Bracewell's fox had been spared his traps only
to end up fleeing the hounds. She would hate that.

Damn. What the hell was he doing, thinking about her
likes and dislikes instead of his work? 'When?'

Bushy brows lowered, Weatherby bent over more maps.
'Two days from now.'

'We'll need beaters from the village.'

'Right. Let them know. They won't want to miss his
lordship dropping of a bit of blunt their way, or the chance

of a stray rabbit or two. Pass the word down at the Bull and Mouth, would ye.'

'Be glad to.'

Weatherby reached for another plug of tobacco and stuffed his clay pipe. Robert braced for the choking smoke while Weatherby went over the rest of his duties for the day.

A half-hour later, he stepped out into a gusty north wind with the brace of pheasant Weatherby deemed ready for his lordship's table. Storm clouds gathered overhead. Another day, he'd go home soaked to the bone. But at least he had employment.

He glanced up at the back of the mansion. The diamond panes stared back like empty eyes. Was she up there somewhere, tucked up warm in her bed dreaming of foxes? Or dreaming of him? His body responded instantly.

Damn it. Why could he not get it through his thick head, she was not for him?

He strode across the courtyard and through into the kitchen where a rush of heat enveloped him. The scent of new-baked bread made his mouth water.

Maisie lifted her head from her churn and grinned. 'Morning, Rob.'

'Good morning.'

Cook bustled out of the scullery and he handed her the rust-coloured birds. 'I suppose you are looking for breakfast, lad?' She set the birds down on the table and planted her hands on her ample hips.

'If you've any to spare.'

Once in a while, Weatherby sent him in here first thing in the morning, knowing he'd be offered a hot meal. Another of the crumbs offered by the higher servants to the lower orders, a greasing of the wheels of servitude. The old gamekeeper had a kind heart beneath his gruff ways.

'Sit you down, then. Maisie, fetch the butter.'

Robert drew up a wooden chair to the scrubbed pine table. While Maisie scurried about setting him a place, Mrs Doncaster tossed two eggs and a thick slice of bacon onto the griddle hung over the fire, then cut off two thick hunks of bread from one of the cottage loaves cooling by the window.

Moments later, she slapped the bread down in front of him and pointed her knife at the pat of butter set out by Maisie. 'There you go, then, you big lummox. Eat hearty if you want to keep that frame of yours from caving in.'

Maisie giggled, then grimaced when the cook glowered in her direction.

Robert pretended not to notice. He stemmed his anticipation of a decently cooked breakfast by slowly buttering the bread. 'It's getting right busy around here.'

'Aye. T'ain't so much the master's guests,' she went on in a low grumble, 'They'n had enough in themselves. 'Tis all them stuck-up maids and valets what'll want feeding and waiting on. The master makes no allowance for that.' Her pudgy hand worked swiftly over the griddle. Deftly, she scooped up the eggs and bacon and dropped them on a plate. She set his plate down with a sharp bang on the table.

At the sound of a throat being cleared from the doorway, the cook turned to face the butler framed in the doorway. 'Good morning, Mr Snively.'

Another battle in the offing?

The grim-faced butler acknowledged the greeting with no more than a flicker of an eyelash. 'Maisie, Miss Bracewell is in the breakfast room looking for tea and toast.'

Not in bed dreaming, then.

'In this house, breakfast above stairs is at eight o'clock,' Cook muttered, handing Maisie a slice of bread and the toasting fork.

'Family is served when they want to be served. I will return in fifteen minutes for the tray,' Snively uttered in awful accents. Receiving no reply, he left.

'Family,' the cook uttered with scorn. 'Hardly. Making out like she's real family. Well, she ain't. Mark my words, she'll come to a bad end.'

A flash of anger shot through his veins. Hot words formed on the tip of his tongue. He swallowed them.

'Good Gawd, Maisie,' Cook yelled. 'Watch what you're doing. You've burned the toast again. Scrape it off quick and slap some butter on it before old Iron Drawers returns and finds nothing ready.' She turned back to Robert. 'You mark my words, blood will out. The mother was no better than she should be, and the daughter will turn out the same. Now, if you're finished, Rob, I gots work to do.'

Seething with rage, he clenched one fist under the table, taking one slow breath after another, angry at her. But worse. Anger he could say nothing in her defence. It was not his place to defend Miss Bracewell. Any sign of interest would fan the flames of gossip.

The sight of congealed egg on his plate turned his stomach. Either that or the vicious words had stolen his appetite. He pushed the plate away. 'Quite finished, Mrs Doncaster. Thanks.'

He rose and picked up his hat and coat. For once he couldn't wait to leave the warmth of the kitchen and get back to his labours.

Outside in the passage, where the servants' stairs led to the bedrooms above, he took a deep breath and fastened his coat buttons, residual anger making his fingers clumsy.

'Rob?'

He turned at Maisie's breathless call. 'Don't you have a breakfast to prepare?' he asked. 'You'll be in trouble if it's not ready.'

'Snively came fer it right after you left.' She closed the gap between them. He backed up until he hit the newel post.

'Cook meant to give you this.' She waved a small package. 'Tea.' She made a dive for his pocket.

He snatched the packet from her hand. 'Give her my thanks.'

Still blocking his path, she peeped up at him from beneath stubby lashes. 'They'll be right busy when the guests arrive. No one will notice me and thee.' She nudged him with a generous hip. 'Perhaps we can have our own party. Ee, but I do fancy you, Rob.' Scarlet blazed on her plump cheeks as she aimed a kiss at his mouth. Jerking back, he fielded her moist lips on his cheek at the same moment he heard a gasp from farther along the passage.

Maisie lifted her chin and glanced over his shoulder. Smirking, she bobbed a curtsy, then sauntered away with an exaggerated sway to her hips. 'Enjoy yer tea, Mr Deveril,' she called over her shoulder.

Wincing, Robert turned to face Frederica, feeling just a little too warm for comfort.

Frederica regarded him gravely from eyes swirling with grey shadows. A silent considering stare. He had no idea what she was thinking. A little jealousy would have been nice.

'She kissed *me*,' he said at last.

'I saw. You are certainly popular.'

Robert huffed out a breath. 'I thought you were eating breakfast?'

'Cook forgot the jam.'

Probably on purpose. He gestured for her to pass and turned to leave.

She grabbed his sleeve, glanced up the hallway and back to him. 'Snively mentioned you were in the kitchen. I wanted to ask you something.'

A pot clattered. They both jumped. Robert raised his eyes to the ceiling and saw no help forthcoming. 'We cannot talk here.' They would put two and two together and unfortunately would make four.

'I'll come to your house,' she murmured. 'Later.'

'No!' he whispered.

'Where, then?'

'Down there.' He caught her elbow, feeling once more the delicate bones beneath his fingers. A shimmer of awareness over his skin. He sucked in a breath and released her. 'The cellar.'

With a nod, she whisked along the hall and down a few steps into the dark. He ducked in after her. 'What did you want?' he murmured, aware of her scent mingling with the smell of coal and mildew.

'I need your help.'

'Ask your uncle.'

'He can't help me in this.'

'What makes you think I can? I told you it is best we not meet again.'

'Y-you s-said…' She gave a little moan of distress. She sounded desperate. His body strained in response, the desire to defend and protect rising rampant.

What the hell? He never let women get to him this way. Yet he couldn't help it with this one. He softened his tone. 'Take a deep breath, then tell me what is wrong.'

Her quick, indrawn gasp was like a knife to his heart. She sounded terrified.

'I need to learn to waltz.'

He retreated up a step, unaccountably disappointed. 'A dancing lesson?'

She touched his arm. An unexpected sensation in the dark. The heat of it travelled straight to his chest. He flinched.

She snatched her hand back as if she too felt scorched. 'I must learn to waltz or I will make an idiot of myself. Can't we still be friends?'

Friends, when the thought of holding her in his arms stirred his blood and drove his brain to the brink of madness?

Somehow he kept his voice calm, glad the dark hid his expression. 'There must be someone else who can teach you.'

She stilled. He felt her stillness as if her heart had stopped beating and had thus stopped his own.

'I'm s-sorry,' she whispered, her voice full of ache, as if her only friend in the world had let her down. 'I was wrong to ask.'

Now he felt guilty, a pain that hit all the way to his heart. 'All right.'

'I beg your pardon?'

'I'll teach you. One lesson.'

He heard her sigh of relief. 'Thank you. When?'

'Tonight. My house.' Footsteps sounded in the passageway. He moved deeper into the dark of the stairwell, protecting her from casual sight with his body. One of her breasts pressed against his arm; the scent of her hair, vanilla and roses, a heady combination, filled his nose. His body quickened. Demanded more. Somehow, he kept his hands off her. Breath held, he waited while the footsteps passed them by. No outraged shout of surprise broke the silence. Nothing but her rapid breaths against his neck. One move that even suggested she wanted to kiss him and he wouldn't be able to resist. She drew him, more than any woman he'd ever met. He worried about her, when he didn't want to care. People he cared for always let him down. He knew that and yet he could deny her nothing.

He was in over his head and drowning.

The sounds faded. He leaned close to her ear. 'Whatever you do, do not let anyone see you leave the house tonight.'

She nodded.

His body shaking with the effort of not kissing her senseless, he released her, strode up the stairs and, with a quick look to make sure all was clear, made the two steps to the back door and out into the yard. He released a shuddering sigh of relief.

Was he mad? Had he actually agreed to meet her again?

She'd looked so vulnerable, so afraid, he couldn't say no. Not and sleep at night.

He'd promised. One dance lesson, but nothing more.

God save him, he'd seek other work. Somewhere far away.

Wrapped in sacking, Pippin's hooves made little sound on the frosty earth. Thick clouds obliterated any light from above, but Frederica found her way to Robert's cottage with ease.

A faint chink of light shone through the shutters. She slid from Pippin's back and tied him to a tree. His hot breath warmed her chilled cheeks as she patted his neck. 'I won't be long.'

Her heart set up a steady thud in her ears. Suddenly unsure, she crept to the door and tapped softly.

Nothing. Perhaps he'd gone out and left a candle burning. Or perhaps he'd changed his mind.

She rapped louder and backed up into the shadows. If the door didn't open by the count of three, she'd leave.

The sound of a bolt being drawn through metal held her suspended between fleeing and staying. Her heartbeat drummed against her ribs.

Light spilled onto the ground in front of the door from his lantern.

God. He was just so beautiful. His shirt, open at the throat and tucked into tight-fitting buckskins, revealed a glimpse of crisp, dark hair at the base of his throat. The dark shadow on his jaw gave him a disreputable air. Frederica swallowed, trying to find enough saliva to speak.

Shaking his head, he started to close the door.

'It is me,' she croaked, stepping closer.

'I'd begun to think you weren't coming after all. Come inside before you are seen.' He leaned forwards, clasped her hand and pulled her over the threshold, and she stumbled into the room.

He'd tidied up. The bed was neatly made, no sign of supper dishes or clothing. The chair and table were pushed back against the wall, leaving an open space in front of the merrily blazing hearth. He'd been waiting for her. Her heart gave a little lurch of happiness.

She twirled around.

His face held a pained expression. He was looking at her legs. His eyes widened as he took in her attire, a pair of Simon's old breeches and one of his shirts. 'What in hell's name are you wearing?'

'I rode. I thought it would be easier than skirts.'

'Good God.'

'I borrowed some of Simon's breeches. He's grown out of them. And one of his shirts,' she said. 'I had to saddle Pippin myself and I need help to mount a lady's saddle. I know I look dreadful.'

'I wouldn't say dreadful.' His gaze reached her face and in the firelight, his eyes seemed alight with embers. 'Certainly...unusual.'

A giddy swirl hit her brain as if the air in the cottage had turned to steam and she laughed, albeit a little breathlessly. 'I always ride astride when I can. I can go so much faster without fear of falling off.'

'You ought to be spanked.' He looked as if he might like to undertake the task himself.

She felt hot all over. He wouldn't, would he? 'You promised me a lesson.'

'In waltzing.'

She eyed him warily. 'Yes.'

His jaw flexed and his mouth flattened. 'Then let us begin. First, have you ever seen a waltz performed or tried it yourself?'

She shook her head.

He huffed out a sigh. 'Then we will begin with the basics. A waltz is a gliding dance in three-four time. When danced well, it is a sensual experience for dancers and watchers alike. Performed badly, and it is simply two people galloping around in circles.'

He ran his eyes from her heels to her head. No doubt expecting her waltz to be of the galloping variety.

'Where did you learn?' she asked.

Her question seemed to catch him off guard. He blinked a couple of times as if trying to come up with a story. He gave a small dismissive gesture with his hand. 'In my misspent youth.' His smile was bitter.

The waltz was considered scandalous by many. He must have had a misspent youth. A flitter of excitement skated through her abdomen. 'Show me.' Her body trembled, awaiting his touch.

He narrowed his eyes. 'First, let me see you move. Go and sit down in the chair by the hearth.'

Puzzled, she strode across the room and dropped on to the seat.

'No,' he said. 'Forget you are dressed like that. Pretend you are wearing the most elegant of gowns. Do it again. This time don't swagger, glide.'

She went back to the centre of the room and walked slowly to the chair and lowered herself into it.

'Better,' he said. 'You are the most beautiful woman in the room. You do not dance with just anyone. Your partners have to be worthy.'

She batted her eyelashes at him and smiled. She didn't feel particularly beautiful, only rather silly.

He shook his head. 'No. Ignore me. Feel it inside yourself. Feel light. Ethereal. Beautiful. Calm. Be completely unconscious of anyone except the person seated beside you.'

'There isn't anyone.'

He glared at her. 'Pretend you are talking to someone.'

When she shook her head, he growled something under his breath. Seconds later he had picked up a broom and stood it next to her chair. 'You are an artist. Use your imagination. This is Lady Stuck-up. You are not visibly aware of anything but her gossip. Yet you know the world is looking at only you.'

She closed her eyes for a moment, imagined a ballroom full of glitter and members of the nobility. She straightened her spine, opened her eyes, but let the images remain. Her companion, a luscious blonde in a diamond tiara and sky-blue gown, spoke in soft tones. Music played in the background. Eyes followed each nod of her head. Aware of Robert's approach, she pretended not to see him, but smiled at something Lady Stuck-up said.

'Miss Bracewell,' Robert said, 'may I ask you to honour me with the next waltz?'

She slowly turned her head to look up at him. A small, devastating smile curved his lips. He held out a hand.

She hesitated for a moment. Would she, the most beautiful woman in the room, dance with this man? Perhaps she would do him the honour, this once. With a slight incline of her head, she rested her hand on his palm.

He stared at her for a moment, as if lost. He was certainly a good actor, playing to her role of *coquette*.

He raised her to her feet, placed her hand on his sleeve and drew her into the centre of the room, his guiding hand almost imperceptible as he steered her to her place, yet full of energy and demand.

How did he do that? She tried to look unconscious of his powerful presence.

He swirled her around, then placed one of her hands beside his lapel, and kept the other firmly grasped. She felt pressure from his other hand between her shoulders. 'The orchestra plays the opening bars,' he murmured. 'Listen to the rhythm. One, two, three. One, two, three. Feel it inside your body.'

He hummed a tune in a light tenor and a shiver raked her shoulders.

'Step back, step side, step around,' he said as he moved in a circle.

Stiff and awkward, she tried to follow his movements. She stumbled. His strong arm held her up.

'S-sorry,' she said.

'You are fine. Follow my lead. Relax.'

'If I could just see what you are doing with your feet...'

An eyebrow went up and he gave her a rueful smile. 'And I used to envy the dancing masters their job.' He released her and she stepped back. After a second's pause, he crossed the room and bowed to the broomstick. 'Dear Lady Stuck-up, would you be so good as to demonstrate to Miss Bracewell?'

Frederica giggled.

He shot her a warning glance. 'Remember, you are a haughty diamond of the first water, not a schoolroom miss.'

Frederica lifted her chin and stared down her nose at him. His look of approval gave her confidence. She maintained her indifferent expression as he picked up the broom and twirled around the room. At first, she wanted to laugh, but as she watched his lithe body and manly grace, her blood quickened and her insides fluttered in a rush of pleasurable thrills.

Silly girl. He isn't interested. He'd made it quite plain. She wiped her palms on her breeches. Watch his feet. Learn.

Gradually the pattern became clear, and she tapped her foot in time to his soft hum.

He stopped and cast poor Lady Stuck-up to the corner. He grinned at her. 'Do you see?'

'I think so.' Oh, she hoped so, or he'd think her such a dolt.

'Very well, we will try again.' Once more he encircled her in his arms. A tremble shook her frame.

'Don't be nervous. Remember, you are a willow, you are elegant, you glide, you do not hop like a frog.'

She chuckled at the image.

He frowned and she resumed her haughty pose.

'Above all, you are bold and confident,' he instructed.

As bold as her mama. The thought bolstered her courage. She took a deep breath.

'First the opening.' He hummed a few bars, then with the gentlest touch, he led her into the dance.

This time, she felt his directions, subtle tugs and pushes of hand and arm and body guided her steps. She floated as if immersed in the River Wynch's swirling eddies.

'Very nice,' he said.

She stumbled.

He laughed. A wonderful, warm sound. It touched her heart with the sweetest echo of pain.

'Next lesson,' he said. 'How to converse with your partner. Keep the music in your mind, let your feet listen to it.'

Now her feet had ears?

'You dance divinely, Miss Bracewell.'

'As do you, Mr Deveril.'

'Uh-uh.' He shook his head at her with a smile. 'A mere gracious thank you will do. And if you make a misstep, never apologise. After all, the man is in charge of the dance. If you falter, his is the error.'

And so it went, over and over, his chiding and guiding, her occasionally stumbling until a ridiculous conversation about the price of corn escalated to nonsense.

And she was doing it. Dancing the waltz, gliding and twirling and talking nonsense.

They laughed as he swirled her around in a complex set of steps and brought her to a breathtaking halt.

He stared down at her, his dark eyes full of laughter, his handsome face the most relaxed she'd ever seen it. Her breath caught in her throat.

His expression softened, eyelids lowered, his lips took on a sensuous cast. Unable to bear the uncertainty, she slipped her hand up to his neck and raised her mouth to his.

Who kissed whom, she wasn't sure, but the kiss was blissful, gentle and infinitely sweet. His chest rose on a deep breath and the pressure against her mouth increased. His tongue traced the seam of her lips and she opened for him.

The taste of him filled her mouth, the scent of him invaded her pores and, swept up on a tide of sensations, she clung to him.

Strong hands caressed her back, her hips, her ribs. So delicious. Her skin warmed and cooled as his touch trailed a sensual path of delight. One hand cupped her buttocks, pressed her against the evidence of his arousal, while the other strayed to brush the underside of her breast, then slid up to cup her fullness. Her breasts tightened.

She gasped.

On a groan, he broke away.

She clung to his shoulders. 'Don't stop. Not now.'

He held her close, cradled against his chest. 'We must not.'

She stroked his jaw, felt the springy beard, which softened its angular lines. 'How can it be wrong when it feels so wonderful?'

In the old days, the words would have been all the permission Robert needed. But this wasn't the old days. She was too young, too inexperienced and he was the wrong man. 'No. You came here to learn the waltz. Now you must go.'

'But I want you, Robert.' She flung her arms around his neck, ran her tongue around the edge of his ear.

His body shivered. She'd learned his sensual lessons too well. 'You say that now. But what about later, when ardour cools?'

'I don't care about later.'

This was desire talking, her newly discovered feminine

power. How many times had he seen it happen to débutantes in their first Season? Not that he had ever partaken of such forbidden fruit. No matter what she said, she was still innocent in so many ways. While she might have lain with some youth without experience, or some blundering man, she'd not yet been jaded by sordid affairs.

'Please, Robert.'

The agony of denial made his body clench unbearably. Lust for a woman had never ridden him this hard. There had always been another waiting in the wings. This one was out of bounds.

She'd lain down with him once, a small voice whispered. Why not again? One last time. What difference would it make? The insidious whispers drove a wedge between his conscience and his desire. Only the growing sense that if he succumbed he would never want another woman held him back. Was she indeed some other worldly being who held his soul enthralled? The devil's spawn.

My God, was he losing his mind? He pushed her away. 'Answer me this, then?'

Eyes hazy, she blinked. 'What?'

'Who was your first lover?'

'My f-f-first…' Her mouth, red from his kisses, trembled.

'You said you were ruined. By whom?'

Her lashes lowered, hiding her eyes. 'A lady doesn't tell.' Her voice was a low seductive murmur. 'Why do you want to know?'

'Did he break your heart? Is that why you are so reckless? Are you using me to…to get back at him?'

'No.' Her shocked denial rang true. Tears glistened. 'If you don't want me, just tell me and have done.' But now there was heartbreak in her voice.

He'd been too harsh, his tongue too rough. Unable to

bear the pain and confusion in her gaze, he pulled her close, kissed the top of her head, inhaled the scent of her hair, her unique essence, soothed her back and shoulders with his hands. 'I confess I find you irresistible.'

At last she relaxed and he tipped up her chin to look into her face. 'I'm sorry. I should not have asked. I'm trying to do the right thing, instead of what I want.'

She smiled. 'Right for whom?'

'For you, of course.' He cupped her face in his hands and took her lips with his and felt his soul rise to meet hers as she returned the kiss.

When he finally broke the kiss and pulled away to look into her face, she smiled. 'I want this,' she whispered.

After such a declaration, she'd be hurt if he refused. He could see it in her face. She'd feel scorned. Rejected. He couldn't do it. He took a deep breath. Then he would bring her pleasure she sought without taking his and let her go in good conscience. It was the only thing to do and retain a shred of integrity.

Mentally, he shook his head. The right thing to do would be to bundle her out of the door, but it was as close to right as he could get without destroying his fragile little elf. He picked her up and carried her to his cot.

He lay her down on the bed and stretched out beside her.

He captured her sweet mouth in a kiss. She responded by sweeping his mouth with her tongue, then drawing his into her mouth with a gentle suck. His member throbbed a demand.

He unbuttoned her shirt and exposed one perfect breast. God. No stays. Had she planned his seduction? Did he care as he gazed upon her breasts, a perfect fit for his palm? He rubbed the nipple with his thumb and watched it tighten to a rosy bead, heard her indrawn breath with a surge of blood to his loins.

He bent to suckle and she squirmed beneath him, arched her hips against his thigh in silent demand for more. Not so silent. The little cries in the back of her throat, the sounds of wanting, of desire, filled his mind, stole his thoughts, robbed him of control.

His shaft strained against his trousers, pressing for escape, seeking a far sweeter, hotter confinement.

To survive this torment, he'd have to bring her to a climax fast. Still sucking and nipping at her breast, he skimmed his hand between her open thighs, pressed down hard and circled.

At once she cried out, wove her fingers in his hair and quivered. Almost there. Please, God, let her be almost there.

He sucked her other breast, pressing and grinding against her woman's flesh, the heat of it burning his hand, dampness seeping through to his fingers.

So hot. So wet. He needed to be inside her.

His fingers tore at the buttons of his falls. One side undone.

No. He squeezed his eyes shut. He'd lost control with her the first time. This time he would master his urges. He went back to his firm massage of her, only to discover her fingers finishing the job on his buttons, her hand burrowing beneath his shirt and cupping him.

Her nails grazed his balls and his body tightened. Her fingers wandered, explored the base of his shaft. He thought he would explode in her hand.

'It feels so hot,' she said. She curled her hand around him. 'And so hard here. When you are so s-soft under—'

He reached down and grabbed her hand and pulled it free.

She stared up at him. 'Don't you l-like me to touch you?'

Heaven preserve him when she looked at him with those huge, seductive eyes. 'Touch me elsewhere.' His voice sounded harsh, but only because he was hanging by a thread. Her wince cut him to the quick.

He kissed her fingertips. 'I love it when you touch me there, but it will end too soon. For both of us.'

'Oh. I see.' She rubbed her hand over his chest. Through his shirt, his skin tingled with need to feel her skin to skin.

Dear God, he hoped she didn't see how much power she had in the palm of that little hand to bend him to her will. 'Yes. Like that.'

He swooped in for a kiss, anything to take her mind off her exploration of him, and resumed his ministrations with his hand. She sighed and moaned into his mouth. Her teeth grazed his tongue and she sucked his bottom lip. Ah, no. He was too close to the edge. He drew back

'What are you doing?' she asked.

He shook his head. He no longer knew what he was doing. 'Pleasuring you.'

'Take your clothes off,' she whispered. Her breaths came short and fast. She undid his shirt buttons and tugged the fabric free of his breeches. He whipped the shirt off over his head. Her fingertips traced the contours of his chest, then circled his nipples. 'Now your breeches and boots.'

He inhaled a deep breath, saw the heat in her gaze, the anticipation in her tongue licking her lips and sighed.

Why fight it? It would be the last time. He swore it. In seconds he'd stripped out of his clothes. When he turned back, she had her shirt off and was wriggling out of her breeches. In the light from the fire, the triangle of light brown hair at the apex of her thighs glistened with her moisture. For him.

His wood nymph, his exotic, wild woodland creature, glowing in firelight, begging for his touch. An unexpected blessing. A pure light in his blighted life.

Lost. He was lost. And he never wanted to be found.

He tugged her breeches over her feet and flung them aside. Ripped off her stockings in feverish haste. He covered her with his body, thrust inside her. Her heat, the tightness of her flesh, squeezed around the pulsing of his blood inside her body.

A sigh of fulfilment whispered hot breath in his ear.

Pleasure ripped through him, unbearable, the tension too hard and too fast. He surged against her, holding his weight with trembling arms, aware of her joy in the far-off reaches of his mind, but stretched to breaking point with his need for completion.

He came into her, hard and fast and rough, and she met each stroke with a thrust of her own that sent him spiralling to the stars. Together they rode all the way to heaven and the abyss beyond.

He collapsed beside her, face down, and finished against the rough blanket, blissfully satiated, yet wanting more. Disgust welled up inside him. He was what he had always been. A seducer. A rake.

She snuggled into the crook of his shoulder.

'Happy now?' he murmured for something to say, to divert his thoughts from his own sense of disappointment that he was not a better man.

'Very happy,' she said softly.

Moisture leaked from his closed eyes and he brushed it away. Because she was happy? Or because he might never again experience such joy?

While Frederica slept, her even breath a symphony to his ears, Robert watched shadows and licks of flame dance on the ceiling. How to extricate himself without doing her damage? More damage, he thought bitterly. In the old days, he would have sent round a string of pearls with a footman. Jewels were his speciality. This child of nature had no need for baubles and trinkets to enhance her beauty; she needed protection from a cruel harsh world.

And he wanted to be the one to fight her dragons. Even if he was not her first, he wanted to be her last.

Marriage.

Shocked, he inhaled a deep breath. Surely not. He'd never wanted to wed. Never wanted to be tied down to one woman. Was this simply a case of him not being ready to let this one go?

He didn't recall ever feeling this need for possession. Or the urge to protect.

Frederica stirred.

Robert glanced down and found her looking up at him. 'Time to go?' he asked.

She sighed. 'Soon. Robert?'

'Yes, love?' He liked the way the word tasted on his tongue, but it was as far as he dare go for the moment.

'What if I can only dance the waltz with you, here in this room? What if I trip over my feet?'

He pulled her close, felt her fear in the faintest tremor beneath her skin. He kissed her forehead and the tip of her nose, inhaled the musky scent of their loving and the essence of her, outdoors and fresh air with a trace of vanilla. 'You will be fine.'

He'd find a way to make sure of it. 'Come, let us get you dressed.'

The next morning, still feeling blissful, Frederica strolled into the breakfast room and found Snively hovering over the sideboard.

She lifted the lid of a silver platter and helped herself to a couple of gammon rashers. Goodness, she was hungry this morning. Today she would see the results of the dressmaker's efforts at Lady Radthorn's. The riding habit and the gowns would be a boon for her travels. Poor Uncle Mortimer. All that expense for nothing. One day, she would find a way to pay him back. In the meantime she'd do her best to make sure the ball went off without a hitch and keep her own plans a secret.

'Is everything ready for our guests, Snively?' she asked. 'Do you have all the extra help from the village you need to decorate the ballroom?'

'Yes, miss. All is arranged, as we discussed.'

Frederica smiled. There was no one as well organised as Snively. Or so willing to aid her over the years. She would be sorry to leave him behind. 'Thank you so much for your help. You will let me know if you have questions, will you not? Lord Wynchwood will have an apoplexy if we run into problems.'

He afforded her a quick smile. 'All will be well. Oh, I should let you know that his lordship asked that we move your things to the second floor in the morning.'

She stared at him. 'My things?'

'Yes. Next to the other lady who will be staying here. He thought it made more sense with company in the house. I'll set someone on it in the morning.'

So they felt a little guilty at hiding her away. 'I do not want my desk moved. Or my easel.'

A twinkle lit his eyes. 'Don't worry, miss, I'll see to that part myself.'

She grinned back. 'You are a dear. By the way, is there any mail for me this morning?'

'Michael is not yet returned from the village. If there is anything for you, I will see it reaches you directly as always.'

'Thank you.' She selected a slice of toast and went to her usual place at the table facing the window. Beneath a clear blue sky, a hoar frost sparkled like crystals on the lawn. Impossible to catch that glitter with a paint brush. She sighed.

Snively brought her a cup of tea. He glanced at the door and back to her. 'Miss Bracewell, are you thinking of leaving Wynchwood?'

Her heart jumped, heat flashed under her skin, followed by cold. She stifled her gasp and tried to look unconcerned. 'Whatever d-do you m-mean?'

'I've known you a long time, miss. I've watched you grow up. I know what goes on in this family and I've never seen you so happy, or so excited. Not since your uncle let you ride the gelding. You are up to something. And it's my opinion that you are planning to take the money from your drawings and run.'

Heart pounding, she folded her shaking fingers in her lap. Snively had always been her ally in this house, but as her uncle's employee, would he see it as his duty to betray her? His eyes remained kindly but concerned. Dare she give him her trust?

'L-leave? Why would you think so? For the first time, I am to attend a ball and I am to have a whole new fashionable wardrobe in honour of our guests. What can you mean?'

He frowned and stepped back, shaking his head. 'If I spoke out of turn, miss, I beg your pardon. I just wanted to be sure you will be here for your birthday. I have a gift for you, you see.'

She narrowed her eyes. 'For me?' No one ever gave her gifts on her birthday. Unless you counted her annual new gown as a gift.

He shrugged. 'I understood it to be a special day. Your age of majority, so to speak.'

He looked so uncomfortable she wished she'd told him the truth. 'How kind of you, Mr Snively.' The birth of an unwanted child had never been a cause for celebration. She couldn't help her sarcastic little laugh. 'I think my uncle prefers we not make too much fuss.'

A sheen of perspiration formed on his wrinkled brow. He looked as if wild horses were tearing him in two. He once more glanced at the door and leaned forwards and lowered his voice in a conspiratorial manner. 'If by some chance you change your mind, Miss Bracewell, promise me you won't go without speaking to me first. Please? I swear I'll tell no one else.'

He'd never ever let her down. She gave him a reassuring smile. 'If I were to leave, I promise I will tell you beforehand.'

'That is all I can ask, miss.' He bowed and stalked out of the room, and somehow she had the sense she'd hurt his feelings.

Dash it. She'd told him of her longing to study in Italy. He must have guessed she would use the money from her painting to achieve her ambition.

Surely he wouldn't interfere. He'd always helped her in the past. Still, she needed to be careful. She didn't want her uncle guessing her purpose before she was ready. And if Snively had guessed, someone else might too.

The following day, the drawing room after dinner seemed eerily silent. Even the walls seemed to be listening for the sound of the carriage. Frederica let go a long breath.

'Stop your sighing, girl,' Uncle Mortimer said. His eyes gleamed over the top of his book, softening the stern words. 'It is good to see you so anxious to meet your cousin again,

I must say. You are going to make a fine couple. Do this family proud.'

If only he knew. 'Simon said they would be here this afternoon. He's late.'

'They'll be here. The hunt is tomorrow.'

She frowned. 'We don't have enough horses for two extra people.'

'Don't be absurd, child. They will bring their own. Behind the carriage.' He made a sound in his throat like disgust. 'We'll have the stabling of them for a week, though, I'll be bound. They won't think to leave them at the inn in the village.'

'We have lots of room.'

'It isn't the space, girl, it's the cost. And there will be grooms to feed as well as valets and ladies' maids.'

'Just one of each I should think, Uncle. At least, that is all I have provided for.'

'Hmmph.' Uncle Mortimer returned to his book.

About to let out another deep sigh, Frederica stopped herself just in time. She picked up her embroidery and eyed the design. It would have made a lovely addition to the drawing room. It would never be finished. Working right-handed just took too long.

The sounds of wheels on the gravel and the crunch of horses' hooves brought Uncle Mortimer to his feet. 'Here they are at last.'

'Will you greet them at the door, Uncle?' she asked, putting her needlework aside.

'No. No. Too draughty. Snively will bring them in here.' He stood, rocking on his heels, his head cocked to one side, listening to the front door opening and voices in the entrance hall.

The door flew back. 'Uncle,' Simon cried, his round face

beaming. 'Here we are at last. Did you think we were lost on the road?'

Uncle Mortimer shook his nephew's hand and patted him on the shoulder. 'I knew you'd come, dear boy. Eventually. I just hoped you'd not be too late. Need my rest these days, you know. Not been quite the thing.'

The instant gravity on Simon's face was so patently false, Frederica wanted to laugh.

'I know, Uncle. The ague. You wrote to me of it.' He turned to Frederica. He had to turn his whole body, because his shirt points were so high, his head would not turn on his neck. In fact, he didn't appear to have neck or a chin. His head looked as if it had been placed on his shoulders and wrapped with a quantity of intricately knotted white fabric to keep it in place. It made his face look like a cod's head. His valet must have stuffed him into a coat two sizes too small to make him so stiff and rigid.

He bowed. 'Coz. I hope I find you well.'

Good lord, he had put on some weight around the middle, and was that a creak she heard? Some sort of corset?

'Y-yes, Simon. V-v—'

'Very well,' Simon said. 'Splendid.'

Frederica's palm tingled with the urge to box his ears.

Simon turned himself about and looked expectantly at the door. 'I want you to meet my friends, Uncle. Great friends.'

Snively appeared in the doorway. 'Lady Margaret Caldwell and Lord Lullington, my lord.' He promptly withdrew.

Pausing on the threshold, the lady glittered. Dark curls entwined with emeralds framed her face. More emeralds scintillated in the neckline of her low-green silk gown as well as at her wrists and on her fingers. Her dark eyes sparkled as they swept the room, seeming to take in everything at a glance. Lady Margaret held out her hand to Mortimer, who tottered forwards to make his bow.

All Frederica could do was blink. It was like looking at the sun. Compared to this elegant woman she felt distinctly drab even with her new blue gown.

Lady Caldwell sank into an elegant curtsy. 'My lord. How kind of you to invite us to your home.'

Uncle Mortimer flushed red. 'Think nothing of it, my lady. Nothing at all.'

The lady turned to Frederica. She tipped her head to one side. 'And you must be Simon's little cousin.' She held out her hands and when Frederica reached out to take one, Lady Margaret clasped Frederica's between both of her own. 'How glad I am to make your acquaintance. I vow, Simon has told us all about you, hasn't he, Lull?'

The viscount, a lean, aristocratic and tall man in a beautifully tailored black coat, finished making his bow to Uncle Mortimer, then raised his quizzing glass and ran a slow perusal from Frederica's head to her feet. 'Not all, my dear, I am sure,' he said with a lisp.

Frederica felt her face flush scarlet.

'Simon,' exclaimed Lady Margaret, 'Lull is right! You didn't tell us your cousin was so charming. Absolutely delightful.'

Simon stared at Frederica, opened his mouth a couple of times like a landed fish, then nodded. 'By jingo, Lady Caldwell, you are right. New gown, coz?'

'A whole wardrobe of new gowns,' Uncle Mortimer mumbled.

The burn in Frederica's face grew worse.

Viscount Lullington lounged across the room and took Frederica's hand with a small bow. His blue eyes gazed at her from above an aquiline nose. She had the sense he was assessing her worth. 'Delighted to meet you, Miss

Bracewell. Simon has indeed been a songbird regarding your attributes. And I see his notes were true.'

Oh, my. Had he just issued a compliment? And if so, why did his soft lisping voice send a shudder down her spine as if a ghost had walked over her grave?

Swallowing, Frederica curtsied as befit a viscount. 'I am very pleased to make your acquaintance, my lord.'

He patted her hand. 'Call me Lull. Everyone does.'

Not she. She backed up a step or two, looking to Simon for guidance.

He rubbed his hands together. 'Here we are then. All ready for the ball. It will be such a grand time.'

'Oh, it is sure to be, isn't it, Lull?' Lady Margaret took the seat by the fireplace and Frederica returned to the sofa. The men disposed themselves around the room, Lullington beside Lady Margaret and opposite Frederica, Simon beside the window and her uncle in his favourite armchair.

'Without a doubt,' Lullington said, his gaze fixed on Frederica.

Frederica took a slow deep breath. 'W-would you like t-tea?'

'We were waiting to ring for tea until you arrived,' Uncle Mortimer added. 'Didn't expect your arrival so late.'

'By Jove,' Simon said. 'What a good idea. Tea. Just the thing.' He looked at Lullington. 'If you think so, Lull? Do you?'

It seemed Viscount Lullington now pulled Simon's strings. Not a pleasant thought.

'Oh, yes, please,' Lady Caldwell said with a brilliant smile. 'We stopped for dinner when we realised the hour was far advanced, but I would die for a dish of bohea.'

All eyes turned to the lean viscount. He nodded his head. 'Very well. Tea for the ladies. For myself, I'd prefer brandy.'

'Me too,' Simon said.

Frederica got up and rang the bell.

Lady Caldwell smiled up at her. 'I wonder if, while we wait for the tea, you could show me my room. I am desperate to freshen up.'

Oh, dear. She should have thought to ask. 'S-s-s—'

'Surely, she will,' Uncle Mortimer said. 'Show our guest upstairs, Frederica. Don't take too long. My head aches if I drink tea too late in the evening.'

Aware of Lady Caldwell's rustling silks, her lush curves and exquisite face, Frederica found her tongue tied in knots. She would have liked to ask the woman about London, about the museums and the academy of art, but feared her words would only make her a fool. So they walked side by side in silence until they reached the bedroom.

Frederica opened the door and Lady Caldwell breezed in. 'Ah, Forester,' she said to a stiff-looking grey-haired woman standing over a brass-bound trunk, shaking the creases from a gown of a soft rose hue. 'Here you are.' She turned to Frederica. 'Come in, my dear. Fear not, Forester's bark is much worse than her bite.'

Forester played deaf.

Since the words of a polite refusal escaped her, Frederica stepped inside. She perched on the upholstered chair by the door, while Lady Caldwell headed for the dressing room.

'Do you need help, my lady?' Forester asked.

'Fiddle-de-de. If I cannot make water at my age, you best send me to Bedlam.'

Forester's lips pressed together, but she made no comment, continuing to remove items from the chest and put them away, opening and closing drawers, putting scraps of lace here and handkerchiefs there. Such delicate items and so many? Had their guests come for an extended stay? Uncle Mortimer would not be happy.

A soft chuckle made her turn. 'You are gazing at my wardrobe in awe, Miss Bracewell.'

'You have a g-great many gowns.'

Her ladyship laughed. 'So I do. Lullington and I are on a progress, do you see? We are going to visit everyone we know for the next month or two, until the Season starts again. London is flat, there is absolutely nothing to do.' She sat down at the mirror on the dressing table, patted her hair and pinched her cheeks.

'Are you engaged to be married, then?' Frederica asked, then turned red and was glad Lady Caldwell had her back to her as she realised just how impertinent her enquiry sounded.

'La, but you are a country miss,' Lady Caldwell said with a musical laugh. 'I left my husband in London. I am travelling with several companions. I have my maid, as do the other ladies who make up our party. The rest of them are staying at Radthorn's house, as you know, and so for now you are my chaperon. Not a breath of scandal, I assure you.'

The thought of trying to chaperon the sophisticated Lady Caldwell made her want to giggle. The whole arrangement sounded odd, but then Lady Caldwell was clearly a woman of the world.

From out of the trunk Forester pulled a dark blue riding habit with gold epaulettes and lots of frogging.

'Do you ride out with us tomorrow, Lady Caldwell?' Frederica asked.

'Oh, my dear, you must call me Maggie or I vow I shall feel like an ancient crone.'

Put entirely at ease, Frederica laughed. 'No one would use that word to describe you. And thank you. Please call me Frederica.'

Maggie clapped her hands. 'To answer your question, yes, I will join the hunt. Do you go too?'

She nodded. That had been a bone of contention between her and Uncle Mortimer. In the end, she'd agreed, but only if she could stay well to the rear and avoid being present for the kill.

'I shall look forward to keeping you company.' Maggie rose to her feet. 'I can't wait for this masked ball. I love dressing up, don't you? Of course you do. What woman wouldn't? And wait until you see the wonderful men Radthorn has brought with him.' She put a delicate hand to the centre of her chest and gave a languid sigh, then laughed and held out her hand. 'Come, let us go downstairs. Tea must have arrived. I think you and I are going to get along famously.'

Oh, yes, they'd be great friends. Maggie would talk and Frederica would listen and everyone would be happy.

What would her new friend think if she learned that Frederica was an artist? A wanton? And about to go out into the world alone?

Robert tightened Pippin's girth and looked up at Frederica, the first of the riders out of the stable. No longer the secretive little mouse she'd been a day or so ago. The sea-green riding habit was of the very best quality. Its tailored lines suited her slim figure and matched the colour of her eyes. He'd never seen her look so elegant or so happy. She looked utterly charming. Glowing.

Bloody alluring.

He wanted to drag her back to his cottage and hide her away.

'Th-thank you, Robert,' she whispered.

Aye. She'd whisper, with her London guests nearby. And that was just how he wanted it. He touched his cap and pulled it lower on his forehead, keeping a wary eye out for Lullington. Of all the cursed ill luck, he had to be one of the guests. And Maggie, too. He was still having trouble believing it.

He shouldn't have reported for work this morning. He should have sent word of some infectious disease the moment he'd realised who young Bracewell had brought along as guests. But that would have left poor old Weatherby in the lurch.

A visiting groom led out the next animals, a sweet little chestnut mare called Penny and a large black gelding. The mare whickered a soft greeting to Robert. He bit back a curse. Who'd have thought the horse would remember him? Maggie, in a dark blue habit, strolled into the courtyard on Lullington's arm. Robert watched covertly as a groom threw her up. She was too busy conversing with the viscount to notice him, a mere servant. Thank God.

Instead of leaving the task to the groom, Lullington saw to Maggie's tack, his hand touching her thigh lightly in an intimate gesture as he finished. So Maggie had gone to Lullington. Perhaps that's why the viscount had been keen to see Robert disgraced. They had often vied for the same females, usually to Lullington's disadvantage. But unless things had changed, he'd not be able to afford the kind of baubles Maggie liked to add to her collection.

Lullington sprang into the saddle unaided. 'Hey, you there.' He pointed his crop at Robert. 'A stirrup cup for the lady.'

Head lowered, Robert touched his hat and went for the tray of pewter cups set on a bench by the door. Normally Maisie would be out here passing the good cheer around, but something had happened in the kitchen and Snively had assigned Robert the task.

He handed a cup up to Maggie, who nodded a thank you.

Lullington looked down only long enough to grasp his goblet. He leaned closer to Maggie. 'God,' he lisped in a low voice, 'did you see the hack Bracewell is riding? A slug.'

Maggie's answering laugh struck a chord in his memory. It was what had attracted him to her in the first place. Merry and meaningless laughter. Now it left him cold.

He took a cup to Frederica, who bestowed thanks by way of an intimate little smile.

Robert prayed Lullington didn't notice. Damnation, but this was hell.

The last rider out of the stable was the young master on a showy bay. It was Robert's first real look at Frederica's cousin. Clearly greener than grass and still with his mother's milk on his lips, he was just the kind of youth dangling at the edges of society to be impressed with Lullington's smooth style of address. Still, even the daring viscount would not dare gull the lad under his own roof.

Bracewell jobbed at the horse's mouth. It reared in protest. Its wicked flying hooves narrowly missed Pippin. Frederica manoeuvred neatly out of the way. 'Take c-care, Simon.'

Robert caught the bay's bridle and soothed it with some whispered words. 'Stirrup cup, sir?' he asked Bracewell, who seemed unconscious that another had taken control of his mount.

'Yes, by Jove. Good man.' Simon beamed. 'I say, Lullington. Good hunting weather, what?'

'Is it?' Lullington replied, looking up at the clear blue sky.

'You wag,' Bracewell said. 'Always ribbing a fellow. What do you think, Maggie? Are you ready to take the first brush today?'

Frederica winced, causing Pippin to dance sideways.

Lullington, who had drawn close, caught her bridle. 'Steady there,' he said to the horse, his gaze fixed on Frederica. 'My word, Miss Bracewell, you look simply ravishing this morning. I am quite determined not to leave your side—you present such a pretty picture.'

Robert gritted his teeth and handed the last of the stirrup cups up to Bracewell. If he had known Lullington was to be ensconced under the same roof as Frederica, he might have whisked her off to Gretna Green and to hell with the consequences.

No, he wouldn't. Any more than Lullington would. The man was simply enjoying himself putting a pretty miss to the blush. Robert knew, because he'd done it himself. The last thing the viscount wanted was a wife as poor as himself.

He just hoped Frederica would see through the viscount's charm to the rake beneath.

She hadn't seen through Robert, though. The thought gave him a cold feeling in his chest.

Gun over his shoulder, Weatherby marched into the courtyard and approached Bracewell with a touch to his hat. 'Hunt is meeting at the Bull and Mouth, Master Simon. Ye've a half-hour to get there. Deveril here will send the beaters off ahead. You'll have a good day's sport, I promise ye.'

Robert ran around, collecting the goblets from the riders.

'We're off,' Maggie said, her face a picture of eagerness. 'We don't want to miss the start.' She trotted out of the courtyard and down the drive, with Bracewell right behind.

Frederica grimaced as if she'd like to miss the whole thing, but the viscount still retained his grip on her bridle.

He gave it a jerk. The little gelding tossed his head, then broke into a canter with Lullington at Frederica's side.

Ire boiled in Robert's gut. How dare he touch her horse? It was as if he'd taken possession. Robert kept a tight grip on his urge to shout a protest. Lullington couldn't do her much harm if the party stayed together.

When Frederica leaned back and gave the viscount's black a sharp slap on the rump with her crop and the black took off at a gallop, he couldn't hold back his smile. For all her appearance of frailty, his Frederica was a woman to be reckoned with.

His? What the hell was he thinking? That was one thing she could never be. Not in any way, shape or form. And there were going to be no more midnight visits.

He'd made certain. He still felt a sharp pain between his ribs every time he recalled the hurt look on her face. What if they could be friends, as she'd asked? Would it ever be enough? Would he be able to resist her appeal? Damnation, he missed her like the devil already.

It wasn't as if he'd seduced an innocent, he reminded himself, but there were different kinds of innocent. And she was the most vulnerable to a man like him.

'Don't stand there daydreaming,' Weatherby growled. 'Get off, lad. You need a half-hour start on the pack or they'll overrun the fox before midday.'

'We don't want that,' Robert said wryly and set off through the kitchen garden at a jog. He'd take the short cut and be gone from the inn long before the Wynchwood party appeared.

The hounds and red-coated hunters streamed up Gallows Hill far ahead of Frederica and Maggie, but Frederica didn't care.

'Hurry up, Frederica,' Maggie called back, twisting in her saddle. 'We are falling behind.'

That's the idea, Frederica thought, but she urged Pippin to a greater burst of speed. The gelding, who'd fretted at being held back, took the bit and surged forwards. Frederica kept a sharp eye out for rabbit holes.

Fortunately, her slow pace had annoyed Viscount Lullington. He'd galloped ahead, promising to return to see how she was doing the next time the hounds were at a stand.

She caught Maggie up and matched Pippin's speed to the chestnut. They rode side by side over the brow of the hill. Hopefully, they would not see her particular fox this morning.

Far ahead, the hunt master blew the view halloo. It seemed her wish was not to be granted.

'Here we go,' Maggie yelled, her eyes brimming with excitement. 'Come on, if you want to be in on the kill.'

Ugh. 'You go ahead. Pippin is lame. He must have picked up a stone. I will need to dismount and take a look.'

Maggie gave a little grimace of disappointment. 'I'll send Lull or your cousin back to find you if you don't catch us up.'

Frederica waved her crop and watched Maggie fly off down the hill.

Pippin's ears pricked forwards. He strained at the bit.

'I know, old fellow. But we don't want to be there when they catch the fox. Wait a few minutes and then you can gallop.'

A lady in dark green and two men in hunting pink, members of Mr Radthorn's party whom she'd met at the village inn, straggled up to her. She waved them on. The last thing she needed was some well-meaning gentleman poking around in Pippin's hooves. He'd soon realise her excuse was a hum.

She had Pippin walk slowly down the hill, listening to the retreating sounds of baying hounds and the hunting horn. Leaning forwards, she patted her mount's neck. 'What do you think? Are they far enough ahead?'

He tossed his head as if he understood every word.

She laughed. 'Very well.' She dug her heel into his flank and he sprang forwards into a gallop, straining at the bit. Oh, dear. He seemed determined to catch the other horses. The hedge at the bottom of the hill came up fast. Too fast. She hauled on the reins, trying to turn his head. Too late. They were going to have to jump it. Not a good idea in a lady's saddle.

Her heart picked up speed. She eyed the closing distance, judged the horse's pace and steadied herself. Not that the saddle provided much support.

Pippin gathered himself. And they flew. She was going to make it. Beautiful jump. Clean. Clear. The horse landed. Frederica hit the saddle with a bump and jolted sideways. She was flying again. Straight at the ground.

Ouch. She landed on her bottom. Hard. She couldn't breathe. She'd crushed her ribs. Panicked, she clutched her chest. She couldn't inhale. She was dying.

'Steady,' a deep voice said. 'Take it easy.'

A huge rush of air filled her lungs. Her head swam. For a moment she didn't know where she was. Then Robert's anxious face filled her vision. 'Where are you hurt?'

Grateful to feel the air sawing in and out of her lungs, she managed a weak smile. 'Winded.'

'Are you sure that is all?' His hands, gentle, clinical, ran over her arms, legs, back. 'Does it hurt when I touch you?'

'No. It feels lovely.'

He repressed a quick grin. 'Not another word.'

'Why aren't you up front with the villagers?'

'I was. I noticed you hanging back, then Lady Caldwell showed up without you. One of those idiots should have stayed behind.' He sounded furious.

'I'm not a child, you know. I've ridden these fields alone all my life.' She glanced around for Pippin. Not a sign of him.

'Still chasing the leaders,' Robert said.

'I don't know what got into him.'

'Overexcited, I suspect.' Robert held out a hand and pulled her to her feet. 'Can you walk?'

She took a couple of steps. Her legs felt like blancmange and her bottom hurt, but she wasn't injured. 'A little stiff and sore, but I'm fine.'

'Too bad.' His dark eyes sparkled. 'I was hoping for the excuse to carry you in my arms.'

'Now why didn't I think of that?'

'Because you don't play those kinds of games,' he said. 'Good thing too.'

There was no one in sight. The only thing in the middle of the field was them and an oak tree. An oak tree with a very wide and gnarly trunk. As they passed it, a wicked thought popped into her mind. 'Oh, I'm not feeling quite the thing.' She headed for the tree trunk and leaned against it with her arm covering her eyes.

'Are you feeling faint?' he said, peering into her face.

She let her arm fall and laughed up at him. 'No.'

He cursed softly. 'Do you know how beautiful you look?'

'No. But I'm hoping you are going to tell me.' Had she said that? Was it he who made her recklessly wanton, or was it all her bad blood?

He gave an unwilling laugh, his white teeth flashing in the black of his curly beard. 'It seems you do play those games.'

'Why have you given up shaving?' she asked.

He stroked his chin with strong square fingers. Mischief shone in his eyes. 'Don't you like it?'

'I'm not sure.'

He placed his hands against the rough trunk, his broad forearms bracketing her head. She drew in a quick breath at the jolt in her stomach. He leaned in for a kiss and she flung her arms around his neck and melded her body to his. After the strain of the morning, it felt wonderful to be in his arms.

He groaned and deepened the kiss, his mouth working magic against her lips, his hands crushing her close.

He broke away, and she was pleased to see he was breathing just as hard as she. 'Robert—'

'Someone is coming. Listen.'

Hoof beats approaching fast. 'Dash it all,' she muttered.

His dark eyes gleamed. 'You owe me the rest of that kiss, but for now, start walking.'

They stepped out from behind the shelter of the tree as a black horse and rider leading Pippin stopped to open the gate to the field.

'Your rescuer arrives,' Robert said drily.

'Viscount Lullington.'

He nodded. 'Watch that man, Frederica.' His voice held such deep loathing, she couldn't help but glance at his face. His eyes were narrowed and his shoulders tense.

'Do you know him?'

His lip curled. 'I know men like him. He'll take any advantage.'

'Oh, he's not interested in me. He's in love with Lady Caldwell.'

'That kind loves only one person. Himself.'

'Why, Robert,' she said, her smile growing, 'are you jealous?'

He glanced at her, his eyes dark, almost bleak. 'What right do I have for jealousy?'

With a sinking sensation, she realised he'd made no promises to her. 'Just do not trust that man.'

The viscount was almost upon them. She turned to face him as he leaped from his horse and strode to her side. He appeared not to notice Robert. 'Are you all right, Miss Bracewell?'

Wishing him elsewhere, she forced a smile. 'Perfectly fine. Pippin decided I needed a walk.'

He grinned. 'I am all admiration. Your spirit does you credit. I expected tears and gnashing of teeth.'

Federica could almost hear Robert grind *his* teeth. She gestured towards him. 'I was fortunate Mr Deveril came along or I might be less sanguine.'

'Good man,' the viscount said. He dug into his pocket and flipped a coin to land at Robert's feet.

Robert stared at it, his face rigid, pride in his eyes, in the set of his shoulders, then he bent to retrieve the coin from the dirt. He touched his cap and walked away.

She felt sick and faint. As if he'd been shamed and it was all her fault. She longed to call out an apology, but Robert's long legs carried him off at a rapid pace.

Meanwhile the viscount was all kind concern. 'Are you sure you are not hurt, Miss Bracewell?'

Heart aching, she forced herself to answer calmly. 'P-perfectly sure.'

Lullington looked at her face and then at the retreating Robert. 'Has he been with your family long?'

'Just a few weeks,' she said.

'He seems like a competent fellow, if rather bold.'

She glanced up to find him staring at her intently, his pale eyes seeming to see into her mind. His gaze dropped to her mouth and he gave a tight smile. 'Now, Miss Bracewell,

do you think you can re-mount this beast?' He pointed to
Pippin.

Aware of prickling heat creeping up her face, she nodded.
'I can.'

'Pluck to the backbone. Let me give you a hand.'

He led her to Pippin and she noticed how soft the leather
of his gloves and how long and languid his fingers were.
A shudder ran down her spine as if she'd brushed past a
cobweb in the dark. Such nonsense. He was a dandy. A
nobleman. She was wrong to compare him with the hardworking Robert.

With Maisie looking on, her face a picture of envy,
Frederica twisted to look at her back in the mirror. Wings.
Made of the sheerest material and dusted with sequins,
they looked almost real. The gown made her look taller,
more shapely. 'It is supposed to represent Titania from *A
Midsummer Night's Dream*. Mrs Phillips did a wonderful
job.'

'You look like a fairy an' all, miss,' Maisie said. 'My ma
used to tell me about them. Don't walk in the fairy circle,
she always used to say. Toadstools, they was.'

With a smile, Frederica ran her hands down the front of
her sheer gown of browns and soft greens.

Maisie went to work with the hairbrush and Frederica let
her thoughts wander. What would Robert think if he saw
her now? Would he approve? Or would he stare at her with
those fathomless dark eyes and tell her that she looked like
a damned peacock? Pretty, but useless.

She couldn't prevent a small smile. Yes, that was indeed
what the blunt, unpolished man would say. And after
tonight, after her one and only ball, she would never look
like a peacock again. Why, she might even dance the night
away on the arm of a handsome gentleman. She sighed. If

only that gentleman could be Robert, it would be the best night of her life.

A knock sounded on the door. 'Who is it?'

'Maggie. May I come in?'

'Please do.'

Maggie looked simply ravishing. A vision. Frederica felt quite dull and plain as she took in the gauzy trousers and soft veils of midnight-blue covered in sequins. The dress of an exotic eastern harem girl. Bangles jingled on her wrists and around her ankles, and a heavy gold choker fringed with coins hugged her elegant neck. Her eyes, rimmed with kohl, peeped over the top of a gold-edged veil.

The brush was held suspended over Frederica's head as Maisie let her mouth hang open.

'You look beautiful,' Frederica said.

The dark-eyed siren ran her gaze over Frederica. Her finely plucked brows shot up. 'Oh, my dear. You are simply divine.' She floated across the room to finger the fabric. 'Look how cleverly she dags the hem and so much fabric. If I had only thought of it.' She shook her head. 'But no. My curves were never meant to play a wood sprite. I would look like a gnome. My dear, you will be the belle of the ball.'

'Fine feathers make fine birds,' Frederica said with a laugh, quoting one of Mortimer's favourite sayings.

Maisie began brushing again.

'And modest too. So refreshing. My dear, you must come to London. They will adore you.'

Until they discovered who she was, then she would be ostracised. Uncle Mortimer had made that very plain. And that was why she did not understand why Simon's parents were going along with his uncle's betrothal plans. But apparently they were. There was only one way out, she'd realised in the dark of her room late last night. She'd have to tell Simon she was a fallen woman. He'd be so disgusted, he'd have to cry off.

She'd offer to save him a whole lot of embarrassment by disappearing.

She could do it without getting Robert into trouble. No one would need to know who had debauched her, any more than they knew who had debauched her mother.

All she needed was a few private words with Simon and she would be free to live her own life.

Unfortunately, Simon spent all his time glued to the viscount's side while Lord Lullington looked bored nigh unto death.

Tomorrow, after the ball, she'd find a way to get Simon alone.

While Maisie finished brushing Frederica's hair, Maggie wandered around the room, touching the bed, pulling open the curtains to stare out of the window, strolling back to the dressing table. Restless energy rolled off her in waves.

She spun about. 'How will you wear your hair?'

'Miss always has it in a knot,' Maisie said.

Maggie tilted her head to one side. 'Wear it down.'

'Too fine,' Frederica said. 'It doesn't have a scrap of curl.' Unlike the older woman's luxuriant waves.

Maggie picked up the headdress, a simple wreath of silk flowers in yellow, pink and white, wound around with ivy leaves. 'You are wrong. Pin it up at the sides so it falls down your back and leaves your neck and shoulders bare.' With a hairpin, she caught one side up, then added another. She popped the circlet on Frederica's head so it settled high on her brow. 'Like so. What do you think?'

It made her look young and vulnerable, and…well almost pretty. 'I like it.' She smiled at Maggie's reflection. 'I really do. But it will not stay.'

'More pins,' Maggie cried. 'Fasten those pieces we

pulled back to the circlet. That will hold them in place.'
Once more she looked at Frederica like a bird eyeing a
worm. 'Earbobs.'

Frederica blinked. 'I don't have any.'

Maggie looked surprised. 'No? I know. I will lend you
some of mine. Sapphires?' She shook her head. 'Diamonds.
Nothing but diamonds will do. You will provide the colour
and they the light.'

'Oh, no, I couldn't.'

'But you shall.' The lady had a determined gleam in her
eye and a stubborn set to her jaw.

And Frederica could not think of a reason to refuse. She
smiled. 'Then thank you.'

'Oooh. This is so exciting. Wait a moment while I fetch
them.'

'What a nice lady,' Maisie said as Maggie scurried out
of the door. 'And pretty too.'

How nice to have a friend for the first time in her life.
There had been a lot of firsts just lately. 'Very pretty. Thank
you, Maisie, for your help. I am sure there are lots of things
you are needed for downstairs. You can go now.'

'Aye. Mrs Doncaster is fair fit to burst she's that busy.'
Maisie packed up the pins and tidied the dressing table.

'I suppose Cook did not want to lose you to me this
afternoon.'

Maisie grinned. 'Mums the word on that, miss. Oh, and
by the way, I was to tell you that your uncle wants to see you
in the library before the other guests arrive.' She bobbed a
curtsy and headed for the door, standing back for a moment
to allow Maggie to enter carrying a leatherbound case,
before she hurried away.

'Here you are, my dear Frederica.' She set the case down
on the dressing table, and pulled forth a string of the most
gorgeous diamonds, a delicate strand of little teardrops with

earbobs to match. She fastened the necklace around Frederica's throat and stood back to admire. 'Perfect. Now the earrings.' Frederica turned back to the mirror and gasped. 'It is lovely, but I can't wear something so valuable.'

'Nonsense. It is not half as lovely as you, my dear. You will outshine everyone.'

Frederica swung around to face her. 'Oh, no! How can you say such a thing?'

The other woman sighed and patted her hand. 'I'm not much prone to think of others, but for some odd reason I like you.' She laughed. It sounded a little brittle. 'And Lull will be so proud of me when I tell him, he will no doubt buy me the pearls I have been after.'

Frederica couldn't help laughing at her naughty grin.

'And now I must be off,' Maggie said. 'My poor Forester is quite in a fit about my headdress. Apparently, it needs work.' She stood in the doorway and blew a kiss. 'I will see you downstairs.'

Frederica felt rather as if a whirlwind had blown in and out of the room. She took a deep breath. Time to visit Uncle Mortimer. Hopefully he would not be too shocked at this gown.

Simon and Uncle Mortimer rose on her entry into the study. They looked quite splendid. For once, Uncle Mortimer was not wearing his old-fashioned frock coat. Although not in costume, he looked magnificent in a black coat with silver buttons and satin knee breeches. He'd even powdered his best wig. She made her curtsy. 'You wanted to speak with me, Uncle?'

As Mortimer looked her up and down, his pink nose quivered. Oh, dear. Perhaps she would not be attending the ball after all.

'I say, coz,' Simon said, his eyes bulging worse than

usual above his mountain of neckerchief. 'You look splendid. Where did you get the jewels?'

'Lady Caldwell l—l—'

'Lent them to you,' Simon said. 'Most obliging. Is she
not the most delightful of creatures?'

Uncle Mortimer grunted, but gestured her to sit. 'We
need to talk about this evening.'

She perched on the chair. 'Yes, Uncle.'

'Mind your manners and behave as you ought. Do not
mention your mother and things should come off well
enough.'

She stiffened. 'I don't know why Simon wishes to marry
me, when you are all so ashamed of my connections.'

Simon's mouth opened and closed. He gulped. Small
beads of perspiration lined his loose top lip. 'Really, coz.
A pleasure.'

If that was the truth, why did he sound so anxious?

Uncle Mortimer glowered at him before turning his
attention back to Frederica. 'You should be grateful he is
willing to make the sacrifice.'

'Good for the family name,' Simon added, looking as
grave as an undertaker.

'Gratitude is in the eye of the beholder,' Frederica said,
her anger making the words come out in one go.

Mortimer's mouth dropped open. 'Damn stupid saying.' He pointed a shaking finger at her face. 'Listen to
me, young lady. One wrong word out of you, one syllable
astray, and you'll find yourself in the workhouse. Do I
make myself clear?'

'I say. By Jove, Uncle. A bit harsh, what? I'm sure
m'cousin don't need reminding of our charity. She knows
her place.' Simon gave her one of his pleading looks. He
hated a fuss. Frederica wanted to take each end of his stupid
cravat and pull hard.

She certainly wasn't going to get any sense out of him at this moment. He always did what Mortimer said, but if he thought he had any say in her life now or in the future, he was in for a surprise.

She bowed her head to hide her thoughts. 'I understand, Uncle.'

Mortimer looked her up and down. 'What is Lady Radthorn thinking? You are almost naked. I've a damned good mind to lock you in your room.' If truth be told, he'd probably like to drag her into his underground tunnel and feed her worms. Or feed her to the worms.

'No need to make a fuss, Uncle. I'm sure it's all the crack,' Simon said, surprising Frederica. 'You should see what the ladies wear in London.'

'I doubt they are ladies,' Uncle Mortimer grumbled.

She wasn't exactly a lady either. She pressed her lips together to stop from smiling.

Finally composed enough to raise her gaze, she caught both men looking at each other with a sort of satisfied smirk. Now what were they up to? 'Will there be anything else, Uncle?'

'I'll be watching you, girl. Closely. Behave well, and who knows, perhaps Simon will take you to London to see the sights one day.'

Never.

'Off you go. Be downstairs in the hallway ready to meet the guests at seven o'clock with Lady Radthorn.' He flicked his fingers in dismissal.

Doubts about her plan assailed Frederica as she left the room. Simon was so far beneath Uncle's thumb, he'd probably accept her despoiled state without a murmur, if Uncle Mortimer insisted.

In that case, there was nothing else she could do but run.

* * *

Robert cut across the Wynchwood lawn. Light streaming from the downstairs windows made it easy to see his way. Clearly Lord Wynchwood intended to impress his neighbours and his London guests.

Preferring to check out the lie of the land before venturing into the lion's den, Robert pushed through the shrubbery beneath the ballroom windows and from the shadows peered into a room packed with every imaginable creature and assorted figures from history.

All the local gentry were invited, according to Weatherby, as well as the guests down from London. A few years ago he would have been one of them, though he rarely attended such dull affairs. Now here he was, an outsider skulking in the bushes.

Invitation or not, they ought to be honoured by his attendance. He'd found the perfect costume, too—a highwayman. The only person he feared might see through the disguise was Maggie. She might recognise his voice. He'd practised keeping it coarse and rough and with the beard and the waxed moustaches he'd devised from locks of his hair, he defied even his mother to recognise him.

The scrap of black silk he had fashioned for a mask covered the top half of his face. He pulled his borrowed tricorn hat down low on his brow for further concealment.

He took a deep breath. Now or never.

Careful to avoid attracting attention, he worked his way around to the front door, timing his entrance with the arrival of a carriage full of guests. Out stepped a Roman dignitary and his toga-clad lady, a male dressed as an Oriental in loose, flowing robes, who he immediately recognized as Radthorn, and a woman in a Tudor ruff and enormous skirt. Robert followed them in. Snively didn't give him a second glance as they were directed to the antechamber where the ladies could change their shoes and leave their cloaks.

'Really, John,' the Tudor lady whispered having passed off her wrap to Maisie, 'are you sure the Bracewells are quite the thing?' She wrinkled her nose at the faded wallpaper above grimy panelling. 'It is a little dingy.'

Lady Bentham, Robert realised. A merry young widow and John's long-time mistress. John always said his grandmother was up for a lark. She had to be if she permitted him to house his mistress under her roof. If the old lady knew, that was.

Radthorn glanced around, his gaze passing over Robert without a gleam of recognition. 'Old friends of the family. I haven't been here in years.' A smile flashed from beneath his drooping moustache. 'It hasn't changed a bit.'

Robert let his breath go. If his erstwhile best friend didn't recognise him, then it appeared he was safe.

'Why on earth was Lullington so insistent we all come?' Lady Bentham asked. 'It is going to be dreadfully dull.'

Radthorn shrugged. 'You know Lullington. Young Bracewell owes him money and he's not going to let him escape without paying up.'

Robert felt a flash of embarrassment. He'd left a great many debts in his wake. Devil take it, he would pay them no matter how long it took.

John took his lady's arm and with many curses from him and much laughter from her, he helped her tilt her enormous hoop to allow her to pass through the doorway and they headed for the ballroom.

His heart racing more than he liked, Robert trailed them. The Roman tribune and his lady followed hard on his heels.

'Oh, my,' Lady Bentham said, stopping at the entrance

to the grand room that ran the length of the back of the house.

Robert wasn't surprised at her reaction to the swathes of cloth draping the walls and hundreds of candles. He'd spent most of the day helping with them.

'She's beautiful,' Lady Bentham continued. 'Who is she?'

Robert's jaw dropped as he saw that she referred not to the decorations, but to the lady. A vision of loveliness, a glittering queen of the fairies. Frederica. He choked back a gasp.

Dressed in something floating and sheer, she looked enchanting. It didn't take much to imagine the slender limbs beneath the skirts, or the high, pert breasts skimmed by the low-cut bodice. An ethereal queen of the fairies. He half-expected her to use the gossamer wings cunningly attached to the back of her gown and fly off on a breeze.

Every man in the room had the look of a rabid dog as they gazed at her. Only by dint of will did he stop himself from rushing to her side and covering her with his highwayman's cloak.

Her face glowed. Beneath her mask of silk and sequins, her lips were parted in excitement. Yet her eyes held the shadows of absolute terror. Pride filled him. Pride at her beauty and her courage. The beast inside him wanted to proclaim her as his own.

He clenched his jaw instead.

'I had no idea she was so lovely,' Radthorn said, in an awed whisper. 'Simon's cousin. I met her on the hunt this morning. She is making her début under my grandmother's guidance.'

Lady Bentham dug him in the ribs. 'Stop salivating.'

Robert had never seen John look so besotted. He wanted

to strangle his friend with his bare hands. He kept them loose at his sides.

The Roman couple pushed forwards. 'I say there, what's the hold up?'

The last thing he needed was an altercation. Robert extricated himself from the little knot at the door and swaggered in best highwayman style to his chosen location behind a pillar. From here he would observe yet remain unnoticed.

Like every man in the room, he found his gaze drawn to the slight figure in earth tones and diamonds. Like every man in the room, she filled his heart with a strange kind of wonder. He could see it in their eyes. How could any woman look so lovely, so pure, so unattainable?

A sprite come to taunt them all.

How could the man at her side, a cherub-faced idiot in a lion suit and a foolish grin, think himself good enough? Hell. Robert wasn't good enough, but he wasn't going to let that stop him from claiming the first waltz.

He knew the moment she saw him, because she smiled brightly enough to outshine the hundreds of candles. A dozen men around him gasped and clutched their assorted chests of steel and wool and silk, but only he caught the full force of her wide-eyed astonishment.

He bowed and gave a slight shake of his head.

She covered her laugh with her fingers and looked away. His heart thudded wildly. The music started. A cotillion. The lion held out his arm. She placed her hand in his paw.

A growl of protest rumbled in Robert's chest. He almost stepped out from his pillar. Mine. The possessive thought reverberated in his mind, yet he held still, narrow eyed, watching.

The scent of violets wafted beneath his nose. A voluptuous maiden in a veil and the garb of a sultan's consort drifted to his side. 'Oh, my,' she said. 'I do like a tall, strong highwayman. Who are you? Ten String Jack?'

Damnation. Maggie.

'No, yer ladyship. I be the ghost of Mad Jack. Hung I was, up on Gallows Hill yonder.'

Maggie recoiled. 'Lud! How gruesome.' She eyed him up and down. 'You know, I have the strangest feeling I know you from somewhere.' She smiled her radiant, sophisticated, charming smile. A smile as bright as the gold coins on her bangles. The smile she used to hide her disappointments in the life she'd been handed by her parents. Married to an old man as a girl.

He grinned back. 'No, yer ladyship. I live in these parts. You ain't never heard of me.'

'Oh, you foolish creature. I know we have met. Who are you?'

He flashed her a leer and waggled his brows. 'If ye guess right, I'll kiss you. Else ye'll wait until the unmasking.' When he'd be long gone.

'Maggie?' Lullington's imperious voice jerked her head around.

The viscount, splendid as the Sun King in a gold mask and his lean body tightly encased in a suit of white embroidered with gold, crooked a finger. 'Dance, my lady?'

'Coming, Lull.' She hurried off, but not before she cast a glance over her shoulder at Robert. He couldn't resist. He bowed his appreciation. She really was a lovely sight. The loveliest woman in the room save for one.

Not that Frederica's partner did her justice. Pompous ninny. The man knew the steps and performed with dignity, but without grace or feel for the music. The idiot spent most of his time nodding to the other members of the set, or shouting raillery to the other square when all his attention should have been fixed on his partner.

Popinjay.

The back of Robert's neck prickled. Someone was watching him. Nonchalantly, as if seeking refreshment, he turned away from the dance floor. A swift glance found Radthorn's puzzled gaze fixed on his person. Robert pretended not to notice and, walking with a limp, headed for the refreshment table. Glass in hand, he looked again. John's attention was now wholly engaged with a grey-haired lady in the full regalia of the last century and looking as if she had simply pulled out one of her old gowns and wigs. Her long chin reminded him of John's. This must be the doughty grandmother of whom John had spoken often and with great affection. The woman who had taken Frederica in hand.

Thank God the old dear hadn't spoiled Frederica's natural grace and spirit and turned her into a simpering miss like the one dressed as a shepherdess, crook in hand, heading his way.

Robert swung away. He prowled the circumference of the ballroom, avoiding Maggie and the shepherdess with spectacular success until Maggie cornered him beside the orchestra.

'Dance with me,' she said, batting her kohl-rimmed eyelashes.

'Nay, lass,' he growled.

She pouted. 'La, sir. You are very rude.'

Flags of colour flew in her cheeks, a sign of her rare temper. Not good.

He pointed to her flimsy sandals. 'I are mortal afeared of stepping on your pretty little toes.'

She pointed her foot. 'They are pretty, aren't they?' She gazed at his feet. 'And you are wearing very large boots.' She reached up and tapped his chest with her flail. 'But I'll not take it as an excuse, sir.'

He grinned his defeat. 'Then, my lady, your wish is my command.'

He led her into a set still in need of couples and she spent the whole of the dance throwing names at him. When they promenaded down the set, she laughed up at him. 'Why won't you tell me?'

'It's a masked ball. You ain't supposed to know.'

'Infuriating man.' She narrowed her eyes. 'That voice… Are you related to a member of the *ton*?'

'Arr, missy. I'm related to the King of Thieves. Aladdin.'

She shook her fist at him, then groaned as the music concluded. 'I give up, but I will see you later.'

Chuckling at her boldness, Robert stalked back to his pillar. Nearby, Lady Radthorn was engaged in a heated discussion with the master of the house.

'Of course it is necessary. Do you want the world to think the Wynchwoods are country bumpkins?'

'I have no reason to care what the world thinks,' Lord Wynchwood said, wiping his brow. 'You are giving me a headache.'

'Then do as I ask. You requested my help, now you will accept it. We invited all these people from town. They expect to waltz.'

'No.'

'Oh, you are past bearing.'

'And you are overbearing. And foolish.'

The two of them stared at each other in silence. Any man with an iota of common sense would have known Lady Radthorn would not be gainsaid.

Lord Wynchwood sagged. 'All right. I'll give the instruction. But my niece will not waltz. She will stand right here beside me.'

'Nonsense. The gel must dance.'

Robert permitted himself a small smile and positioned himself within easy range of his lordship. The Roman, with whom Frederica had danced the last set, returned her to her spot beside her uncle and Lady Radthorn, who continued to argue that Frederica must dance.

Before anyone could instruct her either way, Robert strode forwards and led her on to the floor to the opening bars of the waltz.

'I say,' her uncle called out.

'Too late,' Robert murmured.

Frederica laughed up at him. 'True to your profession, sir?'

'Aye,' he murmured finding her laugh enough to set wild music soaring in his blood. What was left of his mind he needed for dancing.

She glided in beneath the light touch of his fingers. In his hovel, she'd been earth, grounding him in the here and now. In the ballroom, with the candles playing rainbows among her diamonds and shimmering in the ocean colour of her eyes, she was pure sprite. She floated beneath his fingers, her lips curved in a smile of joy. He felt as if he could fight demons and win.

'R-Robert?'

'Hush,' he murmured into hair scented with vanilla and roses. 'I'm Mad Jack tonight.'

Her smile grew. 'Mad indeed.' Her eyes sparkled. 'You remembered my story.'

'I did.'

Her face dropped. 'But the fox…'

'Safe and sound. Probably up on Gallows Hill, watching the lights and the dancing and wondering whose chickens to steal.'

A gurgle of laughter curled around him. 'How?'

'I trapped the other fox down in the meadow.'

They circled the floor. Despite feigned indifference, he noticed eyes watching him and wondering. Fans fluttered as people asked who he was. He dare not request more than one dance.

'You will be in d-dreadful trouble if you are discovered, but I'm so glad you are here. I had quite decided not to waltz. But I would have been sorry.'

'Me too, sweetheart. You deserve to dance all night.'

He swung her in a dizzying circle, her body, as pliant as a willow, moved in perfect harmony. She felt right in his arms, as if they'd been made for one another. Why had it taken so long to find her? And why now, when he could do nothing about it? After tonight she would be the toast of London. The *ton* despised anything different, except the truly unique. Those they embraced with fervour. For a while. Look at Byron and Brummell. His little wood nymph might well be next.

He caught sight of John watching her with a smile of admiration. His gut clenched. Before long some smooth-talking dissipated rogue would sweep her away with soft words and flattery.

He had no way to prevent it. He could not ask her to give up her life of privilege.

She sighed sweetly. 'I'm so glad you came here tonight.'

He inhaled her scent. 'I couldn't stay away.' He would have been worried knowing how nervous she was.

She glanced up at him and he saw shadows in her gaze. His gut clenched. Something was wrong.

'Meet me in my room, when this dance is over,' she whispered.

He stared at her, startled. 'Are you mad?'

'I owe you the rest of that kiss, remember?'

Arousal gripped him fast and hard. 'It's too dangerous.'

'Please.'

Her husky voice sounded so full of longing, he wanted to kiss those lips right at that moment, lose himself in her magic. He fought the urge to crush her close and smiled down at her instead. 'For a few moments with you, I'd dare anything.'

'My room is on the second floor.'

'I know. I helped with the move this afternoon.'

Her cheeks turned a delicate rose. 'I will make some excuse. Say I need to pin my gown. But R-Robert. Please. Be very careful.'

'Always.'

For the last few moments of the dance, he lost himself in the depths of her sea-witch gaze and allowed himself to dream it would never end. The music came to a close all too soon.

His arms ached when she stepped out of their embrace. His heart felt empty. Yet he must let her go. He led her back to her uncle.

'Where did you learn to waltz?' the old man asked, his chins wobbling and his face a furious red. 'Disgraceful dance. I am shocked.'

'Oh, my dear,' Lady Radthorn said. 'You looked lovely. Quite lovely.'

Other men approached. Robert could smell their interest. Soon she would be surrounded. Flattered. He wanted to draw his ancient pistol and hold them at bay. Instead, he bowed to no one in particular and withdrew.

On his way across the room, he sidestepped the shepherdess. Fortunately, since Lullington had Maggie's full attention on the dance floor, he strolled out of the ballroom unnoticed by anyone but Frederica.

The promised kiss had him hot with lust. Careless of who saw him, he ran up the stairs and slipped into her chamber.

Would she dance a set with another of her admirers before she joined him, or would she come right away? He paced around the bed and back to the fire. Five minutes passed. Then another. Damn it. It was all a tease.

The door opened. He dove for the shadows at the head of the bed.

'R-Robert?'

Joy flooded his veins. He stepped forwards and held out his arms.

She rushed into them and put her mouth up for his kiss. And kiss her he did. Long and sweet, full of his heart and his soul. It wasn't enough. 'Oh, sweetling,' he murmured against her mouth, 'I have wanted to do that all night. You ran a terrible danger meeting me here.'

'It is all right. No one thought anything of it.'

He led her to the chair by the window and sat with her on his lap. He kissed her again, sincerely, tenderly, fiercely.

'R-Robert,' she gasped, when he at last permitted her to take a breath. 'What is the matter?'

He forced himself to speak. 'I just had to tell you how beautiful you look tonight.'

She wound her arms around his neck. 'Thank you. And thank you for being the first to waltz with me. I wasn't nervous at all.'

He smiled down at her. 'I had to see my pupil's début.'

'Thank you.' She kissed his cheek.

He stroked the silky tresses floating down her back. 'I'd risk anything for a moment alone with you. I felt so bad sending you away, but if your uncle ever found out about us, I fear what he might do to you. I can't bear the thought of bringing you harm.'

'I know.' There was sadness in her voice. 'And if my uncle finds out you've been meeting me, you will lose your position.'

He felt like he'd destroyed something precious, but he had no choice. 'I don't care about that, but our worlds are too far apart. I can't offer you the life you deserve. We have to end this here.'

She rested her head on his chest, her sigh a balm to his heart. 'Run away with me.'

Shock ripped through him. And longing. He almost said yes, then he imagined the kind of life he could provide, dragging her from one estate to another, never sure of a roof over their heads. 'You'd lose everything—position, your family. I have no means to support you.'

'I don't care. I hate them.'

God, why was refusing her so hard? He'd never before felt as if he was cutting off his right arm when he gave a woman her *congé*? What was it about this one that had buried itself so deeply under his skin? 'I care.'

'Why don't you just admit that you are tired of me?' Her voice was husky with emotion, but when she gazed into his face her eyes were hard and bright. 'If I hadn't come to ask you teach me to dance, you would not have sought me out, would you?'

He squeezed his eyes shut for a second. He considered asking her to wait until he was well established and become his wife.

A wife? Had he lost his reason? He never stayed with a woman for more than a month or two. It wasn't in his nature. No. He had to be cruel to do the right thing. 'No. I never would have sought you out.'

She pushed away from him.

He let his arms fall away. Felt the chill as she slipped off his lap to stand before him.

'Fine,' she said. 'If that is what you want, then there is nothing more I can say. I wish you well, R-Robert Deveril.' She headed for the door.

For a single mad moment, he considered telling her his story. Of unburdening himself. Oh, hell. What kind of man placed his problems on a woman's slight shoulders? A weakling. 'You'll thank me one day,' he said.

She paused with her hand on the doorknob, not looking back. 'Will I?'

He cracked a hard laugh. 'Probably not. Go ahead. I will follow in a moment or two.'

She turned then, her eyes drinking him in as if for the last time. 'Take care, R-Robert.'

He grinned. 'Don't worry about me. Enjoy the rest of your ball.'

'It won't be the same.' On that wrenching admission, she slipped out into the hall and closed the door.

His heart felt as if someone had torn it in two and stamped on the pieces.

Chapter Eight

Five hellish minutes passed with Robert listening at the chamber door for sounds in the hallway beyond. All he could think about was getting as far away from Wynchwood as possible and drowning himself in brandy. Only a shred of sanity kept him from storming down the stairs.

Heart thudding slow, he continued to listen, angry he'd hurt her. Angry he didn't have a choice.

Hearing nothing, he stepped into the hallway, closed the door swiftly behind him and sauntered for the staircase as if he had every right to be wandering the upper chambers.

A soft click behind him made the hairs on the back of his neck rise. Had someone seen him leave her chamber? If they had, they'd not raised an outcry. Resisting the temptation to turn and look, he continued on his way. A couple in medieval garb ascended the stairs giggling and laughing, clearly looking for privacy. The joys of a masked ball.

Nodding politely, though he doubted they saw him, Robert continued on down the wide staircase, his footsteps drowned by the noise of revelry. The guests had spilled out into the entrance hall where tables sagged beneath punch bowls and glasses. He pushed through towards the front door, narrowly missing treading on Bracewell's lion's tail and dodging a wildly waving tribal spear.

He caught sight of Frederica standing in the doorway to the ballroom, smiling brightly at Radthorn and a couple of his cronies. Too brightly. God, she looked lovely. Something dark rose up in his chest as John smiled down at her, his gaze fixed on her face in undivided attention. An overwhelming desire to snatch her away, to ride off with her, made him clench his fists.

He didn't have the right to take her away from everything she knew and he'd finally convinced her he no longer wanted her. Longing hung around his neck like a chain.

He'd never stop wanting her.

With an effort, he turned away. He'd have to leave Wynchwood. He would never be able to stand in the shadows watching her, seeing her with men like Radthorn and Lullington, and not commit murder.

He stopped at a refreshment table and grabbed a bumper of brandy. It went down in one gulp, burning his gullet. Trust Wynchwood to buy cheap brandy. He needed fresh air. Needed to clear his head. Get a grip, Robert.

There were hundreds more women waiting to be plucked.

Except he didn't want any of them. For his sins, he only wanted one.

He continued his progress to the door.

'Ladies and gentlemen.' A voice rang out above the hubbub of talking and music. 'May I have your attention?' Lord Wynchwood's voice. 'I have an announcement. Please gather in the ballroom.'

The crowd around Robert craned their necks in the direction of the voice, pressing closer, surging forwards.

Robert pushed against the tide.

'I say,' said a pirate. 'You are going the wrong way.'

'You stepped on my skirts,' a queen said crossly, tugging at her train.

'Excuse me,' he said, shifting his foot.

Someone shoved him. His hat and wig slipped. He grabbed at it. Other faces turned his way, curious.

Damn. Any moment now, his behaviour was going to garner unwanted attention. He let himself be carried along with the flow into the ballroom, slowly inching his way closer to the bank of French windows, which he'd earlier made sure were closed but not locked.

He looked up to see Frederica standing on the orchestra dais beside her uncle. She looked mutinous and worried. What the hell was going on?

Jammed between a Roman senator and a black cat and blocked by Queen Elizabeth's enormous hoops, he wasn't going anywhere without causing a stir. He remained still, watching Frederica, who looked more unhappy than when he'd left her upstairs, if that was possible.

Someone bumped him. He braced himself to withstand the shoves of those around him.

'Quiet, please,' Lord Wynchwood yelled. The buzz of conversation died away. A trickle of sweat ran down Robert's back as the temperature in the room increased along with the level of curiosity.

'Thank you,' Wynchwood said. 'It is my very great pleasure to announce the betrothal of my ward, Miss Frederica Bracewell, to my heir, Mr Simon Bracewell.'

Betrothed? All around him, people shouted their congratulations and exclaimed their surprise, while Robert felt as if a black hole had opened in front of his feet and he was falling in. His vision darkened, his heart seemed to still in his chest. Betrothed?

The cold steel of betrayal knifed through his chest, an

edge so finely honed, so cold and sharp, the pain almost drove him to his knees.

Why hadn't she told him? Had she tried, just now, and lost her nerve? Is that why she asked him to run away with her?

Was that the reason she'd come to him in the first place, as a means to escape an unwanted marriage? Would she now confess her sins? At any moment he expected to hear her inform her uncle that she was no longer chaste.

Not that she'd been chaste when she came to him, but they were not to know that.

God, she'd even offered to pay him. To sit as a model. Was that all she had wanted to pay for? Was it? Was she like every other woman in his life, simply using him? She'd certainly betrayed his trust by not telling him the truth.

He pushed blindly through the crowd, squeezing between hot bodies, his nose filled with the stink of perfumes and powdered wigs. The crowd parted with cross looks and grumbles. His stomach roiled with self-disgust. He'd allowed himself to be used.

He felt sick.

A scream rang out.

Once more silence reigned in the ballroom. The room seemed to hold its breath. Nothing moved, except Robert, pressing steadily ahead, the doors filling his vision like the Holy Grail to a Templar Knight.

'My emeralds,' a woman's voice cried. 'I've been robbed.'

Exclamations of horror rippled around the room. People looked at each other in shock, checked their jewels, glanced at each other in suspicion.

Barely aware, and uncaring, Robert drew the curtains aside. He needed air. Something to clear his head, something to stem the tide of icy blackness rising up from his chest and threatening annihilation.

'Stop the highwayman,' a male voice cried out from behind him. Lullington?

A crocodile with a fat belly barred his path.

Surprised, Robert shouldered him aside and grabbed the door handle. The crocodile gripped his wrist. Anger rose up. Robert swung his fist. It connected to bone and soft flesh with a satisfying crunch. The man landed on his tail with a howl. Robert pulled open the door, only to have it slammed shut by the weight of the oriental man and an enormously fat monk.

'Oh, no, you don't,' John Radthorn said, breathing hard beneath his conical hat. 'No one leaves until we find the jewels.'

Jewels? Right. Someone had yelled something about stolen emeralds. He glanced around at the suspicious faces, John's, Simon Bracewell's, his lion head gone, Lord Wynch-wood's. 'I don't have your bloody jewels,' he said. 'But I do have an urgent appointment.'

'Search him,' someone said.

'Go to hell,' Robert growled.

John Radthorn raised a brow. 'No one leaves this house until they are searched and unmasked.' His voice was quiet, but full of determination.

His disguise wouldn't hold up in front of John. Not unmasked.

He pulled his pistol from his belt. 'Stand back, damn you. I haven't got your jewels. I'm leaving.'

People gasped, men muttered, but as one the crowd pulled back, leaving a glittering Lullington in the empty space, with Maggie a few feet behind him. The viscount's lip curled. 'A highwayman. How appropriate. 'Tis my belief he is our thief.'

Bloody hell and damnation. 'I've stolen nothing. I'll let you search me. Then I'm going.'

Lullington minced forwards. 'Perhaps he handed his ill-gotten gains off to an accomplice.' He moved to check Robert's pockets despite the pistol.

The man had courage. But Robert already knew that.

'Not you,' Robert growled and shoved the pistol in Lullington's face.

The viscount halted with a nasty smile on his lips and recognition in his eyes.

He knew.

Robert's heart picked up speed. He glanced around, caught Radthorn's intense stare and nodded at him. 'You do it. I've nothing to hide.'

Men in the crowd surged closer. Robert waved his pistol. 'Who wants a ball in their head? I'll drop the first of ye like a stone.'

'My God,' Wynchwood said. 'That man works for me.'

Inwardly, Robert groaned, even as he smiled and bowed. 'My lord. Thank you for a very pleasant evening. I would recommend a little less water in the punch.'

A half-smile kicked up John's mouth as he moved in. Robert held his hands away from his body, watching the men crowding closer. Off to his right, still on the dais, a small figure in green-and-brown earth tones stared down at him. Her eyes were huge in her pale face.

Radthorn would find nothing and Robert would leave her to her betrothal ball. His lip curled. Once he was gone, she could announce her ruin with his blessing.

John patted the pockets in his coat, ran a hand across his waistcoat and his hips. 'No jewels,' he said.

'Then why is he holding us at bay with a gun?' Lullington lisped, waving a languid hand. 'I suggest we call the magistrate and have him searched properly by the local constable.'

A man dressed as King Charles the First, but looking more like a spaniel, popped through the throng. 'I am the magistrate. You,' he said to Robert, 'will put down your pistol and submit to a proper search of your person.'

'That was a proper search,' John said, his voice strained.

Robert glanced at him, saw concern in his friend's eyes and his stomach hit the floor. John had found something.

A hiss of steel whipped his head around. It was Lullington pulling a sword from his costume's scabbard.

He held the sword tip against Robert's throat. 'It is my guess the rogue's pistol isn't loaded.' He showed his teeth. 'Is it?'

'Do ye dare to find out?' Robert said, pressing his pistol's muzzle against Lullington's chest.

Several men lunged forwards.

'One more step,' Robert said. 'And this man is dead.'

They stopped cold.

Lullington gave a soft laugh and pressed the blade to Robert's throat. He felt the sting as the blade nicked his flesh. 'Shoot, then.'

Curse him. Robert tossed the pistol aside. Loaded or not, he'd not shoot a man in cold blood.

He held his arms wide. 'Search me again, then, if you must.'

'Oh, I think I must,' Lullington said softly. He raised his voice. 'I saw him upstairs a while ago.'

Hades.

The crowd around them muttered.

Robert kept his face impassive and let Lullington pat him down. The moment the viscount announced he did not have the emeralds, he would dive through the glass. But he needed space. He needed Lullington clear of the door.

He moved into the semicircle of watchers, putting John between him and the door. John would let him past.

Lullington slowly ran his hands down Robert's body, his legs, his arms, checking the cuffs on his coat. Robert lifted his gaze and saw how Frederica clung to the music stand. She actually had the gall to look worried. As if she actually cared.

Or was she worried he'd give her away?

Lullington swung him around and felt through the folds of his cloak. 'Aha,' he cried.

Robert froze. It couldn't be. He could not have found the jewels.

Maggie put her hand over her mouth and shook her head.

Lullington pulled forth a strand of emeralds and diamonds. Robert recognised them. Maggie had worn them often in his company.

'A strange thing to keep in your pocket, sir,' Lullington lisped.

'Someone put them there,' Robert said. 'I did not take them.'

'What were you doing upstairs, then?' Lullington asked. 'In the same wing where Lady Caldwell's chamber is located.'

Robert clenched his fists. The bastard. He must have seen Robert in the upstairs hall and then planted the necklace in his pocket in the crowded ballroom. He recalled the bump. Robert glanced around. Every face stared back with an expression of suspicion. It was White's all over again.

'It is possible that the real thief hid them on this man's person, meaning to claim them later,' Radthorn said. The pity in his eyes made Robert feel sick, but at least John wasn't abandoning him.

He glanced towards the podium, dreading Frederica's reaction. She was gone. No doubt she thought him guilty.

'Arrest him,' Lullington said to the magistrate. 'There is no doubt he is guilty.' He held the necklace high to the gasps of the crowd. 'You really should be more careful whom you employ, Lord Wynchwood.'

His sneering gaze rested on Robert. The bugger was enjoying himself. Robert eyed the door two steps away. A fist in the viscount's gut might make him a little less smug and give him enough time to escape.

'Someone fetch a rope,' the magistrate said. A footman scurried off. People turned to watch him go.

Lullington handed the necklace to Maggie, whose pallor had taken on a greenish cast.

The momentary distraction was all Robert needed. He leaped for the door handle, wrenched the door open. Lullington grabbed at his cloak and yanked. Robert tore the damned thing free. Too late. Three men leaped on his back. He hit the ground chest first. The air rushed out of his lungs as all three men sat on his back.

'Bring the rope,' one of them yelled. The other two grabbed his arms.

Robert shook off one, kicked another in the groin and struggled to his feet with the third hanging on to his sleeve.

'Hold him,' someone yelled. Three more men latched on to his arms and dragged him to the floor. His hat went skidding across the tiles. Robert, gasping for breath beneath the pile of men, stared at a gap in the tangle of arms and legs where John's face appeared. 'What the deuce is going on, Robin?' he whispered.

Robert shook his head. 'I did not steal that necklace.'

John winced. 'Hold still, then, man. Don't make it worse. I'll see what I can do.'

Submit to the final indignity. Rage welled up inside him. Blast it, John was right. The odds were against him. There was no sense in getting beaten as well as arrested. Robert took a deep breath and lay still.

'Stand him up,' the magistrate said, his flowing wig all askew, the footman at his side, rope in hand. 'Let me have a look at him.'

The men hauled Robert to his feet. He came face to face with Frederica. Robert pretended not to see her. He kept his chin low in hopes of hiding his face from those that might know him.

The footman fastened a rope around his wrists and pulled it tight.

'An emerald necklace isn't the only thing you are hiding is it, my lord?' Lullington murmured in Robert's ear so no one else could hear.

'Shut your damned mouth,' Robert muttered.

Lullington smiled. 'If you don't want your family name dragged through the mud,' he whispered, 'you'll proclaim your guilt like a man.'

'I'll see you in hell,' Robert whispered.

Lullington held his scented handkerchief beneath his nose, muffling his words. 'I'm sure you will. But you will arrive first.'

'What is he saying?' the magistrate said, leaning forwards.

'Think about it, Robert,' Lullington murmured. 'I'll give you 'til morning to admit your guilt. If not, I'll really unmask you.' He used his forefinger and thumb to pull Robert's mask over his head.

Maggie stared at him. 'Robert?' she whispered in disbelief. Her eyes rolled up in her head and she collapsed in a heap beside the magistrate's high red heels.

One of the ladies near her, a dark-haired woman in a

toga, bent to chafe her hand. Robert saw all of that from the corner of his eye, but it was Frederica's reaction holding him captive and rigid.

At the moment Maggie fainted, the pallor of her skin blanched to translucent white, as if every drop of blood in her veins had drained away, but instead of fainting or screaming, she backed away with an expression of terrible hurt.

Even at this distance he felt her shock and horror. Revulsion oozed from her pores and made his skin feel slimy.

He wanted to deny the theft, but Lullington's threat held him silent. It really didn't matter what she thought. He had far more pressing problems.

She shook her head, stumbled over the crocodile's stupid tail, then turned and fled up the stairs.

He watched her disappear until someone tapped him on the shoulder. John, looking as sick as a horse. 'I'll take my grandmother home and come back later.'

Robert nodded, feeling a little less isolated.

Everyone else, except the triumphant-looking Lullington and the two footmen clenched on Robert's arms, huddled over Maggie's inert body, proffering smelling salts, vinaigrettes and fans. What a bloody farce. If his position weren't quite so desperate, he might have laughed.

'Take Lady Caldwell into the drawing room,' Lady Radthorn directed. She raised her head and peered through her lorgnette at Robert. 'Fine mess you are in, young man.'

'Grandmama, please, let us go home,' John said.

'Throw that vermin in the cellar,' the magistrate said. 'We can't have a fellow like him ruining our evening.' He puffed out his chest. 'I will get to the bottom of the matter in the morning.'

'Ain't got no cellar,' Michael the footman said, looking blank.

'The coal cellar,' Wynchwood said, mopping his brow with a handkerchief. 'Oh, my lord. I feel faint. My health cannot stand the shock. Where are the smelling salts?' He staggered after Maggie's entourage.

'Did you really think by posing as a gamekeeper you could hide from me?' Lullington murmured into Robert's ear.

Robert said nothing.

'Pay your debt or it will either be the gallows,' Lullington said with an infuriating smile, 'or trans-portation.'

A cold chill settled on Robert's shoulders. In that case, he'd count himself lucky to be hanged.

'The only question is,' Lullington continued, 'under which name do you want to be tried?'

Lullington knew Robert would do anything to protect his family's name—he could see it in the other man's face. He knew Lullington had never liked him, but he'd never thought the man so vindictive as to accuse a man of a crime he didn't commit and make it impossible for him to deny it.

'You bastard. I'm working to get your money.'

Lullington's thin lips curled in a sneer. 'I think I prefer this method of settling your debts, my friend. I shall enjoy telling my cousin.'

Michael, the footmen and a man from the village swung Robert around, hustled him down the back stairs and in short order shoved him into the cellar. Lumps of coal rolled beneath his feet. Stumbling forwards, Robert slammed into the wall head first. Stars circled in front of his eyes. Thick dust choked his throat. Coughing, he struggled to remain upright.

The door banged shut. A bolt slid home. The key turned in the lock.

Damp chill seeped through his coat and into his skin. He waited for his vision to adjust to the dark. It didn't. Not one crack of light penetrated his cell.

The beating of his heart filled his ears, a slow steady thud. His ears rang from the blow to his head.

What an idiot he was to have given Lullington such an easy opportunity. If he'd been thinking with his brain instead of what was in his trousers, he would never have risked coming here tonight. And for what?

A woman who was betrothed to another man.

Why would Robert steal from the guests of his employer? She felt as if the ground beneath her feet rocked and swayed to a rhythm she didn't know. She'd thought him perfect, a down-to-earth man, honest and straightforward. She'd trusted him.

It was her fault he'd gained entry to the hall. Her fault he had access to Lady Caldwell's chamber. He never would have been tempted if she hadn't allowed him come to her room. Unless he had planned it all along.

Her heart clenched. She didn't want to believe it. *Men are ruled by their needs,* she'd heard.

Apparently their needs included priceless gems.

And why had Lady Caldwell said his name and then fainted? Did she know him? She kneaded her temples.

At first, he'd denied his guilt. He'd stared at her, willing her to believe him. Was it the truth? Or was he hoping the spell he'd spun would keep her entranced?

If so, sadly he was right. She couldn't bear the thought of him locked up in the coal cellar. She got up from the bed and paced to the window.

Lady Caldwell had her jewels back, so no real harm had

been done, had it? Perhaps she could convince her to let the matter drop.

But first, she wanted to hear what Robert had to say. He owed her the truth.

Chapter Nine

Robert cursed and gripped the shovel hard between his knees and once more began grinding the ropes against the dull edge of the blade.

He allowed himself a wry smile. The magistrate had done him a favour, putting him in a place he knew only too well. With a bit of luck, he'd be long gone before they came to fetch him in the morning. He huffed out a breath. His escape wouldn't help prove his innocence. It would probably make matters worse, but without the evidence, namely Robert's person, the viscount would be unable to prove the identity of the so-called thief. And John would deny it, Robert was sure, even if Maggie supported Lullington.

What would it matter once he was gone? He'd lost any chance of a future here and this way, his family would never know for certain that the man arrested was him. They'd only have Lullington's word.

He sawed back and forth. The first strands of the rope gave way. He still half-expected Wynchwood to stomp down here accusing him of debauching his niece. Well, if it got her out of a marriage she didn't want, good luck to her. Her cousin was an idiot. He wasn't going to stay around to find out if she succeeded. The last thing he wanted was for his father to hear his son was not only a debaucher of innocents, but a thief to boot.

He'd thought she was different from all those other women he'd known. That she liked him for himself, not what she could get from him.

It didn't matter. He was leaving. He would never see her again. Just as he'd planned.

One thing was sure, he wasn't going to let Lullington get away with his ridiculous accusation. Once free, he'd find Maggie and get her to withdraw the charges. He was not going through the rest of his life with this hanging over him.

He sawed harder and faster. The edge of the shovel scored his wrist.

Pain tore up his arm. He clenched his jaw, bit back a curse, blinking away the welling moisture in his eyes. He did not want his guard lured down here by a noise.

Awkwardly, he wiped his face on his upper sleeve. The shovel fell to the flagstones with a clang.

Hell.

He listened. A muffled silence greeted his ears. It was like being entombed alive, or how he imagined being entombed alive. Dark, silent, damp and cold, with the only noise his rasping breath and pounding heart.

Don't think, you idiot. Just get this bloody rope off. He scrabbled among the lumps of coal for his shovel.

The back stairs creaked beneath Frederica's feet as she felt for each step with her foot. Creeping around Wynchwood in the dark was something she had done as a child, looking for food when sent to bed without supper for some transgression or other. Tonight it seemed far scarier, far more risky with so many strangers in the house and something other than food on her mind. Robert.

A thief. He hadn't offered one word of explanation after the gems' discovery, once Lullington muttered something in his ear. He'd stood there, sullen and angry, the very picture of guilt.

Her stomach heaved again. Was that why he'd befriended her, made love to her? So he could steal from her family?

Had she been so utterly taken in?

And here she was planning to set up on her own. If she was so easily duped, here in a house where she was protected, how would she manage on her own?

Whatever he was, whatever he'd done, she wanted the truth. Deep in her heart, she prayed there was some explanation.

Frederica tiptoed along the passage toward a sliver of light cast on the flagstones by the ajar kitchen door. Knowing William, she'd find him taking his ease by the fire instead of standing on guard outside a locked cellar door. Her tale of noises below her chamber window and fears of a possible accomplice should send the footman out into the night chasing shadows, wanting to satisfy her foolish womanly fears.

If she played her part right.

With shaking fingers, she pulled her wrap closer about her and pushed the door open. The figure on the settle by the hearth straightened. Sharp eyes observed her over a tankard.

She stared at him, mouth agape. 'Mr Snively?'

'I wondered how long it would be before you put in an appearance,' Snively said.

She winced. 'I thought William was guarding the prisoner.'

He set his mug down on the hearthstone. 'I sent him to bed with a belly full of his lordship's best porter.'

'Oh.'

'Come to see Robert, have you? You've been getting far too close to that young man, you have.'

Nothing slipped past Mr Snively. 'I wanted to speak to him. Ask him what happened.' She twined her fingers together. 'I just can't believe he would do such a thing.'

'No more do I,' Snively said. 'That there lass and the viscount are up to something.'

'Lady Caldwell, you mean?'

'I do, Miss Wynchwood. There have been some late-night visitations between those two. And the way his lordship looked at Robert Deveril, I could see there was bad blood between them. Old bad blood, or my name's not Joshua Snively.'

A little bud of hope unfurled in Frederica's chest. 'Do you think they put the jewels in his pocket to make him look guilty?' She frowned. It didn't make sense, or answer the question of how they knew Robert. Or why they would deliberately incriminate him? Or why he'd let them? But it was a relief to know that Mr Snively shared her doubts. She plunked down on to a chair. 'What should we do?'

'If he runs, he'll never prove his innocence. If he is innocent, that is. He'll be a hunted man.'

Frederica's blood chilled. 'What is the alternative?'

'Damned if I know,' Snively said, scratching at his chin. 'If he stays, he'll hang for sure.'

She couldn't bear the thought of Robert being hanged, even if she was his dupe. 'Then we must set him free.'

He nodded. 'We've another matter to discuss too, miss. This business of your betrothal. You don't want to marry Master Simon, do you?'

Even though she'd hinted to Snively that she had no

desire to marry her cousin, astonishment didn't begin to describe the emotion whirling in her head to hear Snively speak so boldly of family matters.

He narrowed his eyes. 'If you do, I'll say no more.'

Frederica found her tongue. 'No. I do not want to marry my cousin.'

'Ah. Fair shook the wind out of my sails when I heard the announcement, it did.' He glowered. 'Something's gone wrong. Your uncle received a letter from Bliss two days ago. I'm thinking it's behind this rush to marry you off.'

'Who is Bliss?'

'A London lawyer with information of interest. I can't say any more.'

Could he sound any more mysterious? 'I don't have time for this now.'

'It's important.'

'I can't see how it is more important than a man's life.'

'You would if you knew,' Snively muttered.

'Knew what?' She felt like screaming—he was being so secretive.

'I'm not at liberty to say, miss. Not yet. But something has to be done.'

It did and it would. She was leaving for London. Tomorrow. She'd use the first instalment from her drawings and buy a passage to Italy. The publisher could forward the rest of her money to Florence.

In the meantime, she had to do something about Robert. 'Can you saddle Pippin and leave him at the gate? I will talk to Robert and explain that running is his only course.'

'I doubt he'll need any encouragement,' Snively said. 'I'll do as you bid, miss, but you and I needs to talk after.'

'First thing in the morning.'

'You'll need these.' He handed her a candle, a knife and a key. 'Tell him to be as far from here as possible by

morning. And he's to keep mum about your part in letting
him go.'

Frederica felt her jaw drop. This was not the man she
knew, the stiff and starchy Wynchwood butler. Not only
had his accent changed, his personality had undergone a
metamorphosis. It was all very odd. But right now she didn't
have time to think of anything except Robert and securing
his freedom.

She dashed down the cellar steps to the coal room. At
the door she paused to listen.

'R-Robert?' she whispered through the keyhole.

A metallic clang and then a crunching sound emanated
from the other side of the door.

'R-Robert. It is Frederica. Can you hear me?'

'I can indeed.' He sounded impatient. 'Go back to
bed.'

'I'm going to open the door.'

'All right,' he said slowly.

The key turned easily in the lock. The bolt was stiff in
its hasp and she flinched every time the metal squeaked,
despite knowing no one could hear. The moment it shot
back, the door flew open.

Blinking, Robert stood in the doorway illuminated in
the light of her candle. Coal dust streaked his face and his
eyes were red-rimmed.

'I—I… Are you all right?'

A wry smile twisted his lips. 'Aren't you taking rather
a risk, Miss Bracewell? Opening the door to a desperate
criminal?'

'Did you really steal the necklace? You denied it at
first.'

He stiffened slightly, so imperceptibly it almost seemed
a trick of the wavering light. He lifted an arrogant brow.
'And if I told you I did not steal it, would you believe me?'

He leaned one shoulder against the dusty wall, the picture of arrogance and insouciance. The picture of a rogue.

It was as if he didn't care if she believed him or not. She glared at him fiercely. 'If you tell me you are innocent, then, yes, I believe you.' She realised it was true. Despite everything, she trusted him, as she had trusted few others in her life.

He stared at her for a long moment as if trying to decide whether or not to believe her. 'I have a question of my own. Why did you say nothing about your betrothal?' While the expression was still uncaring, she heard an edge in his voice.

'I had no idea it would be announced tonight.'

'That wasn't my question.'

How could she possibly explain? 'I'm not going to marry my cousin Simon.'

'You'll forgive me if I say the arrangements looked pretty firm from where I was standing.'

'How could I denounce poor Simon in front of all those people? I couldn't make him a laughing stock, even if he is an idiot.'

'Poor Simon indeed.' The corner of his lip lifted in a mocking smile. 'When did you plan to tell him of his cuckolding, before or after the wedding?'

A trickle of shame slid through her belly. He must have seen it in her eyes because his smile grew all the more cynical.

'Why are you being so horrid?' she said.

'Am I being horrid? Then run away, Frederica.' He jerked his chin. 'Back to your noble friends. To your betrothed. You should not be here with the likes of me.'

She gasped.

A shadow passed across his eyes. Bleakness. The announcement of her betrothal must have hurt him. Could that be reason enough for theft? So he could depart Wynch-wood with money in his pocket? Lord, she hoped not.

'I told them repeatedly I would not marry my cousin. But they wouldn't listen.'

'Really.' He tilted his head, his dark eyes intent on her face. His jaw flexed. 'Did you think to use me to make them change their minds? Tell them I'd stolen your virtue?'

She winced. Put like that it sounded cold and calculating. Still, he deserved the truth. 'I thought of it afterwards. And only as a last resort.'

He flattened his back against the wall and stared up into the dark above his head. 'Do you think it will work?' He sounded dreadfully tired.

She stooped and set the candle on the floor. 'Actually, no. I have another plan.' She reached into her pocket and pulled the knife she'd taken from the kitchen out of her pocket. 'I'm booking a passage for Florence.'

He looked down at the knife and up at her face. 'Italy? Was that where you wanted to go when you asked me to run away with you?' He sounded bemused.

'An art teacher I've been writing to has offered to take me as a student if he likes my work. We could go together.' She shrugged as if it didn't matter either way. 'If you wanted to.' She didn't want him to know how hurt she'd been at his rejection. 'Turn around. Let me set you free. If they find you guilty, they will hang you.'

He jerked his hands from behind his back. 'I used the shovel to cut the rope.'

The lace at his wrist was black and bloody. 'And hurt yourself in the process.'

'It's nothing. You should go now before someone finds you here.'

'But what will you do?'

His face became grim. 'I need to speak to Maggie.'

Something sharp pierced her ribs at the familiar name. 'You do know her.'

He cursed under his breath 'Yes. I do. And I didn't steal her damned jewels.'

'Then why say nothing?'

He cracked a bitter laugh. 'You don't want to know.' He grasped her shoulders and turned her around, pushed her towards the door. 'It's time you left.'

He preferred Lady Caldwell's help to hers. The realisation cut her to the quick. And he still hadn't given her any answers. She whirled around. 'I'm not going until you tell me what is going on. What is Lady Caldwell to you?'

The Robert she knew seemed to disappear; another man, relaxed, charming, at ease, took shape before her. He had a dangerous smile on his lips. A smile warm enough to melt a woman's heart. Another woman's heart, for this was not her Robert.

He raised a cocky brow. 'Little girl, you couldn't get much closer than Maggie and me at one time.'

'Lovers.'

He bowed. 'A gentleman never tells.'

The pain almost knocked her off her feet. She clenched her hands, felt the skin tighten over her knuckles and the breath held in her chest like a hard lump of coal. She forced herself to ignore it, to focus on his words, not her hurt. 'And yet you stole her necklace?'

'Let it lay, Miss Bracewell. Forget we ever met. Get married. Have children. Or go to Italy if you must. Be happy, but for God's sake go.' He turned away, his shoulders set and stiff as if he was angry. But the note in his voice wasn't anger, it was bleakness.

'You are a gentleman, aren't you?'

'Once. No more.'

'How can that be?'

'I did something dishonourable. I seduced a lady and refused to wed her.'

The words hung in the damp, coal-dust-laden air.

Robert had never said those words out loud. Never. They were like daggers to his heart, nails in his coffin. But as she'd gazed at him with hope in her eyes, he knew he didn't have the right to drag her down into the hell-pit that was now his life. Better she hate him than follow him into the abyss.

He turned, expecting to see disgust in her elfin face. Instead he saw puzzlement.

'W-why?'

The stutter was back, betraying her nerves. Good. She should be nervous. 'I didn't want to get married.'

'Oh.' She looked shocked.

As well she might. He took a deep breath and found his chest tight. 'I am a rake.'

'But not a thief.'

'No, but nor am I a good man. And after tonight I will be a wanted criminal.'

'But you didn't take the necklace. They have to tell the truth.'

He shook his head, his throat too full of something hot and hard for speech.

A fissure cracked in the ice that seemed to encircle his heart. The pain of it sent him spinning away, made his eyes blur, his heart feeling too large for his chest. It was as if the coal piled at the end of the cellar had been lifted from his shoulders and been put back where it belonged. She trusted him.

He grabbed her shoulder. Tipped her chin so he could look in her eyes. 'Don't get involved.'

'Then stand up for yourself, R-Robert.'

'The evidence is against me, I'm afraid. Who will believe me, a gamekeeper against a peer of the realm?'

She winced. 'How did the necklace get in your pocket?'

All questions he'd asked himself. He took a deep breath. 'I believe Lullington put it there.'

'Because he hates you. I saw it in his face. He is jealous of you—' her voice caught and she took a deep shaky breath '—because of Maggie.'

He narrowed his eyes. 'What do you know about Maggie?'

'That she spoke your name, just before she fainted. She knows you.'

If she trusted him enough to believe him about the necklace, he had to do the honour of telling her some of the truth. 'It was Lullington's cousin whose virtue I stole.' Not that she'd had any, but that was the way it appeared.

She pursed her lips. 'It isn't a very honourable way to punish you.'

He cracked a laugh, couldn't help it. 'He's a clever man. This is the one way he can do it, without sullying the lady's name.'

Her beautiful eyes stared at him. He tried to maintain dispassion, tried not to let the trustful gaze suck the truth about his banishment from his throat even as it ate through every defence he'd built over the years. He didn't want her pity.

He caught her around the shoulders and pressed a brief kiss to her lips. 'You must go now. Forget we ever met.'

A noise sounded out in the passage. They both swung around to face the intruder. Hell. Now he'd never be able to speak to Maggie. He pushed Frederica behind the opening door and picked up the shovel.

'Robert?'

He let his weapon fall. 'Maggie?'

Her buxom figure glided through the door. She paused when she saw Frederica frozen in the light of the candle.

'La, Robert,' she drawled, 'I see you haven't changed. But isn't she a little young even for you, darling? On the other hand, you always did have an eye for something special and this one is quite unique. I'm madly jealous.'

Frederica backed up a step, her gaze flickering back and forth between them, her eyes large and hurt and grave.

'How did you get down here?' Robert asked.

'There was no guard in the kitchen. I hoped to find you alone.' Maggie looked shamefaced and, now he looked more closely, rather pale.

'Why?'

'Dash it, Robert, there's no need to look so Friday-faced. I wanted to apologise. I had no wish to get you into trouble.'

'*You* planted the necklace on me? Not Lullington?' He felt as if those he cared about most were bludgeoning him from all sides. He clenched his fists. 'God damn it, Maggie. Why?'

Maggie flinched. And so did Frederica. She must have heard the shock in his voice, the note of betrayal. Naturally, she wouldn't understand that he and Maggie had been friends as well as lovers. In some perverse way, Maggie's betrayal hurt worse than Father's. At least that hadn't surprised him.

'I had no idea it was you,' Maggie cried. 'Oh, I saw through your highwayman disguise, but I thought you were the saucy gamekeeper. How could I know you were my Robert out for a lark?'

Frederica gasped. Robert inwardly winced. 'I'm not your Robert.'

'You know what I mean. I thought you were a cheeky

servant. I knew you'd leave before the unmasking.' She tossed her head. 'Dash it all. This is so confusing. What are you doing playing at gamekeeper anyway?' She cast a sidelong glance at Frederica. 'Or shall I make my own guesses?'

'That's enough,' Robert snapped. 'Even if you didn't know it was me, why incriminate an innocent man? A theft like that means the gallows.'

'The necklace wasn't supposed to be found. You were to walk outside where my groom was waiting to relieve you of the necklace. He was to engage you in a bit of a scuffle, or get you drunk or something. Then it was to disappear. Lull ruined everything.' She sounded distraught.

'So Lullington is not in on your little scheme.'

'It was his idea.' She caught her bottom lip in her teeth. 'The emeralds are paste. They have to disappear before my husband finds out. I don't know why he changed the plan.'

'Lullington always plays his own game. You know that.'

Her chin thrust forwards. 'He's been good to me. Kind and generous since you left.'

Robert snorted. 'He's a rake.'

She stamped a foot. 'So were you.'

Robert recoiled from her vehemence. He held up a placating hand. 'How came you to be in such a fix that you needed to steal your own necklace?'

Frederica moved forwards, as though she too wanted to know the answer. Her face was white and pinched. He wanted to hold her. To offer comfort. He didn't dare. Maggie had already guessed about them. He didn't want to give her proof.

'You know what Caldwell is like about my gambling. I

had a run of bad luck. Lull would have given me the money, but he was short of funds.'

'So you pawned it.'

She nodded.

He glanced at Frederica, standing silently in the shadows, her thoughts hidden by an unusually blank expression. 'Were you planning to claim the insurance?'

Maggie gave a bitter laugh. 'My husband is the only one who could benefit from that. No. Just before I left to come here, he told me he'd noticed the clasp needed repairs and promised to send it to the goldsmith on my return. I was terrified. If he discovers I pawned it to pay off gambling debts, he will lock me away in the country. He threatened it last time. This time he will do it.'

Robert stifled a curse. 'Well, you are in a pretty fix now. The emeralds are recovered. And very publically, too.'

'I know.' She twisted her hands together.

Frederica moved into the circle of light. 'You must t-tell the magistrate the t-truth,' she said. 'You cannot allow R-Robert to take the blame.'

Her fierceness took him by surprise. The sense of being swept up out of harm's way by the arms of an angel was strangely uplifting to say the least. He wanted to hug her. Instead, he raised a brow at Maggie.

She wrung her hands. 'I'll tell the magistrate I don't wish to prosecute,' Maggie said. 'I can't tell him I planted them on you, but I can convince Lull to let the matter drop.'

'I don't need Lullington to do me any favours, but dropping the charges would work.'

'Is this a private party?' said a drawling voice from the doorway. 'Or can anyone join?' A lithe, tall man leaned against the doorpost, a bottle in one hand and two glasses dangling from the other.

John. Robert groaned. How many more people from

his past would join him in his cell? All it wanted was Lullington to complete the nightmare. 'Radthorn, what are you doing here?'

'I dropped the ladies at home, then returned to see if you needed help.'

'By giving me enough brandy so I won't notice when they hang me?' He gave a hard laugh. 'I'm surprised you are prepared to acknowledge you know me.'

John stiffened. 'Er, Robert…about that afternoon. You took me by surprise. I didn't expect to see you out in the street. We were meeting at White's.'

'What are you talking about?' Frederica asked, her eyes suspicious.

'The day he got sent to Coventry,' Maggie said. 'Lull told me all about it.'

'He would,' Robert said.

'It was all over Town,' Maggie said. 'The son of one of the most powerful dukes in the land thrown out of the fold?' She shrugged. 'It was on everyone's lips.'

'A duke's son?' Bemusement dawned on Frederica's face and then horror.

'A second son, Frederica,' he said, reaching out a hand. 'I'm banished. My father disowned me.'

She spun away, avoiding his touch. Then she turned back, her soft mouth twisted in pain. It almost killed him to see her hurting even if he couldn't understand the source of her pain.

'You have to leave here tonight,' she said, clearly anxious to be rid of him. 'If Viscount Lullington deliberately implicated you, there is no guarantee he will back down.'

Maggie opened her mouth to protest.

'Miss Bracewell is right,' John said. 'Lullington would love to spear you with his proverbial rapier. Come home with me and we'll find a way to sort out the mess. The duke—'

'No,' Robert said.

'What about Charlie?' Maggie asked.

Charlie had been less than charitable the last time they met. He shook his head. 'Forget about my family.'

A grating noise had everyone looking up.

'Snively,' Frederica said. 'Unbarring the trapdoor. Pippin should be waiting at the end of the drive.'

John looked startled. 'Enterprising young lady, I see. Robert, let me offer you refuge until we get this sorted out. Do you think you can find your way to Radthorn Grange? You can stay in the east wing.'

Another person who believed in his innocence. His best and oldest friend. A man he would trust with his life. Robert let go a breath. 'All right. I'll meet you at the gate. Then we can decide on what to do next.'

'Let Pippin go when you are done with him. He'll find his way home,' Frederica said. She looked at him for a long moment, moisture glistening in her eyes. 'I just want you to know, I am not getting married.'

Amid the tears he saw hope. Yet he could not be swayed by those eyes or that lovely mouth. He could not tie her to a man without honour. He could not let the ache to fill his empty nights be her downfall, no matter how much he desired her. 'You are safe here,' he said softly. 'Get married, have children and be happy.'

She stared at him as if he'd handed her a death sentence.

'You had better get going,' John said. 'Who knows who else might decide to visit you?' They all knew he meant Lullington.

Frederica turned away, but the pained expression on her face sliced through his chest like a sword. At that moment he would have much preferred to face the viscount's blade.

She was better off without him. He might never clear his name. He'd certainly never be accepted back into society. He forced himself to scramble up the coal heap, holding his breath against the clouds of dust, and pulled himself out into the fresh air.

Chapter Ten

Frederica turned back to see his legs disappear through the trapdoor. Tears she hadn't wanted him to see stung the back of her eyes. Obviously, he couldn't wait to see her married to Simon. He'd said she belonged here.

Of course she did. He was a duke's son. One step from royalty. Far above her touch.

And all this time she'd thought him no better than herself. One of the lesser mortals. A man within her reach. How he must have laughed behind his hand at the way she'd fallen for his charm.

The tears threatened to well over again. To hide them, she picked up the three-cornered hat lying at her feet, then rounded on Maggie who was talking in a low voice to Lord Radthorn. 'You will do as you promised, won't you?' Her voice sounded damp.

Lady Caldwell's wide eyes darted a glance at Lord Radthorn before she answered, 'Robert is not the man for you, my dear. He's a charming rake, but a rake all the same.'

Radthorn shook his head. 'But he's too much of a

gentleman to betray you, Maggie. I'm damned if I'll let you make him an outlaw.'

Maggie folded in on herself, her shoulders hunching, her hands twisting at her waist, her pretty face looking years older. 'I already said I would withdraw the charges. But my husband is going to murder me.'

Radthorn put an arm around her shoulders. 'Don't worry, Lull with think of something.'

Maggie wiped her eyes with the heel of her hand. 'Yes.' A tremulous smile curved her lips. 'He usually does.'

'Of course he does,' Radthorn said cheerfully. He patted her shoulder.

She smiled up at him ruefully. 'I never meant for anyone else to be harmed, John. You know that, don't you?'

Such endearing sweetness curved her lips, Frederica could see why Robert had loved her. Her heart squeezed pitifully, but she forced a practical smile. 'That's it, then. We are d-done here. I'll lock the d-door. With luck it will be morning before anyone notices he's gone.'

Radthorn nodded. 'Good idea. You need to get back upstairs, Maggie. I've no wish for pistols at dawn if Lull finds you missing and comes looking.'

Maggie laughed and fluttered her lashes, no doubt cheered by the thought of men fighting a duel over her. She took Lord Radthorn's arm and the two of them walked out of the cellar.

All's well that ends well. Not quite. Maggie would be fine. Robert would be fine. And she was betrothed. Hah. In a pig's eye.

She dropped the hat on the floor.

The son of a duke and the Wynchwood Whore's bastard daughter—he must have thought her such a fool.

Suddenly, she felt drained. Empty. As hollow as a drum

in her chest, and yet there was a hard ball of something else in there making it hard to breath. A sense of loss.

She didn't want to think about it or she might start crying in earnest. And never stop. Tears never did the slightest bit of good.

Frederica left the cell and locked the door behind her. The affair with Robert must be viewed as one of life's lessons. She would never again give her heart to a handsome man. She had no heart left to give. Robert had taken it with him.

She marched up the stairs. With Robert rescued, she needed to know what her uncle was about, announcing the betrothal without warning. Did it have something to do with a letter from the London lawyer as Snively had hinted? Perhaps she should find out in case there was more bad news in the offing.

On silent feet, she stole along the corridor past the drawing room and crept into her uncle's dark study. If there was a letter from this mysterious lawyer, it would be here.

She lit a candle. The desk was cluttered with paper. A quick search turned up nothing. She pulled on the right-hand drawer. It was locked. If Uncle kept to old habits… yes, here was the key in the inkwell. It turned in the lock.

The drawer was full of papers. She unfolded the one on the top, an official-looking thing with a seal. She almost dropped her light. It was a special wedding licence. Made out for her and Simon, dated the day he left London. She picked up the next sheet of paper. A letter. From the vicar. Agreeing to perform the ceremony—tomorrow. She gulped.

They couldn't force her to marry Simon. Could they?

Did she dare stay and find out?

Umm. No. She needed to leave. Now. Tonight. And there was only one person she trusted to help her.

* * *

Raindrops ran down the nursery's diamond window panes. Low-hanging clouds hid Radthorn Grange's acres from Robert's view. He swung around at the sound of the door opening.

'Only me,' John said, tossing a pile of clothes on the cot on which Robert had spent a restless night. 'Why you insist on wearing these rags is beyond me. I would happily lend you some of mine.'

'Because no one will give me work if I dress like a damned dandy,' Robert said.

John winced.

Robert focused on undoing the buttons of his frilled highwayman shirt to avoid seeing his friend's embarrassment and softened his tone. 'Thank you for fetching them. I'll be off as soon as I'm dressed.'

'You might want to hear the latest.'

Robert glanced up. John's face was half-puzzled and half-amused. 'What?'

'Wynchwood Place is in utter turmoil. You are a wanted man.'

'Hardly news.'

'It's not what you think. Maggie worked her magic on Lull. He agreed that the jewels in your pocket weren't Maggie's at all and said they must have been part of your costume. For a moment I thought all would be well, until they discovered you missing, along with Miss Bracewell. Now you are wanted for kidnapping.'

Robert's stomach pitched. 'The little fool.'

'It gets worse. The silver plate has gone. They found signs of a struggle in the butler's pantry and the butler is also missing. Apparently done away with by a desperate criminal. You.'

Robert's jaw dropped. 'Bloody hell? Are you saying he stole the silver and ran off with Frederica?'

'It looks like it.'

Robert's mouth went dry. 'My God.'

'I know.' John gave him a pained looked. 'They found your hat in the butler's pantry. It seems your Miss Butter-never-passed-my-lips Bracewell neatly took a leaf out of Maggie's book and left you to carry the blame for her abduction. No wonder she was so keen to set you free.'

'She wouldn't do that.' She couldn't have.

What did Snively have to do with it? Was he the one who'd had her virginity? That old man? Disgust rose like bile in his throat even as he shook his head in denial.

What other explanation could there be? She'd seen her chance and used him to take the blame. The cunning little witch.

He struck out with his fist at the wall. Felt pain in his knuckles, felt the vibration up his arm and all the way to his chest.

Damn it all. After Father's betrayal, he'd sworn to trust no one. To rely only on himself. He'd forgotten his own rules.

But Snively! How could she? Jealousy pricked like the point of a knife. He forced himself to think. Where would they have gone? She'd talked of Italy, which meant a port. Or was that a smokescreen? A lie to put him off the scent, if indeed he had any ideas of following her.

One thing was certain, they would have to fence the silver. And London was the most likely place.

'Where does Wynchwood presume we are headed?'

'Ah, that's where things start to get interesting.'

'Out with it, man. I don't have time for puzzles.'

John sighed. 'You spoil everything. Listen to this. Young Simon was in such a dither when I found him in his room packing he muttered something about finding them at a Mr Bliss's office near Lincoln's Inn Fields.'

'A lawyer?' It made no sense at all.

John shrugged. 'I was just about to question him further when Lullington joined us. He hustled me out of the door.'

'Meaning he is in Bracewell's confidence.'

'I assume so. Even old Wynchwood is headed for town and he hasn't been there for years. It all sounds a bit like a Minerva novel, don't you think.' John chuckled, clearly vastly entertained.

'If Wynchwood's for London, I am too.'

'What I don't understand is why Lullington is tagging along?' John mused.

'Lullington is short of funds.'

'I don't see how this would help.'

'I really don't care about Lullington. If Wynchwood thinks Mr Bliss's office is the place to look for the runaway pair, I am going there too. I have to clear my name, John. I won't let anyone turn me into a criminal.'

John clapped him on the shoulder. 'Nor you should. Come with me to the magistrate and we can clear the whole thing up.'

'Can we? Or will they accuse me of doing away with her too?'

'Ouch.'

'Quite. I'll catch the first stage that goes through Swanlea.'

'I think not,' John replied. 'I'll take you up in my carriage, as my groom.'

Robert raised a brow.

'You insisted on dressing like that.' John grinned. 'I'm going to enjoy giving you orders.'

'Bastard.'

'Numbskull. Why the hell didn't you come to me before?'

For the first time in a long time Robert didn't feel completely alone. But his growing rage at Frederica's dirty trick left little room for softer emotions.

'Right. Let's be off.'

A duke's son. Again the realisation twisted Frederica's insides painfully. It was as if her mind refused to believe what she'd heard. Standing at the window of the private parlour Snively had procured at a down-at-heel inn near Lincoln's Inn, she took a deep, calming breath. Dash it. She kept letting thoughts of Robert creep into her mind the way shadows creep into a valley at night. Thoughts of what she'd hoped.

If wishes were horses, then beggars would ride. She had many wishes. But horses were in short supply.

From one side of the mullioned window, she peered into the narrow street, careful to ensure no one would see her from below. Snowflakes floated past the window, turning grey when they hit the cobbles, then melted away. It would make an interesting drawing. If only she could settle.

After visiting the publisher to arrange for the payment of her money, Snively had gone to find a friend he thought might prove useful. She paced to the blazing hearth on the other side of the room and held out her hands to its warmth.

Robert *had* tried to warn her off. She just hadn't wanted to hear. She'd thought he was trying to protect her because he thought her too good for him. Quite the opposite. In the end, she'd seduced him. Used his wicked male urges against him. Her body flashed hot, then cold.

What man would resist a wanton? He'd tried to be honourable and she'd behaved with all the morals of a barn cat. If only he'd told her who he was, she would never have harboured such foolish ideas. It had to be his lack of trust that made her chest ache as if her breastbone was pressing against her heart.

The door flew open.

Frederica jumped. She swung around.

'I told you to keep this door locked,' Snively said, hanging his hat on the hook on the back of the door and shooting her a glare under his brows much as he'd done when she was a child tracking mud across the hall floor.

'What did you discover?'

'None of the Wynchwoods have called on Bliss as yet.' He dropped into a chair beside the hearth. 'An old friend of mine is watching the place.'

They'd arrived in London yesterday and so far there had been no sign of pursuit. 'Perhaps you are wrong about Uncle Mortimer,' she said, sitting opposite, clenching her hands in her lap to keep them still.

He wiped his brow with a large white handkerchief and stuffed it back in his pocket. 'I'd be right glad if I was, miss. My nose tells me otherwise. 'Tis my guess he knows your father left a letter to be opened on your birthday.'

'My father?' Her chest squeezed. She couldn't breathe. It was like falling off Pippin, the ground rushing up to meet her. 'My father left a letter?' she gasped. 'You know who he is? Why didn't you tell me?'

Snively's face turned red. Beads of sweat broke out on his brow. 'A slip of the tongue, miss. Forget it.'

'No. I need to know what this is all about.'

'I can't tell you.'

She had never seen Snively sweat as he was doing now.

She voiced her greatest fear. 'At least tell me he is not some horrid murderer.'

'I've said more than I ought, but I'll say this. You needs to find out for yourself. Tomorrow at the lawyer's office.'

'And if I don't?'

He pressed his lips together. 'You'll be sorry.'

Pieces of a puzzle fell into place in her mind. 'You said you went to see Mr Bliss because he could arrange an account on which I could draw. It isn't true, is it? He is the lawyer who wrote to my uncle.'

He tugged mightily at his stock. 'Yes.'

'Then where is the money for the drawings?'

'Waiting for you at the publishing house,' he squeezed out.

'Then we don't need to see this Mr Bliss. I will book passage to Italy immediately.'

'Don't, miss. Please. You must read the document Mr Bliss has for you.' His jowls wobbled. He dabbed at his brow. 'Sworn to secrecy, I was. But I assure you, you will not be sorry.'

'I'm sorry I trusted you.'

He gazed at her with hurt eyes.

'Dash it. If my father wanted to contact me, he could have done so years ago.'

Snively cringed. 'It's all explained in the letter.'

She huffed out a breath. 'I don't even know his name.'

'He swore me to secrecy.'

Because of who she was? She felt sick. 'I don't need to know and I need to be on a ship before Uncle Mortimer finds me.'

'You'll regret it,' he said.

She glared at him.

He let out a sigh. 'Joshua Snively don't blab. Not with a thousand pound on the line. And Bliss will not see it paid to me if I say one word. Your father trusted me. Now so must you.'

Life had seemed much simpler less than a week ago. Did

she really want to know the identity of her father? Lady Radthorn's talk of her mother's wildness before her marriage meant this man could be anyone. A shiver ran down her spine. Perhaps the man was a criminal. Or married and ashamed. Or...what? And why should she care when her father had never paid her the slightest heed until now?

Should she trust in Snively's assurances that all would be well or her own instinct to run?

This was like one of Shakespeare's plays where everyone pretended to be someone else. The only thing she knew for sure was that if she didn't leave England she might never have her chance to learn her craft. And yet Snively had always been a good friend and right now he looked terribly upset.

She huffed a sigh. 'Very well. I'll wait one day to read this letter. But no matter what happens, I am leaving right afterwards.'

'Fair dos,' Snively said, looking hugely relieved. 'I'll go find us a ship. In the meantime, lay low.' He pushed to his feet with a grunt

'Thank you.'

He rubbed his chin. 'Your pa paid me well for this job, miss. But after all these years watching over you from a distance, I've come to think of you as one of my own.'

She reached out and squeezed his hand. 'Thank you, Mr Snively. I do wish you'd tell who my father is so it won't come as too much of a surprise.' Or a horrid shock.

'I gave my word. Tomorrow is soon enough, never you fear.' His dark eyes twinkled. 'Now when have I ever steered you wrong?'

She took a deep breath. Tomorrow it would be.

'Radthorn!'

On his perch at the back of John's curricle, Robert

cringed at the sound of his mother's voice. His heart plummeted. 'Pretend you don't see her,' Robert hissed in John's ear, careful to keep his head low.

'Can't,' John muttered, neatly pulling into the curb on Bond Street. 'Take their heads, Parks,' he said in a louder voice.

Robert leaped down, and, keeping the horses between him and the diminutive lady on the footpath, ran to the bridles. He shifted so he could see his mother as she raised her face to look at his friend. She looked elegant as always, but beneath her jaunty red-plumed bonnet her face seemed more lined than Robert remembered. More careworn. Damn Charlie. Or was it the girls running her ragged? He prayed she didn't look hagged because of him.

'I didn't think you were due in town for another week, John?' she said, her voice calm and cool. 'How is your grandmother?'

'Very well, your Grace.'

'And you, Robert?' she said, raising her voice. 'Why have you not called to see me?'

Startled, Robert jerked the bridle. He must have been mistaken. She couldn't possibly recognise him like this. He patted the horse's flank.

'You jobbed at the bits,' Mother scolded, appearing at the curb in front of him.

John's rueful chuckle carried above the noises in the street while Robert drank in the sight of his beloved mother's face, her fine grey eyes holding sadness and pleasure, her lips curved in an encouraging smile.

His throat burned and his arms longed to hug her slim shoulders. 'Father won't like it if you acknowledge me,' he said roughly, bitterly.

Her eyes widened. She drew in a quick breath. 'I knew

you'd had an argument, but I thought it was you who left in a temper. Charlie hasn't looked me in the eye since.'

Charlie wouldn't. He'd agreed with Father. 'You had best move on,' he said, seeing her footman lingering a few yards farther down the pavement.

'Come home with me, to Meadowbrook, and I'll talk to the Duke. Sort it out.'

A lump rose in his throat. He swallowed and shook his head. 'Please go, your Grace, before someone sees you talking to a groom and gets suspicious about the low company you keep. I certainly don't want another episode like the one at White's.'

Her gaze took in his garb and her eyes filled with pity. He felt ashamed to cut such a disreputable figure in her presence. 'I'm so angry with your father,' she said softly. 'How you must have suffered. Come home. I'll make him put it right.'

He stiffened, the events of that day rushing through his veins like poison. 'What happened was my own fault, Mother. I must be the one to make it right. But what Father said…well, I'm sorry, it was unforgivable.'

'As proud as ever.' She shook her head sadly. 'We cannot talk here. Your father is still at Meadowbrook. I came to town to visit an old friend who is ill. Call on me in the morning at the town house.'

'I'm in a bit of a scrape. I will not bring more disgrace to the family.' He couldn't help his smile. 'Are the girls well? How is Hal?' The youngest son, born long after the other children and most beloved by his father.

Her eyes misted. 'All are well. They miss you.'

His throat felt raw and full. 'I miss them too. And Charlie?'

She shook her head. 'He went to Durn on business.'

'Good God.' Durn was the gloomiest of the Duke's

properties, located in the wilds of Yorkshire. No one ever went to Durn willingly.

Mother smiled wearily. 'I worry for him. He is not happy.'

A chill entered Robert's chest. 'I'm supposed to feel sorry for him?' He headed back to his seat.

Mother looked up at John over the horses' backs. 'I'm glad you found him for me, John. Keep him safe.'

'Always at your service, your Grace,' John said. He flicked his leader with his whip and the curricle moved out into the traffic. Robert stared straight ahead, not daring to look back in case he did something rash like leaping down and giving her a hug. No doubt some bright spark would take him by the collar to the nearest constable for assaulting a lady.

'Damn,' he muttered.

'Quite,' John said. 'Bloody well, quite.'

And damn him for a fool for getting tangled in another woman's toils. And still he kept not wanting to believe what she'd done.

They left Mayfair and entered the city. Here the bustle was all about commerce, the businessmen purposeful and the poor more ragged. John pulled up outside a well-maintained bow-fronted office with a sign proudly proclaiming the name of Mr Edward Bliss. A fellow leaning against the wall on the opposite side of the street ran a knowing eye over the horses. 'Hold 'em for you, mister?'

'Get a move on, Parks,' John chortled.

Robert glowered. 'Ask if either of them have visited,' he muttered and leaped down to take the nags' heads.

John stabbed his whip in the holder and stepped down. In the unhurried saunter of the polished gentleman, he entered the solicitor's office.

The wall-lounger sloped off.

John was back in less than a moment. He shook his head imperceptibly. Robert wasn't surprised. Neither Snively nor Frederica was a fool. Still, he'd had to try.

'You didn't say who was asking?' he said, when they were on their way again.

'As we agreed,' John said. 'Where now?'

'Drop me off at the Angel. I'll start by looking in all the inns within walking distance of here. And then try farther afield.'

'I'll come with you.'

'There isn't a prig in the City who will talk to you looking like that,' Robert said. 'And besides, I want you to check on ships to Italy. See if any left in the last day or two and if any are due to sail within the next few days.'

'Do you want me to look at the list of passengers?' John said, grinning over his shoulder, then executing a nice weave between a baker's van and a hackney.

'Thank you,' Robert said with feeling.

'What are friends for? You don't know how I kicked myself after that meeting outside Whitols.'

'Water under the bridge and far out to sea,' Robert said, clapping him on the shoulder, then cursing as he realised his *faux pas*.

John laughed. 'I'll leave these tits with the groom at the inn and we'll begin the hunt.'

A knock sounded at the door. Mindful of Snively's strictures, Frederica approached it cautiously, listening. 'Who is it?'

'Chambermaid, miss. To make up the fire.'

The voice was familiar. Betty had been in and out several times during the day. Frederica turned the key and stepped back.

The maid bustled in with a coal scuttle. 'A man was

asking after you and the other gentleman, miss. Described you he did.'

Frederica's heart gave a warning thump. 'What man?'

'Young 'un. Handsome too.'

'What did you tell him?' They had given false names at the inn.

'Nothing, miss. As your friend requested. Thought I better let you know.' The girl emptied half her bucket on the embers in the grate and poked at them vigorously.

The thumping in her chest picked up speed. 'Yes. Thank you.' She fumbled in her reticule and found some coins. Her fingers encountered Snively's pistol primed and ready to fire.

The girl rose to her feet. 'Will that be all, mum?'

Frederica nodded and pressed a sixpence in the girl's ready palm.

'Tell no one I am here.'

'No, miss.'

Frederica opened the door and the girl and her coal scuttle slipped out.

Frederica swung the door closed. It stopped short of the frame. The toe of a scuffed brown boot appeared in the crack.

Frederica backed away, watching the door swing open.

'Miss Bracewell. This is a pleasure,' said a voice full of anger.

Chapter Eleven

'R-Robert?' Frederica sat down heavily on the sofa instead of running and throwing her arms around his neck as she wanted, because this was the Robert of weeks ago. Dark. Aloof. He looked as if he wanted to throttle her. 'What are you d-doing here?'

He stalked in, his eyes raging, his expression murderous. 'You didn't think you'd get away with it, did you? That I'd accept your blame?'

He kicked the door shut with his heel and crossed his arms over his chest. 'Or did you think I wouldn't find out until they had me clapped up in prison?'

Her heart thumped madly against her ribs. 'I don't know what you mean. I helped you escape.'

His lip curled in disgust. 'While you and Snively helped yourself to his lordship's family heirlooms.'

She gasped, shocked by the fury in his eyes as much as his words. She gulped a breath. 'Don't be r-ridiculous.'

'Then you won't mind coming with me to the magistrate and clearing this whole thing up, will you?'

She clutched her reticule against her chest, felt the weight of the pistol inside. Snively had warned her that she had enemies in the Bracewells, but she hadn't expected Robert to be one of them too. Trying to look natural, unconcerned, she tucked the reticule between her and the sofa arm, fiddling with the strings as she spoke. 'You are talking in riddles. Isn't it rather dangerous for you here in London? Or did Lady Caldwell keep her promise and have the charges dropped?'

He snorted. 'You know very well there is little Maggie can do about what you and your partner in crime have laid at my door. You are coming with me to Bow Street and you are going to admit the whole wretched scheme. Where is the silver? Have you sold it?'

'Silver?'

'The Wynchwood family plate you and Snively ran off with.'

He was talking nonsense, but she did not doubt his intention to hand her over to the authorities.

She eased her hand inside her reticule and gripped the pistol firmly. 'I took nothing that was not mine.'

'Don't play the innocent with me. I know better, don't I?'

Heat rose to her cheeks. He made everything sound so horrid. Sordid. She might have known he'd use her past against her. Everyone did.

She drew out the pistol and cocked it with her thumb, just as Snively had shown her.

Robert started back. Then he grinned, an unpleasant curl of his lips. 'You don't think I'm scared of that little pop?'

Her hand shook. Her heart galloped. She felt hot all over. Shoot Robert? She couldn't. She just needed to hold him at bay until Snively came. She levelled the pistol at his chest and swallowed. 'In the r-right spot, it will do significant d-damage,' she said, her voice shaking.

He took a step towards her.

'Stay where you are.' *Don't make me do this.*

He lunged and knocked the pistol aside, then wrenched it from her hand. 'If you are going to threaten a man with a pistol, you had better fire it right away.' He released the cock and slipped the pistol in his pocket.

She crumpled against the sofa back, a little ashamed of her cowardice and a lot relieved. She couldn't have shot him, no matter what. 'I won't go back. I would sooner you shot me than marry Simon.'

He narrowed his eyes. 'Damn Simon. Where is the silver? Tell me the truth or I swear you are going straight to Bow Street. You and your accomplice.'

She glared down her nose at him. 'We did not take any silver.'

'Are you telling me Snively did this without your knowledge?'

He was shouting. She struck the sofa cushion with her fist. 'You are mad. I'm no thief, any more than you are. And anyway, what concern is it of yours if I did take the silver?'

His jaw hardened. His voice lowered to a growl. 'You made it my business when you let them think I'd taken you with me. I am charged with abduction.'

She gasped. 'What?'

'When they found me gone and you gone, they assumed I had stolen you away, just as you planned.'

'No!'

'They found the evidence you left, my hat, blood, and the silver gone. You must have taken it.'

'We didn't.' She stared at him. 'Why would Uncle Mortimer make it look as if we had stolen the silverware?'

A startled expression crossed his face. 'Your uncle lied?'

'What else can it be? I swear to you, I came away from Wynchwood with nothing but the clothes on my back and my portfolio.'

Anger leached from his face, leaving only mortification, his cheekbones stained red. 'Oh, hell,' he said. He passed a hand over his face. 'I thought… Forgive me.'

He looked so devastated that she nodded, though she wasn't sure how she felt after his accusations.

He sat down beside her on the sofa, his eyes full of regret. 'Could Lullington have taken it to pay Maggie's debts?'

Maggie. As before, the casual use of his lover's name made her chest squeeze. Jealousy, when she had no right to be jealous. She forced herself to think, instead of feeling hurt. 'The silver isn't worth much at all. And he could have had it without stealing it, too. Simon would have been only too glad to settle his debts with some old plates and cutlery.'

'Bloody hell.'

She frowned. 'They are saying you abducted me?'

'It appears so.' He laughed softly, and shook his head. 'You know my father always predicted I'd come to a bad end.'

He sounded so resigned it hurt her to hear it.

'I will go to Bow Street,' she said bravely. 'Tell them I'm safe and say I stole the silver.'

He picked up her hand and kissed the back. The brief brush of his lip sent a hot shiver down her back. 'If you do that you'll be forced back to Wynchwood. I thought you might be on a ship to Italy by now.'

And she would have been, if Snively hadn't been so excised about her father's letter.

'Where does Snively fit into all of this?' Robert said. 'Is he another of your lovers? Was *he* your first?' He spoke lightly, as if he didn't care, but she heard an edge of distaste.

A horrid feeling invaded the pit of her stomach. It writhed as if full of snakes. It was her fault he thought her a bawd, but the suggestion made her feel sullied. She wanted to tell him to leave. But he was knee deep in her midden and he deserved the truth. 'We aren't lovers. Mr Snively is…was employed by my father to watch over me until the terms of my uncle's guardianship ended.' She raised her gaze to meet his. 'It seems my father left a letter that I am to receive on my twenty-fifth birthday. It will reveal his identity. Quite truthfully, I'm not sure I care, but Mr Snively thinks it is important and he also thinks my uncle somehow learned of its existence.'

Robert frowned as he listened to her explanation. 'All this fuss and intrigue over a letter? Where is this letter?'

'A solicitor called Bliss—'

Robert straightened. 'The name Bracewell let slip in Radthorn's presence.'

'Then Mr Snively is right. My uncle has learned of the letter's existence.' Her shoulders drooped, but she forced a smile. 'It is odd of my uncle to go to such lengths to keep me from learning my father's identity, when I'd almost prefer not to know. I would have left as soon as I have my money from the publisher, but Mr Snively has his heart set on my making an appearance at the solicitor's office in the morning.'

She got up and paced to the window, standing to one side to look out.

'Mr Snively believes that if my uncle catches me before his authority ends, he will do anything to marry me to my cousin,' she said quietly.

Anger surged in his veins. 'Against your will?'

She nodded. 'Uncle Mortimer could have me declared

incompetent and locked away until I agree.' Her lips twisted in an unusually bitter line. 'After all, what gently bred woman wants to run off to Italy and p-p-paint when she could m-marry and have children and be happy.'

Robert felt sick hearing almost his own words.

Her eyes darkened, became huge in her face. 'Or they might use my mother's promiscuity against me.' She raised her gaze to meet his. 'Lady Caldwell no doubt guessed about us.'

'Damnation, this is a pretty tangle.' His voice sounded harsh. He wanted to offer aid, but had none to give. As a wanted man, he could barely help himself. 'Where is Snively now?'

'Booking a passage to Italy. He has a friend watching for my uncle outside the solicitor's office.'

The wall-lounger, no doubt. 'Snively should know your uncle is on his way.'

Robert watched her pace around the room, forcing himself to remain where he was instead of taking her in his arms. He was a complication she could not afford.

'I should leave London tonight,' she muttered. 'Forget about the letter. My father never wanted me any more than my mother did. I was an embarrassment when I was born and nothing has changed.'

'And yet you are curious to know who he is.'

'Curiosity killed the cat,' she murmured softly. The tragic set to her mouth made his stomach sink. There was something here he didn't quite understand.

The door slammed back.

Robert leaped to his feet, his hand going for the pistol in his pocket. Too late.

Snively, looking belligerent, had a pistol pointed at Robert's chest.

'To what do we owe this pleasure, Deveril?'

'Is this a private party?' another voice said and John entered with a pistol pointed at Snively. 'Or can anyone join?'

'Oh, r-really,' Frederica said. 'I have never seen anything so r-ridiculous. Come in, Lord R-Radthorn, and close the door before we have the whole inn crowding in here with loaded weapons.'

A rare grin creased the corners of Snively's eyes. He tucked his pistol in his pocket. Robert gave John a nod, and his friend did the same.

'It appears we have a problem,' Frederica said to Snively. 'Robert has been accused of running off from Wynchwood with me and the silver.'

Snively pinched his lower lip between this thumb and forefinger. 'Aye. So I hear at Bow Street. They, too, are watching the solicitor's office for both of you.'

'Wynchwood must have laid information against me,' Robert said. 'He must have reached Town.'

'Could be Lullington,' John said.

Robert wanted to curse. 'We need a plan.'

At almost midnight, the private parlour was stuffy. Frederica looked pale and at the end of her tether. Robert felt as if he hadn't slept for a week.

'All r-right,' Frederica said. 'So we have all agreed on what we cannot do. Does anyone have any idea of how we should p-proceed?'

The other men, Radthorn and Snively, stopped arguing and looked at her.

'They are watching Bliss's office at all points of the compass,' Snively pointed out. 'There is no way into the building without being seen.'

'Why not a ladder?' Radthorn said. 'Wait until the small hours, climb in through a window. Miss Wynchwood could walk down the stairs from the inside first thing in the morning. *Voilà.*'

'A baby could spot a ladder,' Snively said scornfully. 'What about a disguise?'

'I have an idea,' Robert said. It had been niggling away in his mind all evening. But it was risky. Everyone looked at him expectantly. 'A decoy.'

Snively frowned. 'What sort of decoy?'

'Someone disguised to look like Miss Wynchwood trying to look like someone else,' Robert said.

John gave a soft whistle through his teeth. Snively looked thoroughly mystified.

Swiftly, Robert organised his thoughts. 'We dress another woman to look like Miss Bracewell in disguise. One of us will escort that woman along the street. The watchers will spot the decoy and give pursuit when she runs off, giving the real Miss Bracewell the opportunity to slip inside the office unseen.'

'It might just work,' John mused. 'Lullington will be the hardest to fool.'

Snively perked up. 'I can make a bit of a diversion in the street. Make 'em really confused.'

'We will need someone of Miss Bracewell's height and build,' John said. 'Make her look as if she is wearing a disguise, while Miss Bracewell should look ordinary.'

'Puts Miss Bracewell at terrible risk,' Snively said heavily.

They all stared at Frederica and her face went bright red. 'What about the chambermaid?'

'The lass who let me in earlier?' Robert mused. 'She's about your height and build. Do you think you could charm her into helping us, John?'

John snorted. 'Along with the promise of a guinea or two.'

'We'll need a hat with a veil and a heavy cloak,' Snively added.

'For me?' Frederica asked.

'No,' Robert said. 'You will look like any other woman out shopping. Perhaps a close-brimmed bonnet to hide your face, but that is all. I think this will work.' For weeks he'd felt as if he'd been marking time, going through the motions of living, except for the interludes with Frederica. Now energy coursed through his veins. 'John, find the maid. Snively, your diversion will have to be big enough to distract the men waiting in front of the office.'

'Leave it to me.'

'Then we will plan for mid-afternoon when the streets are crowded. I will go there ahead of time to see if I can spot them and their locations. We will meet back here around midday. Are we agreed?'

Heads nodded.

'Tomorrow, then, gentlemen.'

Despite her cheerful front, Robert worried that all was not well with Frederica. When her blush had subsided, she'd looked paler than before. Her eyes showed strain.

He hung back as the room cleared. 'Are you all right?'

'I'm sorry you got dragged into my troubles.' Her brave smile pierced his heart. 'Whatever happens, you must not take any chances. I could not bear it if you were arrested.'

'A duke's son doesn't get arrested,' he said with a smile and a note of confidence he didn't quite feel. 'Or at least, not for long.' He reached out and took her hand. Her fingers were icy, chilled to the bone, despite the warmth of the room. 'You are freezing.' He drew her nearer the fire and stirred the coals.

She shivered again and stretched her fingers against the

heat. 'Robert…' she smiled up at him '…thank you for trying to help me.'

The words held real gratitude. The look of longing in her eyes as she gazed at him weakened his resolve to leave at once and seek lodgings with John. It seemed with this woman, he had no will. 'It is no more than any man would do.' He spoke briskly, matter-of-factly, in case she read his longing to pull her close and kiss away her fears.

After a moment or two, she turned back to the fire, staring into the flames, her shoulders hunched. Drained of all spirit.

He dropped to the seat beside her on the sofa. 'Are you unwell?'

'I'm fine.' She turned to face him. 'I just wish I had left yesterday.'

He put an arm around her shoulder. 'Don't you want to know your father's name? Hear what he has to say?'

She rested her head on his shoulder. God, it felt so right, her looking to him for comfort and support. His chest ached with the pain of knowing he would never see her again after tomorrow.

'I don't know.' She shivered, her teeth chattering until she clenched her jaw.

He pressed the back of his hand against her cheek, felt the chill of her skin. 'You are freezing. You need something to warm you from the inside.'

He rose and rang the bell. A lackey came to the door and Robert told him what he needed. While he waited for the man's return, he pilfered the counterpane off the bed in the adjoining chamber and tucked it around her shoulders. He knelt before her, chafing her hands. From the rigid expression on her face he guessed that this girl, who he thought of as fearless, was deeply distressed.

He ran a finger down her cheek. 'I'm sorry I suspected

you of trying to pin the blame on me. I should have known better.'

She smiled, her lips tinged with blue. 'Yes. You should have.'

There was the spirit he sought. The fight. Yet her eyes remained shadowed.

He brought her hands to his mouth, warmed them with his breath, kissed the fragile bones that wrought such magic with charcoal and paper. 'Everything will be fine. I promise.'

She looked away, staring into the fire. Took a deep breath.

A little colour returned to her cheeks. 'I will be glad when it is over, that is all.' She gave him a watery smile.

The sight made his chest feel overly full as if his heart had grown too large to be contained.

A knock of the door heralded the arrival of the wine. Robert took the tray to the hearth, filled the small kettle with madeira, spooned in cinnamon and cloves and added a pinch of mace. He heaped in generous spoonfuls of sugar, then hung the pot on the crane above the fire.

Soon the liquid began to simmer and the room filled with a sweet, heady fragrance as he stirred.

'Now, Miss Bracewell,' he said, pouring the mixture into a glass, 'you will oblige me by drinking this. It will warm you. Then we will tuck you up in bed.'

'I don't feel the slightest bit tired. Will you stay a while? I—I find I don't want to be alone.' The soft pleading in her eyes sent hot fire leaping in his blood. Every nerve ending in his body urged him to accept. He fought desire, tempered it with kindness.

'I'll stay for a while. Until you fall asleep.'

'You may be here all night, then.' She took the glass from his hand and sniffed at the contents.

'Go ahead. Drink. I promise not to poison you.'

She laughed then. 'Silly R-Robert.'

God. He loved the way she laughed and adored the way she said his name with that tiny hesitation. It saddened him to think he might never hear either sound again.

She sipped at the mixture and wrinkled her nose.

'Too hot?' he asked.

'No. I've never tasted anything like it before.'

'Drink it to please me.'

She took another taste and another, sipping delicately, her lips turning the colour of rubies from the wine, her cheeks flushing. 'I like it.'

One glass and she'd be sleeping like a baby. And then he'd leave.

Frederica sipped the rest of the wine in silence, her hands cupped around the glass bowl, her eyes focused deep within. He felt an odd desire to ask her if she'd miss him. Not once in all his years on the town had he wanted a woman to remember him once their affair was over. He preferred to think of them moving on, as he moved on to some new alliance. Just the thought of her sitting like this beside a warm fire in quiet companionship with another man caused his heart to still.

Even if he wasn't the first man in her life, he felt closer to her than he'd felt to anyone, except maybe Charlie. And that had been years ago.

He got up from the floor, and sat beside her on the sofa, tucking her into the hollow of his arm. She leaned back against his shoulder. 'Mmm,' she murmured, taking another sip. 'It really is quite delicious.'

It was no good thinking of the future. He needed to mine what enjoyment he could glean from today in full measure. The knowledge that they could at least be friends.

This evening would make for a pleasant memory. For them both.

Her eyelids slid closed and the glass, with only the dregs left in the bottom, tilted. The covering around her shoulders rose and fell with each deepening breath.

The evening was about to end. With a sense of loss, he slowly removed the glass from her grasp and set it on the floor.

She was sleeping. Time to put her to bed and honourably depart.

Chapter Twelve

Carefully, he slid from beneath her and propped her in the corner of the sofa. She looked vulnerable and young. He couldn't leave her here, sitting up, still clothed. He scooped her up in his arms, still bundled in the counterpane, her head lolling on his chest, her breathing wine-laden and heavy. He carried her through to the bedroom and lay her down on her side on the bed. She made no movement as he pulled down the covering and undid the laces down the back of her bodice. Her nape, so elegant, so delicate, so pale in the candlelight, begged his touch. He pressed his lips to the top of her spine and rolled her on her back.

Her eyelids, crescented by dusky lashes, fluttered. Her head lolled on the pillow.

'Hush,' he whispered. 'Sleep. You are safe.'

Held fast by the drugging effect of the wine, her lips parted on a sigh. Her eyes remained closed. The skin of her eyelids was as translucent as the finest porcelain.

Inch by inch, he eased the gown off her softly rounded shoulders and releasing her arms. He pushed the bodice down to her waist, keeping his mind fixed on the task, not on the rise of pale breasts above her chemise and stays. Practical front fastening stays for the girl who dressed without the help of a maid. It took no time at all to unlace them and pull them free.

The gown he worked carefully over her lovely hips and down her legs. He tossed it aside and went to work on her shoes. How he loved her elegantly arched feet inside the practical woollen stockings, the curve of her calf, the gentle bend of her knee. So pretty. And soft. And lost to him.

Beneath her shift, her veiled body tempted his ardour. The rosy peaked rise of high small breasts. The darker triangle of soft fur between her thighs. Granite hard with desire, he allowed himself no more than a glimpse before he covered her up.

He leaned over and kissed her forehead. 'Sweet dreams, little elf,' he murmured.

Her eyelids flew up. She caught at his sleeve. 'You are leaving?'

Damn it. It was as if she had a sixth sense where he was concerned. 'Sleep. It will be a busy day tomorrow. You will need your strength.'

Eyes wide open, she stared at him. 'You said you would stay.'

'I thought you were asleep.' He sat down on the edge of the bed.

'Lord R-Robert?' she said.

He turned back with a frown. 'What is this lord business?'

'That is your title, is it not?'

'I'm Robert to my friends.'

'Is that what we are?' she asked in a small voice. 'Friends?'

Friends. Lovers. And so much more. 'Yes,' he said firmly,

knowing that was all she could be. If he didn't draw back now, he might never be able to let her go.

'Do you have to leave?' she murmured. 'I feel so much better with you here.'

Dear God, she was impossible to resist when she looked at him with such trust.

She trusted him. And needed him. It had been years since he felt needed. He liked it. He stroked a wisp of hair back from her forehead, felt the warmth of her skin. 'If you sleep now, it will all seem much less worrisome in the light of day.'

His gaze fixed on her face, he kissed the inside of her wrist. A shiver ran through her. Imperceptible to anyone else, he felt her desire like a bolt of lightning through his body. He was rock hard and aching.

'Lie beside me until I sleep?' she asked.

Did she have any idea what she was doing to him? Of course she did, the little minx. But she didn't understand that as a practised seducer he had a will of iron honed by years of practice. More experienced women than she had failed to break his control.

He stretched out beside her on the bed, cradled her in one arm. 'Now, close your eyes,' he said.

She snuggled against him. God, it felt good. Never had he experienced anything like this sense of companionship with a woman. Holding her, feeling her warmth, the tickle of her hair against his cheek, the pressure of her elbow against his ribs, the swell of her hip against his thigh filled him with contentment, with the desire to protect. Not in the way a man would protect any woman from harm, but the primal need to shelter and ward.

He would remember her always. Just like this.

Unless he stayed with her.

Something inside him snapped, like a cord pulled too

tight, it whipped back at him, flayed at his soul. If he stayed, how would he support them? He could not live on the money she made from painting and keep any shred of himself.

'Come with me to Italy,' she urged sleepily.

Did she read minds? Or only his? The temptation to say yes burned in his throat.

'What would I do?'

'You could carry my bags,' she said, her eyelashes flicking up, a mischievous smile curving her lips. 'Guard me from the *banditti* I hear are rife in the hills, while I earn money painting portraits of rich travellers against the backdrop of famous landmarks.'

He laughed to hide his discomfort as even this vision of himself tempted unbearably. She'd cast her wood-sprite spell, soft, seditious strands of longing, until he lay before her like a willing captive ready to do ought to please her. Had he sunk so low he no longer cared what he became? 'Is that all you want of me?'

'You could bring me my chocolate in bed every morning.' She cast him a knowing little elfin smile that said far too much.

His groin tightened. He caught her and pulled her close. 'Only if I can lie beside you and make wicked love to you as you drink it,' he growled.

She wriggled with pleasure.

Her hands went to the handkerchief at his throat and pulled at the knot.

This was a game he had played many times. But it felt so much more important with her. It wasn't a game. It wasn't casual. Each time he made love to her, it made leaving that much harder. He closed his hands around hers and she stilled.

'Don't deny me our farewell, Robert,' she said quietly. 'Don't deny us our last night together.'

'Sweetheart, it's the wine talking.'

'I need you, Robert. I'm so afraid.'

He stared at her in shock, at the panic in her eyes and the tremble of her full lips.

'My father,' she choked out. 'How do I know he's not some dreadful criminal? A murderer?' A tear rolled down her face.

'Ahh, sweetheart, is this what saps at your courage?'

'It is like some macabre tale,' she whispered. 'You have to know the outcome, but you know it will be terrible.' She dashed the tear away with the heel of her hand. 'I'm such a coward.' Her voice broke and she started to sob.

He cradled her against his chest, held her close and listened to her soft little choking sounds, felt her body shiver and shake and had nothing to say except, 'Hush.' Over and over, he whispered the same sound, rocking her against his chest.

At last her tears stopped and she took a deep breath.

Finally he dared speak. 'No matter who your father is, you are you. A talented and wonderful woman.'

'Nothing good ever comes from bad. What if I'm tainted by two evil parents? My mother and my father?'

'Good God. You are tormenting yourself.'

She shook her head and looked up at him with a smile so sad it sliced right through the wall of his chest to carve a wound in his heart.

What could he say? He dare not give into something she would regret. 'Look at Henry the Eighth. He was a horror. And if I'm remembering correctly, Ann Boleyn was no saint. But their daughter Elizabeth was England's greatest Queen. And besides, shouldn't you give your father a chance to speak for himself?'

A small silence greeted his words, followed by a determined nod. 'Thank you. You are right. If I don't do this, I will always wonder.'

She rolled towards him, then propped herself up on one elbow. She brushed his cheek with the back of her hand. 'I missed you dreadfully, you know.' She said it as if it had been weeks, not a day or two. But he knew what she meant; he'd missed her damnably too. He had filled the empty space with anger.

'Love me, please, R-Robert. One last time.'

He was undone by her tiny smile of hope, her sweet smile. He'd never been a saint. Never been able to resist a woman's plea. Why start now? He melded his lips to hers, felt the quiver of her body against his chest, the heady spiral of desire in his limbs and he took her mouth in greedy thrusts of his tongue while his hand drew her shift up her thighs. He cupped her in his palm and she rotated her hips.

Eager. Giving and damnably sexy. 'Little witch.'

She laughed into his mouth and her hands went to his shirt. She tore it from the waistband of his breeches and wrenched it up.

He lifted his hands from her body and let her pull it over his head. 'Always in a hurry,' he said.

'Oh, yes,' she said, raking her gaze over his chest and down to his breeches.

His body went rock hard at the admiration and lust in her gaze, but it was the soft little smile on her lips that sent him beyond thought. He captured her mouth in his, swept it with his tongue, melded his body to her soft, feminine curves and set reason adrift.

She clung to his neck with her arms as his mouth wooed her lips. He felt as if he could lose himself within her for ever.

He lay her down and sat on the edge of the bed to yank off his boots while she traced circles on his back with so light a touch his muscles quivered and flinched in delight and torture.

'Hussy,' he said.

'I must take after my mother,' she laughed, her fingertips exploring a particularly sensitive spot just below his ribs. He groaned, stood up and divested himself of his breeches and stockings before whipping around and catching her fingers in his hand. A wicked smile curved her lips.

'Think you can play with me, do you?' he growled, lifting her hand to his lips. He nuzzled her forefinger free, then drew it into his mouth with a swift suck.

Her indrawn gasp brought a smile to his lips and a throb of blood to his groin.

He lifted her hands over her head and ran his gaze over her much as she had viewed him a few moments before, taking in the taut perfection of her small breasts, the tightly furled nipples, the tiny waist beneath the upraised ribs, the hollow of her navel. 'Where to start,' he said.

'You look ready to eat me,' she gasped.

'Oh, now there's an idea.' He let his gaze drop to the triangle of curls at the apex of her thighs, her female mystery beneath the fine lawn of her chemise, her lovely pale thighs above the tops of her stockings and the plain garters of brown. He'd seen garters of roses and lace, and none had ever looked so erotic as these.

Her wrists captured in one hand, he lowered his head, swirled each budded nipple with his tongue and watched her hips squirm in delight and longing. He trailed his tongue down between the valley of her breasts and dipped his tongue into her navel. How sweet she smelled, vanilla and roses and aroused woman. A scent to drive a man over the edge before he was ready. How rough the filmy fabric felt against his tongue compared to the silk of her skin beneath.

'R-Robert,' she gasped and there was shock in her voice, and laughter and below all of that wicked seduction.

'What, sweet?' he murmured against her belly. 'Do you want me to stop?'

He blew a warm breath against her skin.

'Oh,' she squeaked. 'No.'

He grazed his jaw against the soft swell of her belly, delighting in her arching spine.

And then he reached his goal. The centre of her femininity. A musky scent filled his nostrils, powerfully erotic. A film of sheer fabric and a nest of pale brown curls hid his prize.

He licked at the shadowed crease, parting her folds with his tongue, rubbing the lawn against her most sensitive spot and felt her writhe and jerk.

With his free hand he raised her chemise, slowly, pausing to run a finger beneath her garter, and all the while he licked and nuzzled and breathed against her feminine flesh.

She moaned, low and guttural. The primitive sound hit him deep in his chest and zinged its way to his pulsing shaft, the blood beating hot and heavy, the demand for entry, the urgings of the feral beast in what was left of his brain.

A master of seduction never let the beast out of its cage, though he had never found it so difficult as now to remain in control, to keep from plunging into her and driving to the hilt.

Letting go of her wrists, he lifted the chemise to her waist and bared her most sensitive place to his tongue, licking and nipping at her clitoris, revelling in her cries of anguished pleasure. Her fingers burrowed into his hair and her hips pressed up to meet his mouth. He placed his hands beneath her buttocks, kneaded the firm, silky flesh, gauged the roundness, the sweet perfection, and raised her higher, opened her for better access and plunged his tongue into her hot, wet depths. She let out a moan of pure joy.

All passion, his Frederica. All womanly desire. God, he wanted to be inside her heat, feel her tight around his aching flesh.

But this was for her. He worshipped at the shrine of her core, flicking her swollen bud with his tongue, grazing it with his teeth when she wriggled, employed every art he knew to keep her on the brink, until her hands fell away from him, her legs lay wide in submission and she whispered, 'Now, R-Robert.'

A demand that went straight to his shaft. He'd never been this hard. But this was for her. He flickered his tongue across her clitoris, then suckled.

Shuddering, trembling, she shattered on a cry.

He raised himself up to watch languid bliss replace the tightness in her face, to watch a rosy glow infuse her pale skin.

Her eyelids fluttered open and she smiled. 'You are wonderful.'

And he felt like a lad again, pure, unsullied and terribly proud. 'I aim to please.'

'But you did not—' she said.

He kissed her, felt her taste herself on his mouth and eased the head of his shaft into her entrance.

'Oh, my,' she whispered.

Eyes fixed on her face, he concentrated on the blinding sensations of joining her in her pleasure, absorbed the tiny pulses of the aftershock of her orgasm, stroking the walls of her tight sheath fraction by fraction with minute shifts of his hips.

Bringing all of his skill into play as never before, the urge to take her, to drive into her, to lose himself in lust, grew ever stronger. Her body called to him as no woman's had ever done. Her gaze, so full of trust and something he couldn't name, tore at his will. Shook him to the very depths.

Left him primal.

His woman.

The words pounded hot in his veins, setting a rhythm that rode him hard. And still he circled his hips, fighting every instinct with the last atom of his will.

Her eyes widened in shock. Her expression tightened. 'What are you doing to me?' she moaned.

She was almost there. Thank God.

He bared his teeth. 'Bringing you more pleasure,' he panted. Making her his. Binding them together.

The thought sent him over the edge of reason.

He drove into her.

She lifted her hips. He pounded into her body. Her inner walls tightened around his shaft, drawing him deeper. He thrust harder. Faster. Nothing existed but the feral force of their mating.

And then he exploded.

He lost himself in the pure blinding bliss that seemed to go on and on. He shuddered and managed to roll to one side before he collapsed.

Never did he recall such a powerful joining.

Or so much loss of control.

He opened his eyes and looked at her. Had she also reached her climax? God. Why didn't he know?

But the expression on her face was pure satiation. Relieved, he let his eyes close on a groan.

'Thank you,' she murmured. 'That was lovely.'

He heaved himself up on one elbow, kissed her eyelids,

her cheekbone, the corner of her mouth. 'You were wonderful. Sleep now.'

He tucked his arm beneath her head and drew her close. She lay still in his arms, her breathing slowing. She snuggled closer.

'R-Robert?'

'Mmm...'

'I love you.'

Blood roared in his head and a pounding shook his chest. It was as if a fissure had cracked in a wall and bricks were crashing down. Those same words hovered on his tongue.

He stiffened against them. Kept them behind his teeth. She was too young, too innocent. And he too unworthy. Cast out by his peers. Even if he believed in love, and he wasn't sure he did, he was not the man for her.

Frederica turned her face away.

Damnation. He'd hesitated too long. Left it too late to say something teasing, the kind of thing he said to all his lovers. *How lucky I am.* Or, *You are the sweetest woman I know.*

'I'm sorry,' he said instead.

'It doesn't matter,' she said.

But there was heartbreak in her voice. He reached out, then let his hand fall away. What she thought of as love was merely the afterglow. When the fire cooled she'd move on. Or he would.

It was the way it worked.

He just wished that the thought of it didn't make him feel physically ill. Or wish he was wrong.

But the glow was still there, bright and enticing. If only he believed it would last. It never did.

But he could stay until it dimmed. Until they tired of each other. He could find work in Italy just as easily as he could find employment in England, could he not? Mother could no doubt be persuaded to use her influence to help him find a position at the consulate in Florence. He could support them both while Frederica painted until her heart was content.

Until the glow faded. It might take a while. Longer than most. They would laze in the heat, travel around the country looking at paintings and ancient monuments. Now the war with the French was over, there were lots of places he longed to see. Perhaps they could even go to Paris. Why not? He had nothing keeping him in England. And until she found someone more worthy of her love, he could keep her safe.

He leant over her and kissed her cheek. 'Let us see what tomorrow brings.'

With a muffler covering the lower half of his face, Robert peered around the corner. Everything was set. While he couldn't see her, he knew Frederica and John were standing in the shadows of an alley a few yards from Bliss's front door. When the hue and cry started, John would whisk her in. Robert was escorting the disguised maid because Lullington would know him despite the drunken stagger he planned to affect.

A fussy-looking lawyer in his wig and gown bustled up the street. A skinny, shabbily dressed clerk with red-and-yellow-striped stockings scurried along behind him, his arms loaded with tomes, his floppy hat falling over his eyes. A trickle of recognition played at the fringes of Robert's memory. He shook his head. Legal types had been coming and going to the various solicitors' offices all morning. He must have seen this pair before. They headed straight for Bliss's door.

'Damn,' Robert said. He hadn't reckoned on strangers being in the office when Frederica entered.

'Oooh,' moaned Betty behind him. 'I think maybe this is a bad idea. What if they arrests me?'

'Ten shillings,' Robert said, doubling her price.

'How much longer does we have to wait?'

Robert turned back and gave her the quick once over. With her rather ridiculous coal-scuttle bonnet and a dress obviously far too big, she looked like a woman in disguise.

The panic in her blue eyes said if they didn't go now, she was going to balk no matter how much money he offered.

Robert put one arm around her waist, and grabbed her hand. 'Remember, follow whatever I do. And when I say run, you run back the way we came.'

They staggered into the street and wove among the lawyers and city gentlemen. A loiterer leaned on Bliss's office wall. He straightened. He'd seen Betty. Another, on the other side of the street, headed for the curb. The traffic would slow him, but it wouldn't take him long to cross to their side.

'Are you ready?' Robert whispered, aware of the violent tremble of Betty's hand. His heart picked up speed. His muscles tensed, ready to run. 'Keep walking. Just a little bit farther.'

There. Stepping out of the alley, Frederica.

Robert frowned. What the hell was she doing? With a dark cloak and a hood pulled up over her head shielding her face, she looked more suspicious than he and Betty did. She was supposed to be wearing a blonde wig and trotting along as if she was simply out shopping, not looking as if she was a spy for the French.

And where the hell was John?

The man on the other side of the street spotted her.

Robert quickened his pace. Something had gone wrong. He had to get to her before they did. She must have lost her nerve and decided to cover her face.

'Now,' he said to Betty. 'Run.'

With the shriek she'd practised in the inn, she turned and fled with the first man Robert had seen racing after her.

The second man had his gaze fixed on Frederica.

Robert started to run towards her.

A brewer's dray lumbered on to the street. Its driver, with Snively beside him, sped along the street. The diversion.

But was it too late? Robert pushed himself to greater efforts. The gap between him and Frederica closed. Too slowly. The other man would get to her first. He lengthened his stride. Put his head down, bunching his fists, pumping his arms. He dodged an elderly couple with a curse.

A third man appeared between Frederica and Bliss's front door, his arms outstretched ready to catch her.

A barrel bounced off the cart, and then another. Before many seconds passed, beer was running in the gutters and every man, woman and child on the street turned to gape.

Everyone except Robert and Frederica, and the man blocking her path.

Robert hit him at a run. Knocked him to the ground. Robert grabbed Frederica's hand and dragged her along.

'Stop, thief,' someone yelled.

Bastards.

'Run,' he said to Frederica. He looked over his shoulder. Lullington had dodged the fallen man, Wynchwood was puffing along the pavement behind him. Robert smiled grimly. Too late.

He pulled open the door and thrust Frederica inside. A quick glance at the lock. No damn key.

The outer office was empty. Another door led into the inner sanctum where Bliss no doubt hid himself away. The lawyer and his clerk must have gone inside. Damn it all.

He thrust Frederica ahead of him. 'Through there.'

Behind them the outer door opened. 'Robert Deveril,' a voice rang out in stentorian tones, 'I arrest you in the name of the law for theft and kidnapping.'

'Go on,' he urged Frederica and whirled around, pulling his pistol from his pocket.

Frederica stopped short.

'Don't wait for me,' Robert yelled.

He levelled his pistol at the first man through the door and cocked it. Lullington, followed by Wynchwood, pushed their way in.

'Stand back, all of you,' Robert growled. 'This lady has legitimate business with Mr Bliss.'

'The game is up, Deveril,' Lullington said, a triumphant light in his blue eyes.

Robert curled his lip. 'Not yet it isn't.'

'Don't make it any worse for yourself, lad,' the runner said.

'Arrest him at once,' Wynchwood cried, his face red and dripping with sweat, one hand clutching his heaving chest. 'She is my niece. Don't let her get away.'

Out of the corner of his eye, Robert saw Frederica preparing to throw off her hood. Lullington was staring at her in a very odd manner.

'Through that door,' he said. 'I'll hold them off here.'

'Jump him,' the runner said.

'Which one of you *gentlemen* is accusing my son of theft?'

Robert's jaw dropped at the sound of the familiar voice and his head whipped around. He looked into the face of…*'Mother?'*

'May I not visit my lawyer in privacy without all this hullaballoo?' she said. 'I'll have your heads, sirrahs.'

The Bow Street runner faltered in the face of her regal rage.

'Your Grace!' Lullington choked out. He made a leg. 'I beg your pardon. I thought—'

'I know what you thought. I sent for Lady Caldwell after I spoke with Lord Radthorn earlier this morning. While I laud your attempts to help a lady in distress, I do not approve of your methods. Pig's blood indeed.'

Robert gaped at her.

Lullington made a choking sound.

'What is going on here?' Wynchwood said, still game. 'Arrest him, I say.'

Robert closed his eyes briefly. The lawyer and his clerk. They had to be John and Frederica. That's why they'd seemed so damned familiar. They were already inside with Bliss. 'Good God, Mother. If Father caught wind of this—'

Wynchwood pushed the runner forwards. 'That man abducted my niece. I demand—'

'Who is this fat flawn, Robert?' the duchess said in a voice as cold as ice. 'I am certainly no niece of his.' She sniffed. 'Nor would I admit any relationship to such an ill-mannered fellow.'

Lullington's face showed grim amusement. 'Capotted, by Gad. Your Grace, allow me to introduce Lord Wynchwood. Her Grace the Duchess of Stantford. Robert Deveril's mother.'

Wynchwood snatched the wig from his head and threw it down. 'What has the duchess to do with the kidnapping of my niece?'

Lullington curled his lip. 'Where is she, Robert?'

'Actually,' her Grace said, 'I can answer that question,

my lord. She is no doubt speaking with Mr Bliss.' She smiled serenely. 'Robert, do tell this gentleman of the law to go away. I find it quite tiresome with so many people crowding this room.'

Robert raised his brows at the gentleman in question, who was mopping his florid brow with a very large handkerchief.

'Beg your pardon, your Grace,' the runner said. He abased himself and backed out of the door in a swirl of chill air from the outside.

'Get back here,' Wynchwood howled. 'Do your duty. Arrest this man.'

Her Grace drew herself up to her full height. 'Are you accusing my son of stealing silver plate, or was it a string of emeralds, Lord Wynchwood?' Her astonishment was palpable.

Wynchwood looked to Lullington for support.

'He didn't,' Lullington said. 'We were simply trying to stop Miss Bracewell from reaching this office. A hue and cry seemed the only way.'

Snively chose that moment to stomp into the office. 'Waste of good beer that. I knew it would never work.'

He stopped short and stared at the duchess. 'Where's Miss Bracewell?'

Her Grace nodded to the closed door. 'In there.'

'Congratulations, your Grace,' Lullington drawled, his lisp no longer in evidence. 'You have us all at *point non plus.*'

'That was certainly my intention.' A gleam of mischief shone in her eyes.

Robert wanted to shake her. 'I'll murder John for involving you in this.'

She cast him a haughty look. 'Your manners have not improved in your absence, my dearest Robert.'

Robert felt like a boy again beneath that searing glance. 'I'm sorry, Mama, but you could have been badly hurt.'

'By this pack of lily-livered fools? I think not.'

'Thank you, your Grace,' Lullington said.

'Oh, do stop it, Lullington. I knew you when you wore short coats.'

Robert grinned as Lullington flushed. His mother was a force to be reckoned with and stronger men than Lullington had been ploughed down by her will.

'As for you, Robert,' her Grace continued, 'you should have been the one to bring Miss Bracewell to me. Not John.'

Dash it. When would she realise he was banished?

A footman in ducal livery entered the office. 'Ah, Frompton,' her Grace said, 'your timing is excellent. Your arm, if you please. I have had enough adventure for today. It is time I went home. Robert, you will visit me tomorrow afternoon. Without fail.' She swept out.

The men looked at each other, Wynchwood on the verge of apoplexy, Snively wary, Lullington picking at a fleck of lint on his coat and a glint of wry amusement in his usually cold eyes.

The door to the inner office opened. They all turned to watch. Frederica minus her wig, looking decidedly rakish in breeches and striped stockings, sauntered out. Radthorn, now out of his disguise, hovered behind her along with a bewigged and gowned man. The real lawyer. Clutching a rolled document.

Robert looked at Frederica's face. She didn't look too upset. In fact, she looked almost gleeful.

He tucked his pistol in his coat pocket, but kept his hand on the grip.

Wynchwood hobbled forwards. 'There you are, Frederica. You will return home at once.'

'Now see here,' Snively said, bristling.

A half smile curved her lips as she caught Robert's eyes, the elfish little smile that had enchanted him almost from the first. His heart contracted. He kept his face calm, refused to acknowledge the longing to go to her. Instead, he drew back against the wall, ready to act should any of the Wynchwood clan attempt to take her against her will.

'First I must tender my apologies to Miss Bracewell,' Mr Bliss said in a wheezy voice. 'One of my clerks thought to line his pockets by informing Lord Wynchwood of the existence of a very important document held in this office.'

Snively glared. 'Glad to hear you admitting to blabbing and not blaming me.'

Bliss inserted a finger in his cravat and tugged. 'Fortunately, no harm was done, Mr Snively. The terms of the payment to you are not affected by this unfortunate occurrence.'

Snively nodded grimly.

'What does the document say?' Robert asked.

Frederica smiled at him. He grinned back.

'This is all very irregular,' Wynchwood said. His tongue swiped his dry lips. 'This young woman is my ward. I demand she return home with me at once. I have the law on my side.'

'Not any more, Uncle Mortimer. Today is my birthday. Mr Bliss has confirmed that your guardianship ended at midnight.'

Lullington, who had ranged himself beside Robert, nudged him with an elbow. 'Spirited girl.'

'Why the hell are you chasing her?' Robert asked, confused.

'Young Bracewell is a friend.'

'Like hell,' Robert said, ire a burning ember in his chest. 'You saw a way to line your pockets.'

The viscount's cheek muscles flickered. 'You heard your mother, I was doing it for Maggie.'

'Very altruistic. You might fool Maggie and my mother, but I'm no green 'un. You plotted the false kidnapping charges. Why?'

'You deserved it after what you did to Catherine.'

The women they had fought over years before. Robert had won. They'd been idiots to even consider losing their lives over a woman, but Lullington had hated losing and Robert had fuelled his temper by gloating. They'd been enemies ever since. But Robert had never realised how much Lullington's resentment had festered.

'What about your cousin? Are you harbouring ill will about her too?'

The viscount gave a hard laugh. 'When your brother showed her his blunt, she admitted it was all her fault.'

Robert stared at him. 'Charlie?'

'He dragged her before her parents and forced the story out of her. She'd planned it all, hoping to bag a duke. The family married her off with a very nice settlement provided by your brother.'

Righteous Charlie had come through for him. Believed him. What a surprise? 'Glad to hear it.'

'I'd wager you are, since once more you came out of it scot-free.'

Hardly. Robert was about to take issue, when Mr Bliss put his pince-nez on his nose and cleared his throat dramatically.

The room fell silent.

Bliss unrolled the scroll.

A small piece of paper fluttered to the floor. Frederica bent to pick it up. She unfolded it.

'Oh,' she gasped.

Robert couldn't see what it was.

She glanced up at Snively. 'This is one of my drawings.' She touched it with a fingertip. 'Of a pigeon? How did it get here?'

'Your father saw you walking in the village one day, the day he set me to watch over you,' Snively said. 'You dropped it. He kept it with him until the day he passed on. He was also an artist. Some of his pictures of India received acclaim.'

Her eyes filled with tears. 'He came looking for me?' she whispered.

'Ahem,' Bliss said, drawing attention back to him. He glared at the assembled company over his spectacles.

Read the damned document, Robert wanted to yell. He held his tongue and assuaged his impatience by keeping a close eye on Wynchwood.

'I have already relayed the gist of this to Miss Bracewell, but she wanted you all to hear it too.' He looked around. Robert bunched his fists but managed to remain still.

'Her father, Lord Abernathy—'

A ripple of disbelief ran around the room. Wynchwood's jaw dropped.

Abernathy? Her father was a lord? Robert combed his memory. Wasn't he…the richest of all the Indian nabobs? Richer than Croesus of Greek mythology. His name was still mentioned in the clubs with awe and envy.

His throat dried.

Bliss raised a silencing hand. 'The Earl of Abernathy left his entire fortune to his daughter. Miss Frederica Bracewell has proved her identity. Unfortunately, Lord Abernathy was unable to claim his daughter in his lifetime. The circumstances surrounding their relationship are unfortunate and not to be described here.' He glared at Wynchwood. 'But as a younger son with no prospects, he was shipped off to India. Only later did he inherit his title. By the time he received word of his daughter's birth, her mother was dead.'

'Should have let *him* marry the gel,' Lord Wynchwood muttered.

'Should have consulted a fortune teller,' Lullington murmured.

Robert barely restrained himself from strangling the bastard.

Bliss clapped his hands for silence. 'Because of the guardianship arrangements made by her legal father, Abernathy could do nothing until those arrangements ended. He feared when the Bracewells learned of his plans to leave her his fortune they would find a way to spend it.' He glared at Lord Wynchwood, who turned the colour of a beetroot. 'It seems he was right.'

Misty-eyed Frederica placed a hand to her throat. 'I still can't believe my father was a nobleman.'

Robert could see that she was happier about discovering her father was a worthwhile man than about the fortune she'd inherited. She really was a remarkable woman. She deserved a good man.

He felt as if someone had knocked him down and run over his chest with a coach and four.

He was not that man.

Bliss smiled at Frederica kindly and handed her the roll of parchment. 'The details are all in here.'

Wynchwood groaned. 'I should have married you to Simon years ago.'

'Too late, I'm afraid,' Frederica said.

At that moment the outer door opened and young Simon barged in. 'Uncle,' he cried. 'I have brought the special licence. We can marry tomorrow.'

Lullington cracked a laugh. 'Always behind the time, young Bracewell.'

Robert returned a grim smile to this sally. He could not let Lullington know what this meant to him or the viscount would have a field day.

Simon's smile faded as he stared at his uncle. 'I say, what is going on?'

'Ingratitude is going on,' Lord Wynchwood proclaimed, his face drained of colour for once. He looked as if he might collapse. He lurched towards Frederica.

Robert straightened, and imposed his body between Frederica and her uncle.

'All these years,' Wynchwood shouted past Robert, waving his fist. 'I fed you. Clothed you. And this is how I'm repaid?'

'You treated her more like a pariah,' Robert said, shoving him back gently.

'Can I do whatever I want with the money?' Frederica asked.

Bliss nodded and whispered something in her ear. Her eyes widened. Her mouth formed a perfect O. 'My word,' she uttered.

Bliss nodded. 'Do not worry, I will advise you.'

'As will I,' Snively said with a warning note in his voice.

God, they were going to tear at her like dogs over a carcass. He felt sick. Well, he wouldn't be one of those looking for scraps.

Frederica turned a shoulder to the room and murmured something to Bliss. He shook his head. She stiffened. Bliss wrung his hands, then bowed in submission. She cast a considering gaze on the company. 'I thank you for your kind offer of marriage, Simon, but no. Nevertheless, I do owe the Bracewells a great debt. After all, you could have dropped me off at the nearest workhouse and my father might never have found me.'

Robert cursed under his breath. What foolishness was she about? She should have them tossed out on their ears. 'Don't let them sponge on you.'

She gave him a gentle smile. 'They are family. And families must take care of each other, mustn't they, R-Robert?'

'Not always.'

The stubborn set of her jaw told him she wouldn't listen and she continued in a clear voice. 'I have asked Mr Bliss to set up a monthly allowance for Simon on the understanding he is not to use it for gaming.'

Lullington paled. 'I'm done here,' he said in Robert's ear. 'You win again, it seems.'

If this was winning, he'd hate to lose. Robert shrugged. Frederica had won. She'd have her freedom. To paint. To travel. To live life as she pleased. It was the best possible outcome.

She didn't need him at all.

'What is owed to you will be paid, Viscount Lullington,' Frederica called out.

The viscount swung around with a dumbfounded expression. 'You honour me, Miss Bracewell.'

She was too soft-hearted by far.

She cast Lullington a saucy smile. 'I suggest you find a way to relieve Lady Caldwell of her other encumbrance, for I do believe the two of you would make a good match of it.'

With a soft laugh, Lullington made her a flourishing bow. 'Do you recommend poison or a bullet?'

Frederica cast him a mischievous look. 'Ending up on the gallows will not help your suit.'

Her face changed, lost its happy expression as her gaze fell on Robert. He started to back away.

'R-Robert—'

'No,' Robert said. He wasn't a man who could be bought. He went where he willed. He always had. 'I want nothing.' He would not be a jackal snapping at her heels. Or a lap dog dancing on hind legs for crumbs.

And yet still his heart pounded, drumming out evil hope. He headed for the door, feeling as though his feet were trapped in quicksand and he was slowly sinking.

'Why not?' she asked with a catch in her voice.

He let his expression cool, curled his lip and turned to face her. 'It has been a pleasure knowing you, Miss Brace-well, but I value my freedom.'

Her eyes sparkled. Tears. The sight of them burned acid in his gut, but he kept his gaze steady, his smile cynical and bored.

A crystal drop rolled down her cheek, and yet she bravely smiled. 'Then I must wish you well.'

'This is outrageous,' Wynchwood yelled. 'A woman can't be trusted—'

'Say one more word,' Robert growled in the old man's ear as he passed, 'and you will find yourself on the pavement on your arse with a bloody nose. Be glad she's not visiting upon you the kind of misery she's endured at your hands all these years. She's rich enough to see you ruined.'

The old gentleman shriveled, backing away. 'Prepos-terous,' he muttered. 'Gave her everything.' He glanced around to see if anyone had heard.

Frederica would have to watch this family of hers, but it wasn't his business. He headed for the door with Lullington and John hard on his heels.

Out in the street the three men stared at each other.

'So, Mountford, once more you land on your feet,' Lullington said, looking sour.

Feeling rather more as if he had holes blown in his chest

with a shotgun, Robert glared at the dandy. 'Why the hell are you whining? Your debts will be paid.'

'I'd have got a whole lot more if you hadn't robbed the Wynchwoods of their due. Perhaps I should woo the rich woman you rejected back there.'

Robert cursed vilely. 'Go near her and I'll—' He lunged, fists clenched.

Lullington dodged back and released the catch on his swordstick. 'Fisticuffs? You always were a ruffian.'

John stepped between them. 'Enough. It won't matter who kills who, the other one will end up at the end of a rope. Where's the sense in that?'

'I had hoped to see him carted off to Newgate this morning,' Lullington said. 'Having a duke for a father won't protect you for ever, Mountford. I'll be there the next time you put a foot wrong.'

'With trumped-up evidence, no doubt.' Robert stared down his nose. 'You are lucky charges weren't brought against you. If it weren't for Maggie, I would have.'

'Leave her out of this.'

'And leave Miss Bracewell out of your schemes. She's had enough people taking advantage.' Himself included, damn it. Hopefully she'd find someone a little less jaded. A man with less to regret in his past. He took a deep breath. 'Look, I doubt this will make any difference, but I am sorry about your cousin. She's no less a schemer than you are, and deserved to be put in her place, but I shouldn't have let it go so far. I'm glad she found a husband. And I'm glad Maggie has you looking out for her.'

Lullington's eyes widened, no doubt as surprised as Robert by the apology.

'That doesn't mean I won't do everything in my power to keep you away from Miss Bracewell,' Robert continued.

'Including using my family's power.' A threat if ever he'd made one.

Lullington looked down at the ground, his fingers playing with his quizzing glass, then raised his eyes to Robert's face. 'All right. We'll call it a stalemate. Just stay out of my business in future, or next time I won't fail.' He turned to John and bowed. 'I bid you good day.'

'Bloody bastard,' Robert muttered, watching Lullington twirl his gold-headed cane as he strolled away looking every inch a mincing tulip of fashion.

'Never mind him. What about you?' John said at his shoulder.

'God knows. See Mother tomorrow, I suppose. Look for work.'

'You made her cry.' Robert knew John wasn't referring to his mother.

'She'll recover. They always do.'

But would he? Somehow he felt as if he'd left a piece of himself inside the tawdry little office.

Chapter Thirteen

It was a good few moments before Robert could bring himself to ring the bell at Mountford House. He'd never expected to set foot in the place again. He'd never wanted to. Except for a yearning that would not be denied. Not now, as he stood on the doorstep.

He took a deep breath and pulled the bell, listened to the tolling deep in the servants' quarters.

Grimshaw opened the door. Not a flicker passed across his face at the sight of Robert. The man was imperturbable, as all dukes' servants should be. 'Lord Robert, good to see you again.'

'Thank you, Grimshaw.' He handed over his hat.

'Her Grace is in the blue drawing room.'

'I know the way. No need to announce me. I believe I am expected.'

The butler bowed.

Expected.

How formal it sounded.

But he was the black sheep. Not returning home, but merely paying a courtesy call. It hadn't taken too many hours of staring into a brandy glass to realise he would not remain in England. Even if Frederica had gone to Italy, her face would haunt him in every field and wood. He might be tempted to follow her.

Early this morning, he'd drafted a note declining his mother's invitation, but in the end he hadn't the heart to send it. So here he was, prepared for tears and admonishments and a final farewell.

He stared at the drawing room door. Did he knock?

Hell. She had called him her son.

He turned the handle and walked in.

As always she looked beautiful for her age. A little pale, a little sad, a little more fragile, but there was a welcome on her lips and in her eyes.

'Mama.' He started forwards.

A movement jerked his gaze from his mother to a figure rising from a chair on the other side of the room.

Father. Bile rose in his throat. He was not even to have this moment alone with his mother.

He bowed and then met his father's gaze. 'Your Grace. Forgive me. I was unaware of your presence.' Heartsick, he turned to leave.

'Robert, wait.' His father's voice.

He stilled. 'My son. Please. I'm sorry.'

Robert turned slowly. Never in his life had he heard his father retract his word or offer an apology. He darted a glance at Mother. Her face showed nothing.

His father strode forwards, hand outstretched. 'Can you forgive what I did?' he asked. 'Your mother cannot.'

His father's brown eyes pleaded. It was as far as he would go. Far further than Robert would ever have expected.

He grasped the offered hand, felt its strength and its tremble. 'Father.' It was all he could manage without breaking down, without bringing shame on them both.

Somehow he choked down the lump in his throat. 'I'm sorry, Father. I should never have helped Charlie to join the army. It was wrong. I could not have borne it if he had come to any real harm.'

Father's eyes moistened. He raised a hand. 'I know, my boy. I should not have blamed you. Charlie and I had a long talk. Youth believes itself invincible. I had forgotten. I'm glad you finally came home.'

'Come here, Robert,' Mother said. 'Let me look at you.'

He strode to stand in front of her and took both her hands in his and kissed them.

'Oh, my son. I've missed you greatly. Sit down. I want to hear what you have been doing. Radthorn told me a little, but I gather you have been employed in the country?'

He sat beside her on the sofa. She retained hold of his hand as if she feared he might run from the room as he had done so often as a boy.

'Gamekeeping,' he said with a wary look at Father who had taken the chair beside the hearth.

'Learned a lot, did you?' Father asked. He sounded eager.

'Yes.'

'You always did like the land,' Father said in satisfied tones.

He'd noticed? Robert tried to hold his jaw in place. He wasn't sure he succeeded from the knowing gleam in his father's eye.

'Your mother pointed it out,' Father said, with a fond glance at his wife. 'I should have realised. Lord knows there are enough estates to worry about.'

Robert stiffened. 'They go with the title.' He turned to Mother. 'I want nothing of Charlie's.'

'I know,' she said, her grey eyes sorrowful.

The tension inside him eased. He could almost feel her arms around his shoulders, the way he had as a boy when hurt by his father's lack of interest. 'I'm leaving for America,' he announced, suddenly coming to a decision.

'Why America?' Father said. 'We just lost a war with them. Go to Canada, my boy. I've some contacts there. I'll give you letters of introduction.'

Naturally Father would be glad to see his awkward complication gone. Or was he really trying to help? He swallowed the old bitterness and took the offer at face value. 'Thank you, your Grace.'

The clock in the hall chimed. 'Good lord, is that the time?' the duke said. 'I'll be late for the House.'

Robert rose. 'It was good to see you again, your Grace.'

Father clapped him on the shoulder. 'You've done well, my boy. Surprised me.' He cleared his throat. 'But for your swift action, we might well have lost Charles.'

This was the thanks Robert had wanted all those months ago. The recognition that he would never cause his brother harm and that he was just as important to his family as his brother. The anger clutching at his heart seeped away at the sight of his father's distress. A hot lump of emotion scoured the back of his throat. He managed a nod.

The duke smiled sadly at his wife. 'Your mother believes Charles will come about now we have found you again.' His grim face said he wasn't quite sure.

Robert glanced at his mother. 'What is wrong with Charlie?'

His mother sighed. 'We have rarely seen him since your departure. And not heard a word from him since he left for Durn after New Years' Day. He'll come to his senses.'

Father closed his eyes briefly. 'I was wrong to try to drive a wedge between my sons. Dem me…' He turned away, but not before Robert saw the moisture in the old man's eyes. So the duke really did have a heart.

His own felt a little less bruised. 'It doesn't matter, Father. You did what you thought was right. For the good of the family.'

'Hmmph,' said Mother.

The duke kissed his wife's hand and straightened his shoulders. 'If you need that recommendation, let me know, but I'd be very happy if you decided to stay.' He strode from the room, not quite as tall as Robert remembered. Not quite as self-assured.

Her grace watched him go with a sad expression. 'Pride is a difficult thing,' she said softly. 'It is so hard to go back.'

'I'm grateful for your help,' Robert said. 'With Father. And Miss Bracewell. Though you should not have put yourself in such danger. If anything had happened to you...'

His mother raised an elegant hand and lightly touched his cheek. 'I haven't had so much excitement in years. Her mother and I were friends, you know. I had a long talk with Miss Bracewell when John brought her here yesterday morning.'

Robert frowned. 'I don't know what John thought he was about.'

'Helping you. You always did command the respect of your peers, even if you never realised it. Poor John, he was devastated when he realised he'd practically cut you outside White's. You have forgiven him, haven't you?'

'Of course.'

'Write to me from Canada, won't you, dear, if you must go. I will miss you.'

His chest tightened. 'I must, but I will miss you, too, Mama. And the others.'

'They will be sorry not to have seen you. Come home

to us when you can. You will always be welcome, Robert. Have no doubt.'

He took his mother's hand in his and leaned to kiss her cheek. The familiar lavender scent washed through him followed by the same calm she'd instilled in him as an angry and confused boy.

'Thank you,' he murmured.

'And so Miss Bracewell goes to Italy alone.'

Robert felt a faint prickle of unease at the back of his neck. 'That was her plan.'

'You are not putting her aside because you think her unworthy? Because she was born on the wrong side of the blanket?' Mother asked a little hesitantly.

He stiffened at the faint tone of censure in her voice. 'Good God, no! I—well, to put it bluntly, she is far above my touch, and I won't be a parasite.'

Mother smiled sadly. 'My proud, beautiful boy.'

Robert felt as if he'd missed something. 'Snively will make sure she is safe.'

A crease developed between her fine brows. 'I am surprised at you though, Robert, seducing an innocent and then abandoning her.'

His cheeks stung as if she had slapped him across the face. 'You are wrong, Mother. I was not her first lover.'

'Are you sure?'

'What the hell do you think I am? She told me....' Damn it, what had she said? *I'm not so very innocent.* 'Frederica was not a maid when I met her.' His face fired scarlet. He couldn't believe he was having this conversation with his mother. 'A man knows these things.'

'But Robert, you also know she quite often rides astride, like a boy.'

The truth hit him like a body blow. Shock jarred him off kilter.

His mother looked at him silently, her lips pursed.

Dear God. He'd seduced an innocent. He really was a blackguard. 'I have to go.'

She raised a brow. 'I should think you do. But, Robert, a piece of advice. Pride and love don't make good bedmates.'

And with that incomprehensible admonition ringing in his ears he kissed her and left.

Sitting at the table in her private parlour, Frederica jabbed her fork into the roast beef on her plate, lifted it to her mouth, and then put it down again. She just didn't feel hungry.

She left the table and moved to the sofa by the hearth. The sofa where she'd sat just the other night in Robert's arms. She'd been so contented, secure. Without him, she would never have been brave enough to face the lawyer. So why did she now feel so uneasy? The worst was over.

Wealthy beyond her wildest imaginings, she could do anything she wanted. Snively had hired a maid for her and a lady's companion to accompany them on their journey. The old man had beamed when she asked him to go with her as her major domo. Everything was perfect.

Or it would be if Robert hadn't walked way.

Because he wanted his freedom.

Maggie had kindly told her a little bit about his past. The parade of women through his life. She was just one of many. He was a rake.

The piper must be paid. Or was it *no good crying over spilt milk*? He didn't want her. He'd said so in front of everyone.

She sighed and gazed at the trunks standing in the middle of the parlour floor all packed and ready to go at any moment.

A knock came at the door.

The man for the trunks.

She went to the door and unlocked it.

'R-Robert?'

He looked so handsome in his gentleman's clothing, dark blue coat and cream waistcoat and newly shaved.

'May I come in? We need to talk,' he said grimly. He inhaled a quick breath as if he had something unpleasant to say. 'I just left my mother.'

She backed away cautiously. 'W-what is it?'

'There is something I have to ask you. I want the truth.'

She perched on the sofa's edge, wary, uncomfortable. 'What did you want to know?'

He kept her hand clasped in his. 'Were you indeed a virgin before we met?'

His mother had betrayed her confidence. A confidence the formidable lady had extracted with a cleverness that had left Frederica in awe. But her Grace had promised to say nothing to her son.

'She had no right to tell you.'

He drew in a sharp breath. He looked appalled. 'We must be married right away.'

Married. Her heart gave a happy little lurch. Her gaze took in the tightness of his mouth, the darkness in his eyes, and she knew it would be a mistake.

She attempted a laugh. It sounded brittle instead of light and carefree. 'La, this is sudden, my lord. Such a declaration.'

He glowered. 'On my honour, I must make this right.'

'Must?' She'd spoken to him of love and he spoke of honour. She pulled her hand from his grasp. 'Why must you?'

'It is obvious. I took your innocence. I can do nothing else.'

'I was never an innocent, Robert. I have eyes in my head. I saw the beasts in the fields. I can read. I knew what men looked like and what happens between a man and woman.'

'Good God, woman, it doesn't matter what you knew. I debauched you. It is my duty.'

'Duty?' The word was a shriek in her head. It hurt worse than years of hearing her family's horrid slights. She lifted her chin and put chill in her voice. 'Why is it your duty to marry the daughter of the Wynchwood Whore?'

'That has nothing to do with it.'

'Did the thought of the money make you change your mind?' she said cruelly, knowing it would hurt him as much as he was hurting her.

'I don't want a penny of your damned money.'

'To hell with duty, then. I don't need your name to make me respectable.' She clenched her fists in the folds of her skirt and turned her face away. 'My wealth will do that. I will never marry. I'll take my pleasure where I want and with whom I want. The way my mother did.'

He flinched. 'You can't mean that.'

Drawing in a breath to garner every ounce of her strength, she turned to look at him. 'Yes, R-Robert. I do. Think back. I wanted you. I seduced *you*. Now, I don't want you any more. Surely you of all people can understand?'

A muscle in his jaw flickered. There was anger in his eyes and something else. Anguish? Surely not. The pain in her chest grew so bad she thought she might fall to her knees, but she must not, for then he would know what it cost her to send him away. He'd know and he'd try to change her mind.

To tie the man she loved to her in wedlock against his

will, knowing he didn't love her... It didn't bear thinking about.

Frederica got up and went to the door of her adjoining bedroom, unable to look at his beautiful face in case she weakened. Hand on the doorknob, she spoke quietly, calmly. 'I must ask you to leave. Please, do not come here again. I will not see you.'

She went inside and shut the door.

She stood rigid and shaking on the other side. No tears. No sobbing. He mustn't guess how much she was wounded.

After a moment or two, she heard the outside door close.

He'd be glad she refused him. Later.

He'd be thankful for his escape.

She sank down on to the bed and buried her face in the pillow and sobbed.

She didn't want him.

Furious, Robert slammed out of the parlour. He'd offered her his name and she'd given him his *congé*.

Now he knew how all those women in his life had felt.

God damn, it hurt.

He tore down the stairs in fury.

Why wouldn't she let him put things right? She'd talked of wanting other men and thrown him out. His body shook. His heart raged. His fists opened and closed. Wanting to strangle her. To make her listen to reason.

He needed a drink. Something to take away the turmoil in his head.

On his way to the taproom, he collided with Snively. He glared at him and pushed by.

Snively grabbed his sleeve. 'You been up there upsetting her again?'

'Hardly,' Robert said. 'She doesn't give a tinker's cuss for me.'

'Hoity-toity bugger. Up in the boughs, are we?'

Robert brushed him off. 'You've no idea what you are talking about.'

'I know she looks like she lost half a crown and found a penny.'

Robert paused.

'She ain't eating much either.'

'What are you saying?'

'She's miserable when she should be as happy as a grig.'

'What has that to do with me?'

Snively shrugged. 'I wouldn't know. You're the man who understands women.'

'Understand them? No one understands them.'

'Maybe not. Can I buy you a drink?' Snively walked to the bar, pulled out a pipe and shoved it between his teeth. 'I'd have a little think before you acts with haste.'

'Think about what? I asked her to marry me. She turned me down.'

'Happen you're right. Though I never saw her look so down as when you left the lawyer's office. Went down on your knees did you? Begged for forgiveness after what you said?' The older man looked at him sideways and sighed. 'Too high in the instep for that, I reckon. You a duke's son and all and her nothing but a base-born child.'

Robert slammed his fist on the bar. Tankards jumped and rattled. 'That has nothing to do with anything. I offered her my name.'

'Not good enough, my lord.' Snively shook his grey head.

'Drink, sir?' asked the barman, wiping at the bar in front of Robert with a rag.

'Brandy,' Robert said. 'For two.'

The barman poured and moved away. Robert downed his drink in one gulp. It didn't make him feel one iota better. 'What do you suggest, then?'

Snively's eyes twinkled. 'If you don't know, I'm sure I don't.'

Robert's fingers curled around his glass. He wished the slender stem was Snively's neck. 'Fat lot of help you are.'

'All right. Why do you want to marry her?'

'Because it's the right thing to do.'

'Empty words.' The old man turned away. 'You don't deserve her. Bugger off.'

He picked up his glass and wandered to the settle by the hearth where he picked up a discarded newspaper and proceeded to immerse himself in its pages.

Robert signalled for another brandy and when it came he stared into its depths. Why else would he want to marry her? He liked her. He felt good when he was with her. Hell, he felt terrible when she wasn't around.

It was as if they were joined by an invisible thread attached to his heart and the further it was stretched, the more painfully tight it became. Was that what people called love?

He raised the glass to his lips. Then put it down.

Love was romantic nonsense.

Wasn't it?

What had Mother said—pride and love make bad bedfellows? Was that his problem? Was he too proud?

Or did he fear she'd reject his love, the way Father had?

Which meant taking a terrible risk.

What if he couldn't have her any other way? What if she met some handsome Italian count and fell into bed with him? Or worse, married him?

She had said she loved him.

How could he offer her anything less?

And if she turned him down again?

At least he'd be able to look at his face in the mirror and not be disgusted by his cowardice.

He glanced over at Snively, who had finished his drink and was now dozing with the newspaper over his face. No help there.

He climbed back up the stairs and let himself in quietly.

The remains of her supper still lay on the table beside the window. She hadn't eaten more than a mouthful or two. The sight gave him heart. Perhaps Snively was right. She wasn't happy.

Silently, he tried her bedroom door. Locked. He knocked.

'I'm finished with the supper dishes,' she called out. 'You can take them away.'

Her voice sounded thick and damp as if she'd been crying. A good sign? The tightness in his chest said not

'I've not come for the dishes,' he said. 'I've come to make a confession.'

Silence.

'Frederica, there is one more thing I need to say.'

Frederica stared at the door. When would he stop torturing her? 'G-go away.'

'Please, sweetling. It won't take more than a minute or two.'

Ah, how could she resist the plea in his voice? She wasn't going to change her mind, though. Whatever he said. Not even if he tied her up and stood her in front of the altar. All she had to do was remain calm. Strong. In control.

She ran to the mirror. Her eyes were red, her cheeks

blotchy. She dipped a cloth in the ewer and dabbed at her tear-streaked face.

He tapped on the door. 'Frederica.'

'A moment if you please.'

A quick smooth of her gown, an extra pin in her hair. She looked in the mirror and shook her head. He'd know she'd been crying. She fixed a cool smile on her face and opened the door.

He stood a little back from the door, dark, aloof, his face grim. Much as she'd seen him that first day by the river, except in his fine clothes he looked every inch the duke's second son. Generations of knights lived in his bearing.

Inside, she began to shake.

Did he now hope to force his will on her? The way her uncle had intended with her cousin?

She kept her face calm, politely interested. 'Lord Robert, back so soon? I really cannot think of anything else that needs to be said.'

'There is one thing.' His voice was deep and dark and her insides quivered at the sound; her wicked body yearned for his touch.

'I'll hear no more talk of duty and honour. I have neither. Please close the door on the way out.'

She went to the sofa and gazed into the fire's depths, waiting for the slam of the door.

Instead, she heard his step across the floor as he drew near. She held herself rigid, ready to resist a seduction if necessary, primed herself to be deaf to his words.

A faint rustle and a small thud sounded behind her.

She couldn't stop herself—she turned to look.

He was on one knee, his head bowed, so that all she could see of him was dark waves of hair and the breadth of his shoulders.

She started to rise.

'Lady, grant me one boon,' he said softly. 'Hear me out.'

She sank back on the seat, too amazed to do more than stare at his lowered head.

'I am sorry,' he said quietly. 'I came to you in pride. Now I come to you in humility.'

'R-Robert, no,' she whispered. Never had she wanted this proud man to abase himself before her. 'P-please, get up.'

He didn't move, didn't raise his head, didn't look at her, but knelt before her like some knight of old before his liege, humbled, penitent.

She couldn't breathe the sight pained her so much.

'You said my offer wasn't enough. I thought you meant I wasn't good enough. It hurt. My pride was hurt. But far worse was the sense of loss deep in my soul. Only when I realised that I stood to lose you forever did I realise my greatest wrong. I offered so little of myself in return for the priceless gift you bring to my heart.'

'Oh, R-Robert,' she breathed, unable to believe what she was hearing.

He looked up then and the humility and love shining in his eyes almost sent her to pieces.

She reached out.

He took her hand, kissed the back of it with gentle reverence. 'It was family pride that kept your parents apart and pride that set me adrift from my family's love.'

He looked up and gazed into her face. He looked beautiful and sad. 'Today I walked away too proud to beg for what I needed. I let pride speak instead of saying what was in my heart. Can you forgive me, Frederica, for being such an arrogant fool? If you can, I beg that I may spend the rest of my life trying to win your love. I will abide by your wishes. If you send me away, I will never trouble you more. But I want you to know, I love you with all my heart.'

These were the words she had longed to hear. And the truth shone in his eyes and rang in his voice.

Her heart swelled with joy. And yet how could she let him make such a sacrifice? By marrying her he would be giving up his place in society, possibly in his family, if what she knew of the duke was half true.

She had turned him away because he spoke only of duty; now he spoke of love, but she still wasn't convinced it was right. She loved him too well to ruin his life.

She was a bastard. Illegitimate. Unwanted. He was the son of a duke.

She would bring him nothing but shame.

Frederica slid off the seat onto her knees and cupped his cheeks in her hands, felt the warmth of his skin and the faint haze of stubble, inhaled the scent of his cologne. 'Don't do this.'

'Ah, sweetheart,' he said. 'If you won't have me as your husband, I'll come as your servant. You can pay me to carry your bags, arrange for your carriage, keep the damned *banditti* at bay.'

'You would do that for me?'

'I would do that and more to remain at your side. To protect you when asked. To serve when needed.'

Tears blocked her throat and burned the backs of her eyes. 'And will you bring me chocolate in bed in the morning?' she whispered huskily.

'I will.' He smiled. 'As long as I get to lie beside you as you drink it.'

'Oh, R-Robert, are you sure this is what you want? I will never be entirely respectable, you know.'

'As sure as I am of needing my next breath to live. I love you, elf. Without you, I'm a shell. An empty husk. It took a while to get it through my thick skull, but without you, I might as well not breathe. You are my life.'

She pressed her lips to his, and his arms came around her. 'Marry me,' he whispered against her mouth. 'Please.'

'Yes, R-Robert. I will.'

He cradled her nape and she dissolved against his lips and his hard body.

'Here? Or in Italy?' she asked.

'Wherever your heart desires, my love,' he answered and then couldn't help a soft chuckle, 'though I am sure my mother will never forgive me if I don't let her welcome her new daughter-in-law properly. And I would like you to meet my twin.'

'Then England it is. I find I like your mother very much. I'll let Snively know.'

'Later.'

Then there was no more talking because his lips devoured hers and ecstasy carried all thought away.

Three days later, Robert stood on the steps of St George's in Hanover Square with his wife of five minutes and gazed at the crowds madly cheering him and his bride. It was a cold January day, but inside he felt warm.

When he'd told his parents of his wedding plans, he hadn't expected such an elaborate affair, but ducal pride required they celebrate in grand style.

It was right. Frederica deserved the homage.

He raised her small hand to his lips. 'Happy?' he asked, smiling down at her glowing face.

'Never more so,' she answered.

A figure pushed through the crowds and up the steps. Two days' growth of beard shadowed his jaw, his coat was rumpled, his neckcloth limp. He had his gazed fixed on Robert's face.

Charlie. Late. Which really wasn't like him. Their mother had been frantic.

When Charlie reached the top step, he hesitated, then thrust out his hand. 'Congratulations.' His expression said he wasn't sure Robert would take it.

The idiot. He grabbed the large hand and pulled his brother close, slapping him on the back. 'Glad you made it.' His voice sounded thick and husky.

His brother pulled away and cleared his throat. 'I would have been here sooner, but my horse threw a shoe. Had to walk miles for a replacement.'

'A fine tale,' Father said, coming up behind them.

Charlie shook his hand. 'It is true.'

'Better late than never,' Robert said with a sympathetic grin at his brother.

Charlie glanced towards Frederica.

'Let me introduce my wife. Darling, this is my brother Charles.'

Frederica's eyes widened. Her gaze ran over Charlie and she smiled. 'You are even more alike than your p-portrait suggests. I would like to paint you some time. You'd make a wonderful Zeus.'

A growl rose in Robert's throat.

She laughed. 'Draped in a sheet, R-Robert.'

He grinned and pressed a kiss to her wrist. 'Fully clothed.'

Charlie's eyes goggled.

'Family joke,' Robert said.

'Who would have thought *you* would ever marry?' Charlie said. His cheeks turned red.

'I did,' Mother said. 'Welcome, my son.'

Charlie enfolded her in a bear hug. In the next moment they were surrounded by the rest of the Mountford clan. His chattering sisters, who'd been bridesmaids, his youngest brother, whose voice gave no sign of breaking for all that he already topped Robert's chin in height.

It was a good feeling. And Frederica looked thoroughly at home and happy. As she deserved.

The bridal carriage rolled up to the steps.

'I'll see you back at Mountford House,' Charlie said.

''Fraid not. We've a ship to catch.'

'To Italy,' Frederica said.

Charlie looked worried. 'I need to ask your opinion.'

'Whatever it is, Charlie,' Robert said, 'you'll have to deal with it yourself.'

Charlie looked stunned. And just a bit terrified. Robert looked at him. 'It's a woman.'

Charlie nodded.

'Then I definitely can't help you. I don't understand them at all.'

He snatched his wife from the bosom of his family and escorted her into the waiting carriage. They waved from the windows until they turned the corner at the end of the street.

Robert pulled her on to his lap and kissed her soundly. After a long while, he let her go.

She snuggled against his shoulder. 'Your brother really would make a wonderful Zeus.'

'No.'

She grinned up at him. 'Then I suppose I must make do with you. Probably better,' she added hastily at his glare.

He would do. He would do his best to make her believe that for the rest of her life.

'I love you, sweet wife.'

'I love you, dear R-Robert.' She kissed his cheek and wriggled on his lap.

He groaned. 'How long before we board ship?'

'An hour, I think.'

It was going to be the longest hour of his life unless he found a way to fill up the time.

He untied the ribbons of her bonnet and tossed the confection aside. 'That's better. Now I can see your face.'

She laughed up at him, her pretty lips inviting his kisses.

He cradled her nape and plundered her delicious mouth, and many minutes passed before the need for breath forced him to raise his head. He rested his chin on the top of her head. 'You are sure this is what you want?' he asked. It wasn't so much that he doubted it, he just liked the warmth her confirmation gave him.

'I can't quite believe it,' she said softly. 'It is as if every dream I ever had has come true. But, R-Robert, are you sure you won't be bored?'

'Not a chance. I'll be too busy keeping you entertained. And naked.'

A laugh bubbled up from her throat. A warm, encouraging sound. 'I can't wait.'

Nor could he. He let his hand slide up one slim calf beneath her skirts.

She sighed. 'But you do realise I will be occupied with classes during the day,' she said softly.

'I do.' He nuzzled her neck. 'I'll be busy too. Father has asked me to look at some properties he is thinking of buying. And I've some other commissions to undertake for him.' Robert had been delighted at the request. He could finally play a part in his family's endeavours.

'R-Robert,' she said hesitantly, 'when we come back, do you think we could buy a house in the country? A place good for raising children?'

His wandering hand stilled. A bubble of hope he never knew resided there tightened his chest. 'I didn't think you wanted children?'

'I didn't. Before. But now I think I do. We'd be a real f-family. I like the countryside. I could have a studio. You could farm, breed horses, if you'd like to, that is.' She sounded worried, as if she feared he might not be pleased.

'Lady Robert,' he said, laughing, but with his heart full of tenderness, 'you never cease to amaze me. That is *exactly* what I would like.' He tipped her chin. 'But right now I have the overwhelming desire to kiss you again.'

Looking pleased, she placed her palm against his jaw. 'R-Robert, did I tell you I love you?'

'Not in the last five minutes.'

'Well, I do.'

'And I love you, elf.'

He kissed her delicious mouth, promising her a future of love and happiness the best way he knew.

MILLS & BOON®

Want to get more from Mills & Boon?

Here's what's available to you if you join the exclusive **Mills & Boon eBook Club** today:

✦ *Convenience – choose your books each month*
✦ *Exclusive – receive your books a month before anywhere else*
✦ *Flexibility – change your subscription at any time*
✦ *Variety – gain access to eBook-only series*
✦ *Value – subscriptions from just £1.99 a month*

So visit **www.millsandboon.co.uk/esubs** today to be a part of this exclusive eBook Club!

The World of Mills & Boon

There's a Mills & Boon® series that's perfect for you. There are ten different series to choose from and new titles every month, so whether you're looking for glamorous seduction, Regency rakes, homespun heroes or sizzling erotica, we'll give you plenty of inspiration for your next read.

By Request
Relive the romance with the best of the best
12 stories every month

Cherish™
Experience the ultimate rush of falling in love.
12 new stories every month

INTRIGUE...
A seductive combination of danger and desire...
7 new stories every month

Desire™
Passionate and dramatic love stories
6 new stories every month

nocturne™
An exhilarating underworld of dark desires
3 new stories every month

Which series will you try next?

Awaken the romance of the past...
6 new stories every month

Medical Romance

The ultimate in romantic medical drama
6 new stories every month

MODERN™

Power, passion and irresistible temptation
8 new stories every month

MODERN tempted™

True love and temptation!
4 new stories every month

You can also buy Mills & Boon® eBooks at
www.millsandboon.co.uk